THE
JANUS FILE

THE JANUS FILE

DAVID WEBER & JACOB HOLO

SF

THE JANUS FILE

This is a work of fiction. All the characters and events portrayed in this book are fictional, and any resemblance to real people or incidents is purely coincidental.

A Baen Books Original

Baen Publishing Enterprises
P.O. Box 1403
Riverdale, NY 10471
www.baen.com

ISBN: 978-1-9821-9215-0

Cover art by Kurt Miller

First printing, October 2022

Distributed by Simon & Schuster
1230 Avenue of the Americas
New York, NY 10020

Library of Congress Cataloging-in-Publication Data

Names: Weber, David, 1952– author. | Holo, Jacob, author.
Title: The Janus file / David Weber & Jacob Holo.
Description: Riverdale, NY : Baen, [2022] | Series: Gordian Division
Identifiers: LCCN 2022030085 | ISBN 9781982192150 (hardcover) | ISBN
    9781625798787 (ebook)
Subjects: LCGFT: Science fiction. | Novels.
Classification: LCC PS3573.E217 J36 2022 | DDC 813/.54—dc23/eng/20220624
LC record available at https://lccn.loc.gov/2022030085

Pages by Joy Freeman (www.pagesbyjoy.com)
Printed in the United States of America
10 9 8 7 6 5 4 3 2 1

To Ken. Memory Eternal.

BACKGROUND OF EXOTIC PLACES

SATURN IS THE MOST BEAUTIFUL PLANET IN THE WHOLE SOLAR system, or so those who live on it claim. Certainly, the ornate majesty of its many splendid rings bejewels the gas giant in ways no other planet can match, and its plethora of richly varied moons provide suitable dance partners to such a lavishly decorated debutante.

But beauty alone did not bring humanity to Saturn. Matter and energy did, and by those measures, Saturn and its flock of moons bask in decadent wealth. Fortune seekers cannot claim that wealth as easily as the riches within the comfortable and familiar gravity well of Earth, but countless treasure troves exist for those with the will to seek them.

And seek them humanity has.

As we approach the fourth millennium, humanity's fingerprints have spread across the solar system, and even beyond. The terraforming of Earth's only moon has already been completed, and ambitious terraforming projects toil within the atmospheres of Venus and Mars, gradually transforming those worlds, as well. Great machines loom over the planet Mercury, ready to transform the airless rock into a solar-collecting swarm around the Sun...if the legal hurdles are ever fully cleared. Artificial habitats and great vessels dot the solar system from one end to the other, and the light and data of a thriving society fill the vacuum between worlds.

By comparison, Saturn and its moons appear much as they have since ancient times. Naturally, given the extent of humanity's expansion, a wide variety of technological constructs orbit the gas giant, and cities and facilities of varying sizes are sprinkled across its moons. The largest of them is the dome of Promise City, situated at the heart of a cluster of gargantuan machines on the cold, shrouded moon of Titan, where the nitrogen-rich atmosphere and lakes of liquid methane have barely been touched by local terraforming efforts.

These and many others might be expected, but a closer examination of Saturn's environs reveals more striking changes. For one, the co-orbital moons of Janus and Epimetheus, once famous for swapping orbits every four years, are gone, replaced by a wide shoal zone interspersed with massive industrial printers and mobile factories maneuvering around the skeletons of active construction projects. The resources of the Atlas Shoal are a pittance compared to the original mass of the two devoured moons, but to see the results of that grand labor, one must travel into the atmosphere of Saturn itself.

Specifically, to the cloud band at plus forty latitude, which enjoys relatively calm weather on a planet known for its fierce winds. There one may spy a speck of white floating amongst the clouds. Travel a little closer, and the immense scale of the object quickly becomes apparent.

Locals call it the "Shark Fin," for the megastructure does indeed resemble the downturned fin of a colossal aquatic monster. The official designation is Janus-Epimetheus, named in honor of the two moons sacrificed to its construction, and often shortened to simply "Janus." Its outer surface is a pristine white, and its rounded bow cuts through tan clouds of ammonia ice near the top, and reddish-orange thunderheads of ammonium hydrosulfide near the bottom. In total, Janus measures one hundred kilometers in height and two hundred kilometers across the widest point of its flattened, oval crown. Natural gravity is a pleasant 1.065 times Earth's, and external pressure near the top is roughly one atmosphere.

Janus does not travel through this sea of golden and rust-colored clouds alone, but it stands above the rest for being the largest and most ambitious habitat by far. Over a billion physical and abstract citizens call Janus their home, for this is the thriving heart of the Saturn State, as well as its seat of governance.

The shining towers of Ballast Heights, capital city of the Saturn State, sprawl atop the Shark Fin's crown, close to and a little behind the prow. Almost every building's cross section takes the form of an elongated teardrop when viewed from above, allowing the city to weather the windy seasons with minimal fuss.

Three towers stretch skyward above the rest, their upper levels coated in dozens of giant dishes and precision lasers shielded behind glass domes to protect the equipment from gusts of wind. All of the dishes and lasers point toward the heavens, and data packets and abstract citizens alike come and go through these transceiver towers in a continuous ballet of photons and electrons. Each tower's infostructure buffers thousands of connectomes at a time, the digital minds of these citizens paused for a short interval as they await transmission off-world, while separate infostructures accept the new arrivals by placing them in a run-state before staff welcome them cordially to Janus.

All of this is routine on the worlds of the Consolidated System Government. Boring even. But only because we at LifeBeam turn the extraordinary into the everyday.

A virtual banner flutters behind the pinnacle of one of these three towers, declaring our company's name in bold, electric blue letters while our slogan of TRAVEL LIGHT! hovers below.

The physical mechanisms of our infostructure stretch from the top of the tower all the way down to the lowest subbasement in a solid column of robust computational engineering. Redundant systems work in trios, constantly checking and rechecking not only their own work, but that of their neighbors, and emergency backups stand ready to activate within moments in the event of a catastrophic failure.

The tower's systems are drastically—one might say *obsessively*—overengineered against any conceivable failure. They have to be, for their cargo is life itself.

—*A LifeBeam Travel Guide to Saturn*

PROLOGUE

EIGHTY-THREE LIGHT-MINUTES FROM SATURN, A CONSTRUCT FAR
smaller than Janus but still impressive orbited the planet Earth.
The dark blue hull of Argus Station took the form of a fat cylinder, and over nine million officers of the Consolidated System
Police worked on or from there, including the heads of the six
specialized divisions that supplemented the rank and file.

Gordian Division was the newest addition, having been formed
less than eight months ago after a calamity known as the Gordian
Knot had almost destroyed sixteen universes, including the one
the citizens of SysGov called home. The division, charged with
enforcing time travel and transdimensional laws, might have been
small compared to the more established elements of SysPol, but
the monumental challenges before them—and a clear understanding of the countermeasures those challenges required—had led
to the division's rapid growth.

Several levels near Argus Station's south pole had been allocated
to the Gordian Division, having stood empty for several decades,
and much of the space had already been filled with offices, labs,
engineering bays, and hangars for time machines called TTVs or
transtemporal vehicles. This influx of personnel brought with it
the side effect of attracting clusters of civilian businesses eager
to support the new division—

—and make a little Esteem in the process.

LifeBeam was one such business, and a newly constructed transceiver tower descended from Argus Station's south pole for the exclusive use of Gordian Division abstract and synthetic personnel. The company had constructed an expansive waiting lounge at the tower's base, far larger than was required for current traffic levels, but perhaps this was an investment in what many saw as Gordian Division's inevitable rise in the future.

Two men sat on a couch near the outer wall with a virtual image displaying the blue globe of Earth beneath their feet. These two men, the chief scientist and lead engineer of Gordian Division, were the only occupants of the lounge, and both were oblivious to the crime that was about to happen.

"Time." Doctor Andover-Chen said the single word with a grand gesture of his arms as faint mathematical equations danced under the glassy skin of his synthoid body.

Joachim Delacroix looked over with a perplexed face. His own synthoid was externally accurate to his original human body, complete with freckled face and unruly reddish-blond hair. Both men wore the gray-green uniforms of Gordian Division with golden eye and sword flashes at the shoulder.

"What about it?" Delacroix asked finally, not sure what to expect from the eccentric scientist.

"Where does the arrow of time come from? What force drives it forward?"

"Are you asking me?"

"It's more a question to myself, but if you'd like to take a stab at it, I wouldn't mind."

"What brought this on?" Delacroix dodged.

"I find myself with time to think," Andover-Chen explained. "And so I wonder, *why* do I have time to think?"

"Are you really that bored?" Delacroix checked a timer in his virtual vision. "We've only been here twelve minutes."

"Twelve minutes. And what are those, really? Why does the universe even need time? Why not exist simply as a collection of spatial dimensions?"

"I don't know, but it'd be pretty boring without it."

"Or perhaps two dimensions of time?" Andover-Chen mused. "Why can't time be structurally like a sheet instead of a line? And why only one direction?"

"Sorry, but you're outside my specialty. I just do impellers."

"And that's exactly my point."

"It is?" Delacroix raised an eyebrow, not sure where his colleague was going with this.

"Why, yes." The scientist turned to him. "We travel through time. We bend the chronotons around us to our will. But do we really *understand* the fundamental nature of time?"

"Well, if *you* don't, then none of us do."

"And so"—Andover-Chen spread his arms once more—"I find myself wondering about time."

"I think I have a pretty good grasp on what twelve minutes is."

"As do I." Andover-Chen's expression turned sour, and he crossed his arms and leaned back on the couch. "Are they ready for us yet?"

"I think they're still waiting for the last transit confirmation."

"I wish they wouldn't call us in here until they're ready. If there's one thing about time I'm sure about, it's that I loathe wasting it."

"That makes two of us," Delacroix agreed.

"By the way"—Andover-Chen knuckled him in the shoulder—"is it just me, or have you been in a better mood lately?"

"You think so?" Delacroix asked.

"Yes. I started noticing it after we returned from Saturn the last time."

"Oh." He thought on this for a moment. "Yeah, I guess you're right."

"Any particular reason?"

Delacroix hesitated.

"Sorry," Andover-Chen said. "I didn't mean to pry."

"No, it's all right." He sighed. "I've just had a lot on my mind recently. Been going around feeling like my head isn't screwed on straight, you know?"

"Oh, I know how that can be sometimes." Andover-Chen flashed an encouraging smile.

"I guess it's just..." Delacroix hesitated again, then nodded. "It's just that I've experienced a lot of trouble coming to terms with Selene's death."

"Of course, you have. That's only natural." The scientist nodded knowingly. "Ah, Selene. I wish I'd known her better. She must have been a remarkable woman, given what you've told me."

"She was," Delacroix agreed. "Better than I deserved. And

as painful as it's been waking up without her every morning, I think I'm finally coming to terms with life without her."

"Good for you." Andover-Chen clapped him on the shoulder and gave it a gentle squeeze.

"I'm not done healing. Not by a long shot. But I do feel like I've made the first significant step forward in months. In a way, this is the first time I've felt even close to normal since she was killed."

"Well, you look the part, take it from me."

"Thanks." Delacroix gave him a half smile. "You want to know the trick I came up with?"

"Sure. Let's hear it."

"I asked myself if Selene would be proud of the way I've been acting recently, and the answer was no."

"That seems rather harsh."

"But it's the truth. I've been yearning for something I can't ever have again." Delacroix shook his head. "And that's no way to live. I have to heal, and the only way to do that is to first *accept* my new reality."

"Too true." Andover-Chen sighed. "Still, the healing process is a long one."

"But I'm confident that *time*"—Delacroix's eyes twinkled with mischief—"will heal my wounds."

Andover-Chen laughed.

A three-note chime played across their virtual hearing.

"Will Doctor Andover-Chen and Chief Engineer Delacroix please head to Outbound Transmission? The last of your relay confirmations just came in."

"It's time to go." Delacroix stood up.

"And so it is."

The two men headed through the open arch marked OUT-BOUND where LifeBeam technicians guided each of them into separate caskets. Delacroix clicked through the virtual prompts to authorize the suspension and transmission of his connectome, then eased down flat and closed his eyes. The top sealed him in, and he willingly placed his connectome into a paused state.

The casket's infostructure interfaced with his synthetic body, extracted the connectome, and moved it to a data buffer await-ing outbound transmission along with Andover-Chen's. A crane retrieved their caskets, now with dataless synthoids, and stored them in a secure holding area for when the two would eventually transmit back to Argus Station.

The outbound transmission laser locked onto a target reception dish on a LifeBeam relay station two light-seconds away. Both sides confirmed the transmission timing and coordinates. A clock ticked down to zero, and a precision laser fired the two connectomes to the relay station.

The two Gordian connectomes passed through eight more relay stations before arriving at Kronos Station, the SysPol headquarters orbiting Saturn. There, the same process played out between the LifeBeam tower on Kronos and the one rising above Ballast Heights.

Both sides confirmed the timing and coordinates, a timer reached zero, and a final laser fired the photons of Andover-Chen and Joachim Delacroix down to the Janus megastructure.

But an unexpected maintenance routine activated in the reception dish, forcing a shutdown of the primary infostructure as well as the two secondary support infostructures. Backup systems detected the fault within nanoseconds and immediately initiated recovery procedures, but the shutdown process refused all commands to abort.

With all three systems in control of the dish unresponsive to external commands, backup systems initiated an emergency purge of the infostructure and restored all code to default. This process would take three whole seconds, after which the dish would be restarted and normal operations could resume.

But it was already too late.

Andover-Chen and Delacroix arrived less than a second after the dish shut down, and the photons of their minds rebounded off the inert collection dish and scattered into the clouds of Saturn.

TEN DAYS EARLIER

CHAPTER ONE

UNDER-DIRECTOR JONAS SHIGEKI OF THE DEPARTMENT OF TEMPORAL Investigation was not from SysGov. In fact, he wasn't even from the same *universe*. He'd been born on a version of Earth governed by the System Cooperative Administration, or the Admin for short, and yet he found himself sitting at a round conference room table near the core of Argus Station, surrounded by seven titans of SysGov society: the SysPol Chief of Police and his six division commissioners.

Jonas swept his gaze across the occupants, taking in the extraordinary people he'd come to know in the months he'd spent in this foreign universe. He was but a simple human of meat and neurons who had only recently celebrated his thirty-fifth birthday. He was a veritable youngster by SysGov standards, forced to deal with century-old veterans who'd transitioned into immortal synthoid bodies, purely abstract existences with no physical avatars, and a war hero plucked from 1958 in his own universe!

He was so totally, overwhelmingly, *ridiculously* out of his depth that he felt a desire to laugh at the absurdity.

And yet he had them *exactly* where he wanted them.

He sat there clad in the blue uniform and peaked cap of an Admin Peacekeeper with his long black hair bound in a ponytail, though he'd pushed his cap back to the point where it looked ready to fall off if he leaned back too far.

The moment to strike had finally arrived.

"These selections seem"—he paused for dramatic effect—"safe."

"Safe?" Chief Oliver Lamont echoed, sounding as if he didn't comprehend the problem. The bicentennial synthoid tugged his darker blue uniform straight and creased the dark skin of his brow.

"Conservative," Jonas clarified.

Lamont glanced at the five SysPol detective profiles hovering in their shared virtual vision over the center of the table. He frowned and turned back to Jonas.

"I'm sorry, Director. I fail to see the problem."

"Would you instead prefer an officer from a different division?" asked Commissioner Vesna Tyrel, head of the detectives of Themis Division. She watched him with piercing gray eyes, and her long snow-white hair framed the pale, flawless skin of her oval face.

"Not at all. I think the choice of Themis is an inspired one." Jonas gestured around the table with an open hand. "Almost all interactions between the Admin and SysGov have taken place like this, at the highest echelons of our governments. That's fine as a starting point, but we must eventually move on from there by allowing our societies to mingle at lower levels, and I whole-heartedly agree that pairing a DTI agent with a Themis detective is a superb next step."

Jonas' eyes flicked to Commissioner Klaus-Wilhelm von Schröder, head of the Gordian Division. Besides Jonas, he was the youngest person at the table, and yet his growing influence over the other division heads had led them all here.

Relations between the DTI and the Gordian Division, not to mention SysGov and the Admin in general, were on the upswing after a successful joint military operation against the ill-fated—and now *obliterated*—Dynasty universe. Interactions had become so cordial between the two time-travel enforcement agencies that Commissioner Schröder and Director-General Csaba Shigeki, Jonas' own father, took time out of their busy schedules to meet face-to-face on a weekly rotation, alternating which universe they met in for what amounted to informal "working lunches."

Schröder had proposed an initial pilot for an officer exchange program at one of those lunches. SysGov President Byakko, once she learned of his initiative, had taken it several steps further by offering the Admin free rein on selecting both sides of the partnership, the timing of the exchange, where the two would fit within the SysPol organization—basically *everything*—as a means to help alleviate the Admin's phobias concerning some SysGov technologies and cultural practices. Shigeki Senior had latched onto the gracious gesture with gusto and had appointed Jonas to oversee the pair's selection.

It was an important task, and one Jonas took extremely seriously, though he could forgive those around him for thinking otherwise.

"So, Themis Division it is," Tyrel reiterated. "But you find these five options unsatisfactory?"

"Oh, I wouldn't go that far." Jonas gave the list a casual wave.

"But you're also not the biggest fan of them? Why is that, exactly?" Commissioner Peng Fa asked, his glowing blue eyes narrowing from his virtual seat across the table. His digital avatar's skin was the black of night, and he wore the dark red of Arete Division's first responders. Of all the commissioners, he was the most antagonistic during these meetings, perhaps because the Admin tightly regulated its AIs, a practice many in SysGov characterized as slavery.

Jonas smiled pleasantly at the abstract commissioner.

"They seem a bit...suboptimal to me, shall we say?"

"I'm still not sure what the problem is," Lamont said. "Are these detectives not up to the task at hand?"

"Oh, heavens no!" Jonas assured them. "All five are qualified for the program, though perhaps they're a little *too* qualified."

"I wasn't aware that could be a problem," Lamont admitted.

"Recall what I just said about the 'upper echelons' of our societies. We're trying to get *away* from that here." He pointed to the profiles. "These five are...too experienced. I feel a more junior pairing will benefit us here."

"'Too experienced.'" Lamont grimaced sourly as he stared at the profiles. "'More junior.'"

"Yes," Jonas agreed brightly. "Just so."

"I suppose I could give it another try," Tyrel said with something reminiscent of a weary sigh. "Perhaps I can have another batch picked out for us to review in three days?"

"Oh, I hardly think that's necessary," Jonas said.

"I'm sorry?" Tyrel blinked, the confusion inflicting Lamont now spreading to her.

"Why don't we pick out someone right now?" Jonas offered.

"Now?" Tyrel raised both eyebrows.

"Sure. Why not?"

"But I need time to request a new round of volunteers and vet their applications." She turned to Lamont. "Chief?"

"Let's just get this over with," Lamont grumbled.

"But, sir?"

"The Admin has final say in the selection. Isn't that right, Klaus?"

"That was the agreement, sir, yes," Schröder said neutrally. "I believe the president characterized her approach as 'a small token of friendship and trust to the Admin for the lives they lost fighting alongside us.'"

"She did indeed," Lamont breathed, staring blankly at a distant patch of wall.

Jonas supposed the SysGov president had seen the officer exchange program as an opportunity to score some political points with the Admin chief executor, but what she'd *actually* done—wittingly or otherwise—was place all the program's strings in his hands.

"We will honor her wishes," Lamont continued, "regardless of any... misgivings we may have." He turned to Jonas. "Director, this is your show."

"Thank you, Chief." Jonas leaned in with a forearm on the table. "First, Commissioner Tyrel, would you mind pulling up the full detective roster?"

"All right."

The five profiles vanished, and a massive spreadsheet of names appeared over the table.

"Now filter for detectives with five or fewer years of experience. Aged forty or younger. Oh, and if you wouldn't mind displaying each detective's current location, please."

"Easy enough."

The table shrank considerably, but each line was still too small to read.

"Are the rows numbered?" Jonas asked as his implants analyzed the list. "It's a little hard to tell."

"They are."

"How about..." Jonas held up his hand, and a number flashed into existence. "Three hundred and twenty-two. Who's on that row?"

"Did you really just generate a value at random?"

"Maybe."

"Chief?" Tyrel protested.

"Just do what he asks," Lamont groaned.

Tyrel shook her head, but opened the profile regardless. She paused and regarded it with trepidation.

It was a short profile.

Very short.

"Seems we're looking at a Detective Isaac—"

❖   ❖   ❖

"—Cho!" Isaac smiled at his twin sister. "It has a good ring to it, don't you think?"

"If you say so," Nina Cho dismissed with a roll of her eyes as they headed toward the Argus Station hangar.

Both Cho twins wore the standard dark blue of SysPol with the Themis Division's golden eye and magnifying glass at their shoulders. They were on the short and slender side of SysGov norms, though not overly so, with sharp brown eyes and black hair cut short.

"*Detective* Isaac Cho," he repeated. "Not 'acting' detective. Not 'deputy' detective. Just straight-up full detective. And you, too! *Specialist* Nina Cho! No more 'acting specialist' for you." He let out a content, satisfied sigh. "It's been a long road, but here we are at last."

"Yup."

Isaac turned to her. "You don't seem excited."

"And why should I be?"

"Because we made it!" Isaac threw up his arms in triumph. "Ten long years! Five in the academy and five more as 'acting' officers. That's a whole *third* of our lives invested in this, and we *made* it!"

"Yup."

Isaac frowned and dropped his arms. "Somehow I thought you'd be happier."

"I am happy," Nina said with a shrug. "I just resent what a god-awful hassle it was having to come all the way to Earth for a five-hour induction ceremony."

"Actually"—Isaac opened a file above his palm—"only four hours and seventeen minutes."

"You timed it?" She gave him a disgusted look.

"No, I *recorded* it."

"Of course, you would." She shook her head.

"Want a copy?" He offered her the file.

"Hell no!" She pushed his hand away.

"Suit yourself." Isaac closed the virtual display. "I thought Commissioner Tyrel's opening speech was very inspirational. Definitely worth a rewatch."

The twins stepped into the hangar where the elliptical, eighty-meter-long SysPol corvette sat in its cradle with the prog-steel open at the nose and a ramp extruded down to the deck. They checked in with a deck officer clad in the patrol fleet black of Argo Division, who confirmed their identities and authorized them to board the corvette bound for Saturn. They climbed the ramp and were about to step into the forward cargo hold when virtual barriers materialized in front of Isaac, forming a police cordon between him and the corvette's interior.

"Umm." He regarded the cordon curiously, then poked it with a finger. Alarms blared in his virtual hearing, and he winced. "Well, that's not good."

"What did you do this time?" Nina asked, walking through the cordon without incident.

"What do you mean, 'this time'?" Isaac shot back.

The deck officer hurried over and switched off the alarm. She opened an interface in front of her and scrolled down until she found Isaac's boarding entry.

"That can't be right," she said, tilting her head to the side.

"What can't be?" Isaac asked.

"Seems your boarding pass has been revoked."

"Are you sure? There must be some mistake. I'm scheduled to leave for Saturn with my sister." He gestured to Nina. "We requested transport on the same ship, but I can take another ride if we're causing trouble."

"Sorry, Detective, but that's not the problem. Your outbound authorization has been yanked in its *entirety*."

"Oh." Isaac glanced over the cordon again. "Any indication why?"

"Not that I can see."

A private alert blinked to life in the corner of Isaac's vision, indicating an urgent message, and he stared at it, wondering at its timing, before finally opening it. He had to read it three times before the contents set in, and his eyes grew wider with each pass.

"This says I'm to report to the Chief of Police immediately?!"

"Oh my God! You *did* do something!" Nina accused with a gleeful gleam in her eyes.

"Did not!"

"They probably didn't like you recording the ceremony," Nina said with a wry grin.

"No," Isaac stressed. "That's allowed. I checked beforehand."

"Then why have you been called to the boss's office?"

"I ... rightfully don't know."

"You should probably find out, then."

"But ..."

"Best not keep the boss waiting. Especially when it's the *big* boss."

"But, I ... we're supposed to ... I mean ..." He looked over to the deck officer, who nodded in agreement with his sister.

"Nothing I can do for you here, Detective," she said in manner of an apology.

"Yes, I suppose not." Isaac closed the message and straightened his posture. "Well, sis, I guess I'll see you back on Kronos. Have a safe journey."

"*Zhù hǎo yùn,*" Nina said as both a goodbye and a wish for good luck, though her tonal subtext gave the phrase a touch of biting humor.

"Yes, I think I'll need some of that," Isaac replied dryly, then turned and headed for the nearest counter-grav tube.

✧   ✧   ✧

The tube dropped Isaac off near the heart of Argus Station. He looked around the circular space, gathered his bearings, and followed the virtual arrows down one of several spoking corridors. Room labels hovered over doors on either side, and he stopped at one marked EXECUTIVE CONFERENCE ROOM 6: OCCUPIED near the end of the corridor. He submitted his ID to the door's infosystem, but the door only buzzed at him and blinked red.

"Argus?" he asked. "I was told to meet the Chief of Police here. May I come in?"

"Chief Lamont will be with you shortly," replied the station's nonsentient attendant. "Please wait here, Detective."

A programmable-steel chair formed out of the wall to one side of the room label.

Isaac sat down and waited while his mind churned through

recent events, searching for some explanation for why his departure
had been canceled, but try as he might, he couldn't think of a
single reason that made sense, and that went double for why the
Chief of Police would want to see a detective as junior as he was.

"Hey, Cephalie?" he asked. "Any idea what this is all about?"

"Not a clue."

An avatar of a miniature woman appeared on his left thigh,
standing about a third of the way up his chest. Today, Encephalon wore a long, red coat with blue gloves, a blue bow tie, and
a small blue hat with a single red rose pinned in it. The lenses
of her circular wireframe glasses were opaque, and she pushed
them higher up the bridge of her nose.

Cephalie was a purely synthetic mind as well as Isaac's integrated companion, and they'd been happily paired for all five of
the years since he'd received his wetware implants upon becoming an adult at the age of twenty-five. She'd once been a SysPol
officer herself, and Isaac suspected from the start her interest
in him had been based more on a desire for mentorship than
companionship.

Which he didn't have any problems with; he'd benefited richly
from her wealth of knowledge and experience on more than a
few cases already.

"Not even a *little* clue?" Isaac asked.

"I've been asking around since Lamont messaged you. Even
tried looking up his schedule to see what meeting he's in, but
Argus gave me a slap on the wrist and told me—in no uncertain
terms—to mind my own business."

"But this *is* our business," Isaac protested.

"I know that, and you know that, but *Argus*?" She planted
her hands on her hips and shook her head. "Overbearing number
crunchers. What can you do about them?"

"Nothing but wait, I suppose." He settled deeper into the
chair's prog-foam cushion. "Thanks for trying."

"My pleasure." Her glasses twinkled, and she vanished.

Isaac exhaled slowly and drummed his fingers on his thighs.
He glanced sideways at the closed door, cleared his throat, and
continued to wait.

And wait.

And wait some more.

Finally, the door chimed at him.

"Chief Lamont will see you now."

"Thank you, Argus." He rose from his seat, straightened his uniform, and walked up to the door. Prog-steel split open down the middle, and he took one step inside—

—and froze.

Chief Lamont and all six division commissioners watched him from their seats at the table, and the weight of their gazes turned his legs to stone. Isaac had expected Lamont, had braced himself for a face-to-face meeting with the man in charge of SysPol, but what were all *six* of the commissioners doing here? He could maybe understand Commissioner Tyrel's presence, since he worked in her division, but why would any of the others want to see him?

His mind raced in a quest to find an answer, and he began to wonder how much trouble he'd landed himself in. His eyes gravitated to an empty chair at Lamont's left, pulled back and still spinning. Had someone just left through the room's rear exit?

Lamont, perhaps sensing his unease, beckoned him forward with a hand.

"Detective Cho, please come in."

Isaac became acutely aware of his motionless feet.

"Oh. Right." He stepped forward and stood at attention next to the table as the door sealed shut behind him. "Sorry, sir. I'm just rather surprised to find myself standing here."

"So are we, as it turns out."

Isaac wasn't sure what to make of that statement, but he kept his mouth shut and waited for the chief to continue.

"Detective, I'm sure you're wondering why we've called you here today. It's really quite simple. We're considering you for a special assignment, though I can't reveal the nature of the assignment at this time."

"A special assignment?" Isaac pointed to his chest. "Me?"

"Yes, Detective. You."

The stress from a few moments ago melted off him. This was better than he could have hoped for!

"I'm honored you would even consider me, sir, but are you sure I'm suitable for this assignment? My probationary period only ended today."

"We're well aware of your record," Lamont said. "After a careful and lengthy review process—"

Commissioner Tyrel put a hand to her forehead and started rubbing her temples.

"—we've decided you meet some of the necessary requirements. For the next step, we have a series of questions we'd like to ask you. Do you have any problems with that?"

"Of course not, sir. Ask away."

"Thank you. I appreciate your understanding, Detective. First, would you please give us your take on the Admin?"

Isaac blinked. "The Admin, sir?"

"Yes. What do you think of them?"

"Well, I don't really know what to say, sir. To be perfectly honest, I haven't given them much thought. Certainly, I've seen them in the news, but I've never met anyone from the Admin before, nor have I studied—or had reason *to* study—any of the unclassified reports we have on them. I don't think I'm qualified to offer anything approaching a proper analysis."

"Be that as it may, please, indulge us." Lamont spread his palms. "All we're looking for is your opinion of them. Not an analysis."

"I see, sir," Isaac replied, stalling for time more than anything.

Lamont and the others wanted to hear a particular answer from him, and the prize for the correct response was this mysterious assignment. That much seemed clear to Isaac, but he had no idea what answer they wanted, and he was woefully unequipped to even speculate on the matter. He glanced to Tyrel, thinking he might see some hint from his division's commissioner, but she gazed sullenly down at the table surface, as if shadowed by a thunderhead of impending doom. The woman's positivity from when she'd opened the induction ceremony had vanished, and Isaac took no comfort in the dark expression on her face.

He returned his gaze to Lamont.

There was only one thing to do. Only one thing he *could* do, and that was to be as truthful and forthcoming as he could.

"I think they're a bunch of thugs, sir," Isaac began. "Ignorant, brutish thugs. I haven't seen much of the Admin, but what I've seen disgusts me. The militarism, the xenophobia, the AI slavery, the way they unfairly swindled us out of our drive tech. Their government seems to be made up of thugs who believe might makes right and the ends justify the means. Oh, and the less said about their prisons the better! Can you believe they forcefully extract people's connectomes and dump them into unsupervised abstractions? What kind of a 'civilized' society does something like that?"

Isaac hadn't realized how loud his voice had grown near the end. He cleared his throat, straightened his posture, and waited. The room was silent for long, uncomfortable seconds.

Lamont's jaw twitched, and Isaac's heart sank. An icy chill ran down his spine as he realized this wasn't anything close to the answer the chief had been hoping for.

"So, yes," Isaac added to fill the silence. "That's my honest opinion, sir."

"And so it is. Thank you for your"—Lamont smiled without joy or humor—"candid response. Please wait outside while we discuss your answer."

✧   ✧   ✧

Jonas Shigeki couldn't believe his good fortune. The number he'd given Tyrel may not have been as random as he'd led them to believe, but it was *still* random, though filtered by a few more parameters than the ones he'd listed. He lacked access to the detailed backgrounds in Themis Division's official roster, and as such, he'd fully expected to have to go through this exercise a few times before he found a detective with all the traits *he* was looking for.

But to find the ideal candidate on the first try! Remarkable!

While Lamont and the commissioners had scrutinized Isaac Cho's meager professional record, Jonas had instead run a quick search through the young detective's *social* profiles, and that's where he found the key traits he'd been looking for. Oh, had he found them in *spades*!

Cho's impromptu rant about the Admin's failings—some of which Jonas even agreed with—only made him a better choice. He especially liked the part about how the DTI had "swindled" the transdimensional drive tech from Gordian; he was proud of that one, since he'd led the effort. Regardless, what was the point in selecting someone who *already* held a neutral or even positive outlook on the Admin? No, a little negativity—as long as it wasn't entrenched—provided a far better starting point, because success in the officer exchange program would play out in how those attitudes *changed*.

All it'll take is the right two people, he thought. *And now I have* both *of them!*

The conference room's rear door split open, and Jonas strode in with all the swagger of a general about to accept his foe's unconditional surrender. He spun his chair around, dropped into it, and leaned back into the comfortable padding.

"So," he said to Lamont with a wide grin, "what did you think?"

"Perhaps we should select someone else."

"Really?" Jonas asked with faux surprise. "You didn't like him?"

Lamont paused for a moment, and the aura of despair over the table grew thicker, almost palpable. Expectations for the officer exchange program had officially hit rock bottom, and Jonas worked to hide his elation.

It's called controlling expectations, people, he thought, suppressing an inward smile. *Try it sometime. Success will be measured against what you* expect *we'll achieve, and right now you all think I'm steering the ship straight into a looming asteroid.*

"You *did* hear what he said about your government?" Tyrel asked gently.

"Of course, but he didn't say anything disqualifying," Jonas countered. "To the contrary, I feel some of his criticisms are perfectly valid. There's room for improvement in the Admin, just as there is in any government, and I'd like to remind everyone that our current chief executor was elected on a reformist platform. I dare say it wouldn't be too hard to find people in the *Admin* who shared Detective Cho's views, just as I'm sure your government has its share of vocal detractors."

"That may be so," Tyrel said, "but perhaps he's not the best choice for *this* program."

"I have to agree." Lamont turned to Jonas. "Why don't you pick someone else out of the roster? We can keep looking until we find a better candidate. I'll go ahead and clear my schedule for the next—"

"Why go through the trouble?" Jonas interrupted.

"Well . . ." Lamont paused as if unsure how to make the problem any more obvious. "To be blunt, I don't think he'll work out."

"Respectfully, I'm forced to disagree. I think he's perfect."

"By what measure?" Tyrel asked pointedly.

"By the only one that matters, which is how likely this program is to succeed."

"Chief?" Tyrel stressed, her brow creased with worry.

"He has the final say," Lamont told her. "Director, are you sure about this?"

"Absolutely."

"Are you *sure*?" Lamont pointed at the door the detective was waiting outside.

"Oh, yes." Jonas gave the door a casual wave. "He'll do fine."

Lamont leaned back in his seat, a troubled look on his face.

"So"—Jonas placed his forearm on the table and leaned in—"would you like to tell him the good news? Or shall I?"

CHAPTER TWO

"YES, YOU SEE HERE?" CEPHALIE POINTED HER CANE AT AN OLD-fashioned blackboard floating over Isaac's knee. The blackboard displayed a chalky animated rendition of his meeting with the commissioners. "Right...there."

The image paused with his "thugs" comment frozen in his speech bubble.

"I couldn't say *nothing*," Isaac defended.

"True. True." Cephalie clacked her virtual cane atop his thigh. "But you also could have held back a bit. Played your hand more cautiously."

"Yeah, you're probably right." Isaac leaned back in his seat outside the conference room. "The chief said they had a 'series of questions' but he only asked the one. That's not a good sign." He ran rough fingers through his hair and took a deep, calming breath. "You think there'll be any repercussions?"

"I wouldn't stress over this if I were you." Cephalie banished the blackboard with a wave of her cane. "You're not getting this special assignment, whatever it may be, but they're not going to *punish* you for a botched interview. And even if they did, what's the worst they could do? A rotation on Neptune might do you some good."

"Please don't give them any ideas."

Isaac tapped his fingers on the knee opposite Cephalie and took another deep breath. He tried to focus his mind on something else as he waited, but his thoughts kept drifting back to the displeased expression on Lamont's face.

"They're coming out," Cephalie said several minutes later. She vanished from his knee as the door split open.

Isaac rose to attention and watched the physical commissioners file out of the room. Tyrel shook her head as she exited and didn't bother looking his way as her feet carried her automatically to her next appointment. Jamieson Hawke, commissioner of Argo Division, came up alongside her and gave her a comforting pat on the shoulder.

"It'll be all right, Vesna."

"No, it *won't*," was all she said as the two headed down the corridor.

The physical commissioners headed off, and Lamont stepped out after them followed by a young man wearing Admin Peacekeeper blues. Isaac's heartbeat quickened when they stopped in front of him.

Oh dear . . .

"Detective Cho, a pleasure to make your acquaintance." The Admin official smiled warmly and extended a hand. "My name is Jonas Shigeki. I'm the Under-Director of Foreign Affairs within the Admin's Department of Temporal Investigation."

"Hello, Director." Isaac grasped the man's hand and shook it.

Jonas took a step back and turned to Lamont with an expectant smile.

"Well, Chief?" He gestured to Isaac. "Would you like to do the honors?"

"Yes, I suppose I should."

"Sir?" Isaac looked to the chief.

"Congratulations, Detective," Lamont said, though his tone made it sound like he was inviting Isaac to a funeral.

"Sir?"

"You've been selected to participate in an officer exchange program with the Admin."

"Me?" Isaac's eyes bugged out.

"Yes," Lamont said dryly. "You."

"Am I being sent to the Admin?" Isaac asked, a hint of dread in his tone.

"No," Lamont corrected quickly. "Your assignment to Kronos Station remains unchanged. However, you'll be working with a DTI special agent from now on. She'll act as your deputy for the next three months."

"With options to extend the duration," Jonas pointed out.

"Yes," Lamont conceded. "If this goes well."

"As I have every confidence it will."

"A DTI agent?" Isaac asked. "Assigned to *me*?"

"That's right," Lamont said. "Agent Susan Cantrell will be granted the rank of 'acting deputy detective' while she serves within SysGov space. She'll be a full member of the System Police, from a legal perspective, with all the rights and responsibilities that implies and for the full duration of her stay."

"I've been assigned a deputy?" Isaac creased his brow. "Starting when?"

"In, oh"—Jonas summoned a clock over his palm—"about an hour, let's say. How's three o'clock sound to everyone?"

"An *hour*?" Isaac shook his head, struggling with the barrage of revelations. "Sir, I haven't prepared for this. I've never had a deputy before, and I don't know the first thing about working with an Admin agent. I'm a *terrible* choice for this assignment!"

"Please," Jonas reassured. "No need to be modest."

"Director, I—" Isaac began.

"Chief, if you'll excuse me," Jonas cut in. "I'd like to head down to our ambassadorial dock and make sure Agent Cantrell is ready."

"Yes, that's quite all right."

"I'd take the detective with me, but I'm sure you'd enjoy a private word with him before his new assignment begins."

"I would indeed, yes."

"In that case"—he backed away and gave them both a wave—"*zhù hǎo yùn!*"

Isaac and Lamont waited for the director to disappear down the counter-grav tube at the far end of the corridor.

"His English is pretty good," Isaac said, impressed with the director's farewell when compared to Admin speakers he'd caught in the news. Those last three words originated from the Old Chinese "zhù hǎo yùn" meaning "good luck," but the linguistic foundation for SysGov's Modern English came from a fusion of both Old English and Old Chinese, with the tonal vowels of Old Chinese being adapted to serve as a subtle undercurrent to the language. This versatility allowed tonal inflection to imbue those three simple words with a wide variety of meanings.

"Yes," Lamont agreed, "and it's my understanding he stopped using translation software a few months back."

"I see." Isaac nodded, waited for his superior to continue, and only spoke up when he didn't. "Sir, about this assignment."

"Yes, I know."

"Pardon me for saying this, but you don't seem happy with the arrangement."

"That's because I'm not." He faced Isaac. "Don't take this the wrong way, but you weren't our first choice."

"No offense taken, sir. *I* don't think I'm a good choice either. But I'll do the absolute best job I can under these circumstances."

"I'm glad to hear it."

Isaac glanced down the hall once more.

"So, it was the director who chose me?"

"That's right."

"Any idea why?"

"No, and that bothers me."

"Hmm." Isaac pondered what this could mean. "Anything I should be on my toes about?"

"I doubt it," Lamont dismissed. "Again, don't take offense, but you're not important enough for the Admin to take *that* kind of interest in you."

"Again, none taken, sir."

"Honestly, I think the director is being straight with us about his intentions. He wants this to succeed and is doing everything he can to make that happen." Lamont shook his head. "In his own misguided way. If the president hadn't handed all our leverage over, maybe we could have avoided this."

"Sir, do you have the service record for the agent I'm to be paired with?"

"Ah, yes. Of course." Lamont held up his palm, and a file transfer opened. "Here you go."

"Thank you, sir." He accepted the file.

"And here are our latest reports on Admin culture. Make sure you read them."

"I will, sir. Thank you."

"And here are a few more on the DTI and some of the other organizations within their government, profiles on their political leaders, analyses on current social climate, reviews of recent terrorist attacks, and so on."

"Yes, thank you." Isaac frowned as he accepted the mountain of documentation.

"Oh, and you should take these as well." A trio of gray-green files appeared between them. "You technically don't have clearance for these, but I'll see to it you're granted retroactive approval."

Isaac hesitated for a moment as he eyed the classified Gordian documents, but he reached out and accepted them.

"Are you sure I'll need all this, sir?"

"Would you rather dive into this assignment less prepared?"

"No, sir. Point taken." Isaac opened Susan Cantrell's service record and skimmed the digest. "A 'STAND' agent?" He read on, only vaguely familiar with the term. "'Special Training And Nonorganic Deployment.'"

"Yes. The Admin feels one of their synthoids would experience less culture shock over here, and I think they at least have *that* much right."

"But wouldn't they want to pair her to someone with roughly the same age and level of experience?"

"Actually, you're about the same age."

"Oh?" Isaac scrolled up a bit. "Oh, I see. Thirty-two? Quite young to have a synthetic body, at least by our standards."

"And someone like her is even rarer in the Admin." Lamont crossed his arms. "The director has assured us she's exceptionally skilled at her job and highly motivated for this post. Her service record, at least, reflects well on her professionally."

"I see." Isaac closed the file. He'd review it later in more detail. "Anything else, sir?"

"One more thing before you leave."

"Yes, sir?"

"Whatever you do around her." Lamont planted his hands on Isaac's shoulders. "Whatever you say to her."

"Yes, sir?"

"Remember this one thing." Lamont leaned in. "Do *not* embarrass us."

✧   ✧   ✧

"I can do that." Isaac twisted to look at Cephalie, now perched on his shoulder. "You think I can do that, right?"

"Oh, *sure*," she said, then chuckled. "Just be yourself. You'll do fine."

"Are you trying to make me doubt myself?"

His descent through the counter-grav tube slowed, and his path arced out through an opening until both feet came to rest in a wide circular space near the station's southern pole. The walls were Peacekeeper blue with a white line running through the middle, indicating this area had been set aside for Admin use. He followed the virtual markers down the widest of the adjacent passages to a guarded doorway at the far end. The emblem of a silver shield covered most of the doorway.

"Holler if you need anything," Cephalie said before vanishing.

"Right."

Two gray-skinned, yellow-eyed synthoids in Peacekeeper blues, one male and one female, stood watch on either side of the doorway. Both carried nasty-looking rifles and were flanked by a pair of drones the size of large dogs but with guns for faces.

Such a friendly bunch, Isaac thought. *I should be grateful they didn't put me in their sights as soon as I showed up.*

He stopped in front of the two synthoids, who regarded him with calculated indifference.

"Detective Isaac Cho, reporting per Director Shigeki's request." He offered them his SysPol ID file.

The woman checked his credentials while the man opened a communications window.

"Yes?" Jonas Shigeki said on the other end of the window.

"You asked to be notified when Detective Cho arrived."

"I did. And?"

"Detective Cho has arrived."

"Splendid. Send him on in."

"Yes, sir."

The window closed, and the two synthoids exchanged looks.

"His ID checks out," the woman reported. They nodded to each other and placed their palms against infosystem pads on either side of the doorway. The silver shield emblem split down the middle and opened to reveal a wide hangar bay. A single craft slightly larger than a standard pattern corvette rested in a prog-steel cradle. The vessel vaguely resembled a manta ray with its wide delta wing and the long tail of its dimension-rending impeller spike.

"Director Shigeki will see you now." She pointed at the vessel with her thumb. "He's in the chronoport."

"Thank you." Isaac walked in and managed not to flinch when the door sealed shut behind him. He headed over to the open ramp underneath the chronoport's nose. Modular weapon systems hung from hardpoints beneath the wings, including a pair of outboard laser pods and four box launchers for guided missiles.

Two Peacekeepers descended the ramp: Jonas Shigeki and a young woman Isaac assumed to be Susan Cantrell. He'd half expected her synthetic body to feature the gray skin and yellow eyes found on many Admin synthoids, but then he thought of her young age, and he also seemed to recall hearing somewhere that newer Admin synthoids featured lifelike cosmetic skin now that their society had become acquainted with the concept.

She was beautiful, too, with a lean, athletic body. She wore her red hair in a pixie cut, and her hazel eyes caught his. In an earlier era, someone in Isaac's shoes might have considered her stunning, but he came from a society where medical science for the young, synthetic bodies for the old, and avatars for the abstract made the idealized human form a common occurrence, and her looks barely registered beyond casual acknowledgement.

She's better looking than I expected, he thought.

The three of them met at the base of the ramp, and Susan retrieved her peaked cap from under her arm and fitted it back into place. She held herself with poise and confidence, and her face carried a look of cool professionalism, but underneath Isaac thought he saw a hint of something else. Nervousness, perhaps? That wouldn't surprise him; *he* was nervous, too.

"Detective Cho, thank you for coming." Jonas placed a hand on Susan's shoulder and urged her forward. "Allow me to introduce DTI Special Agent Susan Cantrell, one of our best STANDs. Agent, this is Detective Isaac Cho of the Themis Division."

"A pleasure, sir." Susan extended a hand.

"Likewise, Agent," Isaac replied, and shook her hand. Or tried to. She may have looked delicate, but her hand only moved when *she* moved it.

"And is your integrated companion with you?" Jonas asked.

"Why, yes. She is." Isaac tapped his shoulder, and Cephalie's avatar materialized. "This is my IC, Encephalon."

"Nice to meet you as well." Susan nodded to the avatar, and Isaac breathed an inner sigh of relief. She hadn't freaked out at the sight of a free-roaming artificial intelligence. That was a good start.

"Please, call me Cephalie." She gave Susan a wave, then vanished.

"Splendid." Jonas rubbed his hands together. "Just a few brief pieces of business, then I think we can get the two of you underway."

"Yes, about that," Isaac said. "I missed my original flight to Saturn."

"Not a problem," Jonas assured them. "I spoke with Commissioner Hawke a few minutes ago about your travel situation. Regrettably, he informed me there aren't any patrol fleet craft scheduled to leave for Saturn in the next few days, so he helped me book passage for the two of you on a civilian saucer. Once we're done here, a SysPol corvette will rendezvous with the saucer and drop you off."

"Ah. Good," Isaac remarked. Nine days on a civilian transport didn't sound bad at all.

"Now, just a few things I'd like to point out." Jonas gestured down the length of Susan's body. "Agent Cantrell's synthoid is the first in a new model series. Built with SysGov collaborations in mind, it features the latest Admin technology and is fully compatible with your infostructures. Agent, how's it working out for you?"

"Perfectly, sir. No issues to report."

"Wonderful. I'm actually a little jealous. You're about to be the first person from our universe to *truly* experience SysGov." He flashed a half smile at Isaac. "As you may be aware, most Admin citizens, myself included, can only process virtual sight and sound. But Agent Cantrell has no such restrictions; she's now able to experience *any* SysGov abstraction in its entirety."

"That's good to hear," Isaac remarked. "Our investigations sometimes include work in abstractions, so I'm glad that won't present any technical hurdles."

"It won't, sir," Susan said with confidence. "You can count on it."

"Furthermore," Jonas continued, "in addition to her standard kit, which we've already sent to the Argo corvette, we've given Agent Cantrell a wide selection of Admin pattern files, all adapted for compatibility with SysGov printers. If there's anything she needs in terms of repair parts or additional equipment, she has the printing pattern for it."

"Sounds very prudent." Isaac nodded at this, though he wasn't sure what the director meant by "standard kit."

"That said, hopefully most won't be needed," Susan said. "It'd be nice not to have my legs blown off again."

"Your legs?" Isaac blinked. "Again?"

"It's a long story," she said as if it were nothing, though having one's legs blown off didn't sound like nothing to Isaac, synthoid body or no.

"Our work in the DTI can sometimes be a bit . . . rougher than what you're used to," Jonas explained. "And STANDs often serve as the tip of the Peacekeeper spear."

"So I've heard," Isaac said.

"The important part is if her body is damaged, you won't need to call us for spares."

"Which works out for me," Susan said. "I'd hate to be stuck here without legs."

"I'm sure we can avoid that," Isaac stressed.

"Well then." Jonas clapped his hands together. "I believe that's everything I wanted to cover." He passed a destination to the two of them. "The corvette's waiting for you two. Good luck out there. Oh, and agent?"

"Yes, sir?"

Jonas placed a hand on Susan's shoulder. The two made eye contact, and their facial expressions and body language made it look like they were having a conversation even though their lips weren't moving.

Admin closed-circuit chat, Isaac noted, recalling another tidbit he'd read about SysGov's multiverse neighbor. *They're making sure the conversation's private by avoiding any wireless transmissions.*

Susan gave the director a quizzical expression, but then nodded to him. He smiled, removed his hand, and headed up the ramp.

"Shall we head out, sir?" Susan asked him.

"Yes. Let's," Isaac replied, though he grimaced a little at the whole "sir" thing. He led the way out of the hangar and back to the counter-grav tube. He stepped out into the open shaft, but Susan hesitated for a moment before joining him.

"This is a bit weird." She looked around the tube as they sped up through the station.

"How so?" he asked.

"No artificial gravity where I come from."

"Ah. Of course."

A secondary tube branched off the main one, taking them in

a long arcing path around the station's circumference until they arrived at their destination hangar. The elliptical SysPol corvette sat in its cradle, and a virtual image provided a view of space beyond the closed airlock. He could see the full coin of Earth's moon rising over the corvette, white clouds swirling across its bluish landscape. Greenery dotted the surface here and there, and the thin silver band of its orbital ring glinted in the sunlight.

Isaac headed for the corvette, then stopped and turned back to Susan when he realized she wasn't following.

"Something wrong?" he asked.

"Is that Luna?"

"Yes?" He glanced at the distant orb, then back to her. "And?"

"It's *blue*."

"Yes?"

"Why is it blue?"

"Well, umm." He turned back to it, then back to her once more. "Why wouldn't it be?"

"It's all gray where I come from."

"Oh, right!" He snapped his fingers. "Luna didn't always have oceans and an atmosphere."

"You just remembered that?"

"Well, it was terraformed long before I was born." He shrugged. "This is normal for me."

"I see." She gazed at the distant moon, then let out a slow, sad sigh.

"You okay?" He walked back over to her.

"Yeah. It just hit me, that's all."

"What did?"

"How far away from home I am."

"I can understand that." He nodded, then gave her a warm smile. "Welcome to SysGov. If you think a moon with an atmosphere is something, just wait until we reach Saturn."

CHAPTER THREE

ISAAC AND SUSAN CROSSED THE BOARDING TUNNEL BETWEEN THE SysPol corvette and the much larger *Arcturus*, a luxury saucer owned and operated by the Polaris Traveler corporation. Both craft hovered near each other with drives off and artificial gravity on, though the *Arcturus* would ease its gravity back to zero once it resumed acceleration toward Saturn. None of the passengers would feel a thing, since its five wide, circular decks were aligned with "up" as the direction of travel.

Two Polaris employees, one physical and one abstract, waited for them at the far end of the boarding tunnel. The tunnel sealed off and retracted back to the corvette, which began to ease away from the larger vessel.

"Welcome aboard, Detective. Agent." The abstract greeter gave them a polite bow of her head. She was using the avatar of an attractive baseline woman in a pastel green Polaris uniform. "My name's Amelia. I'm in charge of Guest Services here on the *Arcturus*. If there's anything you need while within our care, please don't hesitate to call on me. I guarantee I'll come 'running.'"

"Thank you, Amelia," Isaac replied. "We'll do our best not to cause you any trouble. Has my IC arrived yet?"

"Yes, Detective, Encephalon transmitted in ahead of you. She's already checked in. Now"—Amelia summoned an interface with their itineraries—"I have you both down for transport to Kronos Station. Is that correct?"

"Yes, that's right."

"Wonderful." Amelia checked a few boxes. "Our next stop will be Ballast Heights on Janus. Would you like me to arrange a connecting flight for you or shall I contact the station directly and have them pick you up en route?"

"The latter, please."

"Very good, sir." She jotted down a few notes. "And I take it you'd like the young woman's cargo container to follow the same route?"

"Her... cargo container?" Isaac asked.

"That would be my kit," Susan clarified. "And yes, it should come with me."

"How much stuff is in your kit?"

"Just the standard equipment for a STAND in the field, sir." She looked over at him. "Do you wish to inspect it?"

"Yes, actually."

"That's easy enough to arrange," Amelia assured them. "I'll have it moved to a satellite cargo hold where you can access the contents in private, though"—she held up a stern finger—"I must ask that you *not* remove any of its contents from the cargo hold, given what's inside."

"Of course," Susan said. "That won't be a problem."

"Thank you for your understanding." Amelia dipped her head again.

What exactly is in that kit? Isaac wondered. *And why does everyone here seem to know what's in it besides me?*

"Here are your room keycodes and a map of the ship."

Isaac and Susan accepted the files.

"The ship is currently operating under Janus Standard Time, and our dining halls will be opening soon. Just to point out a few of your options, there will be live classical music in the Deck One Observation Dome, while Deck Five's Cyber-Acoustic Rave is geared toward guests in a more... energetic mood. We're also hosting an amateur karaoke night in the Deck Three Starboard Hall, with some very exciting prizes for the winners."

"Would you like me to show you to your rooms?" The physical greeter placed a hand over his heart and dipped his head. "My name's Jamal, by the way."

"No, that'll be all right," Isaac said. "We'll make our way to her cargo container next."

"Understood, sir." Jamal indicated the location on their maps and provided an access keycode. "Here's everything you'll need."

"Is there any other way we can make your stay more pleasant?" Amelia asked.

"No, I'm sure we can manage the rest."

"Very good." Amelia bowed once more, a little deeper this time. "Again, welcome aboard the *Arcturus*. Please enjoy your time in our care."

Amelia vanished, and Jamal headed off down the gently curving corridor. Isaac pulled up the container's location and started down the corridor in the opposite direction.

"Is that typical?" Susan asked once they were alone.

"What do you mean?"

"They didn't seem bothered by the fact we're cops."

"Should they have been?"

"I suppose not," she conceded. "I'm just used to a different kind of reception."

"Less friendly and more combative?"

"Sometimes. It depends on who we're dealing with and which planet we're on. Mars and Luna are particularly bad where I come from."

"I see." Isaac scratched at his temple. "Haven't you been briefed on SysGov culture?"

"A little. To be honest, my appointment to this position was approved before I even realized what was going on. The whole process just flew by, and then I found myself here. It gave me the impression things were being rushed through before anyone had time to object. That said, sir, let me assure you I have the utmost enthusiasm for this post. It's an honor to be here."

"I had a similar experience with my appointment being rushed." He shrugged. "I guess that's something we have in common."

"I suppose so, sir."

"You can stop that, by the way."

"Stop what, sir?"

"The whole 'sir' thing. I know you're assigned as my deputy, but there's no need to be so formal. Please, call me Isaac."

"Is that an order?"

"I . . ." Isaac stumbled mentally. What sort of question was that? "Well, no. Not an order, per se. More like a suggestion or a request. Yes, that's it! A request. From one coworker to another."

"I see, s—"

His eye twitched.

"I see...Isaac," she replied slowly. It sounded like it took effort.

"There. That's not so bad, now is it?"

"No, s—" Her jaw tightened. "No."

"And would you mind if I called you Susan?"

"If you prefer."

"I—" He paused again and frowned. "What would *you* prefer?"

She let out a long, slow sigh.

"Agent Cantrell?"

"Susan is fine."

"Are you certain?"

"Yes, s—" She cut herself off and sighed again. "Yes."

"Am I making you uncomfortable?"

"I'll adapt."

Isaac grimaced at the nonanswer but decided to move on. He offered her two files.

"What're these?" she asked, copying the files.

"The first is your badge," he explained. "The transmit feature will identify you as a SysPol officer to anyone in your general vicinity. The second is my personal key for SysPol security chat. It will allow the two of us to converse about sensitive matters while in public, if it proves necessary. We'll be able to understand each other, but our speech will come across as gibberish to anyone else."

"Thank you. I'm sure both will come in handy."

"Also"—he looked her up and down—"about your uniform."

"What about it?"

"In Themis Division, we're allowed to wear civilian clothing while on duty."

"Is that a requirement?" Susan eyed Isaac's own uniform.

"Well, no. Simply an option."

"Do you wear civilian clothing while on duty?"

"Uhh, no. I normally wear this." He tugged on his SysPol blues.

"Then I would prefer to wear my Peacekeeper uniform while on duty."

"Are you sure about that? You're going to stick out in that outfit. The virtual badge will suffice as official identification."

"But that's the whole point of the Peacekeeper uniform. To mark me as separate from civilians and to identify the organization I serve."

"Yes, granted, but..." Isaac trailed off and shook his head. "Never mind."

What was *wrong* with her?

They arrived at the satellite cargo hold, and Isaac palmed the door open. A rectangular cargo container sat upright in the middle of the stark chamber. It stood taller than both of them, though not by much in Susan's case, and the outer surface declared its origin in bold Peacekeeper blue with white borders and a silver shield on the front.

"Your kit?" Isaac asked.

"Yes, indeed!" Susan's eyes gleamed with excitement. She jogged over to the container, crossed her arms, and leaned her shoulder against it with a broad smile on her lips.

The crack in her strict demeanor caught Isaac by surprise, and he wondered why she seemed almost giddy in the presence of her equipment. Clearly, this represented a part of her job she took pride in.

"Would you like to see what's inside?" She knocked on the container.

"Of course. That's why I'm here."

"All right, then!" She placed her hand on a control pad, and the container's exterior turned transparent.

"Oh." Isaac's eyes widened. "Oh dear."

"This"—Susan thumped the side with her fist—"is my Type-99 STAND combat frame! Brand-new model! Better than the venerable Type-92s in every respect!"

"A...combat frame?" Isaac asked, feeling numb.

"Yes! For use in operations too hazardous for my general purpose synthoid! When needed, my connectome case is manually transferred to the combat frame, and I take direct control of this beauty!"

Isaac had seen video of Admin combat frames in action, and those skeletal machines must have been modeled after someone's idea of death incarnate. *This* one represented a departure from those earlier designs. Its humanoid body possessed a lithe athleticism, and its current variskin configuration gave it a blue body with white racing stripes and a small silver shield at the shoulder.

It looked...friendlier than those mechanical death skeletons.

Yes, friendlier.

Except for all the *weapons*.

"The Type-99 is an absolute speed demon, with powerful maneuvering boosters in the legs, shoulders, and forearms. It's the fastest combat frame yet, featuring modular weapon hardpoints that can be configured to handle *any* situation. Here you can see the default configuration: heavy rail-rifle on the right arm, shoulder-mounted grenade launcher, and left arm incinerator."

"It has a *flamethrower*?"

"Yes!" Susan beamed at him. "Perfect for when things get up close and personal with the bad guys!"

"Susan?"

"The rail-rifle comes with a precision stabilizer mount. Perfect for long-range sniping, and the guided grenades provide options for enemies hiding behind cover. With this loadout, the Type-99 is lethal at *any* range!"

"Susan?"

"And it's not defenseless, either! Besides its agility, which is *considerable*, the armor is composed of over two *thousand* independent microplates of malmetal, capable of reconfiguring on the fly to form useful, solid objects or seal any armor breach almost instantly!" She thumped the container again. "In conclusion, the Type-99 represents the *pinnacle* of Admin law enforcement lethality!"

"Law enforcement?" he echoed weakly. "Lethality?"

"Yes!"

"*Susan?*" Isaac strained.

"Yes?"

"Has anyone explained to you what we do in the Themis Division?"

"Well, not in detail, now that you mention it." She took on a thoughtful look and rubbed her chin. "The under-director described your division as analogous to DTI Suppression counterterrorism ops, but with a scope that covered the whole solar system."

"And what do those operations entail?"

"Well, first we investigate terrorist attacks. Try to track down the perpetrators."

"Okay. Good so far. We do some of that, too."

"And then we head over to where the baddies are hiding and blow them up."

"Right." Isaac nodded. "I think I see where the disconnect is."

"The disconnect?" Susan tilted her head.

"We in Themis Division—which you are now serving in, by the way—are the detectives of SysPol. We investigate crimes, we collect evidence, we identify the guilty, and we bring them in so that justice may be served."

"Of course."

"*Alive*," Isaac stressed.

"Oh." Susan took a guilty sidestep away from the container.

"We in Themis do not dispense justice. We indict those we believe are guilty, but we do not decide their punishments. That duty is left to the courts, while any punishment is doled out by the Panoptics Division. Lethal force should only be used as a last resort. Yes, we are authorized to use it, but its application normally means we have failed in some other way. I don't even carry a gun while on duty, let alone an abomination like this!" He indicated the combat frame.

"How do you bring in criminals, then? With your bare hands?"

"I utilize a LENS. A Lawful Enforcement and Neutralization System. A *nonlethal* neutralization system. It's a SysPol drone specific to Themis, which Cephalie controls for me most of the time."

"I see." Susan gave the combat frame a forlorn look. But then her eyes brightened and she turned back to him. "What if the criminals counteract the LENS in some manner?"

"Then we call in the SysPol's heavy hitters for backup. The Arete First Responders or—God forbid—the Argo Patrol Fleet! When a situation escalates to the point where brute force is required, we step aside and let the experts take over, but it's our job to do everything in our power to ensure matters do *not* escalate in the first place."

"I see," she repeated. She gave the combat frame one more glance, and her shoulders slumped ever so slightly. "Does this mean I can't even carry a weapon while on duty?"

"No," Isaac corrected, trying not to sound annoyed. "Themis detectives are permitted to carry sidearms while on duty, though they must select from a preapproved list of SysPol patterns. A very limited list."

"May I see the list, then?"

"Why?"

"Because I like to be prepared."

"We're on a luxury saucer in the middle of open space. There's nothing to worry about."

"That may be so, but I'm...ill at ease without a weapon."

"You inhabit a cutting edge synthoid. You *are* a weapon!"

"Still..." She gave him a sad look.

"Fine," Isaac huffed. He looked away as he sent her the file. "Pick anything off this list. I'll arrange for it to be printed for you."

"Thank you."

"Now, if you'll excuse me, I'm going to check into my room."

✧   ✧   ✧

The door opened, and Isaac plodded into his room. It was a nice room, all things considered, with tasteful abstract and physical art dotting a spacious floorplan, all culminating in a wide view of outer space at the back.

"You certainly took your time," Cephalie tittered from atop a complimentary fruit bowl on the table.

Cephalie's words and the room's decor barely registered in his mind as he trudged over to the bed. His knees made contact with the side, which acted as a fulcrum for his whole body to lever down until his face planted into the sheets.

"That bad, huh?"

"Mmm-fnng-rrgng-ghrmm," he groaned into the sheets.

"What?"

Isaac rolled over onto his back and vented a frustrated breath.

"Something on your mind?" Cephalie teleported to his chest.

"Oh, my goodness! She's such a thug!"

"Aww," Cephalie cooed. "Is the big bad Admin Peacekeeper too much for you?"

"You wouldn't say that if you'd been there." Isaac sat up, and Cephalie floated down to his thigh. "Did you see what's in her kit?"

"I might have taken a peek." Cephalie twirled her cane. "Nasty piece of hardware."

"It has a *flamethrower!*"

"Yeah, I saw. Kind of hard to miss."

"What in the worlds does she need a flamethrower for?"

"I don't know. Thinking back, I could have used a flamethrower on a few cases."

Isaac glared at her.

"Only saying," she defended. "You know, hypothetically."

"Well, I have no intention of using it!" Isaac placed both palms on his forehead. "As soon as we get to Kronos, that thing is getting shoved into the deepest, darkest pit of our logistics centers, never to see the light of day again!"

"That seems a tad excessive."

"And do you know what she said when I asked her to call me Isaac?"

"No."

"She said 'Is that an order?'" His mouth gaped as he shook his head. "What kind of person says something like that?"

"Would the answer you're looking for be 'an Admin thug'?" Cephalie offered.

"Exactly!"

"I think you're being too hard on her."

"Oh, there's more!" Isaac continued, undeterred. "Guess the first thing she asked about when I stressed that it's our job to bring criminals in alive?"

"Umm?" Cephalie held her cane across her shoulders. "I give up."

"Guns. As in, can she carry one while on duty."

"I don't know. Makes sense to me. Girl's all alone in a strange universe. Feels good to pack some heat at the hip. Even if it's not a flamethrower."

"Uhhh!" Isaac flopped down onto his back.

Cephalie walked up to his face and poked his nose with her cane. Despite the virtual nature of the interaction, his wetware allowed him to "feel" the jab.

"You think I'm overreacting, don't you?"

"Maybe a touch." She held her thumb and forefinger close.

Isaac sucked in a long, slow breath, then let it all out.

"Come on," she urged. "Stop moping and get up."

"Fine." He sat up, and she floated over to his shoulder. He raised his hand and summoned the reports Lamont gave him.

"Going to do some reading?"

"Yeah. Maybe working through these will help me deal with Susan better."

"That's the spirit."

Isaac selected the Admin cultural overview, opened it, even read the first line, but then stopped.

"You know what? No." He closed the file abruptly.

"No, what?"

"I'm not going to read them." He turned to Cephalie. "I'm not going to let some analyst tell me what to think of the Admin or its people. Because that's part of the problem; I let all those news articles influence my opinion, and now my brain goes straight to the worst possible interpretation every time she opens her mouth. And look at me! I'm working with someone from the Admin who's here because they want to coexist with us! Who's in a better position than me to learn what they're really like?

"So, no. I'm not going to read those reports. I'm going to leave my—and everyone else's—biases at the door and let my experiences with her form my own opinion."

"Are you sure that's wise?" she asked. "Lamont gave you those files because he wanted you to review them."

"Cephalie, if nothing else, the last day has taught me one *very* important lesson."

"And what's that?"

He turned to the miniature woman on his shoulder.

"Our leaders don't have a clue."

CHAPTER FOUR

SUSAN STEPPED INTO HER PRIVATE ROOM WITH HER BACK STRAIGHT and head held high. She looked every bit the proper Admin Peace-keeper, all the way up to the moment the door sealed shut behind her.

Finally, she was alone.

Susan pressed her back against the door and let out a long, slow sigh as she slid down, every artificial muscle in her body loosening until her butt smooshed against the carpet.

She removed her peaked cap, threw it like a Frisbee to land on a nearby table, and ran fingers through her short hair.

"He probably thinks I'm some sort of thug," she moaned.

This was, she had to admit, not an unfair assessment. She was a STAND, after all. She'd voluntarily given up her frail flesh to become a living weapon, a construct that forever teetered on the edge of what it meant to be human, all in service of the System Cooperative Administration and the laws and ideals it fought to uphold.

She was a blunt instrument, not an ambassador. *That* much was painfully obvious.

"'Is that an order?'" She rolled her eyes. "What the hell was I thinking?"

She drew in another deep breath and sighed once more, slouching lower against the door.

It was a common misconception that a connectome *only*

consisted of a neural map. This was not the case. While the technology existed in both SysGov and the Admin to extract a hyper-accurate neural map that replicated a person's "wet" brain, this alone could not produce a complete representation of the individual. There were also the physiological and biochemical aspects of human personalities to consider, such as how smiling could improve a person's mood or how a deep breath could produce a calming effect.

In order to overcome this obstacle, a simulator was attached to the connectomes of post-organic citizens. This software package mimicked organic bodily functions that impacted personality, forming a feedback loop with the connectome's neural map.

As with any piece of software, this simulator could be modified far more easily than an organic body, but strict legal hurdles existed in both SysGov and the Admin for anyone wishing to perform such invasive self-modification. Susan had exactly zero interest in that; she may have come to terms with her synthoid inhumanity, but she clung to what little humanity remained with selfish zeal. The only modifications she'd received were those required by her position as a STAND, such as edits to her pain response. Other than those, her synthoid remained set for maximum fidelity.

And so, when Susan sighed after totally blowing it with her new partner, the act made her feel better.

At least a little.

"What a *day*," she breathed, pushing herself up off the floor. She walked a lap around the room, took some comfort in the blue suitcase on the bed, home to a few modest personal effects. She continued on, paused to admire an oil painting of a city floating over Venus, then stopped at the massive window on the far side.

She gazed out into the starry void, hugged her arms under her breasts, then leaned close to the concave glass and looked up.

An oblong tan orb shone "high" above the ship, distant yet bright.

Saturn.

Her destination.

"Farther than I've ever been." She stepped away and took a moment to consider how she'd come to be here.

✧   ✧   ✧

"Come in, Agent."

The malmetal door split open, and Susan stepped briskly into the conference room deep in the subbasement bowels of the DTI tower. She stopped beneath a single overhead light in front of a long, rectangular table, the rest of the room consigned to the shadows. A natural human would have struggled to spot—let alone *identify*—the other people in the room, but her synthoid eyes adjusted instantly.

From left to right, she saw Jonas Shigeki, Under-Director of Foreign Affairs, Dahvid Kloss, Under-Director of Espionage, Katja Hinnerkopf, Under-Director of Technology, and STAND Special Agent James Noxon. Someone inexperienced with the DTI might have been puzzled to see these four together, but Susan knew better. For whatever reason, she now found herself hauled before the "inner circle," and the only person missing was the man in charge, Director-General Csaba Shigeki.

What could this possibly be about? she wondered. *Have I done something wrong?*

Her interactions with the inner circle ranged from limited to nonexistent, which made their presence here all the more puzzling.

Hinnerkopf may have been the Under-Director of Technology, but the compact, stern woman spent most of her time and energy focused on their chronoports, not equipment as comparatively mundane as synthoids.

Jonas Shigeki had been the Under-Director of Suppression until recently, in charge of the DTI's planetary network of time drive suppression towers, but that was before everyone found out they had a technologically superior neighbor eyeballing them from across the multiverse! Susan had served all ten of her years at the DTI in Suppression, but she'd never once met him in person until today.

She'd fought alongside Agent Noxon during a few tough DTI ground missions, and she'd found him focused, dedicated, and extremely capable, if a little cold.

And then there was Dahvid Kloss.

Susan had been interrogated by him once; she hadn't been the *target* of his investigation, thankfully, but his ruthless pursuit of the leak in their organization had left a lasting impression. She could safely say of all the people she'd met within the DTI, Dahvid Kloss was the only one she genuinely feared.

"Agent," Kloss began as he leaned in, "we are assessing you for possible reassignment in your capacity as a STAND. We will ask you a series of questions, and you will answer them truthfully and completely, to the best of your abilities. Furthermore, this meeting's contents are confidential, DTI under-director rank or higher with yourself and Agent Noxon as approved exceptions. You will not discuss any aspect of this meeting with unapproved personnel. Breaking confidentiality may result in punishment up to and including dishonorable discharge from the Peacekeepers. Are these instructions clear?"

"Perfectly clear, sir."

Possible reassignment? she thought. *Either I've done something very, very wrong...or very, very right.*

"Good. Then let's begin." Kloss placed his hand on the table, and a virtual chart appeared to his right, blurred by a privacy filter. "According to your file, you've been a STAND for nine years. In fact, you're one of the youngest STAND applicants on record, enlisting in the Peacekeepers at the age of twenty and transitioning to a synthoid at twenty-three. What motivated your decision to enlist?"

"The Byrgius Blight, sir."

"Ah, of course," Hinnerkopf said, and Noxon nodded approvingly at her side.

Susan hadn't always been a staunch supporter of the Admin; in fact, she'd been the complete opposite all the way up to her third year at Byrgius University, situated in the lunar crater of the same name. She'd been a bright-eyed idealist at the time, immersed in the melting pot of cultures at Byrgius. No problem was too large or too complex for the enlightened insight of her professors.

Or so it had seemed.

People came from all over the solar system to attend the university because, despite its location within Luna's hotbed of violence, time had transformed it into a symbol for those who wished to reform the Admin, not through bloodshed, but by the slow changing of hearts and the winning of elections.

Her world had appeared so much easier to fix back then, but she soon learned a hard, vital lesson. Some people reserved their hottest rage not for their enemies, but rather for those they viewed as traitors amongst their own people.

And that irrational, black-hearted hatred had led Free Luna terrorists to unleash a voracious nanotech strain within the Lunarian dormitories. The self-replicating blight started as a modest seed, but it grew quickly, devouring anyone and anything it touched. Walls oozed down like wax under a flame, and students writhed in unspeakable agony as tiny machines ate them alive from the inside, reducing them to quivering puddles of meat.

Susan had been asleep in an adjacent dormitory when the alarms sounded. A section of the campus began to depressurize, and emergency bulkheads sealed off her only means of escape, trapping her inside the same area as the blight. She would have died that day were it not for the Peacekeeper teams that had braved the infestation time and time again to save as many students as they could.

She remembered the STANDs most of all. They stood tall and fearless in the face of the blight, pushing it back with their incinerators, holding the line as flesh-and-blood operators rushed student after student to safety.

Not every STAND made it out of Byrgius alive that day, but not one of them—not a *single* one—fell back until the last of the students who could be saved had *been* saved. Then—and *only* then—did the STANDs pull back, allowing the Admin cruiser high overhead to scour the site clean with laser fire.

Susan would never forget that day, nor would she ever forgive the madness of the Admin's enemies. Some problems couldn't be solved with kind words and an understanding heart.

"If memory serves, I applied to the Peacekeepers about a month after the attack," Susan added.

"And your decision to join STAND three years later?" Kloss asked.

"I set that goal for myself the day I enlisted."

"Why?"

"It seemed the best place for me to make a difference, sir."

"Wasn't that a bit hasty?"

"Sir?"

"Let me rephrase the question. Why would you, a young woman with her whole life ahead of her, willingly submit yourself to such hazardous work? Most STANDs 'retire' from service when they're killed in the line of duty."

"I knew that at the time, sir."

"And yet you still volunteered."

"Yes, sir."

"Why?"

"Byrgius, sir."

Kloss drummed his fingers on the table, clearly unsatisfied with the repeated answer.

"Very well," he said at last, then glanced once more to his obscured chart. "What is your opinion of the Yanluo Restrictions? Specifically, the Restrictions on AI development."

"It is part of our duties as Peacekeepers to enforce the Restrictions against AI development."

"Yes, but what is your opinion of them?"

"Sir?" Susan asked, not sure what he was looking for.

"What do you think of them?"

"My opinion doesn't matter, sir. It is my sworn duty as a Peacekeeper to enforce the Restrictions."

"But are they good laws?"

"They're . . . important laws?" she asked more than answered.

"Important, you say?" Kloss exhaled an irate breath. "And if the Restrictions were amended to allow for unfettered AI development?"

"Then I will enforce those new Restrictions. As is my sworn duty."

"But what is your *opinion* of them?"

"I don't really have one when it comes to AI Restrictions. I do have some strong opinions about self-replicators, if you'd like to hear those, sir."

"No, that won't be necessary." Kloss checked his chart again. "Moving on, what is your opinion of SysGov? Can you at least try to give me that?"

"Gladly, sir. Our intelligence on SysGov ground forces is limited at this point. However, it is believed that SysPol's Arete Division serves as the closest analogue to—"

"Stop," Kloss groaned wearily. "You misunderstood the question yet again."

"Sir?"

"I'm not interested in their military. I'm asking about their people."

"Their civilians, sir?"

"Yes."

"You're asking me?" Susan said, bewildered.

"*Yes.*"

"But why?"

"I ask the questions here, Agent. Not you."

"Sorry, sir." She snapped her eyes forward. "I don't feel I'm qualified to give an answer."

"Agent, you *will* answer the question."

"They're ..." Susan struggled to come up with something. Anything. "Weird?"

"Weird," Kloss repeated.

"Maybe a little naive?"

"Naive, you say."

"When it comes to how they use their tech, sir."

"Weird and naive." He turned to Jonas. "Are you even listening?"

"To every word, Dahvid," Jonas replied, sounding bored.

"Care to ask any questions of your own?"

"Look, Dahvid. This is your pointless exercise, not mine."

"And you still think she's our best option?"

"I wouldn't have picked her otherwise."

"But to base our candidate solely on—"

"Common ground," Jonas cut in. "That's the key, and that's why this is going to work."

"His approach is unorthodox," Hinnerkopf said. "However, I must admit I'm interested to see the results."

"And I'll vouch for Agent Cantrell's dedication and professionalism," Noxon said. "She's one of our finest agents."

"Yes," Kloss agreed. "In STAND. I'm sure she's a great walking, talking demolition zone, but have any of you considered that's not what we need in a representative?"

"A what, sir?" Susan asked suddenly.

"You"—Kloss pointed a fierce finger at her—"stay out of this!"

"Yes, sir," she replied in a mousy voice.

"You worry too much," Jonas said.

"I'm the Director of Espionage! It's my job to worry!"

"Oh, don't get so worked up," Jonas urged. "The risk for us is minimal. If I turn out to be wrong and this whole thing doesn't pan out, they'll blame me for the failure. Not the Admin as a whole. Just me."

"You're not half as clever as you think you are," Kloss seethed.

"Maybe so." Jonas leaned back with spread hands. "But who

secured that new drive tech deal? Who led the first ever joint mission? Face it, Dahvid. I have a proven record here. No one on our side understands them like I do. Not even you."

"Perhaps," Kloss fumed, backing off a little. "But I still say we should bring the boss in on this."

"Seriously, Kloss?" Hinnerkopf scolded. "Do you really want to tell the director we need our hands held on this decision?"

"Well, no."

"He delegated this task to us," Jonas pointed out. "And this is an issue for Foreign Affairs, so I'm well within my authority here."

"Yes, but . . ." Kloss glanced at Susan, then turned back to Jonas. "Can we at least tell her what the common ground is?"

"No," Jonas said. "It has to come up naturally. We don't want this to look staged."

"It *is* staged!"

"But we don't want it to *look* that way."

"Fine," Kloss relented, then threw up his hands. "Fine! My objections have been noted. The rest of this is on your head." He faced Susan with fire in his eyes. "You're dismissed."

✧   ✧   ✧

Susan slumped against the window in her room and stared out into space.

"Kloss was right," she muttered. "They should have picked someone else."

She shook her head and pushed off the window, then finished her circuit of the room. The word DELIVERY floated over a section of wall with the line ASK ME ANYTHING! glowing underneath. She stepped up to the display.

"Hello, Agent Cantrell," the friendly woman's voice said in her virtual hearing. "How may I be of service?"

"Umm. Hello."

"Hello."

Susan frowned at the wall. "Are you an AI?"

"No, Agent. I'm but a simple attendant program. Would you like to speak to a live Guest Services specialist?"

"No, that's fine." She looked the wall up and down. She didn't see any seams or obvious differences other than the floating text. "What is this?"

"This is your room's personal delivery port. From here, you may order and receive a wide variety of items from our many shops and restaurants as well as send and receive packages with other guests."

"Oh, so I can order room service from here?"

"That's correct. Would you like to place an order?"

"Umm, yes, actually." She perked up a little. Some food might help put her in a better mood, and she didn't feel like leaving her room. "Got any ice cream?"

"We have a selection of exciting artisan desserts created nightly by our gourmet chefs, some of which include ice cream."

"Pass."

"We also have the full catalog of Flavor-Sparkle brand ice cream patterns available for your print-on-demand culinary pleasure."

"Yeah, that sounds more like it. How about chocolate with big chunks of chocolate fudge in it? Got that?"

"I believe I've found a match for you. Is this what you're looking for?"

A virtual glass bowl appeared in front of her, filled to the brim with rich, chunky ice cream and topped with a dollop of whipped cream and three Maraschino cherries.

"Yeah. That'll work, but bigger and without all the frilly bits on top. Can I have a whole tub of the stuff?"

"I'm sorry, but I'm not sure what you mean by 'tub.'"

"Oh, I was thinking a container this tall and this wide." She gestured with her hands.

"That would be about six liters of ice cream. Is this correct?"

"Yeah," she smiled guiltily. "I'm in a *really* bad mood."

"Your order has been confirmed and placed in the printing queue."

A picture and text description of her order appeared on the wall and a timer began ticking down the seconds. She'd have her ice cream in less than four minutes.

"Nice!"

"How else may I be of service?"

"Do you print out guns, too?"

"I'm sorry. We don't provide that service."

"Figured." She shrugged. "Guess I have to go through Isaac for mine. That's all I need right now, thanks."

"It was my pleasure, Agent Cantrell."

The display on the wall dimmed.

"Guess I'll just window shop tonight." Susan knelt against the wall by the delivery port and opened the catalog Isaac gave her. A list of over fifty pistols appeared before her. "Doesn't seem so limited to me."

She sorted by quantity in service and opened the top entry.

"Popular Arsenals PA13N burst pistol." She skimmed through the entry. "The 'Watchman,' huh. Famous for its reliability and ease of use. Adjustable fire rate and spread pattern. Enhanced projectile auto-guidance. Nonlethal, though. Wonder what it shoots." She opened the ammo detail popup. "Fires cased microbot colonies designed to infiltrate the target and render them sedate. Effective against organic targets and most—but not all—synthoid architectures. Hmm, sounds like a liability to me. Let's see here... microbots include limited self-repli—nope! Not picking you!"

She closed the entry and filtered anything similar off the list. Then she browsed through the reduced list, hunting for the gun that spoke to her soul, but an oval opened in the wall before she found her new best friend. She reached up and grabbed a fat cylinder with the glittery Flavor-Sparkle logo on top and a big spoon stuck to the side.

"Guns and ice cream." She smiled, cradling the tub in her lap. "The night's looking up."

She peeled the top open and spooned a chunky heap of ice cream and fudge into her mouth.

"Mmmmm," she murmured contently, letting the creamy goodness melt away. "Yeah, that's the stuff."

She shoveled in a few mouthfuls, then paged down the list.

"Hmm, what have we here?" She opened the entry. "PA7 'Judicator' heavy pistol. Lethal/nonlethal hybrid. Interesting. Can be loaded with up to three ammo types at once? How does that work?"

She pulled up a virtual model of the gun and spun it around.

"Oh, I see! You load this thing with three magazines. One in the grip, and two running parallel along either side of the barrel." She closed the model. "Let's see here. Ammo can either be automatically prioritized based on target or manually selected. Options include..." She opened the ammo list. "Just about anything, apparently. It's versatile, so that's a plus, but I'm not sure. Seems... overly complicated to me."

She twirled the spoon around in circles, pondering her selection.

"Nah," she declared at last. "Let's see what else we have here."

She'd worked her way through a third of the ice cream by the time she reached the bottom of the list. Nothing had jumped out at her on the way down, so she tried sorting by offensive power.

"Oooh," she breathed. "Hello, sexy."

She expanded the top entry.

"Popular Arsenals PA5 'Neutralizer' anti-synthoid hand cannon. 'When up against heavy armor, neutralize it!'" She smiled broadly. "Where have you been all my life? Let's see here. Lethal against anything with an allergic reaction to big holes. Limited projectile auto-guidance."

She stabbed her spoon into the ice cream, set the container aside, and opened the gun's virtual model. The polished black finish of the long barrel gleamed in the room's light.

"Hmm, I wonder."

She reached up and caressed the surface with her fingertips. It felt real! She closed her fingers around the grip, and the surface adjusted to her hand, "pressing" against her virtual sense of touch. She turned the imaginary gun over, then sighted down the top.

"Simple and effective. Yes, I think we have a winner."

She closed the virtual model, copied the pattern ID into a message, and sent it to Isaac with the caption: "I'd like to carry this one while on duty, if it's all right with you."

CHAPTER FIVE

"I WILL SEE YOUR TEN." KLAUS-WILHELM VON SCHRÖDER TOSSED six chips into the growing pool in the middle of the small, round table. "And I'll raise you fifty."

"Wonderful," Peng grumped, sorting his cards. "Seems our newest commissioner has yet another hot hand."

"He's bluffing," Hawke declared without looking up from his cards.

"No, he's not." Tyrel placed her cards facedown on the table. "I'm certain of it."

"How can you be so sure?" Hawke asked.

"A secret of the trade." Tyrel smiled at her fellow commissioners, all gathered in a modest Argus Station lounge reserved for their private use. "As you may recall, I'm in charge of every detective in the entire solar system."

Peng snorted.

"And yes, Peng," Tyrel continued pointedly. "Before you say anything, my detectives *can* tell their asses from holes in the ground." She raised her nose haughtily. "It's part of their basic training."

"I don't know what you're talking about," Peng said, acting surprised. "I didn't say anything. Did I say anything?"

"You didn't say anything," Hawke muttered, still scrutinizing his cards.

"I didn't say anything."

"You were going to," Tyrel countered.

"Well, if you want to get *technical* about it." Peng rolled his glowing eyes.

"Vesna?" Klaus-Wilhelm asked.

"I fold." She slid her cards forward. "And I suggest you gentlemen do the same."

"Yeah, yeah," Peng muttered, leaning back precariously in his virtual seat, still sorting his virtual cards while the real ones sat facedown on the table in front of him. "Uhhh."

"That bad?" Klaus-Wilhelm asked with the tiniest hint of a smile.

"You know, Klaus," Peng griped, "we said you could pick the entertainment tonight, but I'm noticing a distinct lack of power-ups and procedurally generated loot in this so-called game of yours."

"Sometimes the old games are the best," Vesna defended. "There's a simplistic elegance to the classics."

"'Simplistic elegance'?" Peng frowned at his hand. "Is that what the kids call boredom nowadays?"

"You here to chat or here to play?" Klaus-Wilhelm asked.

"I'm *thinking*." He glanced at his depleted pile of chips and sized it up against the Gordian commissioner's small mountain. "Can we all just accept that I suck at this game and move on?"

"Stay in it," Hawke said. "He's bluffing."

"The phrase 'pride goeth before a fall' comes to mind," Tyrel said.

"And Hawke would know," Klaus-Wilhelm added.

"Oh, too soon, Klaus!" Peng crowed. "Far too soon!"

Klaus-Wilhelm glanced to Hawke, but if the Argo commissioner took any offense, he didn't show it. The two men had butted heads during the Dynasty Crisis, leading Hawke to pull rank and marginalize then *Vice*-Commissioner Klaus-Wilhelm and the rest of Gordian at the moment their expertise was needed most. The result had been a disaster with one of SysPol's *Directive*-class cruisers—the mightiest vessels in their arsenal—lost with all hands and another two fleeing the battle with their tails tucked firmly between their legs.

"Just for that, I'm going to stick this one out." Peng tossed five of his abstract chips onto the pile. "I call."

"Jamieson?" Klaus-Wilhelm asked.

"In my defense, Klaus," Hawke began, finally looking up from his cards, "I did admit I was wrong about you. In fact, I've come to deeply respect the unique insight you, as someone originally pulled from 1958, bring to your post and to SysPol as a whole. Hell, I think it's safe to say none of us would even *be* here if you and Gordian hadn't pulled us out of the fire. Now that I've taken a second look at your record with a...let's call it a clearer head, I see how you've not only adjusted, but *excelled* in the present. You're a tough, adaptable leader, and I find myself thankful you're on our side."

"But you still think I'm bluffing."

"You are *so* bluffing!" Hawke counted out five chips and placed them in a column next to the betting pool. "I call. Let's see those cards!"

"Priority message for Commissioner Schröder," said the Argus Station attendant.

"Oh, for the love of—" Peng threw up his hands. "Why now?"

"No such thing as off duty for us," Tyrel said simply.

Klaus-Wilhelm opened the message header above his palm, and his eyes grew cold.

"My apologies, everyone." He set his cards down and rose from his seat. "I need to take this."

"Klaus, would you mind?" Hawke gestured to the downturned cards. "Before you leave?"

"Of course." He slipped a finger underneath one card and flipped them over as a unit, revealing a full house with aces over kings.

"Oh, come on!" Peng exclaimed.

"He wasn't bluffing," Hawke groused.

"I told you." Tyrel shook her head sadly. "I told you, but you wouldn't listen."

Klaus-Wilhelm stepped into an adjacent room and let the door seal shut behind him. He opened a communications window.

"Is this true, Günther?" he asked gruffly.

"Regrettably so, Commissioner," replied the nonsentient program who also doubled as his secretary. "Both Doctor Andover-Chen and Chief Engineer Delacroix are confirmed dead."

"Permanently?"

It still surprised him when he heard himself asking questions like this. Despite Hawke's compliment, many aspects of thirtieth-century technology, society, and law remained less than clear to him, but he worked to remedy those inadequacies every chance he found. He'd never be as well immersed in this time as someone born to it, but he'd be damned if he'd let that affect his duties in the slightest.

"Fortunately, Doctor Andover-Chen possesses a connectome backup," Günther replied, "and I have already notified the First MindBank of Norfolk of his loss. Once I have the official death certificate from Kronos Station, I will forward it to the bank's headquarters, which will commence the legal work between the bank and SysGov. As long as the doctor did not have any additional stipulations, his revival should follow shortly thereafter."

"Stipulations?"

"Sometimes individuals will place additional requirements on the bank before their connectome can be legally revived, such as specifications for more stringent verification of their original's death. Beyond the government-issued certificate, of course. Other rarer cases involve conditioning revival on the living status of others, though these are outliers."

"Give me an example," Klaus-Wilhelm said, never looking past an opportunity to learn something new.

"A synthoid husband with a backup may not wish to be revived if his organic wife passed away in the same accident. In those cases, the connectome backup is deleted without ever being placed in a run-state, per the wishes of the individual."

"I could see that happening," he said, his voice softer as his mind drifted back to his beloved Yulia's broken body. How she died in his arms with the charred remains of their three daughters nearby, the daughters he'd tricked her into believing she'd saved. He shook the morbid thought away. "If I recall, connectome saving isn't mainstream, so couples with mixed preferences are bound to occur."

"That is correct, Commissioner. Only about one in twenty SysGov citizens utilize the practice."

"Does Andover-Chen have any extra requirements?"

"I cannot say for certain," Günther replied. "These are private arrangements between the individual and the bank. We will have to wait for the First MindBank to provide us with an update. However, I consider it unlikely."

"And once he's revived, will they use the synthoid in storage here on Argus?"

"No, Commissioner."

"Why not?"

"The First MindBank will print out a replica of the synthoid Doctor Andover-Chen inhabited at the time he backed up his connectome, and he will be revived in the same location the save took place. Maintaining this continuity is standard practice for connectome banks following an individual's death."

"I see." Klaus-Wilhelm thought on this and nodded. "Makes sense to bring them back without a jarring change in location. How old is his backup?"

"The doctor made his most recent save six months ago."

"Damn," he breathed. "Gordian Division hasn't been around for much longer. He's going to lose a lot. What about Delacroix?"

"Regrettably, the chief engineer never made a connectome save. He is a permanent loss to us."

"How the hell did this happen?" he demanded.

"The initial report from the Saturn State Police declares the cause of death a connectome transit accident."

"An *accident* suddenly kills two of my best men?" Klaus-Wilhelm growled. "Like hell it was!"

"Sorry, Commissioner. I am only relaying the report's contents."

"*Verdammte Scheiße!*" Klaus-Wilhelm paced over to the window. It wasn't a real window but a virtual one since the room was located near the center of the Argus Station. He stared down at the round, beautiful arch of Earth below his feet.

Andover-Chen had been one of his first hires into the Gordian Division. Back then, *they* had been two leading chronometric physicists, Doctors Matthew Andover and Chen Wang-shu. The two hit it off so well they integrated their minds, a process Klaus-Wilhelm still wasn't entirely clear on, resulting in a singular individual who chose the name Andover-Chen.

Joachim Delacroix's recruitment followed after both Andover-Chen and Raibert Kaminski, one of his top agents, recommended the chronometric engineer. Between Andover-Chen's impeccable science and Joachim Delacroix's meticulous engineering, the two men had proven instrumental in helping to pull Gordian Division up by their collective bootstraps.

And he was supposed to believe both had died in an accident. An *accident*!

Maybe it was, but that didn't make it stink any less.

But what to do about it?

"Who was scheduled to assist them with the impeller testing?" Klaus-Wilhelm asked.

"The doctor specifically requested Agent Kaminski and his team aboard the *Kleio*."

"Naturally." He pulled up a map of the solar system and zoomed in on the TTV *Kleio*'s flight plan. It was puttering along at a comfortable one gee. "Send orders for *Kleio* to shorten its flight time to Saturn as much as possible. I need some familiar eyes on this problem."

"Abstract agents would be able to reach Saturn faster."

"After I just lost two good men to a transmission 'accident'? No way in hell!"

"Understood, Commissioner. Shall I cancel *Kleio*'s impeller testing?"

"No. That's important, too. We're in desperate need of new ships, but Raibert's team needs to look into the deaths as well." He paused and considered the limited resources Gordian Division had out that far. Would four agents and one ship be enough? "What about the other divisions? Are any of them involved yet?"

"Not at the moment," Günther said. "Themis Division has not taken note of the deaths since the initial report from the Saturn State Police classified them as accidents."

"Then we need to fix that. Send a direct message to the Kronos Station commander." Klaus-Wilhelm thought for a moment, then snapped his fingers. "Hargreaves! Send a message straight to Hargreaves. I want the local Themis Division to dig into this, and I want them to keep digging until they hit bedrock. Or whatever the Saturn equivalent is."

"Metallic hydrogen?"

"Yes. That. They're to keep digging until they hit metallic hydrogen, you hear me?"

"Yes, Commissioner. I hear you, and I will include an appropriate reference in the message to Commander Hargreaves."

"This is to be their top priority. Am I clear? Their top priority!"

❖   ❖   ❖

Commander Charles Hargreaves sat at his glass desk positioned at the eye of the pyramid, though technically Kronos Station possessed two such locations, since its SysPol blue hull formed an octahedron, or two pyramids with their bases stuck together. The walls of his office formed a virtual panorama of the surrounding space, with Saturn and the grand sweep of its rings to his back.

"Urgent message for you, Chuck."

Hargreaves stopped reading the latest disappointing field report on the hunt for the Apple Cypher. The broad shoulders of his synthoid body slumped a little, and he let out a tired exhale. He took a moment to compose himself, smoothed back his blond hair, and sat up in his seat.

"Maggie?" he asked.

"Yeah, Chuck?" His integrated companion materialized in his office, taking the form of a beautiful blonde in a barely-there red string bikini. Water beaded on her alabaster skin, and her shoulder-length hair clung to her neckline. A salty ocean breeze tickled his senses, and he calmed a little as her abstract form sat down on the edge of his desk.

He'd met Detail-Magnifier-Supreme eight years ago after his IC at the time left him, citing his "obsessive focus on his job" as the reason for its departure. Hargreaves didn't think of himself as career obsessed. Maybe career minded. Or career conscious. He wouldn't be the commander of an entire state's worth of SysPol officers otherwise.

But obsessed? Hardly.

Back then, Maggie didn't see him as a lost cause either. She'd been working as a civilian contractor for Argo Division at the time, analyzing their logistics processes and proposing optimizations. The two hit it off at a Kronos Station singles mixer, and it wasn't long before she proposed a low-level integration. She even changed her avatar into something more . . . appealing than the literal datasheet it had been before.

One thing led to another, and before he knew it, she'd lured him into a wild night in one of her private abstractions. Their relationship grew from there, and the two had even flirted with the idea of marriage, but he didn't feel that would work out unless either he transitioned to full abstraction or she switched into a synthoid. Neither of them wanted to make the jump, but they still both enjoyed their current arrangement.

"When is it ever not urgent?" Hargreaves asked dully.

"Fair enough." Maggie brushed sand off her thigh. "But this one looks extra urgent."

"Is it *really* urgent, though?" he pressed.

"Can't tell. Haven't opened it."

"Then what makes it look so urgent?"

"It's from Commissioner Schröder." She brought up the message header.

"Uhh," he groaned, shoulders slumping again.

"And it's marked with every priority flag available."

"Yes, that sounds like him." Hargreaves pushed the Apple Cypher report away. "It must be so easy for the commissioners. They can shoot off orders whenever they want, and they don't have to worry about us station commanders mouthing off to their faces because, guess what? I'm over a light-hour away." He frowned at the unopened message. "Almost makes me want to abstract just so I can more easily transmit back to Earth and tell them what I think to their faces."

"You totally should!" She clapped her hands together.

"But I won't. Wouldn't be worth the bother."

"Oh, you tease." She winked at him.

"All right." He blew a breath out the side of his mouth. "Let's see what's so important. Don't want to piss off Lamont's new golden boy."

Maggie grabbed the header and expanded it with a snap of her wrist. Her eyes flicked over the contents with inhuman speed.

"Two Gordian Division agents are dead," she summarized. "Schröder wants it looked into."

"Why aren't we doing that already?"

"SSP declared the deaths accidents."

"They would do that," he groaned with a voice flush with a thousand frustrations. "Hence Schröder's desire for an investigation. Seems like a reasonable next step."

"His message also includes instructions to, and I quote, 'keep digging until you hit metallic hydrogen,' unquote."

"What the hell?" Hargreaves' face twisted as if he'd sucked on a lemon. "We have two dead officers. Does he think I'm not going to take this seriously?"

"I couldn't say. Would you like me to ask him?"

"No." He leaned back, and the chair conformed around him. "No need to antagonize him. Let him know we've received his message and we're on it. Forward his request to Mitch."

"Will do," Maggie said.

"And make sure Mitch knows this one's a priority."

"Higher than the Apple Cypher?"

"Nah." Hargreaves gave the notion a short, dismissive wave. "Not *that* high."

✧   ✧   ✧

Superintendent Mitch was full of opinions, and he considered it his duty to share those opinions with anyone who would listen, which was one of the reasons why he worked in a private corner of the Kronos Station infostructure.

Alone.

Pleasantly alone, in his mind.

He enjoyed the solitude. It helped him concentrate on his job.

Mitch had opinions about names. He'd once dated an AC named Serene Wind Against the Chimes of Reality, and he'd shared with her his opinion on how stupid most AC names were. The date had sped downhill from there.

"Mitch what?" people would ask.

"Just Mitch," he'd reply. So much so he'd considered legally changing his name to "Just Mitch." That would teach them to stop pestering him about his name.

Mitch's vast repository of opinions extended to avatars. As the person in charge of Themis Division for the entire Saturn State, he unfortunately had to attend regular meetings with the other division superintendents, who had requested on multiple occasions that he stop showing up to the meetings without an avatar.

In response, Mitch searched for the most generic stick figure avatar he could find and arrived at the next meeting "wearing" it. His fellow superintendents, clearly lacking a sense of humor, called his attire "offensively simplistic." After that, Mitch started showing up as a giant black monolith with the words SOUND ONLY on the front.

In response, they filed an official complaint to the station commander.

Petty little twerps.

Mitch's opinions covered a wide range of topics, including the many advantages an abstract existence enjoyed over those repulsive walking meat suits organic citizens called bodies. Honestly, why hadn't everyone abstracted by now? It baffled him to no end, and don't even get him started about sex!

Just two disgusting meat sacks gyrating against each other until a spurt of revolting fluid ejaculates out of one and into the other, he thought. If he'd possessed a body, he would have shuddered at the horrible image.

Mitch didn't see the point, and he had opinions—*lots* of opinions—about procreation. If he ever wanted to have kids, he and his abstract partner (a lovely Panoptics Division analyst named Mathematical Adventures Version Eighty) would obtain the appropriate licenses and write the damn code themselves. Not leave evolution to the vagaries of which sperm wins the race!

Mitch was not a popular AC on Kronos Station, except with a select few who understood him, like Charles Hargreaves. Hargreaves didn't like Mitch on a personal level—few people did—but he respected the Themis superintendent's dedication to his job.

Because crime was one of the few things Mitch found more repulsive than sex. It sickened him through and through, made the insides of his mind churn and gurgle until all he wanted to do was find a quiet corner and vomit up all his ones and zeros. SysGov was an advanced, prosperous, peaceful society the likes of which the solar system had never seen, and brain-damaged idiots *still* insisted on mucking up the works!

Mitch didn't want a promotion. Ever. He didn't want a transfer. Ever. All he desired out of life was to stay right where he was and keep kicking crime in the figurative ass.

A priority message arrived from Hargreaves' office, and Mitch opened it immediately. He then pulled up the SSP report from the Ballast Heights transceiver tower.

"An accident," he scoffed, though no one could hear him. "Yeah, right. I mean, what are the odds?"

He threw together a quick mathematical simulation. The odds were *really* low.

He dispatched an order to the SSP team who'd filed the report to return to the tower and remain on site until the SysPol detective arrived. They wouldn't like that, and the detective would get an earful, but he didn't care. If these state troopers would just do their damned jobs and not shrug off the potential homicide of two Gordian agents as "insert most convenient excuse here," then maybe he'd be more inclined to play nice.

But they hadn't and he wasn't.

"Now to pick a detective."

He already knew the kind of mind to look for, and he chuckled when he thought of Commissioner Schröder's words in the attached original message. Yes, if the SSP saw enough excuses to classify it as an accident, then this case might indeed require some digging, and he searched through his detectives on or near Janus for the desired tenacity.

Technically, Mitch wasn't the one who assigned individual detectives to cases; he, as superintendent, assigned a case to a specific *department*, and the department's chief inspector then chose the detective for the job.

Technically.

Realistically, he knew how to manipulate the system to get the results he wanted.

A young detective by the name of Isaac Cho caught his eye for two reasons. First, his track record during his probationary years showed all the hallmarks of a stubborn persistence, of someone who would keep tugging at the threads of a case until he'd solved it or his superior yanked him off the case, and even then, he'd leave with the mournful words, "But the job isn't done yet, Chief."

That's the impression Cho's record gave him. The kid was green, no doubt about that, and he'd yet to prove he possessed the instincts and intuition that could elevate him from a good detective to a great one, but Mitch saw potential in him.

The second reason Cho stood out was because he belonged to Chief Inspector Omar Raviv's department.

Themis departments were positioned dynamically based on their case load. One month, Raviv's detectives might be on Titan, the next they could be in the Atlas Shoal or any number of other locals in the Saturn State. Right now, Raviv's whole department was spread all over Janus-Epimetheus, stretched thin by their hunt for the Apple Cypher.

That meant Cho, who was currently approaching Saturn in a civilian transport, was the only unallotted resource Raviv had. Therefore, if Mitch sent him another case, Raviv would almost assuredly assign it to the only free hand available.

Perfect.

Mitch finalized the orders and transmitted them to Raviv.

✧   ✧   ✧

Chief Inspector Omar Raviv was not having a good day.

He stood in the middle of an SSP situation room located near the top of the First Precinct Tower in Ballast Heights, his head hunched forward slightly, eyes glowering at the virtual wall display. The rest of the situation room was quiet as the dozen senior detectives and analysts all watched the same news feed with him.

"Oh, God! It was horrible!" cried a woman with a hideous blue-and-red scarf. "Hiroki-*chan* only wanted to print a cookie for dessert, but the p-p-printer! The printer!"

"What happened next?" asked a tall and handsome reporter in a black suit with a golden scarf and a wide-brimmed hat.

"It p-printed out an *apple*!" The woman put her face in her hands and began sobbing.

The reporter placed a comforting hand on her shoulder.

"And did your son take a bite?" he asked.

The mother sniffled, composed herself a little, then nodded with solemn intensity.

"Yes, he bit into the apple," she said at last. "Poor thing. We'd talked about the Apple Cypher at home a few times, but it felt like someone else's problem. There's no way it could happen here, but then Hiroki-*chan*...Hiroki-*chan*." The mother began to tear up again. "It wasn't a regular apple! There were all these weird glyphs inside! Oh, God. Is it going to make him sick? Is he going to be okay?"

"I'm sorry. I can't answer that, ma'am."

"Why isn't SysPol doing anything? Why haven't they stopped this maniac? We're living in terror here!"

"We're asking the same questions you are, ma'am. I can assure you." The reporter turned toward the camera. "This is Dimitri Mazurek, reporting for the Saturn Herald from the Third Engine Block. Back to you, Stacy."

The display faded to a view of the Saturn Herald newsroom with Stacy O'Neil, one of the Herald's star anchors, seated across from Omar Raviv. He watched the prerecorded interview of himself, and his eyes narrowed as he took in the caption.

It read: POLICE BAFFLED. APPLE CYPHER HUNT AT A STANDSTILL.

"Thank you, Dimitri." O'Neil leaned toward Raviv, immaculate in her white business suit. She adjusted her long scarf, full of the golds and reds of falling leaves. "Chief Inspector Raviv, is there anything you'd like say to the audience to start us off?"

"Well, Stacy, yes, a few things. First, I can assure your viewers we are doing everything—*everything*—within our power to catch the Apple Cypher. Apprehending this criminal is our main focus here on Janus, and we've mobilized all available Themis departments to bring a swift resolution to the crisis.

"Second, I would like to remind your viewers that our forensic specialists have performed extensive tests on these so-called glyph apples. They're perfectly edible. The glyphs are formed from a simple and harmless coloration available in any food printer, and every printer we've examined has been free of malicious changes. Beyond the obvious replacement of ingredients with apple parts, that is."

He chuckled, but when O'Neil didn't join in, he turned it into an awkward cough.

"Chief Inspector, are you saying people can eat these apples without fear of microtech infections?"

"Yes, Stacy. That's exactly right. I've tried them myself. They're actually quite delicious."

A new caption appeared below the first: SYSPOL MAKES DUBIOUS CLAIM. GLYPH APPLES SAFE TO EAT?

"That's very interesting, Chief Inspector. However, I'm sure our audience is most interested in your efforts to catch the mastermind behind all this. What can you tell us about the lack of progress on the case?"

"Well, Stacy, that's simply not true. We've made considerable progress."

"But every lead so far has turned out to be a dead end."

"True, true, but that's just detective work for you." Raviv put on a brave smile. "You know, I like to think of my detectives as sort of modern-day Thomas Edisons. To quote the inventor, 'I have not failed. I've just found ten thousand ways that won't work.' That's what we're doing here, except we're tracing down leads instead of trying to invent the light bulb."

Another new line appeared: CHIEF INSPECTOR COMPARES DETECTIVES TO FAMOUS SCIENTIST. DO YOU AGREE? CLICK THE LINK TO TAKE OUR SURVEY!

"Mute," the real Raviv grunted, and his recording fell silent.

The situation room was eerily quiet as his interview continued to play without sound, almost as if his subordinates wanted to hear from him first, to gauge how sour his mood had turned before they said anything. He rubbed his aching stomach and contemplated how the universe had conspired to torture him this way.

A month ago, he'd been the happiest man in the entire solar system, newly promoted to chief inspector and fresh back from a honeymoon in the Oort Cloud Citizenry with Elise, the love of his life. He'd married the woman of his dreams and had finally risen to the post he'd long coveted. Everything was going right for him; his horizon glowed with bright possibilities, both large and small.

And then the Apple Cypher had turned his reality into a living hell. He pictured the criminal as a black-cloaked figure with a ridiculous curled mustache, skulking from one Janus city to the next, sprinkling viruses into the infostructure as he traveled.

The image was pure fantasy. They didn't even know if the Apple Cypher was a man, woman, AC, or a group of individuals. They didn't know *anything*, despite the widespread chaos inflicted upon food printers all across Janus-Epimetheus.

Printer vandalism *barely* broke the threshold between prank and crime, or at least crimes SysPol dealt with, but the local media and politicians had stirred everyone into a frenzy over a couple million apples no one ordered, and so SysPol had to respond.

And they'd responded by pushing Raviv forward as their sacrificial lamb for when the public inevitably demanded someone's head roll over Themis Division's "incompetence."

I'll be lucky to get out of this with just a demotion, he thought.

He winced as his stomach acted up again, and he fished a bottle of medibot capsules out of his pocket. He pressed the side tab twice and dropped two capsules into his hand.

"Here, Chief."

Senior Detective Grace Damphart (pronounced Damp-Heart) offered him his refreshed cup of coffee. Black, of course. Coffee didn't need to be a pleasurable experience. It was fuel, pure and simple.

"Thank you, Grace." Raviv took the SysPol-blue mug, a gift from his wife with the golden words CRIMINAL TEARS on the side. He tossed the capsules into his mouth and washed them down with a gulp of coffee. In his gut, the capsule walls broke apart and legions of medibots spread out, resuming their struggle to shore up the walls of his besieged stomach.

"I thought you made a good analogy there, Chief," Damphart added, then glanced around at the other officers. "We really appreciate you sticking up for us. Feels good to know you have our backs."

As one, the room nodded in agreement.

"Wouldn't say it if I didn't mean it," he grunted, rubbing his stomach.

"Still, Chief..." Damphart trailed off. She was a small, nervous-looking woman who normally handled sexual assault cases, but like everyone else in his department, she'd been sucked into the black hole of the hunt for the elusive Apple Cypher.

She may have looked shy and easily cowed, but underneath that tiny, anxious exterior resided a heart of gold—a heart that truly cared for the victims—and a spine of reinforced programmable-steel. Quite literally, in the second case; she'd transitioned to a synthoid after her hundredth birthday, and more than a few criminals had been caught off guard by her enhanced strength and speed.

Raviv had seen the fire in her soul once on Kronos when one of the probationary detectives insisted on calling her Damn-Fart instead of pronouncing her name correctly as Damp-Heart. *He'd* been surprised by her enhancements too, given how fast he'd ended up on his back staring at the ceiling.

One of the incoming feeds dinged, and Damphart glanced to her side.

"We've got an urgent message from Kronos," she reported. "It's from the super."

"Let me see." He pulled the message to his palm and opened it. He read it once, twice, then a third time, all the while the veins pulsed in his neck, and his face grew ever redder. "What. The Actual. Fuck."

"Chief?"

"What the fuck is this?" Raviv blurted, and the whole situation room winced.

"What is what?" Damphart asked.

"Is Mitch trying to get me fired?" he shouted, tossing the message onto a wall for all to see. "I don't have enough detectives as it is, and he's giving us *another* case!"

"Oh my."

"How the fuck are we supposed to handle another case at a time like this?"

"Chief, please try to calm down."

"I need to talk to Mitch about this! We can't take it! No one's free! What does he want me to do, start pulling detectives off the case with the big media spotlight on it?"

"Umm, Chief?"

"The media will see that, and they'll tear me to shreds! They'll say I'm retreating in the face of failure or some other nonsense!"

"Chief?"

"*What?*"

"Actually, we do have one available detective." Damphart offered him a profile, and Raviv regarded it with a dubious frown.

"You mean Isaac?"

"He's almost back to Kronos."

"I need him on the Apple Cypher case, same as everyone else."

"But he's not on the case officially. He's still a free asset."

"Hmm." Raviv looked at the profile as he massaged his stomach. "I don't know," he muttered as he considered the options before him. None of them were good, but perhaps one was less disastrous than the others. "Though, when I think about it, Isaac's not up to speed on the Apple Cypher, so giving him the new case will hurt less than pulling someone else."

"That's my reasoning as well."

"Uh-huh." Raviv rubbed his chin. "Fine. We'll give it to Isaac. Just let him know he's alone on this one. I can't spare anyone else."

"Not to worry, Chief." Damphart gave him a curt nod. "I'll get the order ready for you."

CHAPTER SIX

"MAIL FOR YOU, ISAAC," CEPHALIE CHIMED FROM ATOP THE SALT-shaker.

He finished chewing a mouthful of scrambled eggs, swallowed, and set down his fork. The clinking of utensils against plates and the din of breakfast conversations filled the *Arcturus'* Deck Five Observation Dome. His table sat on the edge of a translucent, peninsula-shaped platform above the wide sweep of the dome's panorama, and Saturn swelled far below his feet as the saucer decelerated.

"Anything good?" He grabbed the bottle next to Cephalie and sprinkled his eggs with hot sauce.

"It's from Raviv. Looks like work."

"I hope so. Some time to unwind is nice, but I'm getting antsy with nothing to do. What's he got for us?"

"Umm, let's see." Cephalie opened the message. "Connectome tower accident. Possible double homicide. Top Gordian agents, too. One of them's a permadeath."

"Fantastic!"

She looked up over the edge of the message and gave him a stern stare.

"Uhh, I mean"—he smiled apologetically—"it's good that Raviv would trust us with a case this important. He wouldn't give a police officer homicide to just anyone."

"Maybe."

"You sound doubtful."

"Initial report from SSP says it's an accident."

"Yeah, right," he scoffed. "When's the last time you and I worked a case that turned out be an accident?"

"Can't seem to recall one."

"Exactly. And that's because someone higher up thinks those agents were murdered. Who was killed?" He forked another bite of scrambled eggs into his mouth.

"Doctor Andover-Chen and Chief Engineer Joachim Delacroix."

"Mmm." He chewed and swallowed, then waved his fork around like a baton. "The doctor I've heard of. Caught one of his interviews after the Dynasty Crisis. Most of the stuff he talked about flew right over my head. Who's the other guy?"

"He's Gordian's top engineer." She shrugged her arms. "*Was* their top engineer, since he's the permadeath. Specialized in transtemporal drive systems. Gordian pulled him over from ART shortly after the division was formed."

"He was with the Antiquities Rescue Trust?" Isaac asked, surprised. He scooped up another helping of eggs and held it aloft. "That's dubious company for a cop."

"Yeah, but Gordian also pulled in just about every time machine in service around the same period, so they needed engineers with experience. Plus, ART got audited *hard* before that. Gordian would have known if Delacroix was clean or not, so I doubt he was involved in any of those nasty ART scandals. Besides, the historians and their security teams were the ones abusing their time travel privileges; I imagine he just worked on their rides."

"Mmm." Isaac nodded, swallowed. "Good point. How were they killed?"

"The dish their beam was aligned with shut down."

"Don't those things have backups?"

"Yeah. Two of them."

"And?"

"Neither kicked in."

"And SSP is calling this an accident?" Isaac made a disgusted face.

"Apparently so."

"Typical." He shook his head and sprinkled more hot sauce on his eggs, then took another bite. "You know, I think they printed out the wrong bottle."

"No, they didn't." Cephalie poked the back of his hand with her cane. "It's not the sauce, Isaac. It's all those taste buds you've killed off with your eating habits."

"I like my food to fight back a little. What's wrong with that?" He picked up the hot sauce bottle and eyeballed the label. "'Atomic' my pale behind. I can barely feel this."

"Dead. Pain. Receptors."

"Yeah, yeah." He turned the bottle over and smacked the base with the palm of his hand. "Where's the transceiver tower?"

"Ballast Heights. The tower's owned and operated by LifeBeam."

"Oh good. That'll save us a trip. Cancel our flight to Kronos and arrange transport to the tower."

"Will do. What about her 'kit'?"

"Umm, no." Isaac frowned at the reminder. "Keep it routed for the station."

"You sure?" Cephalie pushed off the saltshaker and walked over, twirling her cane. "You never know when a heavily armed death machine might come in handy."

"Then it's a good thing we know where to find one." Isaac stirred the sauce into the scrambled eggs until his meal was a uniform red mush. "What's SSP doing right now?"

"Waiting for us to arrive at the tower, per orders from Kronos."

"Great," he sighed. "That'll put them in a cheerful mood, I bet."

"Can't be helped."

"We need to get you a LENS. Ask the *Arcturus* crew if they'll lend us some of their printer capacity before we land."

"On it."

"Just be nice about it this time, okay?"

"What?" Cephalie held up her hands. "I can be nice."

"There's no need for us to commandeer their printers. If they're busy, we can wait. We'll have the nearest SSP precinct print you out one, instead."

"What about Susan's gun?"

"I—" Isaac turned to the side and stared off into space. He let out a resigned sigh. "Yes, that too."

"It's allowed." Cephalie gave her cane a twirl. "Not sure why, but it is."

"It can turn suspects into pink mist!"

"It's not *that* bad." She tapped her cheek with a thoughtful finger. "Close, though."

"What in Saturn's rings does she need a sidearm that powerful for?"

"Hey, don't blame her for the choice."

"And why shouldn't I?"

"Because *you're* the one who gave her the full catalog. *You* set the rules for her"—she poked his hand again—"and she followed them. Not her fault she didn't pick the one you wanted."

"Fine. Whatever." Isaac shook his head, eager to change the subject.

"You going to involve her in any of this? Or you working this case alone?"

"With her, obviously." He scooped up another mouthful of eggs. The heat was . . . unsatisfactory. "Where is she now?"

"In the main concourse, doing a circuit of the shops. Last I spoke with her, she mentioned wanting to pick out a souvenir."

"From a saucer? What for?"

"*Isaac.*"

"What?"

"She's in another *universe*. This is new to her."

"I know that. But a souvenir from a saucer?"

"Look"—Cephalie put her hands on her hips—"do you want me to tell her where to meet us or not?"

"Sure, go ahead."

"Okay, then." She shook her head and opened a comm window. "Was that so hard?"

Isaac glanced down at Saturn. "Wait."

"Yes?" Cephalie asked, her hand hovering next to the window.

"I just had an idea." He flashed a warm smile. "Ask her to meet us in the Deck Three Bow Park. I think she'll appreciate the view better from there."

"And then what happened?" Isaac asked.

He sat with Susan on a bench with a clear view through the *Arcturus*'s bow. A dozen other passengers relaxed on similar benches or stood around the Bow Park's grassy hill as Saturn swelled to fill half the horizon. The ship sped forward without thrust, its bow aligned for the descent through the upper atmosphere and its artificial gravity switched on, though it ebbed away as Saturn's natural gravity took hold.

He'd already reviewed the basics of the case with Susan. There wasn't much to do but wait until they arrived at the transceiver tower, and in the awkward silence that followed, he'd made the mistake of suggesting she share some of her DTI stories.

It's like listening to the same joke over and over again, but no matter how many times I hear it, the punch line never makes me laugh.

"I joined a DTI raid involving four chronoports from Defender Squadron," Susan continued. "I was part of the STAND unit on *Defender-Two*. We traveled into the near present, about twenty hours in the past, and brought in the Free Luna cell at their last known position, right before they *originally* released the gas in the Tycho Crater Capital Building."

"Was this the flesh-eating gas you mentioned or the gas that takes over people's implants?"

"The flesh-eating one. Not a well-designed weapon, though. The microbots didn't replicate very well with only human tissue for parts, so we were able to save most of the victims."

"Well, that's good. What happened next?"

"The past versions of the terrorists were interrogated, and we were able to determine the cell's fallback location in the True Present. It turned out they had a base in an old, abandoned part of the Tycho subway line, near the outskirts of the dome. After that, we returned to the present and..."

Susan trailed off, and a hint of worry creased her brow.

"After that, you...what?" Isaac urged.

She smiled bashfully.

"Don't keep me in suspense," he said. "What happened next?"

"We...blew up the base."

"And the terrorists inside?"

"We blew them up, too."

"Of course, you did," he sighed, unsurprised.

And there's the punch line, he thought.

"They resisted," Susan added.

"How, exactly?"

"They threatened to hit our organic operatives with the gas."

"Ah."

"That's why us STANDs were sent in."

"Mmhmm."

"And we blew them up."

"I see."

"They were *really* bad people," Susan stressed.

"I didn't say they weren't," he replied wearily. "And these terrorists? Not the ones you blew up, but their past versions who hadn't yet committed the crime? What happened to them?"

"We put them back where we found them, before we returned to the True Present to raid their base."

"Doesn't that risk branching the timeline?"

"Not with an interaction that small, no. The differences are absorbed back into the original timeline. Or at least"—she gave him a little shrug—"that's what I've been told. I'm not an expert. But I can tell you our operating doctrine changed significantly after the Gordian Division made contact with us last year. We do our best to minimize our footprint when working in the past."

"Interesting." Isaac leaned back in thought. "From what I gather, Gordian isn't eager to provide Themis with that kind of support. First, our caseload is *way* too large for them to even make a dent in it at their current size. And second, between exploding universes, imploding universes, temporal knots entangling universes, branched timelines trying to destroy *our* universe, and who knows what other nutty stuff they deal with over at Gordian, they don't want to do *any* time traveling if it's the least bit risky."

"I'm not surprised," Susan said. "I wonder if time travel will become stricter for us, too."

"Who can say?"

The saucer flew into a towering thunderhead of tan ammonia ice, which blotted out the sun. Lightning flashed outside, and liquid ammonia ran across the window in thin rivulets until the saucer broke through to reveal a vast sun-kissed expanse of puffy mist. A great cloud chasm yawned open, revealing rusty storms of ammonium hydrosulfide tens of kilometers below.

"Saturn," Susan exhaled with an almost dreamlike quality.

"First time?" Isaac asked.

"First time." She nodded. "Never been to the planet before. There isn't much here back home. Just a colony on Titan, a dozen or so mining colonies on the moons, and a handful of fuel collectors in the atmosphere. I've been as far as Jupiter's moons, personally."

The saucer dipped lower, skimming the cloud tops. The running lights from other spaceships and aircraft twinkled in the distance, and a wide white shape glinted behind a choppy crest of clouds.

"Is that..." She stood and walked up to the window.

"Yes," Isaac said, joining her.

The saucer cruised in, and the great bow of Janus-Epimetheus parted the clouds like an impossibly tall sailing ship. The megastructure floated out into one of the deep cloud canyons, but even then, only the top thirty or forty kilometers of its downturned fin-shaped body could be seen. The rest was obscured by the swirling reddish-orange storm below.

"Amazing," Susan breathed. "Pictures don't do it justice."

"Home sweet home," Isaac sighed.

She turned to him. "You've lived on Janus before?"

"You could say that." He gave her a half smile. "I was born here."

"Oh." She frowned a little.

"Right...there, actually." He pointed to a spot near the prow.

"Sorry. I must seem silly to you, then, reacting like this."

"Not at all," he assured her. "We Saturnites like it when our home impresses people."

The ship slowed, and their flight path took them around the megastructure's upper plateau, a wide oval two hundred kilometers long and fifty wide with towering metropolises rising all across its surface. Hundreds of spacecraft and aircraft took off and landed in a constant flow of traffic along the outer lip.

"How does it stay up? Counter-grav?"

"Nothing so fancy. And nothing that requires a source of power. Just good, old-fashioned buoyancy."

"But two whole moons went into its construction, right? It must be immensely heavy, even if a lot of the interior is empty space. How does it generate enough buoyancy to stay afloat?"

"Tanks full of exotic matter foam." He pointed. "There. See that bulge along the lip? The one right beneath that airport? That's one of them, and there are *thousands* spread all throughout the megastructure, providing it with buoyancy and stability."

"But what if they leak?"

"They can't. That's one of the advantages of using a foam instead of a gas. Sure, you can break it off piece by piece, but a punctured tank is basically a nonissue. Plus, the exotic matter has negative mass. The stuff's more buoyant than *vacuum*. Very space efficient. Let's us jam more inside. Plus, the megastructure's verticality helps, too. External pressure is around ten atmospheres near the bottom, while the interior is consistently Earthlike from top to bottom."

"I see." Susan watched as the saucer flew over Janus, slowing as it approached a city near the bow that towered above the rest. "So you add more of these tanks as Janus grows?"

"Eventually, but we won't have to do that for a while."

"What do you mean?"

"The tanks we have make Janus so light we need added weight to hold it down. Many of the tanks have detachable ballasts built into them."

"Detachable?" Susan pondered this. "Ah. So if there's ever a truly catastrophic failure..." She fluttered her fingers and raised her hand.

"Exactly. We drop the ballasts and float on up." He indicated the dense, towering city below. "Though mostly we add and remove them over time as Janus evolves. That's where the name 'Ballast Heights' comes from. Back then, when the city was founded, Janus was *much* smaller, and that part of the crown did have ballasts underneath it."

"Hey, kids!"

Both Isaac and Susan turned to see a LENS float up behind them with Cephalie riding on top. The spherical body of the LENS resembled a silvery metallic eye slightly larger than the average head, and its tough outer shell of fast-reacting prog-steel shielded its small graviton thruster, internal capacitors, and sensitive equipment.

"Hello, Cephalie," Isaac said.

A portion of the shell eased outward to form a long, blunt pseudopod, and Isaac's left eye twitched when he saw the weapon and magazine belt it held.

"I come bearing gifts," Cephalie announced cheerfully.

Susan's face lit up with a quick moment of glee, but the expression vanished when she realized Isaac was watching, and she hid it behind an indifferent mask.

"Thank you, Cephalie," she said with stiff professionalism.

"My pleasure."

Susan took the hand cannon and placed the holster against her right thigh. The smart fabric in her uniform interfaced with the holster, and the two surfaces locked together. She placed her hand on the pistol's grip, and the holster released automatically. She pulled the weapon out, confirmed it was unloaded, then inspected it while not pointing the barrel at anyone.

She gave the weapon a curt, satisfied nod, though Isaac suspected that was a carefully regulated response for his benefit. She slotted the pistol back into the holster and removed her hand. The holster constricted around the weapon once more.

Isaac picked up the belt from the LENS and held it before him at arm's length, almost as if it reeked with a foul stench.

"Six, seven, eight," he muttered, counting the magazines. "Isn't this a little excessive?"

Cephalie leaped from the LENS to his shoulder and poked him in the neck with her cane. Isaac ignored her.

"Can't be too careful." Susan took the belt from his unresisting hand and looped it around her waist. The two pieces of smart fabric interfaced, then locked into a semi-rigid form.

"I suppose not," Isaac said with mild resignation.

The saucer slowed to a halt over a quintet of circular platforms that sprouted out of a thin, pastel green spire. They descended gently, and Isaac caught sight of a virtual Polaris Traveler company logo rotating over the building's apex.

The saucer came to rest on the landing pad with feathery lightness.

"Attention all guests," a warm feminine voice spoke over their shared virtual hearing. "This is Amelia with Guest Services. The *Arcturus* has just arrived at our private Polaris Traveler spaceport on Ballast Heights, largest city on Janus-Epimetheus. The local time is fourteen hundred twenty-two, and the outdoor temperature is a brisk negative one hundred and thirteen degrees Celsius. Please bundle up if you plan to go outside."

"Ha. Ha," Isaac said dryly.

"If this is your final destination or you have a connecting flight in Ballast Heights, please disembark at this time. We hope you've enjoyed your stay with us. To everyone else, we look forward to serving you as we head next to Promise City on Titan."

"This is our stop," Cephalie said.

"Right." Isaac stepped away, but then paused and turned back to find Susan still gazing out the window. "Something wrong?"

"Not really."

He walked back. "What's on your mind?"

"It looks, I don't know." She frowned, as if searching for the right word. "Less exotic from this angle?"

"It's a city like any other."

"Only it's in the atmosphere of a gas giant."

"Well, yeah. There's that."

"This is going to take some getting used to." She sighed, taking a half step away from the window.

"Welcome to the Shark Fin." He nudged his head toward the exit. "Come on. Let's not keep the state troopers waiting."

CHAPTER SEVEN

"WELL, LOOK WHO FINALLY DECIDED TO SHOW UP!"

Isaac ignored the comment as he followed the LifeBeam receptionist into the meeting room with Susan and his LENS not far behind. Three physical state troopers lounged in high-backed chairs around the long, oval table, distinct in their dark green uniforms and caps, so dark they were almost black. The lone uniformed avatar for an abstract trooper leaned against the wall, and a LifeBeam employee in a light gray business suit sat at the head of the table, a mixture of worry and frustration on his face.

"Thank you," Isaac said to the receptionist. "That will be all."

The receptionist glanced to the seated employee.

"It's all right." He nodded to the receptionist. "I'll take it from here."

"Please let me know if you need anything, sir." She left, and the door sealed shut behind her.

"Took you long enough." The trooper who'd spoken earlier— a big man with a hooked nose—made a show of propping his boots up on the table. "Thought I'd have to transition by the time you got here."

"Thank you for waiting," Isaac said with practiced patience. "I'm Detective Isaac Cho. This is my deputy, Agent Susan Cantrell, and my IC, Encephalon. Who's the ranking trooper here?"

"What's up with you?" the troublemaker asked of Susan. "Kronos run out of uniforms or something?"

"I'm an exchange officer from the Admin's Department of Temporal Investigation," Susan replied levelly.

"Well, good for you! Ain't you special!" The trooper nudged the woman next to him. "Don't you think she's special?"

"She's special, all right."

To Susan's credit, she showed no signs of rising to the jabs or even acknowledging them. Isaac had expected her to conduct herself in a competent manner, but seeing her composure while on duty helped put him at ease. The last thing he needed was a deputy with enough killing power to slaughter everyone in the room in a matter of seconds who took offense at every stupid insult thrown at them.

"Which one of you is in charge?" Isaac let a hint of weariness leak out.

"I am." The third physical trooper stood. "Sergeant Nakayama, Twelfth Precinct."

"And you are?" Isaac gave the LifeBeam employee a curt nod.

"Lee Silas, senior engineering manager for this tower. I was on duty when the incident occurred."

"Is this going to take a while?" the mouthy trooper asked. "I was supposed to go off duty an hour ago."

"Sergeant"—Isaac turned to Nakayama—"if your subordinate has nothing productive to add to this meeting, I suggest he keep his mouth shut."

"Johan, zip it."

"All I'm saying is—"

"*Zip it!*"

Johan grimaced like a man chewing the inside of his cheek. He put his hands behind his head and leaned back farther, but he didn't say another word.

"Thank you." Isaac opened a virtual copy of the accident report. "Sergeant, I reviewed your report on the way down, and I have a few questions I hope you can help me with."

"Fire away."

"First, I see the infostructure was inspected by a Trooper Fleming, but your team's physical inspection of the transceiver equipment seems to be missing. Can you provide me with that part of the report?"

"There isn't one."

"Oh?" Isaac made a note on his copy of the virtual report. "And why is that?"

"I saw no need for a physical inspection. Fleming's review of the infostructure found no sign of malicious intrusion. Everything looked clean, so the only reasonable conclusion is a glitch in the system."

"This was no software glitch!" Silas stormed, face turning red. "That's what I've been trying to tell you, but you won't listen! The backups don't run the same software as the primary for this very reason! It's inconceivable for them to all fail at the same time!"

"Mister Silas, I'll get to you in a moment. You can either wait quietly or wait outside."

Silas took a deep breath and settled deeper into his seat.

"Now," Isaac continued, "is Trooper Fleming present?"

The abstract trooper raised her hand.

"Good. And are you an expert on connectome transmission technology?"

"I . . . well, no."

"Do you have any hands-on experience with said technology?"

"You mean besides using it to get around?"

"Yes. Besides that."

"Well, umm"—Fleming's gaze flicked to Nakayama then back to Isaac—"I once worked for Verified Destinations."

"The LifeBeam competitor? In what capacity?"

"As a traffic monitoring tech."

"And your job functions were?"

"I would make predictions of upcoming peak traffic periods and line up reroutes ahead of time."

"Data analysis, then. And that's all?"

"Yeah," Fleming admitted. "Guess so."

"Then you have no direct experience with transceiver software before today?"

"I . . ." She shrugged. "No, not really."

"Not really, or not at all?"

She sighed. "Not at all."

"Then on what grounds did you conclude this was a software glitch when at least one LifeBeam employee"—he indicated Silas—"who probably has more experience than you with the software, claims it couldn't be?"

"Like I said," Nakayama cut in, "she found no signs of intrusion."

"Yeah, that's right," Fleming added, regaining some of her composure. "All the normal viral attack paths were spotless."

"All the *normal* attack paths." Isaac jotted down another note. "Interesting."

"Fleming is very good at this kind of work," Nakayama said.

"I'm sure she is."

An awkward silence fell over the room as he scribbled in the report's margins.

"Sergeant, besides the missing physical inspection, your report also seems to lack any LifeBeam employee interviews. Would you mind providing me with those?"

Nakayama frowned and crossed his arms.

"Sergeant?"

"We didn't conduct any."

"Then, Sergeant, let me see if I understand the situation. Your team, which doesn't include an expert on this type of equipment, declared the deaths accidents. That declaration was made without performing a physical inspection of the equipment or conducting any interviews with people responsible for said equipment. In fact, it's based solely on an abstract review of the infostructure, which was the least time-consuming option available to your team."

"Accidents happen."

"Indeed, they do. Though I somehow doubt this to be the case here."

"If you're trying to imply—"

"Thank you, Sergeant." Isaac closed the SSP report. "As always, Themis Division appreciates the support SSP provides. Please accept my apologies for any inconvenience we may have caused. Your team may return to their regular duties."

Nakayama's mouth cracked open, as if he wanted to share a few more choice words with Isaac, but then he thought better of it and started out the door.

"Let's get out of here," he growled.

Fleming's avatar vanished, and the other troopers filed out.

"Called us out here and had us sit on our asses for hours just for that shit?" Johan griped under his breath.

The conference room door closed, and they were alone with Lee Silas.

"You don't believe it was an accident, do you?" the LifeBeam manager asked.

"I believe their report is incomplete," Isaac replied simply. "Everything else remains to be seen. Can we start with a visual inspection of the equipment?"

"Oh, yes. Of course." Silas rose eagerly. "This way."

He led them to a nearby counter-grav tube reserved for company employees. He entered his credentials into the abstract interface, then stepped in. Isaac and Susan followed, and gravitons whisked them upward two hundred stories to the highest reaches of the LifeBeam tower.

The tube dropped them off into a corridor barely wide enough for two people to pass each other if they pressed themselves against the walls and sucked in their guts. Infostructure nodes and cabling covered the walls and ceiling, and thick trunks of heavier cables ran underneath the floor grating. Waste heat radiated off the walls, and cooling air blew down on their heads.

"Sorry about the tight squeeze," Silas said. "This part of the tower rarely sees foot traffic, but it'll widen at the end."

He led them to a cramped circle of space at the end of the corridor.

"This is it," Silas declared. "Transceiver 27. That third of the wall is the primary infosystem, and then the two backups are to either side of it."

He opened an interface and pressed a few buttons. Shields along the ceiling parted, providing a direct view of the transceiver itself. Isaac craned his neck at the wide dish receiver and the narrow, focused laser emitter mounted on a pair of heavy gimbals.

"And that's the transceiver itself."

Isaac gestured around the room. "Anything out of the ordinary here?"

"Umm." Silas turned in a circle. "No, nothing. We have dozens just like it. Plus, we keep strict logs of who comes in here. We're the first people here in months."

"Cephalie, have the LENS perform a basic sweep."

"On it."

"How soon do you intend to return the transceiver to service?" Isaac asked.

"Actually, it's running right now. The system was only down for three seconds."

As if in response, the gimbals actuated, and the dish and laser aligned on a new target.

"Do you feel that's wise?" Isaac asked.

"The software was restored to default during those three seconds. After that, we finished processing all pending transits and then closed the transceiver to new ones so we could run our diagnostics."

"And what did you find?"

"The system passed every hardware and software check we threw at it. We couldn't see any reason not to return it to service, so we did."

"Then a hardware failure of some kind seems unlikely?" Isaac asked.

"Yes, I'd tend to agree. We think it was software-related, and the problem was cleared out when the systems were restored to default."

"I'm not seeing any signs of physical intervention," Cephalie reported. "All these surfaces are spotless."

"Good to know," Isaac said. "Mister Silas, do you have a record of the infosystem's contents before you purged them?"

"We do. That's automatic when a fault occurs. We save the entire subsystem state at the moment of failure."

"Can you provide a copy to my LENS?"

"I sure can. One moment."

Silas worked his virtual interface, then Cephalie gave Isaac a thumbs-up from atop the LENS.

"Thank you," Isaac said. "Have your people had a chance to review the fault state?"

"We have, but what we found puzzles us. There's a timestamp error and a few lines of code that are different from what each of the three systems should have contained. The transceiver shouldn't have been able to operate in that state."

"Then it must have been changed recently?"

"More like moments before the Gordian officers tried to transmit."

"Who could make a change like that?"

"Software updates are *very* strictly controlled," Silas said. "Normally, updates are validated by headquarters back on Earth before being sent to us for implementation. Even then, it requires the approval of all three senior engineering managers before we go live with the update."

"Then this mysterious code change, if done through the proper channels, would have required assistance from your HQ?"

"Not quite. We're also allowed to make updates in case of emergencies, though again all three managers need to sign off on it."

"Who can make such approvals for this tower?"

"Easy." Silas tapped his chest. "That would be myself and the other two senior managers. They're a pair of ACs that go by the names of Infinity-Plus-One and Hikari-no-Kage. They both joined at the same time, been with the company for decades. Real pleasures to work with."

"I'll need contact strings for all three of you."

"Sure. Sure." Silas raised his fingers to the interface, then paused and looked up. "Wait a second. You don't think *we* did it, do you?"

"It's my job to consider all possibilities," Isaac said, keeping his voice level. "For the time being, all three of you will need to register any travel plans with SysPol."

"But we wouldn't!" Silas exclaimed, his face twisting in dread. "The three of us are all company lifers! I've gotten *awards* for how well we run this tower! We'd never throw our careers away by trying to kill someone, let alone two cops!"

"Then you have nothing to fear from our investigation."

"Do you really think Silas could have done it?" Susan asked once they left LifeBeam's mid-tower reception foyer. She'd spoken in SysPol security chat, which showed Isaac she knew when to be discreet in public. Another good sign. Foot traffic was light in the pedestrian tunnel connecting LifeBeam to a nearby transportation hub, but the ubiquitous nature of SysGov infostructure meant the walls literally had ears.

"No, but we can't ignore the possibility." Isaac stopped with his back against the wall. "That said, LifeBeam runs its employees through strict psychological evaluations. All the connectome transmission companies do, as required by law. The people reviewing the evaluations are just as vulnerable to errors as the rest of us, but to miss problems with three managers?" He shook his head. "A lot of low-chance events need to line up for this to be an internal job."

"Then you agree it's not an accident?"

"I do, but I also admit that's still a remote possibility. For instance, the three managers could have botched a code change and are trying to cover their tracks. Unlikely, but still something we have to consider."

"Seems like a rather dubious way to travel, if you ask me." Susan looked back at the tower. "Here's a question. Why didn't LifeBeam try to resend the connectomes?"

"They can't," Cephalie said.

"Why not?"

"Because it's illegal to copy a connectome," Isaac pointed out. "With a few exceptions, of course, such as saving a copy at a mindbank. Travel companies like LifeBeam generally aren't allowed to retain copies of the people they transmit."

"There were a *lot* of shenanigans back when the tech was new," Cephalie added. "A few centuries back, a lot of people ended up being copied illegally, and SysGov clamped down hard on the industry as a result."

"It's not much of an issue nowadays," Isaac continued, "but the legal restrictions remain in place."

"So, the transmission lasers are fire and forget?" Susan asked.

"Basically."

"*Very* dubious."

"Connectome transmission is incredibly safe. Safer than physical travel."

"You sure about that?" Susan asked doubtfully.

"Yes, by a healthy margin. Plus, anyone who travels this way can also back themselves up at a mindbank. Accidents do happen, as Nakayama said, but they're rare and typically have a higher body count than this."

"Why's that?"

"Most accidents relate to hardware failure," Cephalie said. "If a transceiver goes down hard, they need time to shift a working unit into place to receive the incoming stream."

"This failure feels...too specific," Isaac added. "The transceiver's off for three seconds, and two Gordian officers just happen to transmit in during that window?"

"Safe or not," Susan began, "you'll never get me to fire my brain photons across the solar system."

"That's just because you're not used to it," Cephalie said. "Think about it. You can travel from Saturn to Earth in nine days or an hour and a half. A lot of people travel this way after going meatless by keeping a spare synthoid stashed in every port."

"I'll keep my connectome right where it is"—Susan knuckled her upper chest—"thank you very much."

"You were quiet in there, by the way," Isaac noted.

"Is that typically how SSP treats a detective?" she asked, some agitation evident in her tone.

"Sometimes." He shrugged. "Sometimes not. It all depends on who we get. A lot of SSP troopers don't like us. Some are of the opinion we fly in, screw everything up, declare victory, then fly out, leaving them with the cleanup. Others resent the authority we can exercise over them. Honestly, I'm used to their drama by now. I do my best to ignore it." He looked up. "By the way, you didn't answer my question."

"Sorry. I prefer to observe how you handle things for now, that's all. To get a feel for the job." She raised an eyebrow. "If that's all right with you."

"Sure, I understand. But know you're welcome to chime in whenever you want. We're partners in this. I'll take the lead, but that doesn't mean you should stay passive." Isaac glanced across the Ballast Heights skyline, its towers gleaming in the sunlight. "And on that subject, what do you think of this case so far?"

"Any technical analysis is better left to experts, but the big hole I see right now is motive. A connectome tower is a high-traffic area, so there's a vast pool of people with potential access to it. The question is, why would any of them want to kill the two Gordian officers?"

Isaac turned back to her and flashed a slim smile.

"What?" she asked. "Did I say something wrong?"

"No. Quite the contrary." He tapped his temple. "It seems we're thinking along the same lines. Yes, I'm wondering about the motive, too. And as you said, we'll leave the technical side of matters to the experts." He opened a comm window to Kronos Station. "Dispatch."

"Themis Dispatch here. How may we be of assistance, Detective Cho?"

"I need data forensics performed on a connectome transceiver fault state." He nodded to Cephalie. "Sending the file now."

"File received, and I see you've already attached your case number. What priority level should I flag this as?"

"Standard. I'll update you if that changes."

"Understood, Detective. Your request is in the queue. Anything else?"

"Not right now."

"Then have a pleasant day, Detective. Dispatch out."

Isaac closed the window.

"Now we wait?" Susan asked.

"Now we hunt for the motive," he corrected. "And we need to remember it's possible only one of them was the target. The other may be collateral damage."

"You mean Delacroix, since he's the permadeath?" Susan asked.

"Most likely, though another possibility is Andover-Chen learned something in the past six months our supposed murderer didn't want him to remember. We don't know enough yet for even an educated guess, so that's what we're going to remedy. Cephalie, what were Andover-Chen and Delacroix transmitting in for?"

"TTV impeller testing." Cephalie conjured a see-through schematic of an elliptical spacecraft with a long spike protruding out of the rear. Brackets highlighted the spike. "Gordian Division has been working to replace the time machines they lost during the Dynasty Crisis. With the recent destruction of several major producers near Earth, Gordian's been looking elsewhere for their time drive needs. Those two were to perform final inspections before one of Gordian's TTVs—the *Kleio*—puts each impeller through its paces."

"And someone might have wanted to prevent or delay those inspections?" Susan theorized.

"It's a possibility," Isaac said. "Where were the inspections to take place?"

"Down at the bottom of the Shark Fin in an industrial town called New Frontier. Gordian has a nine-unit order with Negation Industries and one more being produced by the Trinh Syndicate. Both men have apartments in the city, and temporary offices at the manufacturing facilities."

"Sounds as good a place to start as any." Isaac pushed off the wall. "We'll head there next. Mind ordering our train tickets?"

"Not a problem."

"Time for another trip." Isaac sighed.

"On a *train*?" Susan asked.

✧   ✧   ✧

"I'm on a train," Susan said, staring out the window as another city rose past them.

"Yes?" Isaac asked from his seat along the opposite wall of their private cabin in *Pillar Six*. His virtual sight identified the area as the Rosman Divide, a stalactite city with its towers hanging off one of Janus-Epimetheus' major horizonal divisions. The trains of the Pillar Line ran along the primary structural support pillar extending one hundred kilometers from the center of the crown all the way down to the tip of the fin. Fifteen tracks lined the pillar for most of its height, with trains zipping up or down or along sloping paths that led to major cities farther away.

"I'm on a train"—Susan's eyes narrowed—"on *Saturn*."

"Actually, in Saturn's atmosphere."

"I'm on a train. In Saturn's atmosphere." She shook her head. "That didn't help."

"Maybe focus on the Shark Fin instead?" He shoved the inert LENS over to give himself more room.

"No, I don't think that'll help either." She closed her eyes and pressed the back of her head against the wall. "Where are we heading again?"

"New Frontier. It's an industrial city at the bottom tip of the lowest Epimethean Expansion." Isaac ran a search and perused the results. "It's a fairly small shelf city. About fifty thousand inhabitants. Only one SSP precinct. Large immigrant populations of Lunarians, Terrans, and Jovians living alongside the local Saturnites. Negation Industries put in the original expansion request, and they still have the largest exotic matter factory beneath the city. They're Lunar-based, so I suspect most of the immigrant families work for them. Sounds like a factory town melting pot to me."

"And *your* Luna isn't full of violent political extremists, right?" Susan asked.

"Oh, heavens no!" He chuckled. "Lunarians have a reputation for being a bit...eccentric, though."

"Eccentric by *SysGov* standards?" she asked with a hint of concern.

"Now, Susan. Be nice."

"Sorry."

"A lot of SysGov's wealth is concentrated on Earth's moon, and it's no secret Earth and Luna enjoy a special relationship.

Like a mother doting on her firstborn. I expect the Lunarians and Terrans form the city's upper class."

"That's so different from the Admin." Susan risked another look out the window. "Back home, Lunar violence is as regular as rain on Earth. Most of it stems from their various secessionist movements, fueled by generations of fomenting hatred."

The train descended past a vast parkland full of citizens enjoying themselves under a bright artificial sun. People took leisurely strolls through its rolling hills or swam in the shimmering waters of its central lake. The view went dark as they entered another divide, and then lit up with a glimmering view of the Pillar Palaces, massive estates extending outward from secondary support pillars, each trying to outdo the other in ostentatious opulence.

"Well, I don't think you have anything to worry about," Isaac said. "No Lunar secessionists over here."

"That's good. I'm not in the mood to have my arm blown off again."

"Your arm?" He raised an eyebrow. "Again?"

"It's a long story."

"I thought you said it was your legs."

"What?" She looked perplexed for a moment, but then her face lit up with understanding. "Oh! You mean what I said back when we met? Sorry. Different long story."

"How many times have you lost limbs in the line of duty?"

"Too many!" She let a smile slip out.

Isaac frowned and wondered at the violence in her past but decided not to press her. A zone of darkness flashed by, then Susan turned to watch the crossbeam city of Eighty Bridges rise upward. Buildings extended above and below the intersection of two thick crossbeams that joined secondary support pillars, and lesser structures spread outward from the center in all four directions. Dozens of thin bridges connected the major crossbeams at diagonals and in a radial pattern, making the city's thoroughfares resemble a spider's web of bridges built around a central residential clump.

"Glad I'm not bothered by heights." She leaned toward the window and looked down at the next divide far, far below. "Ever have problems with jumpers?"

"More often than you'd think."

"Oh?"

"A city like Eighty Bridges will have mechs on standby to catch anyone who falls, so a common rite of passage for gang members is to jump off the side of whatever tall structure is available. SSP does their best to discourage jumpers, and some cities have instituted heavier penalties, but the practice is still commonplace. And there are some who do it just for the thrill, knowing they'll survive"—his eyes darkened—"most of the time."

"What do you mean? The mechs don't always catch them in time?"

"Not exactly," Isaac explained. "They're reliable, at least in most cities. Just thinking about a case Raviv and I worked on."

"Who's Raviv?"

"Oh, sorry." He leaned toward her seat. "Chief Inspector Omar Raviv, recently promoted to the post. He's my boss. *Our* boss, now, actually. He was the senior detective I mentored under during my probationary period. He's a solid investigator and a great teacher. I learned a lot from him. Tightly wound, but solid. Very dependable.

"Anyway, he and I were on a jumper case in the Second Engine Block. This poor teenager jumped after being pressured by his 'friends,' but someone sabotaged the mechs."

"Oh, no," Susan gasped. "What happened?"

Isaac smacked his hands together, and Susan winced.

"The mech covering that zone was stuck in a diagnostic cycle at the time. The perp tried to make it look like an accident, but he didn't do a very good job of it. The two were after the same girl, and this idiot thought he could get away with murder."

"But you and Raviv caught him?"

"Yeah. Case ended in the death penalty." He shook his head. "Sometimes, I don't know what these people are thinking. Other times, I don't *want* to know."

Susan nodded, and they both stared out the window for a few quiet minutes.

"What's our first stop when we reach New Frontier?" she asked after a while.

"Their apartments," Isaac said. "We'll check those out first, see what pops up. After that, we'll stop by the impeller manu-facturers."

"Hey, kiddos!" Cephalie materialized above the LENS. "I got something good for you."

"Let's see it," Isaac said, then smiled as the files opened in his virtual sight. "Wonderful! Gordian got back to us."

"Records for their deceased officers?" Susan asked as she opened her own copies.

"Yep. Let's see what we have here."

He started with Doctor Andover-Chen's file. He'd come across most of the man's biographical info before, since the physicist had been in the public eye for some time, so he focused on the parts specific to the Gordian Division.

Andover-Chen's research had been instrumental in resolving the Dynasty Crisis. Specifically, his work on the chronoton bomb had allowed the allied Gordian and DTI attack force to . . . disconnect the Dynasty universe from the SysGov universe. This was the first Isaac had seen about exactly how they'd managed that not-so-minor feat, though, and he felt his eyebrows rising. They'd *created* more transdimensional space between the two to prevent the Dynasty universe's temporal implosion from destroying SysGov?

His eyebrows came down and he frowned as he read on. The notes contained a lot of "chronometric" this and "transdimensional" that as well as a heavy dose of seven-dimension math.

"Ever get the impression you're not speaking the same language as someone else?" he asked.

"*Yes*," Susan groaned. "How does a universe's timeline implode, anyhow? Nobody's ever been able to explain *that* to me."

"I haven't got a clue, either. Cephalie?"

"Don't look at me. I'm just the messenger."

Isaac read on for several minutes, but the throbbing in his temples only grew worse. He pushed the file aside with a sigh.

"I think I'll come back to the doctor later."

"Already ahead of you." Susan adjusted the angle of her interface. "Some interesting stuff in Delacroix's past. He transitioned to a synthoid at the age of fifty-four. Isn't that early for SysGov citizens?"

"It is, though not entirely unheard of. Does it say why?"

"Umm." She scrolled down. "Ah! Here we go. He was involved in an accident at ART. He'd been inspecting a faulty impeller when one of the safety systems failed and the impeller doused him with hard radiation. His organic body was a mess, almost unrecoverable, and first responders performed an emergency extraction of his connectome." She looked up. "They're allowed to do that?"

"If you preapprove the procedure, they can." Isaac tapped the side of his head. "I'm preapproved, but only if my organic body can't be revived. I'm in no rush to go synthetic."

"The transition's not so bad. And it has its perks."

"Anything else stand out to you?"

"A few things." She scrolled down. "His wife, Selene Delacroix, died recently. She was killed during the Dynasty nuclear attack on a factory cluster at the Earth-Luna L5 Lagrange point. Says she worked for the Mitchell Group, specializing in exotic matter engineering."

"Wait a second. That sounds familiar." Isaac pulled Andover-Chen's profile closer and scrolled up. "Yeah, here it is. The Mitchell Group was Gordian's biggest exotic matter supplier during the c-bomb's construction." He grimaced and shook his head. "I remember how shocked everyone was at the news, myself included. A *nuke* going off in the L5 Hub."

"Doesn't happen too often over here?"

"No, thankfully!"

"Here's another intriguing bit," Susan continued. "About a month ago, Delacroix separated from his integrated companion, an AC named Komuso, whom he'd been with most of his adult life."

"Sounds like he was going through rough times."

"No indication it affected his job performance, though," Susan noted. "More like the opposite. He buried himself in his work to cope. Hadn't taken a single day off since his wife died."

"Interesting."

"Any thoughts?"

"Not yet." Isaac leaned back. "We'll see what we find in their apartments."

CHAPTER EIGHT

THE STRUCTURAL PILLAR NARROWED NEAR THE BOTTOM OF THE Shark Fin, and the fifteen tracks thinned down to only two. They transitioned through one last divide, and the train's descent began to slow.

Isaac peered down at New Frontier. The shelf city was built into an oval space that narrowed near the bottom. Seven major levels ringed the structural walls, and bridges crisscrossed the empty space in the center. A lush park covered a full third of the upper shelf, a lake took up another third, and the rest was populated with elaborate estates and carefully manicured gardens. Farther below, the buildings became smaller and more densely packed, and the city's artificial sun failed to reach all of them. The Negation Industries logo scrolled across the factory roof below the city's bottom shelf.

The train eased onto a curved track that brought it into a station one shelf below the top.

"Attention passengers. Thank you for choosing the Pillar Line for your transportation needs today. We are now arriving at New Frontier, Shelf Six. Indoor weather is twenty-two degrees Celsius, pressure is one point oh five atmospheres, and local ventilation is providing a gentle breeze of six kilometers per hour. Outside, the temperature is a chilly negative three degrees Celsius, pressure is nine point eight atmospheres, and wind speeds are gusting at two hundred and seventy kilometers per hour. We hope you enjoyed your time with us, and we look forward to serving you again in the future. All passengers, please prepare to disembark."

"End of the line," Isaac said, rising from his seat.

The car drove off the down ramp onto Shelf One and turned down a narrow street, taking Isaac and Susan farther underneath the upper shelves. The buildings to either side were low and squat, and overhead lights provided inconsistent pools of illumination.

Oasis Apartments came into view at the far end of the street, composed of nine rather taller buildings arranged around a wide cul-de-sac. Each rectangular building extended from the shelf floor all the way up ten stories to the bottom of Shelf Two. Lighting in this part of New Frontier wasn't great to begin with, but the walkways crisscrossing between the apartment structures imposed a foreboding gloom over the street below.

The car parked itself along the lip of the cul-de-sac, and the cabin door split open.

"Vehicle, wait here," Isaac said, climbing out of the car.

"Standing by," replied the car's attendant program.

"They couldn't find a better place to stay?" Susan asked, looking around. A few other cars ringed the cul-de-sac, and they could see half-empty parking garages inside each building's first floor. The walls had once been a uniform ocean blue, but a greasy patina oozed out of open seams in the paneling, and a faint rubbery odor lingered. Active graffiti adorned parts of the walls and sidewalks, some of it obscene, while others displayed large blocky numbers that would change every couple of seconds.

"Maybe they picked the one closest to the factory?" he guessed.

"I thought this place was supposed to be new." She turned to him. "You know, 'New Frontier.'"

"Well, it's not *that* new." He looked around, then shrugged. "It was 'new' enough when this shelf was settled, but that was over twenty years ago. It's clearly fallen out of favor as the city expanded upward with additional shelves."

"I see." She gave the apartments a dubious frown. "What's that coming out of the walls?"

"Degraded prog-steel that should have been replaced years ago."

"Is it dangerous?" she asked with a hint of concern.

"Hardly," Isaac assured her. "Basic prog-steel, like the kind used in civilian construction, can corrode if it isn't maintained. It loses its adaptive qualities, becomes inert."

"So, it's harmless?"

"Very harmless. Come on."

He led the way to the second building on the right with his LENS floating behind and above his shoulder and Susan bringing up the rear. He pinged the door with his police credentials, and it opened into a modest square room with two doors on the far wall.

One split open to reveal a cramped compartment.

"An elevator?" Susan asked.

"Problem?" Isaac turned back with one foot inside.

"I was expecting artificial gravity."

"Counter-grav is for the rich," Isaac replied matter-of-factly. He waited for Susan and the LENS to squeeze in, and they took the elevator up to level four. They stepped out onto a balcony that ringed the building and followed it around to the back to find Andover-Chen's apartment.

"Four-twelve," Susan said.

"Mmhmm." Isaac used the keycode Gordian had provided along with their agent profiles, and the apartment door split open. The entrance led to a clean, spartan interior with gray walls and a floor carpeted in a checkered pattern, all arranged into a main living space, bathroom, and bedroom.

He stepped through the threshold, the infostructure recognized his presence, and abstractions came alive around him. Soft music played in the background; Isaac didn't recognize the composition, but it had a serene, unobtrusive melody. It was the kind of music one might listen to while working to help focus the mind. Perhaps classical Martian?

Isaac walked along one wall covered in abstract picture frames: a young Matthew Andover receiving a diploma, Chen Wang-shu doing the same; Andover giving a speech; Chen lecturing his students; a recent picture of Andover and Chen joining the Gordian Division; Andover-Chen celebrating his/their integration; Andover-Chen accepting an award from President Byakko; Andover-Chen giving an interview; Andover-Chen shaking hands with a short, compact woman in a Peacekeeper uniform, and so on.

"Doesn't the guy have any family?" Susan asked.

"I'm beginning to think he's married to his work."

"And he seems to have a high opinion of himself."

"Maybe, but look at what he accomplished during the Dynasty Crisis. I suppose he's earned the right."

The pictures weren't *all* about Andover-Chen. A photo of Albert Einstein sticking out his tongue floated large and prominent on the far wall, and Isaac guessed the few other black-and-white photos might also be famous scientists.

"What's this one?" She pointed to a wall-height poster squeezed into a corner, almost haphazardly. The poster depicted a dark green lizardman with a grenade bandolier, a pistol-wielding white-furred mouse-alien half the lizardman's height, a lithe golden-hued humanoid with long cranial antennae, and a hulking suit of power armor carrying the result of a wild orgy between a rocket launcher, a machine gun, and a flamethrower. The poster's caption read "Kleio Squad."

"Looks like a gaming group for *Solar Descent*," Isaac said. "That's a popular abstraction here in SysGov. I'm guessing the one with the antennae is the doctor."

"Why do you say that?"

"The picture's focused on him."

"Ah."

Isaac walked over to a wide desk placed against the wall with a trio of powerful infosystems towers jammed underneath. He pulled out the chair and sank into it. A blizzard of charts materialized around him, and he blinked his eyes at the deluge of data assaulting his senses. Mathematical equations, time machine schematics, and graphs that made no sense to him filled his worldview, though he did pick out a few notes the doctor had left for himself, floating above or below the mass of screens. He pulled one close.

"'What if we find a universe where the speed of light is different?'" he read aloud, grimaced, then let it return to its original place and pulled in another one. "'Reminder: Talk to Hinnerkopf about transverse research outpost idea.' Know anything about that?"

"First I've heard of it. The transverse is the space 'in between' universes, in case you were wondering."

"Thanks. I was." He grabbed another and cleared his throat. "'Which next? Accelerated medibot healing ·or drone armor upgrade?'"

"Accelerated healing?" Susan asked. "Drone armor?"

"Perks for his *Solar Descent* character." Isaac rose from the seat and slid it back in. "Cephalie, how about you?"

"The infostructure's clean." She appeared atop the LENS. "Nothing out of the ordinary. His mail buffered from his most recent stay looks normal to me, too. Lots of back-and-forth with Negation Industries and the Trinh Syndicate about the impellers they're working on. Progress reports back to the Gordian commissioner. Work and personal messages between him and Delacroix. All the kind of stuff you'd expect to see from Gordian's top scientist. Plus a few messages to and from Gordian agents Raibert Kaminski and Philosophus about their next gaming session."

"Pull copies of all his correspondence and grab any notes he left to himself. We might need them later."

"Consider it done."

Isaac checked the other two rooms, but besides the expected synthoid charging station and bed, a spare Gordian uniform in the closet, and some basic synthoid care products in the restroom, the two rooms appeared almost unused.

"Delacroix's place next?" Susan asked.

"Yeah, let's move on."

They exited the apartment, and Isaac locked the door behind them. They took a nearby flight of stairs up one level and rounded the corner of the building to where the bridges intersected over the cul-de-sac in a denser pattern, forming an elevated communal platform with a few park benches and basketball court.

A lone teenager dribbled his ball half-heartedly as he paced up the court, a bored frown on his face. He looked over when Isaac and Susan came into view, and every muscle in his body locked up. He missed his next dribble, and the ball bounced past his frozen hand until it rolled to a halt against the platform's guardrail.

<Isaac?> Cephalie sent him privately.

<I see him,> Isaac replied without moving his lips. <Looks like a lone Numbers gang member. Any others around?>

<He's the first one I've seen.>

<Keep an eye on him.>

<Will do.>

The teenager wore a white baggy shirt and pants with bold, black numbers appearing and disappearing at random, as well as round abstraction goggles with reflective lenses and a band around the back of his head. He sidestepped over to his ball and picked it up, trying and failing to look natural while also never taking his eyes off the police.

Isaac had no doubt the gangster was up to no good, and the sudden appearance of a SysPol detective had shocked him, but that didn't mean Isaac could do anything about it, and so he continued around the next building. He turned the corner and caught sight of the door to Delacroix's apartment.

Someone had forced it open.

He whirled around and faced the gangster.

"You there!"

The kid bolted for the stairs.

"Stop! Police!"

The gangster ignored him and sprinted across the platform toward the stairs.

"Cephalie!" Isaac shouted, sending unlock codes for prisoner-restraint functions to the LENS.

The outer eyeball surface of the LENS morphed into an aero-dynamic teardrop, and the internal graviton thruster fired at full power. The LENS darted forward, a silver arrowhead seeking its target. The gangster turned and cried out moments before the tip of the LENS pressed against his ribs.

Malleable prog-steel deformed like soft putty, splashing out-ward to form four pseudopods of mercury-like metal. The flexible arms looped around the gangster's wrists and ankles, stiffened, and he stumbled and fell backward. He would have smacked his head against the guardrail if not for a fifth pseudopod that circled around behind him and, acting like a spring, lowered him slowly—almost lovingly—to the ground.

The prog-steel restraints stiffened further, and the LENS's naked mechanical core floated up and away from it.

"Fuck you!" the gangster spat. "Why the fuck you do that?"

Isaac ignored the kid as he examined the busted door from a distance, arms clasped behind his back.

"Brute force," he muttered. "Did they saw through the lock with a vibro-knife? Not a very sophisticated approach." He peeked inside but couldn't see much without stepping in and risking the destruction of evidence. Instead, he waved his hand over the door, and a virtual police cordon appeared.

"Why the hell you fuckers grab me? I was just shooting hoops, for fuck sake!"

"Then why'd you run?" Isaac walked over to the prone gangster with Susan. "You seemed to be in an awful hurry all of a sudden."

"Let me go, you fuckers! I didn't do anything!"

"Somehow I doubt that." Isaac pointed a thumb over his shoulder. "You know anything about the apartment with the busted door?"

"Go fuck yourself!"

"You sure? Seemed like you might have been watching it. Though I'm curious why you'd hang around *after* it's been robbed."

"I'm not telling you anything! I have rights! You hear me? I have rights!"

"Fine. Have it your way." Isaac opened a comm window. "Dispatch."

"Themis Dispatch here," a friendly male voice said. "How may I assist you, Detective?"

"I need a forensics team at my location, and I have a guest for the SSP to pick up, also at my location."

"Understood, Detective. Let's take care of the 'guest' first. There's an SSP squad copter available and near your location. There, I've routed them to assist you, ETA seven minutes. Do you have an ID for the individual?"

"Kid, what's your name?"

"Fuck you, cop!"

"I have a Mister F.U. Cop standing by for pickup," Isaac said, his tone so dry he could have turned New Frontier into a desert.

The voice on the line snickered. "Is that really the gentleman's name, sir?"

"Hey, I'm just repeating what he told me." Isaac knelt next to the gangster and pulled off his abstraction goggles.

"Give that back!" He squirmed in vain against his restraints. "You can't do that! That's mine! I have rights!"

"These are some nice goggles you have here." Isaac turned them over in his hands. "Cephalie, check the permit on these, would you?"

"Looks legit. Single-use printing pattern registered to a Nathan Skylark, age seventeen. And you're right. They weren't cheap."

"You catch that, Dispatch?"

"I did, and it appears Skylark already has a criminal record."

"Why am I not surprised?" Isaac shook his head at the kid.

"Mostly vandalism," Dispatch added. "Skylark seems to be a small-timer in the Numbers gang."

"You looking to branch out, Nathan?" Isaac asked.

"Fuck you! Fuck all of you!"

"Mister Skylark seems to have a rather limited vocabulary." Dispatch's tone was as dry as Isaac's had been. "I'll attach his criminal record to your case file."

"Much appreciated, Dispatch."

"Now, about that forensics team you've requested...that one's going to be a little harder. There aren't any full physical teams near your location, and even the ones that are *remotely* close aren't going to be free for a while."

"The Apple Cypher case?" Isaac asked.

"Got it first try, Detective."

"Doesn't have to be a full team, then. Looks like an amateurish break-and-enter. This shouldn't be a huge job, so I'll take whatever you can give me."

"Let me see what I can find...aha! I do have one specialist already in New Frontier. I should be able to sneak your request into her queue, since there's hardly any travel time involved. There we go. Looks like she could be ready for you in about half an hour."

"Perfect. I'll take it."

"Entered and accepted. Anything else?"

"Nothing. Thank you."

"Our pleasure, Detective."

Isaac closed the window and stood up.

"Cephalie, have the LENS perform a preliminary forensic pass over the room. We can help give the specialist a head start."

✧   ✧   ✧

A pair of state troopers arrived and took the gangster away without griping about it once, which Isaac appreciated after the unnecessary drama in the transceiver tower. He sat down on a courtside bench and waited for the forensic specialist while Susan stood nearby.

"Anything?" Isaac asked as the LENS floated out of Delacroix's apartment.

"Infostructure's been wiped, and anything of value's been carted off." Cephalie twirled her cane and sat down on top of the LENS, which came to rest beside Isaac on the bench. "I'm leaving the rest to the specialist."

"Check with the apartment. See if they have any surveillance cameras."

"Already did. They have nine cameras per level, but half of them are busted, and the ones that aren't connect to a compromised infostructure. There must be seventeen or so programs floating around in there, all fighting each other to generate fake videos. We're not getting *anything* useful out of that mess."

"Oh well." He shrugged. "It was worth a try. Did you let the apartment know about their problems?"

"All they have is an attendant program watching over things."

"That's it?" Isaac shook his head.

"Yeah, and it didn't seem all that concerned about the break-in or the smashed cameras. It gave me the contact string for the apartment's site manager, and I left a message."

"Hmm."

"This crime could be unrelated," Susan said.

"Why do you say that?" Isaac asked, even though he'd wondered the same thing.

"Skylark doesn't strike me as part of an elite criminal *anything*, and I wouldn't expect some random youth gang to go toe-to-toe with SysPol's newest division."

"Fair point, but the Numbers could be acting as someone's hired muscle."

He checked the time, then opened Andover-Chen's correspondence with Negation Industries and began reading. One prominent topic dealt with a failed impeller inspection and Negation Industries' attempt to ask Andover-Chen to overrule Delacroix. To his credit, Andover-Chen stood firmly by his colleague in public, though he did voice some private concerns to Delacroix that the man was being too strict. Isaac made a note to bring up the impeller when they visited the company.

He continued reading but barely made a dent in the remaining correspondence when the disk-shaped frame of a SysPol conveyor drone floated up to their level with a fat crate slung underneath, secured by a pair of malleable arms.

A slender, dark-haired woman in SysPol blues walked up the steps and waved at him.

"Hey, Isaac!"

"Nina?" Isaac asked, rising from the bench. "What are you doing here?"

"Someone's grandma saw an apple. You?"

"Double homicide."

"You have all the luck," she teased.

"Do not."

"Says the guy who just arrived in a luxury saucer."

"I—" He paused and frowned. He tried to think up a witty retort, but nothing came to mind.

"See? I have a point, don't I?"

"A *small* one."

"Oh, I'm just getting started!" She glanced over at Susan. "What's this about you having a deputy already? And one from the Admin, at that!"

"Friend of yours, Isaac?" Susan asked.

"Sister, actually." He gestured to them in turn. "Susan Cantrell, meet Nina Cho. Nina, Susan."

"Just to be clear, I'm his *older* sister," Nina corrected.

"By all of sixteen minutes," Isaac added with a roll of his eyes.

"Still counts." Nina extended a hand. "Nice to meet you, Susan!"

"Likewise." She shook her hand.

"My little brother hasn't caused you any trouble yet, has he?"

"*Nina.*"

"Well..." Susan frowned uncomfortably at the sudden question. "No?"

"You don't have to cover for him, you know."

"New job, new challenges. That's all."

"Well, just let me know if he does anything unbearable." Nina slapped a hand down on Isaac's shoulder. "*I'll* straighten him out!"

"A-*hem.*" Isaac glowered as he brushed her hand off. "I believe you have a job to do."

"Sure, sure. Where's the crime scene?"

"This way." Susan led her to Delacroix's apartment. "Here's the dead agent's apartment."

"Geez. Talk about a lack of subtlety. They saw through the lock?"

"Looks like it."

Nina turned back to the conveyor drone and whistled.

Six compartments on the crate opened, and six spherical drones that resembled Isaac's LENS hovered over to her.

"In you go, my lovelies!" Nina gestured inside, and the forensics drones floated past her. She summoned a virtual interface, tapped a few keys, then paused to squint at one of the readouts. "You have *got* to be kidding me."

"What's wrong?" Susan asked.

"They sprayed the whole place down with Grime-Away. The walls are dripping with the stuff! Can you believe that?"

"Well, you know what they say," Isaac sighed.

"Know what who says?" Susan asked.

"Grime-Away," he intoned. "Good for grime, great for crime."

"It's an aerosol cleaning mixture," Nina added. "Microbot-based."

"Self-replicating?" Susan asked, sounding worried for some reason.

"No, nothing fancy like that," Nina said, "but the microbots will scour any surface they come into contact with before pooling together and traveling to the nearest reclamation chute. Dirt, grease, skin cells, hair follicles, respiratory spray, fingerprints, shoe prints, you name it. Grime-Away doesn't care. It eats them all."

"Some criminals use the stuff to tidy up after their messes," Isaac added.

"So that's it?" Susan asked. "It's that easy for the bad guys? They spray the place down and destroy all the evidence?"

"Hardly!" Nina cracked her knuckles as four of her drones traveled back into the crate. "These fools see someone use Grime-Away in a movie, and they think it'll work in real life. This is the tool of a criminal who doesn't know any better." She shook her head with a sly half smile. "They don't realize the kinds of toys I have at my disposal. I almost feel sorry for them."

The four drones left the crate, this time with boxy attachments dangling beneath them.

"All this does is slow me down," Nina continued, "and not even by that much."

"You sound confident," Susan noted.

"Because this break-in job has 'novice' written all over it." Nina turned to Isaac. "I thought you'd have a tough one for me."

"Do you *want* a tougher task?" Isaac asked pointedly.

"Honestly, I wouldn't mind. Raviv's had me bouncing around from one tampered food printer to the next since I arrived, and every one of them is the same. Altered pattern files with no indication of how they got there."

"Is the Apple Cypher really that big of a problem?" Isaac asked.

"Not right now," Nina said. "Everyone's overreacting like damn fools over food printer vandalism, but the *implied* threat is the real problem."

"If the criminal can change your food patterns," Susan began, "what might be sabotaged next?"

"Exactly," Nina agreed. "And that's why everyone's freaking out."

"Well, enjoy your non-food-printer assignment while it lasts." Isaac glanced inside. "How long do you think you'll need?"

"Oh, Isaac. You know better than to ask." She smiled sweetly at him. "It'll be done when it's done."

"Figured you'd say that."

"I need to stop by the local precinct after this. Maybe catch you there before I head up the pillar?"

"Sure, if we're around. Need anything from us before we head out?"

"No, I've got this one covered."

"Then we'll leave you to it."

"Should we head for the SSP precinct?" Susan asked. "Question that kid?"

"Not yet. We can hold him for twenty-four hours without charging him, so he's not going anywhere. Let him stew for a while in his cell. Cephalie?"

"Yeah?" She appeared on his shoulder.

"Tell Negation Industries we're paying them a visit."

CHAPTER NINE

THE CAR FOLLOWED A NEARBY DOWN RAMP TO THE INDUSTRIAL sector's roof, unofficially dubbed as "Shelf Zero." Negation Industries took up most of the volume below, but Isaac spotted virtual signs for the Mitchell Group, CounterGravCorp, Reality Controls, Atlas, SourceCode, and the Trinh Syndicate. Beside Negation Industries, the Trinh Syndicate was the only company with an established foothold; all the others looked like they were in the process of setting up new factories, given the large temporary holes cut into Shelf Zero and the masses of factory machinery sitting around up top, awaiting installation.

"This town might be on the threshold of a nice economic boom," Isaac said. "Lot of exotic matter producers moving in."

"Because of the industry lost during the Dynasty Crisis?" Susan asked.

"Most likely."

Their car parked in a small visitor lot next to a round, white-walled guest center. They exited their vehicle and walked in through wide glass doors. A gray carpet guided them straight to a physical receptionist behind a counter while abstractions of Negation Industries products floated to either side: graviton thrusters of varying sizes and outputs, hot singularity reactors for starships and space stations, industrial-grade counter-grav plating, and the prominent spikes of TTV impellers.

They stopped in front of the counter. The receptionist, a young man with a round face and silvery-blond hair, dipped his head to them.

"Hello and welcome to the New Frontier site for Negation Industries. How can I help you?"

"Detective Isaac Cho, SysPol Themis." He pinged the receptionist with his credentials. "My IC called ahead. Vice-President Ortiz should be expecting us."

"One moment, sir. Let me check." He pulled up a virtual itinerary. "Yes, here you are." He opened a comm window and let it ring a few times.

"This had better be important," grunted the low, gravelly voice on the line. "I'm damn sure I set my do-not-disturb flag. Do you have any idea the kind of problems I'm dealing with right now?"

"No, sir." The receptionist rested his cheek on a fist. "Would you like to talk about it?"

"Would I? Production is throwing every excuse in the book at me while running eight percent behind today's quota. Eight percent! Maintenance wants my head because I cut their printer runtime down to what it *should* be. Exotic Printer Seven just faulted out, and now Maintenance is pointing the finger at *me* as the reason we don't have the right spares on standby. IT, in their infinite wisdom, decided *now* is the best time to push out the latest security patch, so Exotic Printers One, Two, and Three are throwing fits and might need to be shut down to have the patches removed. Quality is screaming at me over every little microscopic deviation in what we *have* produced today, and they think it's a *wonderful* idea to chuck half of that down the reclamation chute. And all of those problems hit me in the last two hours! So, yes! I'm a little busy right now!"

"I understand that, sir," the receptionist said with impressive patience, "but there's a Detective Isaac Cho here to see you."

"Oh." The fire and brimstone wheezed out of the voice like a balloon deflating. "Shit. Umm, right. Tell him I'll be right up."

"I will, sir." The receptionist closed the window. "Our VP will be up to see you shortly, Detective. Can I offer you some refreshments while you wait?"

"Sounds like he's under a lot of pressure," Isaac observed.

"It's been like that since the Dynasty Crisis."

"Supply and demand?" Isaac asked. "More demand than you can supply?"

The receptionist nodded. "As problems go, I suppose it's a good one to have."

The door to a counter-grav shaft behind the counter split open, and a stocky man floated up. He wore a black suit with a wide-brimmed hat and the Negation Industries logo pinned to his high collar. An oval amethyst floated above his shoulder, the visualization of his integrated companion. He caught sight of Isaac and company, smoothed out his suit, and walked around the counter.

"Detective, a pleasure." He extended a hand. "Chester Ortiz, Vice-President of Operations here at Negation Industries New Frontier and the account manager for all Gordian Division contracts. At your service, sir."

Isaac shook his hand, then introduced Susan and Cephalie.

"Thank you for taking time out of your busy schedule to meet with us, Mister Ortiz."

"Oh, not at all. It's been a hell of a day for us, and I've been running around like a crazed lunatic, but I still caught the news." He flashed a smile full of grim determination. "What a terrible accident. We were looking forward to having Doctor Andover-Chen back on site with us."

"And Delacroix, too, I imagine."

"Yes." His smile became a little forced. "Him, too."

"Did you have problems with the chief engineer?"

"I didn't mean anything by it, and I suppose it's bad form to speak ill of the dead. He could be a hard man to please at times. That's all."

"What was your relationship with the two agents?"

"Well, as account manager, I'm their point of contact with Negation Industries. I manage the production of their order, deal with any issues or contract disputes that might come up, and generally do my best to keep the customers happy."

"Any social interactions with the two?"

"Nothing besides two celebratory dinners to mark project milestones. We didn't hang out after hours, if that's what you mean." Ortiz motioned to the shaft he'd arrived through. "I'm more than happy to answer any questions you have. Would you like to take this to a private room? Or perhaps you want to see the impellers we're building for the Gordian contract?"

"Let's start with the impellers first," Isaac said. "I'll also need access to their desks and any material they left behind."

"Easy enough. I'll take you there after I've shown you the factory. This way."

They took the shaft down to a six-way junction where gravitational forces swept them sideways through a transparent tube with a view of the factory floor below. Bulky industrial printers, each two or three stories high, sat in rows with a mess of conveyor belts spanning the gaps between them, filled with pallets of partially fabricated products. One of the larger printers was down for maintenance with vivid red virtual marquees declaring a list of faults. Drones, ACs, and physical workers swarmed over it, removing panels and pulling components out.

"Problems?" Isaac asked.

"Just another day on the factory floor," Ortiz replied matter-of-factly. "If the job was easy, anyone could do this. Working with exotic matter requires extreme levels of precision—both on the exotic and normal matter sides—and we've been pushing our equipment hard to keep up with demand. These are all 'standard' printers you're seeing. We haven't passed any exotic ones yet.

"Printing exotic matter is tricky business. Physics gets a little strange when you start plopping negative signs in odd places. Ever let something go and have it fall upward faster and faster?"

"Can't say that I have," Isaac said.

"That'll sometimes happen here. How about pushing an object *up* in order to keep it from *falling* up? Ever do that?"

"Again, no."

"And most people never will, despite how much our society relies on exotic matter."

"Why is that?" Susan asked.

"It's because any finished product has a greater sum of regular matter incorporated into the design, so the mechanism ends up with positive mass. Otherwise, technology with exotic matter would be almost impossible to handle in day-to-day life."

The tube turned downward, taking them below the upper printer level to a massive chamber with twelve giant cylindrical machines crammed together. The tube dropped them off at a high observational balcony overlooking the floor.

"The bread-and-butter of our operations." Ortiz swept a hand across the view. "These twelve exotic matter printers were custom designed and built by our on-site engineering team, and a few of them employ special, proprietary modifications. You won't find faster or higher quality exotic printers anywhere in the Saturn State."

"That's a bold claim."

"But a truthful one."

"Maybe so," Isaac said, "but I couldn't help but notice a few big names establishing a presence below Shelf Zero."

"Oh, *them*." Ortiz chuckled dismissively. "Yes, it seems our competitors are finally waking up. Shame it took them so long. They had to lose whole factories before they started looking for better options. *We* realized Saturn's promise long before the current shortage."

"And why is that?"

"There are a lot of reasons. Hydrogen is the preferred base to begin with when producing exotic matter, and Saturn offers abundant access to hydrogen gas. Furthermore, our printers are optimized for the higher atmospheric pressure this far down the Shark Fin, accelerating the conversion process to give us an edge over the competition."

"What about the other gas giants?" Susan asked. "Why Saturn and not them?"

"Each has its own problems. Both Neptune and Uranus lack much of Saturn's industrial infrastructure, and Jupiter's surface gravity is prohibitively high. A harsh two point five gees versus our pleasant one point one. Plus, all that radiation isn't doing the Jovians any favors, either, whereas Saturn's radiation is quite mild. Barely worth a mention."

"Jupiter's industrial infrastructure is significantly larger than Saturn's, though," Isaac countered.

"True enough. The Galilean moons were colonized long before Saturn, so the Jovians enjoy a head start on us, but I don't think that'll last forever, and the higher-ups in our company agree. Both planetary states bask in a wealth of raw materials, but Jupiter's gravity and radiation place barriers around many of its resources. Those barriers *can* be worked through, but Saturn doesn't have those problems, so why go through all that effort?"

"Interesting." Isaac gazed across the machines below. "Where are the Gordian impellers?"

"Here. Let me show you." Ortiz called up an interface and sent data to their shared virtual vision. The floor vanished, and Isaac realized each cylinder extended half a kilometer down into

Saturn's atmosphere. Sections of the great machines turned trans-lucent, and the spikes of time drive impellers appeared within nine of the units.

"The scope of your contract is for nine impellers?" Isaac asked.

"That's right. Eight of them are ready for testing. We're making a few minor adjustments in preparation for the field tests."

"I understand Gordian purchased ten impellers in total. Why is Negation Industries responsible for only nine of them?"

"Because of all our other orders. We tried to free up the nec-essary capacity, offered discounts to other customers in exchange for delayed production. Some people bit, but not enough. In the end, we settled on a nine-unit order, and Gordian went elsewhere for the last one."

"Fair enough. And the ninth impeller? You said eight are ready for testing."

"Yes, that one," Ortiz huffed. "It's still behind schedule. *Way* behind."

"That particular unit seems to be a bone of contention between you and the Gordian agents."

"With good reason. Andover-Chen and Delacroix inspected all nine units during their visit about six weeks back, and we still hold that all of them met their specifications."

"They disagreed?"

"That they did." Ortiz clenched his jaw. "Look, I don't mind exacting customers; that comes with the territory. But *Delacroix*." He shook his head. "That man went too far in demanding we build a new impeller from scratch instead of adjust the one we'd already built!"

"Was he authorized to make that call?"

"Yeah, unfortunately." Ortiz sighed, nodding slowly. "It's a somewhat gray area in the contract. By the letter of the agree-ment, Gordian Division *does* have the right to specify changes to the impellers if they fall outside a certain percentage of the agreed tolerances. Still a dick move, if you ask me."

"And the ninth impeller fell outside that tolerance range?"

"Yes. *Barely.* We were four percent under the targeted chronoton permeability rate of change, which is why we argued reworking the impeller would bring it firmly within the agreed performance specs. Delacroix rejected that offer outright. I thought I might have a chance getting through to Andover-Chen, but those Gordian chaps just formed ranks, and that was the end of it. I knew I wasn't making headway, so I sucked up the loss and moved on."

"What happened to the failed impeller?"

"We disabled the time drive features, chopped it up, and sold it off as bulk exotic matter. That's standard procedure for us."

"Why not use it for another contract?"

"Generally speaking, we can't because the specifications from contract to contract are too different. Sometimes we can get away with that, but Gordian's the only impeller customer in existence."

"I see. And who bought impeller nine?"

"The Trinh Syndicate."

Isaac raised an eyebrow. "The other company on Saturn with a Gordian contract bought your defective impeller?"

"Yeah, I know. That struck me as a little weird, too, but they put in the highest bid." Ortiz blew out a breath. "Damned frustrating affair all around, if you ask me. But, it's behind us, and we'll finish number nine eventually. If you ask me, his stubbornness didn't make sense. Gordian has been screaming for new impellers, and the fastest way for us to get impeller nine out the door was to rework it, but *nooooo*! It had to be perfect! So now they can wait longer for us to finish the last part of their order."

Isaac jotted down a note to follow up with the Trinh Syndicate.

"Last question for now. Are you aware of any reason why either man would have been killed?"

"Wait a second. You mean they were murdered?" Ortiz seemed genuinely surprised. "I thought it was an accident."

"Please answer the question, Mister Ortiz."

"Sorry. Hmm." He gazed up at the ceiling in thought. "Yeah, I guess it would be funny for a Themis detective to show up for an accident. Sorry, I've had a lot on my mind today." He shook his head. "But no. I can't think of anything, really. Sure, Delacroix could be tough to deal with, but I've handled far worse in the past, trust me. And Andover-Chen was one of the easier customers I've had in years."

"What about the rejected impeller?"

"In this business, you win some, you lose some. All that did was cut into our profit margin. We're still comfortably in the black on this project. I couldn't understand someone being *killed* over it. What would be the point? We're still on track to close this project out as an overall win, just not as big as we were hoping."

"Thank you, Mister Ortiz." Isaac closed his interface. "If you wouldn't mind, I'd like to see their work area next."

✧   ✧   ✧

The Gordian Division office was built into a circular overlook branching downward from the roof of the exotic printer level. The desks sat facing each other in the center of the room's wide, panoramic view with a diagonal counter-grav tube the only obstruction. Ortiz received two urgent calls on the way over and asked to be excused while they sifted through the agents' desks.

"That's quite all right," Isaac said. "I think we have everything we need from you, for the moment."

"Sorry. Call if you need anything."

"We will."

The tube whisked the vice-president away, leaving them alone.

Susan walked over to the wall and gazed down at the exotic printers.

"Let me get this straight"—she crossed her arms and switched to security chat—"Gordian Division gets its impellers from a factory a hundred kilometers down in Saturn's atmosphere?"

"Some of them, anyway."

"And there wasn't an easier place to build the things?"

"Well, there *were* . . . until the Dynasty blew them up."

Isaac sat down in Andover-Chen's chair; he knew it belonged to the doctor because of the virtual portrait showing Andover-Chen shaking hands with SysGov President Byakko and a pair of *Solar Descent* character sheets. The same deluge of incomprehensible charts and equations appeared around him, and Isaac tried to sift through the mess.

"What are you looking for?"

"Anything on that rejected impeller." He pushed through three layers of charts, shoving them over a corner of the desk until he spotted what he was after and pulled the annotated time drive schematic forward. "Here we are. See this?"

"What exactly are we looking at?" Susan asked, stepping over.

"The doctor's own review of the reject. 'Adjustments to rear quarter should increase max CP delta by a few percent. Why not do that? Need to ask Joachim.' Interesting."

"CP delta?"

"Chronoton permeability," Cephalie explained, the LENS

bobbing in the air beside them. "It's how fast the impeller can adjust the flow of chronotons passing through it."

"The important part is the doctor had doubts about Delacroix's decision," Isaac said, "even if they maintained a united front when dealing with Ortiz."

"Wouldn't this impeller decision have rubbed someone the wrong way?"

"Sure, but Negation Industries already absorbed the loss. If someone wanted to prevent all that Esteem from getting flushed down the chute, they acted too late. Besides, Ortiz doesn't strike me as the type. I read him as the kind of person who's bombarded with problems to fix and decisions to make on a constant basis, and he works through them as best he can. He's used to compromises and imperfect solutions, and I don't think he'd dwell on them too much. Rather, he'd simply move on and face down his next set of challenges."

Isaac sifted through the other charts, but nothing caught his eye, so he stood up and walked around to Delacroix's desk.

The difference was stark. An impeller schematic, two inspection reports, and a few open messages were all laid out in a neat row, and a trio of personal photos hovered against the backdrop. He pulled one close and ran a search on the petite young woman with long brunette hair holding Delacroix's hand. The picture looped through a few seconds of them walking toward the camera, waves washing across their bare feet. She turned to him with laughter sparkling in her large brown eyes.

"Selene?" Susan asked.

"Yes."

"Pretty."

Isaac let go, and the photo flew back to its place on the wall. He grabbed the next one showing a closeup of Selene kissing her husband's cheek. The last featured the couple looking out across one of the Venerian aerial cities, although Isaac couldn't tell which one. He shifted in the seat, but something scraped against his left forearm, and he looked down.

"Hmm?" He ran his hand over the chair's armrest, and bits of foam crumbled away.

"Something?"

"Either Negation Industries gave him the worst chair in the office, or Delacroix likes tearing chunks of foam off his armrests."

"Don't your chairs repair themselves?"

"Normally, yes." Isaac twisted in the seat and ran his hand over the back of the chair. He pressed in, and the back gave easily around his hand. "But its prog-foam bladder is depleted." He crouched down and checked under the desk. "Looks like the cleaning remotes missed a spot. There's some more stuck in the corner."

"A sign he was under a lot of stress?" Susan asked.

"I wouldn't read too much into this." Isaac rose and dusted himself off. "He probably did it without thinking. I had this friend back in high school who would get super nervous before exams. He'd stay up all night studying, all the while picking his eyebrow out. Just plucking it one hair at a time, and *only* the right eyebrow. A few times, he showed up to school the next day almost bald over one eye."

"Did the other students poke fun at him for it?"

"Naturally, kids being the little monsters they are." He furrowed his brow and turned to Susan. "Are there high schools in the Admin?"

"Yes."

"Like the ones we have in SysGov?"

"What do you mean?"

"Peaceful. No one shooting at each other."

"*Yes,*" she stressed.

"No heavily armed synthoids roaming the halls?"

"Of course, there are. That what makes them peaceful."

"I see." Isaac shrugged. "Sorry. Foolish of me to ask."

"What's that supposed to mean?" Susan asked, sounding irritated.

"Nothing. We're getting sidetracked." He turned away before she could respond. "Cephalie?"

"Here." She appeared atop the LENS.

"Anything to report?"

"Nothing unusual. More business correspondence and the like. I grabbed copies of everything."

"All right." Isaac spotted a piece of foam stuck to the back of his hand and flicked it off. "We're done here. Let's move on to the Trinh Syndicate."

CHAPTER TEN

"A WORD OF WARNING BEFORE WE GO INSIDE," ISAAC SAID, PLACING a cautionary hand on Susan's shoulder.

"Yes? What is it?"

"It's about the Trinh Syndicate. Or rather, Saturnite syndicates in general." Isaac glanced meaningfully at the modest red building they'd parked next to. The Trinh Syndicate guest center was barely a third the size of the Negation Industries surface building. Virtual gold coins dangled on red strings above the door, tied through the square hole in their centers. They tinkled in a nonexistent wind beneath golden letters spelling TRINH with a long, golden dragon looped around the logo.

"What about them?"

"First understand that the syndicates are, at least on the surface, law-abiding companies."

"But that's not the whole story?" Susan ventured.

"Not even close. You've already seen signs of the gang problems here on Janus, and the syndicates are a big part of that because they use the gangs as disposable muscle for various purposes. Discreetly, of course, and it doesn't help that these companies are internally structured to make criminal prosecution of their leadership all but impossible. Too compartmentalized. In fact, most syndicate members forgo integrated companions for that very reason; easier to keep secrets known to one instead of a few.

Lower-level employees almost always take the fall when SysPol tries to move in."

"And what do the gangs get out of it?"

"Syndicates are known for paying their debts. *Generously.* Gang members are almost always the ones who wind up in jail when a job goes south, but once they've 'paid their debt to society' and are released, the syndicates hire them. Or, at least, the best of them. In that sense, the gangs act as recruiting grounds for future syndicate members, which motivates the gangs to perform well for their future employers. You could say the two parts form a barely concealed criminal ecology."

"Doesn't anyone try to stop this?"

"Stop it?" Isaac chuckled sadly. "They'll just tell you the system is working as intended. Criminals go to jail, then find gainful employment once they've been 'reformed.' See? Everything's on the up-and-up." He grimaced at the guest center. "Perhaps it's true in some cases, but that doesn't mean the syndicates don't bend the prison system to their advantage."

"But then"—she glanced over at the red building—"why would Gordian work with such a company?"

"Because they don't know any better," Isaac grumbled. "Like I said, the syndicates are, on the surface, legitimate businesses, so why not deal with them? Typical Earth-centric mistake if you ask me, made by someone ignorant of the inner workings here in the Saturn State."

"I see." Susan nodded thoughtfully. "I'll keep that in mind."

Isaac led the way inside and stopped in front of two security synthoids standing guard in front of a counter-grav tube. More virtual coins dangled on red cords from the ceiling, and abstract portraits of the company's upper management adorned the walls. The synthoid pair wore shiny black prog-steel armor emblazoned with golden dragons and carried heavy rifles with nonlethal underslung attachments.

"Detective Isaac Cho and company." He transmitted their credentials. "We're here to speak with Melody Quang."

"One moment while I check with her." One of the synthoids opened a comm window obscured by a privacy filter and spoke silently with the other side.

Isaac couldn't see his face behind the reflective visor. He waited for the conversation to finish.

"Junior Manager Quang will see you now." The synthoid snapped the comm window shut and shifted to the side. "Please step into the tube; it'll take you to her."

"Thank you." Isaac walked in, and the tube zipped him down into the bowels of the facility. Unlike Negation Industries, the tube walls were opaque, and no infostructure tickled his senses.

The shaft deposited them in a simple conference room with a long, red-lacquer table and more pictures of Trinh management on the walls. A young woman rose from the head of the table, clothed in a form-fitting red dress with gold dragons dancing across her thin scarf. She wore her black hair in a short bob, and her dark eyes shared the same warmth as her smile.

"Detective Cho, I'm Melody Quang." She shook his hand. "I'm sorry we had to meet under these circumstances. You have my condolences on behalf of the Trinh Syndicate."

"It's not really my place to accept that, since I didn't know the victims, but I appreciate the sentiment."

"Please, have a seat. I imagine you have a lot of questions for me."

"That I do." Isaac settled into a chair at the corner next to Quang. Susan took the next seat, and the LENS hovered behind them. "I'd like to go over your business dealings first. I understand the Trinh Syndicate is handling one of the impeller orders."

"That's right. We're on contract to deliver one of the Gordian Division's new impellers, which we're all very excited about. We're about eighty percent done with it."

"The Negation Industries impellers were due to be tested during this visit. Weren't yours as well?"

"Yes, per the original schedule, but we experienced some delays in the production. Nothing major, and nothing that would invoke a penalty clause, but the impeller won't be test-ready for another four to five weeks."

"Does the Trinh Syndicate have a lot of experience producing time drive components?"

"No, this is our first order, so some delays are to be expected as we work the kinks out of our production process. We've printed a lot of exotic matter products out of this facility, but the impeller has been the most exacting venture for us to date. We actually hired a few ex–Negation Industries engineers, lured them over to our side with lucrative Esteem contracts and signing bonuses. Some people don't appreciate the constant crunch next door, and we welcomed the added expertise. That team's been helping us gain ground on our original schedule, though we still have a long way to go."

"And the two Gordian agents were okay with the delay?"

"More or less," Quang said with an indifferent wave. "Like any customer, they prefer to have everything perfect and delivered yesterday, but they listened and were understanding of the difficulties we've faced. In the current climate, their options are limited, so both sides had strong motives to work through the difficulties in order to deliver a finished product we could all be happy with."

"I understand the Trinh Syndicate purchased a Negation Industries impeller rejected by the Gordian Division. Were you involved?"

"Yes, every step of the way." Quang smiled proudly. "I'm the one who convinced our upper management to move in, and I handled the bidding for our side."

"And why did you decide to purchase the defective unit?"

"Unlike Negation, we regularly handle less demanding contracts. When we considered the cost of modifying the impeller's remains versus producing over a thousand negative tons from scratch, the benefits became clear. I presented the cost analysis to our management, they approved my proposal, and here we are."

"Is the rejected unit held at this facility?"

"No, and calling it a 'unit' is a stretch. Negation broke the impeller down into over fifty chunks before handing the material to us; they were legally required to render it chronometrically inert. Afterward, we transported those chunks to a new production facility we're setting up on Titan, along the southern coast of the Kraken Mare."

"And what does this new facility do?"

"It's our newest site for exotic printers. Beyond that, I can't say."

Isaac looked up from his notes.

"That isn't my project." She flashed a coy smile. "Management keeps me focused on our New Frontier presence, but the rumors coming from Titan are quite exciting. We know we're small-timers when it comes to the exotic industry, but this new facility could help elevate us into the big leagues."

"Big enough to challenge the Mitchell Group or Negation Industries?"

"Maybe not *that* big." She chuckled. "Not yet, at least. But large enough to wrestle with mid-tier competitors like Counter-GravCorp, certainly. Hydrogen serves as the preferred basis for exotic conversion, and methane is four parts hydrogen to one part carbon. The methane lakes on Titan need to be dealt with eventually for the moon to be made habitable, and by establishing a factory on Titan, Trinh will produce exotic matter in a shallower gravity well than Saturn while also receiving a terraforming contribution subsidy."

"Interesting." Isaac jotted down a few notes. "What was your working relationship with the two agents?"

"Andover-Chen was a bit of an oddity. Sharp as they come, but hard to get to know. I'd characterize my relationship with him as strictly business."

"And Delacroix?"

"Joachim was . . . sad." She frowned and lowered her head. "He hid his pain well, but I could see it. His wife's death hit him hard. Tore away one of the focal points of his life, and so he sought refuge by clinging to another focus."

"What do you mean?"

"His work. He spent long hours at our facility. At Negation Industries, too, I imagine. I mentioned it to him a few times. Suggested he rest or spend some leisure time on Shelf Six. He politely declined. There always seemed to be another analysis to review, another report to write. Maybe it helped him cope." She glanced at the wall and sighed. "It makes me sad, thinking about him."

"Why's that?"

"Because, unlike the doctor, he won't be coming back. And because he was making progress. At least, I think he was. He'd fought through the grief of loss, and he seemed ready to begin piecing his life back together."

"Did you have any problems with the two men?"

"Oh, no. Both were great to work with. Demanding, but fair."

"I'd like to see their work area after we're done here."

"Of course." She pointed behind him. "It's right next door. I'll take you there whenever you're ready."

"But before that, I have another topic I'd like to cover with you." Isaac looked her square in the eyes. "Concerning some of your past actions."

"Oh boy." She grinned at him. "Here it comes."

"I'm sure you expected this."

"Yeah, I did. What do you want to know? Besides the fact that I was a typical idiot teenager?"

"I'd like you to tell me about your juvie criminal record."

"You have my file." She smirked at him. "You probably know more about the ins and outs of those crimes than *I* do."

"True, but I'd like to hear it in your own words."

"Honestly, I haven't given those years much thought in a while, so my recollection might be fuzzy." She raised an eyebrow. "You're not trying to get me to lie to a police officer, are you?"

"I'm sure we can chalk up any minor errors to poor recollection."

"Fair enough." She drummed her fingers on the table. "Let's see. I joined the Skulls at the age of fifteen. Participated in a bunch of petty crimes for about five years. Vandalism, surveillance sabotage, pattern copying and trafficking, etcetera. Eventually, I ended up in the juvie panopticosm. I served my time, straightened out my ways, and landed an entry-level position at Trinh. I then worked my way up the ranks from there."

"And the incident that landed you in jail until you were twenty-six?"

"You mean that time I firebombed a police copter?"

"That would be the one."

"That was *hardly* a crime." She laughed it off. "The auto-suppressors put out the fire almost instantly."

"That may be so, but your criminal act served as a distraction for a bank heist."

"Which I had no knowledge of. All I was told was the gang needed me to make some noise at a particular place and time, so I did." She shrugged her shoulders. "Young idiot that I was. I paid the price for my stupidity and moved on. Anything else?"

"Just one final question. Are you aware of any motive someone might have for killing either the doctor or the chief engineer?"

"No, sorry."

Isaac raised an eyebrow. "That was quick."

"I figured you'd ask that one, too." She sighed. "I thought back to the conversations I've had with them, but nothing stands out.

They've accommodated our schedule delays without any penalties, and as the project manager, you cherish clients like that. So, no. Can't think of any reason they might have been killed."

"Very well. That'll be all for now, I believe."

"Then let me show you to their desks."

The syndicate's Gordian Division office overlooked a single exotic printer, smaller than the ones at Negation Industries and more baroque due to a number of modifications jutting out of the main body. The machinery hummed with activity, building up layers of exotic matter around the spiked mechanism within.

"She didn't seem so bad," Susan said, again using security chat while they were undoubtedly being listened to.

"No," he breathed, almost whispered as he gazed down at the machinery below through the outward-slanted window.

"You don't sound convinced."

"Just wary of syndicates in general, that's all." He sighed and turned his back to the window. "Anything?"

"I found more of this stuff." She held up a clump of prog-foam picked off Delacroix's chair.

"At least he's consistent." He gave her a half smile. "Cephalie, how about you?"

"More of the same. Both these gents stayed *very* busy with their work. No signs of infosystem tampering either, just in case you were wondering."

"Thanks. I was."

"Doesn't mean the syndicate didn't. Just that they'd need some skilled people to pull the wool over my eyes."

"And they have access to that sort of talent," Isaac noted, "if they were so inclined."

He walked over to Delacroix's desk and gazed at the pictures of his wife aligned against the partition separating his desk from Andover-Chen's. He drew one to his hand and took in the frozen moment of a happy couple drinking the same strawberry milkshake through two straws.

"What a sad way to go," Susan said, looking at the pictures over his shoulder. "Guy loses his wife, starts pulling it together, then is killed."

"Yeah." He let go of the picture, and it flew back into place. He took one last look around the place and planted his hands on his hips. "Either of you see any reason we should stick around here?"

"Not at the moment," Susan said.

"Me neither," Cephalie said.

"All right. Let's head up."

He called Melody Quang back into the room, thanked her for her cooperation, and took the nearest counter-grav tube back to the surface. One of the security synthoids even gave him a friendly wave on the way out. They'd almost reached their car when Cephalie bolted upright atop the LENS.

"Oh!"

"Don't tell me we forgot something," Isaac growled with one leg in the car.

"No. Nothing like that. Check your mail."

He sat down and opened his inbox.

"Ah!" He beamed at the new message header.

"Good news?" Susan asked, sitting down opposite him.

"We'll see. It's the preliminary forensic report from the LifeBeam tower." He copied the file over to her and opened his original.

Susan tapped the door's interface, and the cabin door contracted shut.

"Vehicle, take us to the New Frontier Police Precinct," Isaac ordered, not looking up from the report.

"Destination set. Departing." The car pulled out of the syndicate parking lot and headed for the nearest up-ramp.

"Looks like the forensics team found unexplained code fragments in the transceiver's fault state," Isaac summarized. "The mystery fragments were flagged for deletion but not yet deleted."

"Could be a virus cleaning up after itself but not yet finished when the system faulted," Cephalie suggested. "That's my read on it, anyway. On their own, these fragments don't tell much of a story."

"But the forensics team concludes they're *not* from a Life-Beam program," Isaac said. "Or, at least, not one written to their exacting standards. Says here they ran a comparison between the fragments and LifeBeam's internal coding standards, which the company provided to them for reference."

"That lack of correlation strongly implies these fragments were from a virus," Cephalie noted.

"It does indeed." Isaac looked up at the other two. "I think we can now confidently say this was a homicide and not an accident, and that an attack virus was the murder weapon."

"The question remains who released the virus and why," Susan said. "We haven't stumbled across anything resembling a motive, and the forensics team doesn't know where the virus came from."

"Not yet," Isaac corrected. "This report is just an update. They make it clear they plan to widen their search to the tower's main infostructure in an attempt to identify the infection vector."

"I'm a little doubtful they'll be able to locate the vector, though," Cephalie cautioned. "From what they've found, this was a *very* sophisticated virus. Look at what it did in the transceivers; it *almost* cleaned itself out when the fault state was recorded. I think we got lucky the forensics team found anything at all."

"Then we may never find out how the virus infected the tower?" Susan asked.

"We'll just have to wait and see," Isaac replied. "Maybe their final report will flag a vector. Maybe it won't."

"And in the meantime?" Susan asked.

"In the meantime"—he smiled at her—"I think we're due for our little chat with Skylark."

CHAPTER ELEVEN

"SO, HE'S A NUMBER," SUSAN SAID, STANDING OUTSIDE ONE OF the NFPD's interrogation rooms. The precinct building was a tall cylinder on Shelf One, situated close enough to the shelf edge for the city's artificial sun to gleam off its metallic walls, and the interrogation rooms were located on the bottom floor.

"That's right."

Isaac glanced into the room; the door was an opaque steel gray, but cameras provided a one-way "window" inside for his virtual vision. Nathan Skylark alternated between slouching in his chair and fidgeting with his abstraction goggles. Isaac saw what he surmised to be a recent growth spurt in the teenager's sunken cheeks, long neck, bony shoulders, and scrawny arms. He looked like a stretched, elongated piece of putty, his silhouette not yet filled in with the muscle and body mass of adulthood.

The kid lacked any wetware implants, which made those goggles his gateway into the surrounding infostructure, and the precinct's selective data isolation had rendered them useless. Citizens of the Saturn State became adults at the age of twenty-five, the age when brain growth halted for most people, and only adults could legally receive wetware. That didn't stop some gangsters from wet-wiring their still-developing brains, and Isaac was relieved to see Skylark was, at the very least, not *that* sort of problem. The pink scar tissue circling his eyes and along the bridge of his nose indicated he relied heavily on his goggles for day-to-day interactions.

"And the Numbers are a gang," Susan continued.

"Yep."

"One of the bigger gangs on Janus."

"And probably the largest Lunarian gang around here. They don't seem to have a strong presence in New Frontier, but they're a major problem higher up the Shark Fin."

"But this same gang is affiliated with a religion?"

"The Sect of the Divine Randomizer. It's a Lunarian faith."

"How does *that* work?"

"Which part? The sect or the gang's relation with it?"

"Both, I guess."

"Well, the sect preaches that there's divine intervention in every random event, be it quantum fluctuations spawning virtual particles or random numbers generated through software. *All* randomness isn't, according to their faith, and that's how their deity—the Divine Randomizer—enacts its will."

"And the Numbers?"

"They're a violent offshoot of the faith." Isaac grimaced. "You see, if you believe the divine can be witnessed in random events, what might you want to see less of?"

"Umm...preplanning?" Susan tried, not sounding sure of herself.

"Order in general. The more chaotic our society is, the closer we all come to the divine, or so their deacons claim. Hence, societal constructs—like *laws* and *police*—are impairments to the free exercise of their faith."

"And they really believe that?" Susan asked incredulously.

"I'm sure there are some true believers—the higher-ranked deacons, for example—but it's my opinion that most of the rank and file join because they're looking for an excuse to do whatever their hearts desire without having to feel guilty about their crimes."

"How does the sect feel about all this?"

"Officially, the Divine Randomizer Sect and the Numbers are unrelated."

"The sect's full of holier-than-thou jerks, if you ask me." Cephalie's avatar blinked into existence atop the LENS. "If they really cared about the gang problem, they'd denounce the Numbers loudly and proudly."

"But they don't," Isaac said. "And likely never will."

"Why do you think that is?" Susan asked.

"Because, in their heart of hearts, those jerks agree with what the Numbers are doing!" Cephalie snapped.

"I feel like there's some unspoken history here," Susan ventured.

"Oh, you'd better believe it! 'Vow of silence' my digital ass!"

"Cephalie had a few run-ins with the sect before we met, and one involved a deacon concealing evidence from her." Isaac cleared his throat. "And on that note, let's see what Skylark has to say for himself."

He used the keycode the desk sergeant provided him, and he and Susan sat down at the table opposite Skylark. The LENS floated in after them, and the kid's eyes darted to the drone.

"State your name for the record," Isaac began, opening a private interface.

"I'm not saying a word while you have that fucking thing here!" Skylark pointed at the LENS. "You're threatening me, and I don't have to take this! I have rights!"

"As a Themis Detective, I'm fully within my authority to have my LENS nearby in case a prisoner turns violent," Isaac stated in an even tone. "Furthermore, you're required to identify yourself when asked by a police officer." His tone grew more forceful. "State. Your. Name."

Skylark crossed his arms and slouched deeper into his seat.

"How's the data isolation treating you?" Isaac asked.

"It sucks!" He tossed his goggles onto the table. "Why the fuck won't you let me connect?"

"I ask because I'm a hair away from walking right out that door and letting you cool off overnight in your cell."

Skylark tried to put on a tough face, but a worried frown leaked through, and he gazed longingly at his goggles.

"Therefore, this is the last time I'll say it." Isaac leaned forward. "State your name for the record."

Skylark bit into his lower lip, eyes locked on his goggles, but then he rediscovered his courage and puffed up.

"Like any of this matters." He shook out his shoulders, trying to act big. "You want my name that badly, you can fucking have it. I'm Horizon-Four." He wagged his eyebrows at Susan. "You know, four is a *very* sacred number." He pressed a splayed hand to his chest. "It's a sign of good fortune and ... virility. Care for a taste?"

"That's your gang alias," Isaac said. "State your *legal* name."

"Why the fuck you care? You already know what it is."

"Do you want to spend the night here or not?"

"Fine! For fuck sake!" He threw up his arms. "It's Nathan Skylark! There! Are you happy now?"

"And, Nathan, have the state troopers informed you of your rights?"

"Yes! Are we done yet?"

"And do you fully understand those rights?"

"Like I care what you cops say. Boring! Can I go now?"

Good enough for the record, Isaac thought and ticked a box on his window. Skylark's file indicated the SSP had already run through the correct procedures—along with a note about his uncooperative attitude—but it didn't hurt to verify, especially when working in an unfamiliar precinct for the first time. What would Raviv say if he botched the case because of inadmissible evidence?

"You talk at all?" Skylark asked Susan, then bobbed his head toward Isaac. "Or does he just keep you around as scenery?"

She didn't dignify the question with a response.

"Nathan," Isaac began, exasperation edging into his voice, "the sooner I have what I want, the sooner you can be on your way. Assuming you've done nothing wrong, that is."

"Really nice scenery." He looked down at Susan's chest and smirked. "Let me guess. He's the brains of this little duo and you're the boobs, am I right?"

Isaac glanced over at Susan to find her normal stoicism intact. If the obnoxious kid's taunts bothered her, she didn't show it.

He cleared his throat.

"Let's start with some basic questions. Why were you at Oasis Apartments earlier today?"

"You know why. I was shooting hoops."

"Do you live there?"

"No."

"Do you have friends or family who live there?"

"No."

"Was anyone else with you?"

"No."

"So, let me see if I have this straight, Nathan. You went over to Oasis, alone, solely because you wanted to play some basketball."

"Yeah."

"All by yourself."

"Sure. Why not?"

"Where do you live?"

"Redstone Estates. Block Three." He smiled at Susan. "That's a gated community, if you didn't know. *Very* upscale."

Isaac confirmed the information against Skylark's record and ran a quick search. "That's up on Shelf Seven," he noted.

"Yeah. So what?"

"You're telling me you went all the way down to Shelf One, alone, because you wanted to play basketball."

"Sure."

"Does this gated community you live in have recreational facilities?"

"Well, yeah."

"And do those facilities include a basketball court?"

"Dunno."

"You don't know," Isaac echoed meaningfully. "You live in an upper-class gated community and you're so clueless about its amenities you traveled to the bottom shelf of this city to an apartment complex where none of your friends or family live, all to play some basketball alone."

"What's so strange about that?"

"Then, if all you said is true, why did you run when I looked at you?"

He turned away and crossed his arms.

"Why did you run?"

"Hey, cutie, I'm dying to know." He gave Susan a lewd smirk. "Is that body real or metal on the inside?"

"Why did you run, Nathan?"

"Come on, no one likes a quiet bitch." He grabbed his crotch. "Betcha I can make you squeal."

Isaac shot a quick sideways glance over to Susan, concerned Skylark might be getting under her skin. *He* certainly felt the urge to reach across the table and thump some sense into the kid, though he'd never do such a thing. He could only imagine how Susan, as the target of these disgusting remarks, felt at the moment. She'd handled herself well so far, but the difference between them—the very *important* difference that Skylark seemed unaware of—was their training.

Isaac knew how to question uncooperative prisoners within the confines of the law.

Susan knew how to use a flamethrower.

An incident involving her losing her temper and painting the walls with the kid's blood might prove ... problematic on so many levels. The more he thought about it, the more worried he became, but then she turned her head his way ever so slightly and raised a subtle, questioning eyebrow. She seemed unperturbed by the juvenile remarks, at least on the surface.

Good, he thought with mild relief. *Good. Perhaps I'm worrying about nothing. She's a professional, after all. A professional in a different field, but that still counts for something. She's dealt with worse scum than this dumb kid.*

By ... blowing them up.

Hmm.

Darn. Now I'm worried again.

Susan saw the concern on his face, and her brow creased in an unspoken question.

Isaac shook his head and turned back to Skylark, more determined than ever to get this interrogation back on track.

"Nathan, I don't think you appreciate the gravity of your situation."

"You don't scare me," he spat. "You've got nothing on me, cop!"

"On the contrary, I have plenty of justification to press charges. When I arrived at room 516, I found evidence of a crime. That alone gives me added authority to issue orders to civilians in the area, yourself included, and the order I gave you was to stop running. But you ran. I could charge you with 'disobeying a lawful order,' but I think I can do better than that."

"So, some guy had his apartment ransacked. So what?" Skylark sneered. "*I* had nothing to do with it. You can't pin this on me."

"Oh." Isaac sat back and regarded the gangster with cool eyes. "You don't know."

And there's the crack I needed, he thought. *Time to wedge his defenses open.*

"Don't know what?" Skylark asked.

"This case isn't about burglary."

"But..." The kid gulped down a breath.

"The apartment belonged to Joachim Delacroix."

"Never heard of him."

"Chief Engineer Delacroix of the Gordian Division. And recently deceased."

"It belonged to a dead cop?" he squeaked, all the bravado draining from his face.

"Correct."

Skylark leaned back and put a hand to his mouth. His eyes darted around erratically, and he bit into the back of one finger.

"Let me lay it out for you. A SysPol officer has been murdered. Someone broke into his apartment. *You* were outside watching the place, and when a cop arrived, you *ran*! Now how do you think that looks to us? Huh, Nathan? How bad does it look for you?"

"I didn't have anything to do with it!"

"With what, Nathan?"

"I . . ." He looked away and chewed on the side of his long finger.

"You think a few hours in here is bad?" Isaac asked. "You're in *way* deeper than you know. You can look forward to spending the rest of your youth in a panopticosm. And this"—he held up the kid's goggles—"won't work in there. No games. No shows. No nothing. Just you, the other inmates, and a *lot* of counseling."

"But I didn't do anything!" He sniveled, tears dripping out of his eyes.

"Then why were you there?"

"I was only supposed to watch the place!" he blubbered. "I swear! That's it! The Numbers didn't even do this job! I can't fucking go to jail! I can't!"

"Then who did the job?"

"The Fanged Wyverns! Shelf One is our turf, but they stripped that guy's apartment, so the deacon asked me to watch over the place in case they tried hitting another. If they did, I was to call in backup so we could scare them off. That's all, I swear!"

"Then the Numbers weren't involved in the theft."

"Fuck no!"

"And the Fanged Wyverns robbed the apartment."

"Yes!"

"Did the Fanged Wyverns murder Delacroix?"

"How the fuck should I know?"

"And you claim you weren't involved in either the burglary or the murder."

"No! A million times no!"

"Then why did you run?"

"You scared me!"

"Why?" Isaac pressed. "You claim you committed no crime. Why did the presence of a police officer scare you?"

"I . . . I . . ."

"Why did you run?"

"I . . ." Tears traced down his cheeks.

"Why did you run?"

"I want my lawyer," he sniveled.

"Why did you run, Nathan?" Isaac snapped, rising from his seat.

"I want my lawyer!" he shouted back.

Isaac paused for a long, deliberate moment, then sat back down in his chair. Skylark started sobbing uncontrollably, all his earlier puffed-up arrogance gone. He wiped under his running nose with a baggy sleeve.

"That's within your rights." Isaac gestured to the LENS. "Cephalie, open a hole in the firewall for his goggles, but lock it down if he tries anything."

"Done," Cephalie said through the LENS's onboard speaker so Skylark could hear.

Isaac pushed the goggles forward with a finger.

"Go ahead."

The kid blew his nose into his sleeve, then picked up the goggles with trembling hands and fitted them over his eyes. He gestured his way through unseen menus.

"He's putting in a legit call," Cephalie said. "And . . . the Skylark family lawyer just transmitted into the precinct. He'd like a word with you."

"I'll bet." Isaac rose from his seat and left the interrogation room.

✧　　✧　　✧

Susan followed Isaac and the LENS out of the room, impressed with how her partner had reduced the gangster to a spineless puddle.

Slimy little brat deserved it, she thought, and she smiled inwardly at how Isaac had shattered the punk's fake bravado. *She'd* wanted to reach across the table and thump some sense into him, but Isaac had remained cool and in control the whole time.

They stepped into an empty interrogation room, and the abstract lawyer appeared before them. He wore an antiquated three-piece suit, black with a long gray tie, and a pair of rectangular wireframes over his dispassionate eyes. In fact, the AC's avatar seemed to be composed wholly of rectangular shapes, from his rigid posture and squared shoulders to his long face and buzzed haircut. He made a show of adjusting his tie, then set his virtual briefcase on the table.

"And you are?" Isaac asked.

"Mister Wall," the abstract lawyer said in a dour tone, "of Wall, Block & Pachelo. I'm on retainer to the Skylark family, and I've come concerning young Nathan Skylark's detention. I've just finished reviewing his file with the NFPD, and I must say, I'm already disturbed by what I've found. I'll need to speak with him in private after this, but I can clearly see his arrest was unwarranted. In fact, I'd go so far as to say it represents an overreach of SysPol's authority and provides the family with grounds for a lawsuit, should they choose to pursue one."

"You really want to go there?"

"Want has nothing to do with this, Detective Cho. The facts are what they are. Nathan Skylark hasn't committed any crimes, and you have no basis for either his arrest or his detention."

"Then you need to check your facts," Isaac challenged. "I caught Nathan fleeing the scene of a crime, and when ordered to stop he continued running. That grants me probable cause to make an arrest."

"I'm sure that was a simple misunderstanding on his part. Did you properly identify yourself as a police officer?"

"I was in uniform and I pinged him with my badge."

"Then perhaps he felt unduly threatened."

"Regardless of how he *felt*, it's his civic duty to follow lawful commands by the police."

"Indeed. *Lawful* commands," Mister Wall stressed. "But does you shouting at him fall within that category?"

"You can twist what happened into a pretzel for all I care," Isaac said. "A forensic specialist is looking over the apartment as we speak, and you better hope there isn't the slightest sniff of him inside. Until I see the results, Skylark isn't going anywhere."

"You haven't charged him with a crime. And you can't retain him for longer than twenty-four hours."

"Then I have that long to make a decision."

"And in response, I'll ensure the remainder of that time is as fruitless as possible. Young Nathan will be exercising his right to remain silent from here on out."

"Have it your way." Isaac crossed his arms. "Let's assume for the moment he was just in the wrong place at the wrong time."

"No assumptions necessary, I assure you."

"Oh, but I *insist*. Not only did we catch him fleeing a crime scene, but he's demonstrated a complete lack of respect to authority figures during his detention. *And* his criminal record shows he has questionable taste in friends."

"Those are problems for his parents and are, to be frank, none of your business."

"You and I don't seem to be seeing eye to eye on where my business ends."

"I can assure you that, in this case, I draw the line exactly where it belongs."

"We'll just have to agree to disagree. But I'm not unreasonable." Isaac turned to the LENS. "Cephalie, prep a release form for Nathan. If the forensics come back without any surprises, we'll let him go early." He turned back to Mister Wall. "Happy?"

"I'll be waiting with bated breath."

"You do that."

The lawyer dipped his head and vanished.

✧   ✧   ✧

"Do you think the Fanged Wyverns broke into Delacroix's apartment?" Susan asked.

"I believe Nathan thinks so," Isaac said. "Nina's forensics report will clear it up, one way or the other. But our guest looks to be little more than a local nuisance. A spoiled rich kid playing at gangster life. All he has is vandalism on his record, so he's the loser they stuck with staking out the apartments."

"He's also wrong about his name," Cephalie said. "To the Numbers, four is considered unlucky because of its phonetic connection to the word for death in Old Chinese."

"Good catch," Isaac said. "His ignorance reinforces my impression he's a nobody."

"He did seem..." Susan searched for the right description. "Like a scrawny little peacock. *Without* much plumage."

"Yeah." Isaac coughed out a laugh. "I was wondering why a gang member would hang out *after* the apartment had been robbed. Nathan's story fits the facts, regardless of how much of a pain it was squeezing it out of him. If the report shows any Numbers were involved, we'll charge him formally. Otherwise, I don't see the point. SSP can deal with him however they like."

"Know much about the Fanged Wyverns?" Susan asked.

"Not at the moment." Isaac opened a virtual window and searched the precinct's database. "Jovian ethnic gang. One I haven't dealt with before. Looks like they're an occasional problem in New Frontier but have a larger presence across the lowest reaches of the Epimethean Expanse. Makes sense."

"Why's that?"

"Large Jovian populations in these parts of the Shark Fin. Quite a few cities around here were founded by Jovian companies looking to branch out into the Saturn State, so like New Frontier, they attracted an immigrant populace." He closed the window. "I get the impression they're a rowdy, if small, gang in this city."

"Why wouldn't the Numbers use a drone or other remote device to keep an eye on the apartment?" Susan asked.

"Because of drone licensing," Cephalie explained. "Only certain types of drones are allowed in certain areas, and you need to be licensed to pilot one. That licensing can be very expensive and time-consuming to acquire."

"Would a gang care, though?"

"They would because drone violations bring SysPol down on their heads," Isaac pointed out. "Those are *federal* crimes, and we don't take kindly to remote-piloted crime. State troopers might have trouble tracking down unlicensed drones, but our forensics teams don't mess around. That's not to say some don't try, but why risk it when you have people like Nathan to boss around?"

"Huh, interesting." She wondered if she should mention Sys-Gov's attitude about drones back home at the DTI. She'd assumed most aspects of SysGov law were laxer than in the Admin, but here the opposite was true. How many crimes could be prevented by tighter restrictions on drones back home?

Then she remembered something else she wanted to ask him.

"Isaac?"

"Yeah?"

"Back in the interrogation room, I noticed you kept looking in my direction."

"Oh." Isaac appeared a little embarrassed for some reason. "That."

"Were you expecting me to help out in some way? I only ask because I want to be sure I'm supporting you to the degree you expect."

"It's nothing. I thought you might rough him up, is all."

"Oh." She considered his comment, then said, "Was I supposed to?"

"What?!" Isaac's eyes grew wide with shock and indignation, and she regretted her words immediately. "No!" he snapped. "No, you should *not* have used your advanced synthoid body to physically assault the defenseless seventeen-year-old kid in our custody!"

"I only meant..." she began, but her foot was firmly planted in her mouth, and she grimaced as the verbal drubbing continued.

"How can you even suggest something like that? I can't believe I'm hearing this! Haven't you been paying attention? Didn't we go over this on the saucer? Why do you insist on acting like this? You really need to get your..."

Susan winced as he laid into her, and she knew she only had herself to blame. But then she realized he was watching something past her. The indignation in his eyes flickered out, replaced with regret, and his mouth gaped open in what might have been in horror. He forced himself to look her in the eyes.

"Susan, I'm so sorry," he said, every word overflowing with genuine apology.

"Uhh?"

"There I go again making bad assumptions." He shook his head, scolding himself. "I should have known you weren't being serious, and I hope you'll forgive my hasty words."

"What?"

A tiny voice cleared her throat.

Susan looked behind her back to find Cephalie standing atop the LENS, a big sign held overhead in her hands.

The sign read: THAT WAS A JOKE, YOU DUMMY!

"Umm." She faced Isaac again. He appeared unsure if he'd smoothed things over adequately.

"It's a bad habit of mine," he confessed. "Sometimes I get so wrapped up in my work I take everything too literally." He gestured to the LENS. "Cephalie, back me up on this."

"Yeah, it's true." She folded the sign and stuffed it in her purse. "He can be *really* dense at times."

"That's not the first time she's used her signs, believe me."

He chuckled, then shook his head again. "And your joke was rather funny."

"My joke?" Susan asked, a moment before what felt like a tiny cane jabbed her in the butt. "Yes. My joke. I'm glad you liked it...eventually."

"But"—Isaac held up a finger—"all that said, I do need to pass on a word of caution."

"Yes?"

"I'm not sure how this works over in the DTI, but we, as Themis detectives, should do our part to uphold our division's public image. Jokes about beating up prisoners, as you can imagine, reflect poorly on both Themis Division and SysPol as a whole. Especially if they're overheard by the wrong people."

"Of course. I understand. I'll keep such suggest—*jokes*," she corrected quickly. "I'll keep such jokes to myself in the future."

"That's for the best." He sighed. "Now, since I've managed to make a complete fool of myself, I need a breather. Maybe get some coffee. Be back in a few."

He stepped out of the interrogation room, leaving Susan alone with Cephalie.

The door sealed shut, and the two looked at each other expectantly.

"That wasn't a joke," Cephalie said as a statement, not a question.

Susan frowned. She wasn't sure how she felt about an AI saving her from yet another social gaffe; she didn't have strong feelings about unregulated AIs, but they were *still* outlawed in the Admin, and she'd torched a rogue infosystem or two in her time with the DTI.

"Why did you do that?"

"Eh?" Cephalie shrugged. "Why not?"

"That's not much of an answer."

"I suppose it isn't." Cephalie leaped to her shoulder and sat down there. Her virtual senses felt the imaginary weight. "But now I'm curious."

"About what?"

"Would you beat up that punk if Isaac ordered you to?"

"Well, not *now*." She rolled her eyes.

"But rewind a bit. Forget this last conversation. Would you have?"

"Maybe," she admitted, somewhat surprised by her own honesty to a bunch of ones and zeros. "I suppose I wouldn't have a problem trying to scare him into cooperating."

"Have you ever roughed up a prisoner?"

"Personally? No."

"Been part of a team that did?"

"Yes, but he was a *really* bad person."

"How bad is really bad?"

"Ever see a toddler's brain leak out of her eye sockets?"

"Eww!" Cephalie exclaimed. "Okay, that qualifies as bad."

"Our squad was up against the clock. We needed to find his second microtech bomb before it was too late."

"And so"—Cephalie spread her palms—"you extracted the information by any means necessary."

"Because it *was* necessary. Otherwise, the bad guys would have won."

"Isaac would disagree. Doing something like that *is* letting the bad guys win. At least in his mind."

"I know." She gazed down at the floor.

"Look, I'm not saying either of you is right or wrong. He's never faced a scenario like that, and you're new to this kind of work."

"*That* much is certain," Susan sighed. "I'm still not sure why I'm even here."

"But who knows?" Cephalie nudged her chin up. "A different, less rigid perspective might prove useful."

She turned to face the AC. "You think so?"

"Sure, I do!" The tiny avatar smiled at her. "I mean, what's the worst that could happen?"

CHAPTER TWELVE

"OH NO! NOT MORE OF THE DAMNED THINGS!"

Isaac's ears perked up at the familiar voice. He turned a corner near the station canteen, fresh steaming cup in his hands. Nina stood facing the wall, shoulders hunched and a hand against her brow.

"Nina?"

"Hey, Isaac," she groaned without looking up.

"Something wrong?"

"Thirteen more."

"More what?"

"Malfunctioning printers." She pressed her forearm against the wall and faced him. "Another thirteen were added to my work queue while I was on your case, all in and around New Frontier. It'll take me *days* to clear through all of them. I swear, this Apple Cypher business is like a hydra."

"But that's just your job. Why sound so depressed?"

"Because now I'm stuck in this smelly armpit of a city!"

"Aren't you being a little overdramatic?"

"You saw Shelf One!"

"It's not *that* bad."

"Says the person who thinks the Howling Bow is a nice place to live," she mocked.

"Because it is," Isaac defended. "It's homey."

"Whatever." She put her back to the wall and crossed her arms. "You have any luck with your case?"

"Mixed. I was hoping your report might shed some light there."

"Check your mail. It's all there, and I think you'll be happy with what I found. Got an ID on one of the thieves."

"Wonderful!" He beamed at her. "I'll share the good news with Susan and Cephalie. Later."

"Take care."

He returned to the interrogation room to find Susan sitting on the edge of the table, chatting with Cephalie.

"We have a forensics report," he started. "Nina's finished with the apartment." He set his mug down, opened the mail, and sent Susan a copy. As he expected from his twin sister, the report was well organized, with information categorized under separate tabs. He started with the FORCED ENTRY tab and expanded it. "The thieves used a Trades'n'Crafts 'Cut-All' Pattern D vibro-knife to saw through the lock. That doesn't tell us much."

"Why not?" Susan asked, opening her copy.

"That specific pattern is public domain," Cephalie explained. "Anyone can print it. No permit required. Trades'n'Crafts places some of their low-end patterns into public domain for promotional reasons."

"Which is why gangs use it as a weapon," Isaac added, scrolling down. "Ah, but this is more interesting. The thieves tried using the keycode first. Nina pulled the door infosystem records, and it shows they entered the same code five times with no luck."

"Sounds like they expected it to work," Susan noted.

"Yes." Isaac traced through the report with a finger. "And the keycode they used was the room's *old* code. But Delacroix put in a request to have it changed near the end of his last visit three weeks ago. It's worth noting that that's the *only* change request on record, so it doesn't appear we're dealing with a habit of his, such as changing keycodes at regular intervals."

"Maybe he expected trouble?" Susan said.

"Maybe," Isaac agreed, nodding. "I'm wondering how the thieves obtained his original keycode in the first place, though. But this explains why they cut through the lock. They didn't *expect* any problems breaking in, and when their code didn't work, they improvised."

"Real clumsily, too," Cephalie added. "That must have created

a ton of noise. I'm surprised NFPD didn't receive a civil distur-
bance call."

Isaac clicked the next tab, and his eyes twinkled.

"Way to go, Nina!" he said with a broad smile. "Positive ID
on one of the thieves. Derrick 'Hatchet Man' Fuller. Age twenty-
three, known Fanged Wyverns member since 2972." He expanded
the criminal's record. "Assault, robbery, intimidation, and the like.
He's already done two years in a juvie panopticosm."

"Sounds like a real piece of work."

"What's more, Nina found traces of three accomplices," Isaac
continued. "She doesn't have positive IDs on them, though. They
might not have criminal records yet, which is not uncommon as
the gangs drop and pick up members."

"What's this tab do?" Susan asked as she clicked her interface.

The interrogation room vanished, and an abstraction of Delacroix's apartment sprang up around them. Numbered icons dotted the
virtual space, ready to expand with detailed information if selected.

"Whoops," Susan uttered.

"No, no. It's fine," Isaac assured her. "I wanted to see this next
anyway. Beats having to drive out there again." He clicked on
one of the floating icons, and translucent outlines appeared on
and underneath Delacroix's desk. "Timeline estimate places the
theft half an hour after the murders. Items stolen include three
TurboCruncher 'Azimuth-G' infosystem towers, a TurboCruncher
'Eclipse-XX' wrist attendant, two Gordian Division uniforms, a
smattering of synthoid care products, a few articles of civilian
clothing, a physical portrait of Delacroix's wife, and two bottles
of Old Frontier redcap whiskey."

Susan chuckled. "That's an odd list."

"The infosystems are what matters. I get the impression these
goons were told to strip the place, top to bottom, without a lot
of detailed instruction." Isaac sighed. "Moving on, we now have
a clear course of action."

"Bring in Fuller?"

"Not quite." He flashed a half smile. "Cephalie, is the precinct
captain in?"

"He is, and he's at his desk right now."

"Splendid." Isaac closed the abstraction and opened the door.
"Let's go have a chat with him."

"You're going to cause trouble, aren't you?"

"What makes you say that?" he asked, feigning ignorance.

Isaac led the way to the precinct's central elevators, and they took one up to the tenth floor. Captain Sylvester Lasky sat at a cluttered desk, straight backed and broad chested, with a wide window behind him overlooking Shelf Zero. His synthoid skin was the same dark green of his uniform, making it difficult to tell where one ended and the other began. Perhaps that was the intended effect—a man who *was* his uniform.

He looked up as Isaac and the others stepped into his office.

"Can I help you, Detective?" Those were the captain's exact words, stiff and formal, though his tone made it sound like he'd actually said, *I don't want a Themis troublemaker in my precinct, but I'm obligated to work with you.*

"Captain, I need your assistance."

"I assigned Lieutenant MacFayden to support your case. Please work with her directly. I'm very busy."

"I'm aware of that. However, I suspect the assistance I require exceeds her authority."

Lasky made a noncommittal grunt in the back of his throat. He closed the virtual reports over his desk and leaned forward.

"What, exactly, is it you need from me?"

"I have evidence at least four members of the Fanged Wyverns are involved in the case. I need them brought in for questioning."

"That doesn't sound so bad." Lasky relaxed a little. "Which ones? There are a lot of Fanged Wyverns in the city."

"All of them, preferably, until we find the ones we're looking for. I don't have positive IDs on all four."

Lasky glowered at him.

"I'm serious, Captain."

"I'm sure you are," Lasky fumed. "Everything must look so binary up on Kronos. The world is either black or white, but down this deep in the Shark Fin, there are many shades of gray. Do you realize what you're asking of me?"

"I believe so."

"Then let me highlight your ignorance. Right now, the New Frontier gangs are relatively calm. We haven't had any major turf wars in months, and violent crime is trending down across the board. The gangs aren't interested in picking fights with us, and we, frankly, don't have the resources to go after every little crime they commit. So we focus on the worst offenders. We make a few examples, and the rest hunker down and play it safe. Everyone wins. The citizens of this fair city experience less crime, my hardworking troopers get harassed by the gangs less, and yes, even the gangs win a little breathing room, a little discretionary enforcement. We've found a comfortable equilibrium.

"And you"—he pointed a large finger at Isaac—"are telling me to rile up the hornet's nest!"

"No, Captain," Isaac said, undeterred. "I'm not ordering you to do anything."

"Then why are you bothering me?"

"Captain, I fully acknowledge this is your precinct, and you're the expert in your city. And so, I'm *asking* for your assistance. I suggested a way to pursue my case's evidence trail, but I welcome your input when it comes to the gangs you regularly deal with."

"Then you don't plan to throw your weight around?"

"No, Captain. I don't, unless I find myself with no other recourse to solve my case. I understand we have different priorities, you with your city and me with this homicide, but they're not mutually exclusive."

Lasky wrinkled his brow. "You sure you're with Themis?"

"Last I checked, Captain."

The big man tapped his fingers on his desk. Then he grinned at Isaac.

"All right. I'll bite. Let's see if we can figure out an approach where you don't make a mess of my city. Got anything other than they're Wyverns?"

"Only one positive ID. Derrick Fuller."

"The Hatchet Man!" Lasky's eyes burned with barely contained fury.

"You know him?"

"Damn right I do. He knifed MacFayden in the leg a few years back and landed himself in prison for assault. The jury went *way* too easy on him, if you ask me. He's kept a low profile since being released."

"Then you're not inclined to 'rile' things up over him?"

"I'll make an exception for that floating turd, and I'm sure MacFayden wouldn't mind another crack at him. Also, we know the scum he floats around with, so we can perform a targeted grab." Lasky paused, then leaned back in his chair. "You want him when we're done?"

"Not unless I can directly tie him to the murders. I figured I'd leave his handling up to your discretion."

"Even better." Lasky keyed open a comm window. "MacFayden, get up here. We've got work to do."

"Right away, boss."

The New Frontier Police Department knew their city well. They knew where the gangs hung out, they maintained unofficial member lists, and they actively cross-referenced every entry with known associations, both lawful and otherwise. That meant when Lasky and MacFayden looked up Fuller, they immediately knew the best places to find him, which gang members he'd been spotted with recently, and where to find *them*.

SSP dispatchers put out calls to all available squad cars and quadcopters, and even more left the station garage. All totaled, they brought in eleven Fanged Wyverns for questioning: Derrick Fuller, four Wyverns unlucky enough to be found with him, and six more known associates the troopers pounced on at other locations. Patrols were out in force looking for another three, but the investigative gears of the precinct had already shuddered into action with those brought in.

Every interrogation room on the ground floor was filled as SSP sergeants questioned the gang members, and Isaac sat in a second-floor command-and-control room with Susan, Cephalie, and Lieutenant MacFayden, a woman who looked tough enough to chew through industrial prog-steel despite the gray at her temples. Images from each room orbited them, and he enlarged one and enabled the sound while nursing his latest cup of coffee.

Derrick Fuller sat across from a sergeant, looking unconcerned. He wore a black hoodie with a subtle scaly pattern and a large neon yellow jaw on the back. His abstraction visor sat on the table.

"We know you did the Oasis job," the sergeant said. "You're in a heap of trouble this time, Fuller."

The gangster didn't make eye contact with the cop. He stared at the wall with a bored expression and picked at an incisor with his thumb as if trying to dislodge a stuck piece of food.

"You have any idea who you stole from? A dead cop, that's who. And not just anyone. We're talking SysPol Gordian Division. You listening to me, Fuller?"

Isaac pulled out and muted the window. Fuller had been with the Fanged Wyverns for eight years and had already done time in jail for them without blabbing. They needed something more potent than additional prison time to loosen his lips, and Isaac didn't see any obvious leverage they could use.

However, the other gangsters might prove more... malleable, he thought as he reviewed their files.

Some of them didn't have criminal records yet, and Isaac suspected three of those had been brought along for their muscles, essentially acting as pack animals to haul away the goods while under Fuller's command. They might not be as interested in prison time as Fuller, and Fanged Wyverns were, on average, less wealthy than the Numbers. Chances were none of these gangsters enjoyed the equivalent of the Skylark family fortune to lean on; no high-priced lawyers coming to *their* rescue, he suspected.

He picked a window at random and listened in on a gangster named Long Lie, age sixteen, no criminal record. His neon yellow hoodie featured a large dragon-like silhouette on the back.

"Where were you from nine to eleven this morning?"

"Home. Playin' games."

"Not at school?"

"Nah."

"Why not?"

"Cuz."

"Which games were you playing?"

"Just one."

"Which one, then?"

"*RealmBuilder.*"

"What were you doing in the game?"

"Buildin' stuff."

"Anyone see you playing?"

"Yeah."

"Who?"

"My ma."

"Anyone else?"

"My sis."

"They see you the whole two hours?"

"One of 'em."

"Which one?"

"My ma."

"Will she tell us the same thing?"

"I guess."

"Well, we're going to call her right now and see if your story checks out. You'd better hope it does."

"Sure. Whatev."

Isaac picked another window, enlarged it and enabled the sound. The caption identified this young man as Yang Zhao, age nineteen, no criminal record. He wore all black except for stylized yellow bite marks on his arms and chest. His muscles strained against a hoodie on the edge of being too small for his bulk.

"What's this?" The cop pulled up Yang's left sleeve, revealing an expensive wearable infosystem. "What the hell is this?"

"What's it look like?" He jerked his arm back.

"You have a permit for that?"

"Sure do."

"Then let's see it, Yang. Show me. Right now. Prove to me you're not a troublemaker."

"It was a gift."

"Gift or not, where's your permit?"

"I don't have it *with* me."

"What kind of permit is it, then? Single use? Limited replication? Destruct and reuse? What kind of permit you got for your wearable?"

"I don't remember."

"The hell you don't!" snapped the cop. "Out in public without your pattern permits. I could charge you right now, if I wanted. Add that to the theft."

"You've got the wrong guy! I didn't steal anything!" Yang tried to sound confident, but his voice cracked.

Isaac zoomed in on the wrist-mounted infosystem and took a sip from his coffee. The camera IDed it as a TurboCruncher Eclipse-XX.

"And we have a winner," Isaac remarked with a mischievous smile.

"Could something like that be in the public domain?" Susan asked.

"Not one that nice," Isaac said. "Public domain patterns are for the poor. Anything else, you need to buy." He opened a private channel to the interrogating cop. "Thank you, Sergeant. Looks like you've got the suspect limbered up for me. I'll take it from here, if you don't mind."

"Not at all. My pleasure."

"What?" Yang asked, his voice cracking again. "What's going on? Who're you talking to?"

"He's all yours, Detective," the cop finished.

"A detective!" Yang blurted. "A *SysPol* detective's here?"

"That's right, Yang. And you're next on his shit list."

The sergeant stood up and departed without another word, leaving the gangster alone with his mounting anxiety.

Isaac sat down across from Yang Zhao with the slow, deliberate patience of a man ready to apply some much-needed pressure—*and* in full possession of the tools necessary to do so. He waited for Susan to take her own seat and for the LENS to float down onto the table. Then and only then did he activate his virtual interface and review it within a long, drawn-out silence.

Yang Zhao shifted in his seat, a deep, nervous frown on his face. His eyes slid from Isaac to Susan and back, and his discomfort grew.

"Let's start with your wrist attendant," Isaac said at last.

"What about it?"

"Where did you get it, really?"

"Like I said, it was a gift."

"Lying to a police officer is serious offense, punishable by up to one year in prison."

"I'm not lying."

"Who gave you the wearable?"

"It was...umm."

"When did you receive it?"

"I don't remember."

"You'd better start remembering." Isaac fixed him with a piercing gaze. "One last chance. Where did you get it?"

"Don't recall." He looked away.

"Enough of this." Isaac gestured the LENS forward. "Check the pattern serial."

The LENS floated over to Yang and extended a mercurial pseudopod to his wrist.

"You can't." Yang jerked his wrist back and stuffed it under his other armpit. "I know how this works. No warrant, no search."

"Which I would have no difficulty obtaining under these circumstances," Isaac informed him patiently. "But I don't even need that to search you under the probable cause statute. I have several good reasons to suspect you've committed a crime, and the statute provides me with limited authority to perform unwarranted searches. We know at least one Fanged Wyvern robbed an Oasis apartment this morning, and we know one of the items stolen matches the wrist attendant in your possession. Now, you can either stick out your wrist or I can have the LENS do it for you."

Yang paused longer than he should have, but with a resigned huff, he stuck out his arm.

"Collect a DNA sample, too," Isaac added.

"What for?" Yang asked.

"To see if you were in the apartment."

"I wasn't." He sat up straighter and raised his chin, some of his confidence returning.

"Then you have nothing to fear," Isaac stated evenly.

"Fine. Take it, then." Yang leaned forward, offering his left cheek. "It's not like I have a choice here."

"No. You don't."

Interesting. You think this is going to exonerate you, Isaac thought. *You might be in for a rude surprise.*

The LENS produced two pseudopods. One removed the wearable infosystem from his wrist and enveloped it in liquid metal, and the second caressed the gangster's cheek. A prog-steel capsule formed around the shed skin cells, which then traveled up the pseudopod back to the LENS's main body and its internal forensics module.

"The pattern serial's been changed," Cephalie reported through her speaker as the LENS set the device on the table. "Someone replaced the manufacturer's code with what looks like a random string of characters. Might be Delacroix's, but I can't be certain. I'll need a few moments to process his DNA."

"Who's Delacroix?" Yang asked.

"Yang Zhao, you've been found in possession of illegally modified property. Do you have anything to say for yourself?"

"Okay, fine." He flashed a smile. "Look, you're right. It wasn't a gift."

"Then how did you obtain it?"

"Well, it was sort of a gift." He leaned in, suddenly all buddy-buddy. "A gift I gave myself. You see, back at our hangout, I saw this pile of goodies. Someone was going to toss that"—he pointed to the wrist attendant—"down the reclamation chute. Can you believe that? So I ... helped myself to it."

"Knowing it was stolen."

"I didn't know that. Just saw it with a pile of stuff about to be thrown out. It looked nice, so I grabbed it."

"What other 'goodies' did you see it with?"

"Oh, let me think." He rubbed his chin and glanced up at the ceiling. "It was an odd pile. Some nice infosystem towers. Two or three, I think. A bunch of clothes. A whiskey bottle."

"Who brought those items into the hangout?"

"Don't know."

"Who wanted those items reclaimed?"

"Don't know."

"Then how do you know they were due to be thrown out?"

"That's what the pile next to the chute is for. Just trying to keep the hangout clean, you know." Yang chuckled. "Some of us Wyverns are slobs!"

"I see." Isaac knew a tall tale when he heard one. Yang's burst of confidence meant he *thought* he'd figured out a way to navigate the mess he'd landed in, and Isaac wasn't about to turn down even more leverage. He glanced to Cephalie's avatar, lounging on the table. "Finished with his DNA yet?"

"I am."

Yang put both hands behind his head and leaned back with a broad grin on his face, reveling in his own brilliance.

"And the results?" Isaac asked.

"His DNA was all over that apartment."

Yang almost slipped out of his chair.

"Why am I not surprised?" Isaac sighed.

"B-b-but! That can't be! There's no way that's mine!"

"And why not, Yang?"

"Because we used—" His jaw clapped shut and his face reddened.

The room was silent for long, uncomfortable seconds before Isaac raised a questioning eyebrow at the gangster.

"Ohh," Yang whimpered, deflating as the magnitude of his error slammed home. "Shit."

"Because you used ... what?" Isaac asked.

"Umm."

"Let me make your situation crystal clear for you." Isaac

knitted his fingers together on the table. "You've been placed at the scene of the crime, you were found in possession of an item stolen from the same scene, and you've lied repeatedly to us. You're in trouble. A *lot* of trouble, and the only way to make matters any better for yourself is to cooperate with us. If you do, I'll pass on a recommendation for leniency."

"But—"

"I'm not finished," Isaac interrupted, and Yang clammed up. "We're not talking about lukewarm, wishy-washy cooperation, either. You've already tried to lie your way out of this. No, I want *everything*, and you can start by giving me the names of the people with you and an explanation for why you hit that apartment."

Yang's mouth hung open as he stared at the table, a pale expression on his face.

"What'll it be? This is the best offer you're going to get all day." Isaac leaned back with an indifferent grunt. "Frankly, I don't care either way. I've got plenty of other gangsters I can lean on after you, so mark my words, I *will* discover the truth."

Yang swallowed audibly, then took a slow, shuddering breath.

"D-detective, sir?" he asked, his tone totally transformed from before. He was ready to beg, and Isaac didn't mind this at all.

"Yes?"

"You promise?" He looked up, eyes filled with fear. "I'll get a good sentence."

"That's not my role. I'm not a judge. Nor am I a prosecutor, though any recommendation I make *will* reach the prosecutor for your case."

"Then you'll recommend a good one?"

"If you cooperate, yes. On that, you have my word." Isaac cleared his throat. "As long as you're not guilty of murder, that is."

"Murder!" Yang cried. "Who said anything about that?!"

"You asked who Delacroix was. Were you being honest there?"

"Yes! Never heard the name in my life!"

"He's the murdered cop you robbed."

The blood drained from Yang's face, and he gulped again.

"I'm waiting."

"Uhh, yeah," Yang uttered, in the process of a stumbling attempt to regain his composure. "Yes, sir, Detective. Where should I, umm, begin, sir?"

"Who was at the apartment?"

"Me, Derrick, Manobu, and Hao. We took Hao's truck."

Isaac checked the list of gangsters at the station and flagged Watanabe Manobu's and Huang Hao's files for further review.

"Why were you there?"

"Derrick gathered us up this morning. Said he was helping a friend move."

Isaac gave the gangster an incredulous glare.

"I swear it's the truth, sir!" Yang pleaded. "I didn't know what any of this was about until it was too late. And yeah, it sounded shady from the start, but what was I supposed to do? It was the Hatchet Man himself giving us orders. You been around the guy? Man, he's *crazy*. Lunatic knifed a cop once! A *cop!*"

"Continue."

"When we got to the apartment, Derrick tried the keycode a couple times, but it didn't work. He started cussing up a storm, and that's when I knew we wasn't there to help nobody 'move.' But I was stuck there with the others. Manobu, he suggested he call his friend, but then Derrick just pulls out his shiv and starts cutting through the damn lock!" He snapped his fingers. "Just like that! I had to plug my ears, it was so loud!"

"And then what?"

"Derrick told us to haul everything not bolted down back to the truck, so we did." Yang's shoulders slumped. "And then Hao grabbed four cans of Grime-Away out of his truck. Man, if I'd still had any doubts what we was really doing, *that* finished 'em off. Derrick said we needed to leave the place 'minty fresh' for his friend, but I knew what was going on."

"Who used the Grime-Away?"

"We all pitched in. I didn't want this coming back to bite me, so I *lathered* the place. Emptied my whole can." He chuckled sadly. "Didn't help in the end, did it? Pissed Hao off, too. He yelled at me for using too much."

"What did you do with the stolen goods?"

"We took all of it back to our hangout on Shelf Two."

"Where?"

"In the alley between the city's reclamation plant and the air processor. Same place the cops picked me up."

"Are the stolen goods still at your hangout?"

"The booze is. Derrick took both bottles for himself, then ordered us to recycle the rest."

"And did you?"

"Yeah. Most of it was easy, but we had to bust up the towers to make 'em fit. They made a lot of racket going down."

"And this?" Isaac held up the wrist attendant.

"I...figured all that hard work was worth a little pay. So, I kept it instead of tossing it down the chute."

"Who changed the pattern serial?"

"Manobu did. I promised to share it with him after, so he hooked me up with this little eyedropper of reprogrammed micro-bots. Just a squeeze or two, and they seep in and reorganize the printed number. Said he'd help me get a forged permit later." Yang blew out a resigned breath. "Turned out to be *too* late."

"Did all four of you know this was a robbery?"

"By the end, we did. Hao and Derrick knew from the start."

"Do you know why this apartment was targeted?"

"No."

"Did any of the others say anything that might indicate why it was targeted?"

"No." Yang shook his head. "Derrick kept saying it was a 'friendly favor' all the way through."

Isaac glanced to Susan. "Let's have a chat with MacFayden."

They both rose from their seats.

"Wait!" Yang pleaded, reaching for him. "I told you all I know, and you promised."

"*If* your story checks out."

The door sealed Yang Zhao inside, and they headed up the stairs to the control center.

"You think he was finally giving us the truth?" Susan asked as they walked.

"That's what my gut says, but you know what they say."

"No, actually, I don't."

"I'm sure you have this one back in the Admin." He gave her a smile. "Trust but verify."

"Ah." She nodded. "Yes, we have that one."

"See? We're not so different."

"I didn't say we were."

"But you and I have both been thinking it."

"Umm. Maybe?" she conceded.

They stepped into the control center, and MacFayden sat up in her seat.

"Yes, Detective?"

"Did you catch the names Yang gave us?"

"I did. We'll collect the wearables off those four as evidence. Our forensics group isn't as well equipped as SysPol, but I think we can hack the security on a few cheap visors without too much trouble."

"You read my mind. Thank you."

"Hell, Detective." She flashed a sharklike grin. "Thank *you*. You're giving me another shot at that bastard Fuller, so I want to see this go well as much as you do—if not *more* so. Care to interrogate the other three scum buckets next?"

"Actually, they can wait. I'm much more interested in what we learned from Yang."

"What's next for us, then?" Susan asked.

"Only the most *glamorous* of pursuits," Isaac said with false enthusiasm. "Time to start digging through the trash."

CHAPTER THIRTEEN

SUSAN CLIMBED OUT OF THE CAR AND SURVEYED THEIR SUR-
roundings. Three SSP copters and two squad cars were parked
along both curbs of a dark Shelf Two street running along the
city's outer circumference, and virtual police cordons glowed in
front of an alley between two city utilities: the reclamation plant
and the air processor. Both were nondescript monolithic blocks
from the outside, built near the Shark Fin's outer wall, which she
could see at the far end of the alley. The hum of machinery filled
her ears, and she sniffed at a curious smell in the air—a strange
mix of chemical odors and something similar to cooked meat.

Two pairs of state troopers stood watch on either side of the
police vehicles, directing pedestrians and vehicles around the
area, and more troopers and drones searched the alley.

"We're not actually digging through the garbage, are we?"
Susan asked.

"Oh, no. Not *us*," Isaac stressed before his face assumed a
thoughtful look. "Well, maybe Cephalie."

"Yeah, yeah," the AC griped, the LENS floating behind them.
"Just keep ordering the drone around."

"Only if SSP needs the help."

Susan followed Isaac through the police cordon and down
the alley, which curved behind the reclamation plant to form a
pocket between the outer wall and the plant.

Susan paused at the threshold and took in the place.

The gangsters had done their best to make the space homey. Several overhead lights—none of which matched—shone down on a bizarre collection of sofas, loungers, recliners, mattresses, cabinets, workbenches, tables, and printers. No two were alike, but everything—*everything*—was in shades of black and yellow, and Fanged Wyvern graffiti covered the walls with giant yellow jaws snapping at the darkness.

Dozens of pipes of varying thickness extended down from the bottom of Shelf Three and ran into the back of the reclamation plant. One of the narrower pipes entered the plant at floor level, and a crude hatch had been installed just above the bend. Mac-Fayden and three more troopers stood around the hatch while a conveyor drone used its tooled arms to probe inside.

Isaac paused next to her and yawned into a fist.

"How long has it been since you slept?" Susan asked.

"I don't know. When did we wake up on the saucer?"

"Sometime yesterday."

"Too long, then." He rubbed an eye with the palm of his hand. "How are you holding up?"

"My body will keep going until it runs out of power, but my connectome needs downtime like everyone else."

Cephalie cleared her throat and waved at her from atop the LENS.

"*Almost* everyone else," she corrected. "At STAND, our superiors stressed the need for regular mental rest, even with our synthetic bodies. I . . . may not have followed those instructions as closely as I should have, initially." She let out a small, embarrassed sigh. "And I've been told I get . . . irritable if I skip too much sleep."

Isaac chuckled. "*That*, I'd rather not see."

She frowned at him, not sure how to take the comment, but he was too busy yawning again to notice.

"You know SSP can handle this, right?" Cephalie said.

"I want to know what they find." He rubbed the side of his face. "But you're right. Let's see what MacFayden has for us, then we'll turn in for the day. We need to check into our hotel at some point, anyway. How's that sound?"

"No complaints here," Susan said.

"All right." Isaac walked up to MacFayden. Graffiti of a giant yellow jawbone chomped at them as they approached. "Anything good?"

"Partially." She put her fists on her hips. "We called ahead and had the utilities shut down this pipe. It and five other lines feed into one of the main hoppers that perform final sorting upstream of the more specialized reclamation units. It also acts as a buffer during peak hours. I have a team searching the hopper, but given the timing, any evidence that reached it is gone."

"Then why 'partially'?"

"Because these kids are dumbasses." She pointed at the ceiling. "See where the pipe comes out? There's another hopper up there built directly into Shelf Three. It provides an initial sorting pass for waste coming from upper shelves to the plant, so the line they cut isn't meant for general waste."

"It's already been sorted once?" Susan ventured.

"You've got it, and what passes through here is more granular. Or it's *meant* to be. Remember how Yang said the towers made a racket going down?" MacFayden knocked on the side of the conveyor with her fist, and it wobbled briefly. "You ready to reel it up, yet?"

"Fewer interruptions would be nice," said the AC operating the conveyor drone. "But yes. I think I've got a firm hold this time."

The conveyor levitated higher with one arm looped around the pipe for support and the other stuffed deep down the hatch. The flexible, prog-steel appendage contracted like a straining muscle, metal screeched against metal, and the arm pulled a busted infosystem free of the pipe. The glossy white shell was cracked and dangled from an infosystem rack broken into three pieces and connected only by cables, but more than a few rack nodes were still slotted into place and appeared intact to Susan's untrained eye.

"Just as I thought." MacFayden's eyes glinted. "One of the towers didn't make it all the way to the hopper." She turned to Isaac. "We'll sweep the rest of their lair tonight, but chances are this is the main prize."

"I'm inclined to agree." Isaac nodded to the lieutenant. "Good work."

"Don't mention it. We'll seal the evidence up and get it back to our lab. You should have a full report in the morning."

"Great. I appreciate the support."

"Hell"—she smiled at him—"*I* appreciate a detective that doesn't walk all over us!"

"It'll be interesting to see what Delacroix kept on it." Susan crossed her arms and leaned against the wall.

"DON'T!" Isaac and MacFayden shouted at the same time.

"Don't what?" Susan asked, her back pressed against the jawbone graffiti.

"Oh, no," Isaac breathed with sad eyes.

"What?" Susan asked. "What's wrong?"

She pulled away from the wall, but something tugged at her back, almost like an adhesive. The resistance wasn't enough to bother her artificial muscles, and she turned to find strands of black and yellow tar stretching from her uniform to the graffiti. A million pictures of microtech horrors flashed through her mind, and she pressed a boot against the wall and kicked off it so fast she almost bowled Isaac over. He staggered back, lost his balance, and landed on his butt.

"What the hell was that?!" She grabbed her uniform's shoulder and tugged it forward, granting her a view of her back. Black and neon yellow tendrils of color spread across the smart fabric. "Oh, no!"

She grasped her collar with firm hands, ready to rip the infected coat off. Her arm muscles switched at maximum power, all limiters removed.

"STOP!" Isaac shouted, holding both hands up toward her.

She froze. Black and yellow streaks spread over her shoulders, down her arms, and around her torso, but she held per position. Isaac would know how to combat whatever nightmarish weapon this was, and she would follow his instructions to the letter.

"Help," she peeped at him.

"It's okay." He rose to his feet and dusted his butt off.

"What do I do?"

"Nothing. You can let go of your collar."

"Are you sure?" She glanced down as yellow and black enveloped her chest.

"The graffiti infected your uniform's firmware with a virus. It's a harmless prank. That's *all*."

"But—"

"Please don't disrobe in front of the troopers."

She looked around. Every state trooper in the hideout was staring at her, and one of them was doing a bad job of hiding his laughter. She wanted to curl up and hide in a dark corner somewhere, but instead she straightened her posture and slowly let go of her collar. She checked her hands and found no signs of microtech infection. She ran a diagnostic on her epidermis, and all the indicators in her virtual vision lit up green.

"Get back to work, you lazy bums!" MacFayden snapped, and Susan's audience found more important things to do.

Susan slumped her shoulders and let out a long, shuddering sigh. She kept sighing until she'd emptied her artificial lungs.

The sigh did nothing to improve her mood.

She gazed down at her uniform. She looked like a bumble bee on the receiving end of an electric shock.

Isaac stepped up to her but maintained an arm's length between them.

"How do I switch it back?" she asked.

"Do you have a way to reload your uniform's firmware?"

"No. All they gave me was the pattern file."

"Then it'll be easiest to toss it and print a fresh one. Also, can you still shut down your uniform's smart features?"

"I should be able to. The switch is hardwired." She reached back into her collar and squeezed a tiny switch at her throat. "There. Should be off."

"Let me test something real quick." He pressed his cuff against her sleeve, jerked his arm back, and checked the cuff. "Okay, good. No longer infectious. That saves us some trouble."

"What sort of trouble?"

"We'd have to throw a tarp over the car seats."

She sighed again and lowered her head.

"Come on." He patted her on the shoulder. "Let's head for the hotel. I think we could both use some rest."

"Fine," she groaned, and followed him out of the alley. They were almost to the car when Cephalie stopped them.

"Raviv is calling. He wants an update on the case." She glanced at Susan meaningfully. "And he wants to hear how you're doing."

"Can this wait?" she asked.

"He's the boss," Isaac said with a grimace. "No point in delaying this."

"I can think of *several* points!"

"I know. Let me talk to him first. Maybe we can keep him from seeing"—he gestured up and down Susan's uniform—"you know."

He stood opposite Susan while Cephalie positioned the LENS to act as a camera. A comm window opened, and Omar Raviv appeared. He was not smiling. In fact, Susan found it difficult to think of an expression more the polar opposite of smiling than Raviv's expression at that moment. It somehow went beyond a mere scowl and became something darker, as if all the man's miseries were pooled in his jaw muscles.

"Isaac," he grunted.

"Hello, sir." Isaac smiled. "Still feels weird calling you that, but you are the boss now."

"You crack that Gordian case yet?"

"No, not yet."

"You going to crack it soon?"

"Hard to say."

"Then you're not free to work on the Apple Cypher case?"

"No, not at the moment."

Raviv let out a pained exhale and rubbed his stomach.

"Are you all right?" Isaac asked.

"Never better. Why?"

"Just making small talk, I guess."

"Stay focused. You need to crack this case and get to hunting apples."

"We *are* focused, I can assure you."

"I need everyone hunting these damned apples. *Everyone.*"

"I understand that."

"You know something, Isaac?" Raviv leaned toward the screen and spoke softer. "I think this case is getting to me."

"Why do you say that?"

"I had a dream last night. I was being chased by man-eating apples. You ever been chased by apples before?"

"Can't say that I have."

"Don't let them catch you." Raviv looked off to the side and shuddered as if recalling something terrible. "They're slow eaters. Takes a *lot* of bites to finish a man off."

"Sir, we're working as fast as we can."

"How's Cantrell been?"

"Fine. No problems to report."

"Is she slowing you down?"

"No, not at all."

"Speeding you up?"

"She's"—his eyes flicked to Susan's, then back to the screen—"still learning our procedures, which is to be expected of someone in her position."

"Then she *is* slowing you down."

"No, she *isn't*."

"Well, it's not like I can do anything about it," Raviv said with a shrug. "Commissioner Tyrel tied my hands on this one. You two are joined at the hip as far as she's concerned."

"That was my understanding as well."

"Is she there? Can I speak to her?"

"She's ... around," Isaac said delicately.

"Then let's see her. She works in my department. I should at least say hello to her."

"Yes, but perhaps tomorrow would be—"

"Can she come into view?"

"Technically, yes, though—"

"Then call her over."

Isaac opened his mouth as if to protest, but then he let out a resigned exhale, clicked his jaw shut, and stepped out of the camera's field of vision. Susan tried to drain some of the apprehension from her face and rounded her way in front of the LENS.

Raviv did a double take. "Agent Cantrell?"

"Yes, sir?" Susan said with a cringe.

"Is that a standard Admin uniform you're wearing?"

"No, sir. I'm having ... wardrobe difficulties."

"You best get that sorted out."

"I intend to, sir. *Believe* me."

"I don't know what kind of slipshod operation the Admin is, but here in SysPol we expect our police to dress professionally."

"Yes, sir. I know, sir. It won't happen again, sir."

"Are you slowing Isaac down?"

"I'm trying not to, sir."

"Because it looks to me like you're slowing him down."

"That's not my intention, sir."

"It better not be. Next time I call, I want to hear all about the progress you two are making, and I will see *you*"—he pointed at her—"in a proper uniform. Is that clear?"

"Perfectly clear, sir."

"Good." He made a shooing gesture. "Now go crack this case."

The comm window closed, and Susan hung her head.

"I think he likes you," Isaac said.

"Oh, *please!*" she moaned.

"No, really." Isaac patted her shoulder. "I've worked with him for years. He's not angry at us. Not really. He just sounds angry when he's stressed."

"But when *isn't* Raviv stressed?" Cephalie asked.

"Hmm." Isaac rubbed his chin. "Yeah. Good point."

✧   ✧   ✧

"Hello, and welcome to . . ." The hotel receptionist trailed off as Susan and Isaac stepped up to the counter. She regarded Susan's uniform with a doubtful eye.

"I'm not in a gang," Susan said wearily. "I'm just having a bad day."

"Oh, I see, ma'am." The receptionist appeared to recover from her initial shock. "If there's anything we at the Top Shelf Hotel can do to make your stay here more enjoyable, please don't hesitate to ask."

"Room, please," Susan muttered.

"Kronos Station should have made our reservations." Isaac transmitted his ID. "Both should be listed under Isaac Cho."

"Let's see." The receptionist opened her interface. "Yes, here you are. Two rooms with an open-ended reservation. Rooms 910 and 912, and Miss Cantrell's travel case has already been delivered to room 912."

"Key, please," Susan muttered.

"Yes, of course. Here are your—"

Susan copied the keycode and shuffled toward the counter-grav tube.

". . . keycodes," the receptionist finished.

"She's had a *really* bad day."

"Yes, I can see that, sir."

Susan took the tube up to floor nine and palmed the lock open on room 912. She stepped in, looked around the boring, beige chamber, and let out an angry groan.

"What the hell is this?"

Her travel case sat in the middle of the floor. Other than that, the room was empty. No chairs, no desk, no artwork on the walls, and no bed. Not even a charging station for her synthoid. Her internal power could last for weeks without charging, at least at her current level of activity, but she liked to stay topped off. How was she supposed to do that without a charger?

She spotted the delivery port in the wall, walked over, and knocked on it.

"Yes, Miss Cantrell?" the receptionist responded in audio only. "Is something wrong?"

"My room is empty."

"Umm. Is that a problem?"

"I don't even see a charger. What kind of hotel is this?"

"I'm sorry, but I don't understand."

"What's there to understand?" she snapped. "How am I supposed to recharge while I sleep?"

"But your room has been furnished according to your preferences. The process is automatic."

"This is most definitely *not* how I prefer things!"

"Susan," Isaac said, his voice coming through a touch softer and more distant. "Did you fill out your travel profile?"

"My *what*?"

"It's a form. The station should have sent it to you."

"I don't remember seeing anything like that."

"Check your mail. I'm sure it's there."

She opened her inbox and ran a search. Sure enough, she'd received a reminder from Kronos Station to set up her profile, which the station would use when booking her travel arrangements. She'd barely given it a thought because she'd been focused on more important matters, like learning how Themis Division operated and *solving the damned case*!

"Yeah, I see it," she sighed. "I didn't fill it out."

"Then that's why your room is empty. Top Shelf belongs to the Ring Suites hotel chain. They all use room preferences, so they print out the furniture and set up your room to order before you arrive. I really like them, because I get to sleep in my favorite bed each night."

"And I don't have a profile." Susan closed her eyes and rested her forehead against the wall. "Hence my empty room."

"It's no big deal. We can swap rooms tonight. Just let me grab a pillow and blanket first. I'll be fine on the floor."

"No, it's all right," Susan sighed. "You need a good night's sleep more than I do. I'll rough it out here."

"You sure?"

"Yeah, it's fine. Can they start printing me some basic furniture tonight? Maybe a bed and charger? I don't need much else."

"We certainly can," the receptionist chimed in. "Perhaps I can interest you in our deluxe Ring Suites Odyssey package—synthoid variant, of course—featuring artwork and furnishings designed by—"

"No."

"Or," the receptionist continued without missing a beat, "I can put in an order for our basic Synthoid's Slumber configuration. All public domain patterns, so there's no additional cost."

"Yeah, that one. Send it up when done."

"Yes, ma'am. Give me a moment...there. I've flagged it as a priority in our system. Each kit will be delivered by drone as soon as it's finished. Is there anything else I can help you with?"

"No," Susan grunted. "That'll be all."

"Then please have a pleasant—"

Susan closed the channel and put her back to the wall.

"What a damn nuisance."

She rubbed her face with both hands, then slapped her cheeks and stood up off the wall. The delivery port interface glowed next to her, and she placed a custom printing order and provided a copy of her uniform pattern. She checked the bathroom, relieved to find at least *it* had been stocked with towels and an assortment of synthoid care products.

SysGov products, though. She eyed the bottles suspiciously. Most formed microbot colonies to actively clean and care for a synthoid cosmetic layer, and at least one listed "self-replication" as a feature.

She shuddered, then shoved the bottles all to the side of the sink. She placed her travel case on the counter and flipped it open.

"Not on my skin."

She took out her Peacekeeper-approved tube cleaner gel first, poured out a cap full, and swished it around in her mouth before drinking it. It left a spearmint-flavored aftertaste, and she smacked her lips as she stripped off her uniform.

She found the reclamation chute next to the delivery port, balled up the black-and-yellow fabric, and tossed it down into oblivion. She then returned to the bathroom, grabbed her skin and hair gels, set the shower temperature and flow pattern, and stepped in.

Scalding water splashed against her chest, and she began lathering her epidermis with the skincare gel. The shower glass fogged up, and she relished the relaxing heat. The water served no purpose other than to spread the cleansing suds, but there was something undeniably soothing about a long, hot shower, even after her transition, and she reveled in it after her rough day.

She rested her head against the glass and let the stream of water beat against the back of her neck. Her mind wandered through the day, touching on all the dumb things she'd said and done, and she cringed at the memories.

She lost track of time, alone in the shower with her thoughts, but she snapped out of it with a start.

"No use sulking over it," she muttered to herself, then rubbed her face.

She turned around twice, let the water wash away any remaining suds, then dispensed a gob of haircare gel into her hand and worked it into her scalp. Bubbles fell across her eyes but caused no irritation, and she finished and then rinsed off.

She switched off the water, grabbed a towel off the rack, and looped it around her chest before tucking it in.

"Wonder if they finished the charger."

She stepped around the corner—

—and froze.

A bed sat in one corner of the room. A black-and-yellow bed with a uniform neatly folded on top. A black-and-yellow uniform with a black-and-yellow peaked cap. Tendrils of alien color radiated out from where the bedposts touched the floor, and the delivery port formed a black-and-yellow sun on the wall.

She knew what Isaac had said about the virus being a prank, but this couldn't be normal! She sidestepped around the discolored floor, careful not to touch *anything*, reached the door, palmed it open, and slipped out.

Someone knocked on Isaac's hotel room door.

"Grfrgn mrgr," he groaned into his pillow.

The person pounded the door so hard he thought it might split open. He rose with a start and blinked around his room with blurry eyes.

"Isaac!"

"Susan?" he grunted. "That you?"

"Yes! Open up, please!"

He checked the time. "It's one in the morning."

"I don't care! I need your help!"

"Okay. Hold on." His fingers found the glass of water by his bedside. He took a sip, blinked his eyes into focus, and rose out of bed. He shambled over to the door, eyes squinting in the gloom, and palmed the release.

The door split open, and he saw Susan as he'd never seen her before: hair damp, droplets of water glistening off her pale flesh, naked except for the towel wrapped tight around the thrust of her perky breasts. Her lips quivered on the edge of words, but her eyes spoke volumes. The rigid formality of Susan-the-Peacekeeper was gone, replaced with gentle nervousness.

"Uh?" Isaac swallowed dryly. "Hello?"

"I need your help," she said softly.

His eyes flicked down to her firm cleavage, then back up to her face, and an absurd train of thought formed in his mind.

Those are fake, he told himself, which was ridiculous, because Susan was a synthoid. *All* of her was artificial!

"My help?" he said weakly.

"There's a problem." She glanced back to her room. "And I'm not sure how to handle it."

Is she coming on to me? he thought. *Is casual sex amongst coworkers a thing in the Admin? That seems unlikely, but here we are. Maybe it's a "work hard, play hard" kind of thing?*

"It's the bed," she added.

"The bed," he squeaked, and his mind raced.

He was not—*completely*—without experience in this area. He'd engaged in his share of hot-blooded, youthful experimentation and had witnessed firsthand the wreckage of relationships ruined by immaturity and inattentiveness. That was simply part of growing up, of learning by doing and—more often than not—failing. But the importance of such physicality had waned as he matured, replaced with a driven emphasis on his education at the academy.

He'd tried to rekindle some of his youthful passion after receiving his wetware at the age of twenty-five. That desire led to an ill-advised tryst with an older—and far more mature—AC, but when the novelty wore off, so too did their mutual interest, and they'd separated only a few weeks in.

Relationships were...something that happened to other people, he'd decided at the time, and he'd redoubled his concentration on his career. Eventually, he knew he would want a family, but he felt no urgency in the matter. He had nothing against the occasional fling, should a suitable opportunity present itself, but those, too, seemed to happen only to other people.

Maybe this is just one big misunderstanding, Isaac wondered.

Susan adjusted the towel, and it dipped lower, revealing a generous portion of moist, pale skin.

She is coming on to me! he thought. *But she's looking at me like she expects something. Oh dear! I never read those cultural files! Are there rules I don't know about? Will I offend her if I say no? Do I even want to say no? What's the correct response here?*

You should have read those files, Isaac! he scolded himself.

He cleared his throat and lowered his voice an octave in what might have passed for suave somewhere in the solar system.

"The bed, you say. Yes, what about it?"

"It's easier to show you."

She took hold of his wrist and yanked him toward her room. "Whoa!"

So assertive! His heart raced as he let himself be pulled along. *I don't know if I'm ready for this!*

They passed through the door, and he stumbled forward into her room. She rested a hand on his shoulder to steady him and pointed.

"The bed."

"What about..." He trailed off as he realized at last what was going on. "Oh. I see."

Black and yellow streaks spiraled outward across the floor and one wall, and a gang-themed uniform sat folded on top of a gang-themed bed.

"You sound disappointed."

"It's nothing." He summoned the room's master control interface. "Can I have a copy of your key, please?"

"Sure." She offered him the file with an open palm, and her towel slipped a little lower.

Is she doing that on purpose?! he vented on the inside, but he pushed the thought away and accessed the room's root functions with her key. He triggered an active purge, and the walls, floor, and bed switched to a gray grid pattern before cycling back to their original beige colors.

"There." He wiped off his hands with a deep frown on his face. "Problem solved."

"That was it?"

"Yup."

"You're mad at me, aren't you?"

"No, no," he assured her, and perhaps this was a small white lie. "Just tired."

"But how did that even happen?"

"Your uniform must have infected their systems when it was reclaimed. Pretty impressive for a gang virus, actually. I'll let the staff know. They shouldn't have any problems cleaning up the mess, and I'll make sure they print you out a new uniform when they're done."

"I'm sorry. I really am." She put a hand to her chest. "I just thought— Well, some SysGov tech makes me nervous, and I wasn't sure if it was dangerous."

Her towel slipped even farther, but Isaac kept his eyes locked on her face.

"I understand," he said. "A lot of this is new to you."

"You've got that right!" she said with a chuckle.

"By the way."

"Yes?"

"You should probably..." He mimed an upward tug with one hand, never letting his eyes wander from hers.

"I should..." She looked down. "Oh!" Her face reddened and she pulled her towel higher. "Sorry! I didn't realize!"

"I know. Trust me, I know."

"I'm so sorry!"

"It's all right," he replied dully. "No harm done."

"This was *very* improper of me!"

"Don't give it another thought." He stepped toward the door. "Anything else?"

"No. And thank you, Isaac. I appreciate how understanding you've been."

"Don't mention it."

The door closed, and he slouched down and shambled back to his room. He sighed, palmed it open, and walked in. The door closed, and he spotted Cephalie seated on the edge of the fruit bowl on the table. She giggled, but then she started kicking her legs over the edge, and her laughter crescendoed into an unrestrained howl of mirth.

"You shut up!" he snapped, then headed into the bathroom to take a cold shower.

CHAPTER FOURTEEN

SUSAN'S FEET TOUCHED DOWN ON THE HOTEL'S GROUND FLOOR outside the counter-grav shaft, and she cradled a small bottle in her left hand. She scanned the foyer, once again clad in her sharp Peacekeeper blues and feeling more comfortable in a public space because of it. Two receptionists were checking guests out while the distant clink of silverware and dishes drew her toward the hotel restaurant.

She followed the breakfast sounds through a pair of archways to a wide-open hall filled with small, circular tables. Guests occupied only a fraction of the room's capacity, and a few stood near a row of food printers or requested custom orders from a trio of chefs. She spotted Isaac sitting at a table in the corner, private reports active around him as he scooped up a mouthful of scrambled eggs from his plate. His inactive LENS sat in the chair beside him.

She walked over.

"Morning, Susan." He set his fork down and shifted the reports aside. "Sleep well?"

"Very," she said, then hesitated for a moment. "And you?"

"Fair. Took me a while to get back to sleep."

"Sorry about that," she said with a frown.

"Don't be." He gestured to the seat opposite him, and she joined him at the table. "Little misunderstandings like that will happen. We'll work through them."

"I know, but it's not just last night. I feel like I'm letting you down, like I'm not pulling my weight."

"Don't be too hard on yourself." He gave her a comforting smile. "I spent five years of my life training to be a SysPol officer and another five working as a probationary detective. I *should* be better than you after all that time and effort."

"Still, I felt an apology was in order." She placed the small, black bottle on the table. "Here."

"Oh?" Isaac spun the bottle around until the skull-and-crossbones label faced him. "'Flavor-Sparkle presents our all new Death Extract.' Huh. I didn't know F.S. made a hot sauce."

"Apparently, they're branching out. Cephalie mentioned you like food with a good kick, so I printed this out for you."

"She did, did she?"

"You don't?"

"Oh no. It's not that. I do like it when my food fights back. I just think Cephalie is prone to exaggeration."

"I see." Susan grimaced. "Then, perhaps..." She reached for the bottle.

"Don't be hasty," Isaac cautioned with another smile. He picked up the bottle and twisted the cap off. "You didn't have to do this, you know."

"But I wanted to."

"And I appreciate the gesture." He sprinkled the death sauce on top of his eggs. "Would you like to try some with me? Maybe grab a plate yourself and we can sample it together? I don't know what those chefs are doing, but both the eggs and hash browns are *very* good this morning."

"I'll pass. Spicy food is one of the few ways I can still feel pain."

"Really?" Isaac asked, sounding genuinely interested. "I wouldn't have guessed."

"Yeah. And because of that, it weirds me out when I try to eat it. I haven't enjoyed anything spicy since I transitioned."

"That's a shame." Isaac set the bottle down and ate a bite of scrambled eggs. "Hmm. Sweeter than I expected. And with an unconventional, almost fruity flavor." He chewed and took on a look of deep contemplation, then his brow furrowed. "And not quite as hot as 'death extract' would lead one to believe. In fact, I'm still waiting for it to hit me."

"Cephalie said you're accustomed to hot food, so I made sure I picked one with extra heat."

"Yes. About that." He picked up the bottle, scrutinized the label, then set it down and took another bite. He chewed it slowly and deliberately, staring off in thought.

"You don't like it?" Susan asked, anxiety building in her. Had she goofed again?

"No, it's something else." He raised the bottle to his nose and sniffed it, then wrinkled his nose.

"What's wrong?"

Isaac drained the dregs in his water glass, then tipped the death sauce bottle over and let the full contents glug into the glass. Golden brown fluid filled the cup halfway.

"Something *is* wrong, isn't it?" Susan said.

Isaac raised the glass to his mouth and drank it all in one go.

"Are you sure that's wise?" she asked, cringing.

He smacked his lips and set the glass down.

"I'm fine," he said. "It's apple juice."

"*What?*" Susan grabbed the bottle and sniffed it. She dabbed the moist rim with a finger and licked it. "Apple. But I swear I picked the right pattern."

"I'm sure you did." Isaac gave her an indifferent shrug. "But we live in apple-blighted times." He licked his lips. "Wow. That may have been the best glass of apple juice I ever drank."

"It was supposed to be death sauce!" she said, glowering at the bottle.

"It's the thought that counts." He glanced down at his eggs sprinkled with apple juice and pushed the plate toward the table center. "On a totally different note, the precinct's forensics team must have pulled an all-nighter. We have reports on the contents of Delacroix's tower and the gangster's wearables."

"Oh, good," Susan remarked, eager for the change in subject. "Anything interesting?"

"Quite a bit, actually." He sent her copies of the files. "The information we received from Yang Zhao turned out to be accurate, so I forwarded a recommendation of leniency to the SSP. I have a feeling that, with the right approach, they might be able to pull him out of the gangs before it's too late."

"He did seem less . . . hardened than some of the others," Susan observed.

"That he did. Anyway, I was skimming the reports over breakfast, and a few details stood out. First, as we assumed, the Fanged Wyverns are acting as the agents for an as-yet-unknown individual or group. Both Fuller and Hao received messages from someone named Ōdachi."

"Do we have any information on this Ōdachi person?"

"No, unfortunately. It's an alias the NFPD has encountered before, though they've never been able to track it down. They've seen it used to pass orders to the Fanged Wyverns and, occasionally, receive reports back."

"Would SysPol have better luck tracing it down?" Susan asked.

"Maybe, if we can catch one of the transmissions while it's happening. But what we have right now isn't enough. The message from Ōdachi, like any other, has a routing record attached to it as it bounces from one infosystem to another on its way from sender to destination, but that record is as fake as they come."

"Useless to us, then."

"Pretty much. But it's confirmation the gangs aren't the real problem. Someone wanted Delacroix's apartment cleaned out. If we can figure out who, we're one step closer to finding the murderer, and I bet that person was afraid of what we might find on Delacroix's hardware."

"Speaking of the tower..."

"Yes, *that* proved to be well worth our efforts yesterday. First, we have some *very* angry messages between Delacroix and a few different people at Negation Industries, all concerning the 'defective' impeller. I get the impression matters became a bit more heated than Ortiz let on."

"Heated enough for murder?"

"No, the Negation Industries angle still doesn't look viable to me. But it does reinforce how irregular they found Delacroix's demands." He tapped one of the reports and smiled. "Especially when combined with the *other* little nugget."

"Which is?"

"Delacroix and the Trinh Syndicate manager, Melody Quang, were in a relationship."

"What sort of relationship?"

"The horizontal kind."

"Oh my." Susan's eyebrows shot up. "She never mentioned that."

"Yeah, and I can see why. Besides the obvious business conflict of sleeping with your customers, of course. We have multiple mail threads and calendar entries corroborating the relationship, and with that, Quang's involvement with Delacroix places a lot of suspicion on his impeller edict." He leaned toward Susan. "Here's what I'm wondering. Did she put the idea in his head? Was the vulnerable man who'd just lost his wife being used for the syndicate's financial gain?"

"The apartment job would benefit her as well," Susan noted. "No tower, no evidence of this relationship."

"Exactly."

"Then Ōdachi could be a Trinh Syndicate alias used to send orders to the Fanged Wyverns."

"A distinct possibility." Isaac sat back in his seat.

"But"—Susan raised a cautionary hand—"we still don't have a motive."

"Also true," Isaac conceded with a quiet sigh.

"Who would benefit from either Delacroix's or Andover-Chen's deaths? It doesn't seem to be Quang. At least with the information we have."

"And that's bugging me. Quang might not be involved in the murders, despite what we found last night. Perhaps she's only interested in covering her tracks on this shady impeller deal, and maybe she did order the apartment burglary as a result. If that's true and she's not involved in the murder, then we may be unduly zeroing in on Delacroix. We need to keep Andover-Chen on our scopes as well, at least until we have solid confirmation of who the actual target was."

"So, what are our next steps?"

"Two things." Isaac held up a finger. "One, we need to have another chat with Quang, and this time we'll be treating her as a potential suspect rather than an investigative lead."

"And two?"

"Something reeks in the Gordian Division." He shook his head. "I have no idea what, but we need to look into—"

"Hey, kiddos!" Cephalie appeared on the table as the LENS levitated off its chair. She peered at the death sauce bottle. "Oh, good grief! Did you use all of it already?" The LENS picked up the bottle with a pseudopod. "You did! What is wrong with you? Are you trying to burn a hole in your stomach?"

"It's not what you think," Isaac defended.

"Well, I guess you liked it." Cephalie nudged Susan's hand with her cane. "Can I pick them or what?"

"Yes, Cephalie," Susan replied blandly. "You did great."

"As I was saying," Isaac continued, "we need to dig deeper into Gordian. Find out where this stench is coming from."

"Then you'll love this bit of news," Cephalie said. "I just transmitted back from the precinct, and guess who's in town and wants to talk to you?"

Isaac shrugged his shoulders.

"None other than Gordian's finest. Agent Raibert Kaminski."

"Kaminski?" Susan exclaimed with a start.

"Yep," Cephalie continued. "The TTV *Kleio* docked at the New Frontier Airport an hour ago. Kaminski's at the precinct now."

"You've heard of him?" Isaac asked Susan.

"I—" She cut herself off before she revealed anything... awkward.

Yes, she knew who Raibert Kaminski was. *Everyone* in the DTI knew. It had only been eight months since the Gordian Division agent had shown up in the heart of the Admin to deliver a dire warning to Director-General Csaba Shigeki. Kaminski and the *Kleio* had been the first SysGov representatives anyone in the Admin had met, and the DTI, being full of people who liked to prepare for the worst, had shifted operations to safeguard against the worst-case scenario: a transdimensional war between SysGov and the Admin.

Susan, for her part, had participated in numerous war games designed to test and refine DTI tactics against the technologically superior SysGov forces, and the *Kleio* had featured heavily in those early simulations. The Admin had possessed little else to build its abstractions with, at the time, and so Susan had participated in dozens of mock SysGov infiltration attempts at the DTI tower as well as mock boarding actions on an abstract version of the *Kleio*, with the goal of seizing the vessel intact.

Not every simulation ended well, and more than one concluded with the *Kleio* detonating a nuclear fail-safe device (which the real version turned out not to have). Susan had also been gunned down by the crew a few times, and she'd blown up the simulated version of Kaminski once or twice, as well.

"Yes," Susan said flatly. "I've heard of him."

Best leave it at that, she told herself. *This way, there's less chance of my foot-in-mouth disease kicking in.*

"I'm not surprised," Isaac said. "The *Kleio* is well known, even outside SysPol circles." He let out a long, slow sigh. "Let's head for the precinct and meet up with our Gordian colleagues."

"Why the long face?" Susan asked.

"Because we're not dealing with civilians here, but a coequal division of SysPol. That relationship blunts some of our investigative authority." He grimaced. "And I don't think Kaminski will like what I have to say. Not one bit."

Isaac's first impression of Raibert Kaminski was one of size. The man possessed a hulking synthoid body: ripped muscles, broad shoulders, and thick neck leading up to a scowling face with long blond hair tied back in a ponytail. The grayish green of his Gordian Division uniform fit him well, though, and the eye-and-sword flash at his shoulder glinted in the NFPD conference room's light.

Isaac's second thought was that Raibert Kaminski knew an Admin uniform when he saw one, and the big man's jaw visibly tensed at the sight of Susan. A seething undercurrent of animosity abruptly permeated the room around him, and Isaac saw the conversation ahead become even more difficult.

"What's she doing here?" Kaminski asked pointedly with a nod toward Susan.

"Agent Cantrell is part of the new officer exchange program," Isaac replied evenly. "She's acting as my deputy."

"Does she have to be here?" Kaminski crossed his arms and leaned back against the wall, eyeing Susan suspiciously.

"She does." Isaac raised an eyebrow. "Is there a problem?"

"No, no, of course not," Kaminski dismissed with all the thespian aptitude of a middle grader. "Just strange to see someone from the fuc—" He grimaced, then cleared his throat. "From the Admin out here on Saturn, is all."

"Hello, Philo," Cephalie said with a sly smile from atop the LENS.

"Cephalie?" The avatar of Kaminski's integrated companion materialized beside him. Philosophus took the form of a huge, redheaded, red-bearded Viking with a peculiar helmet. The helmet came with a pair of horns, as Isaac would expect from someone emulating an ancient Viking, but the material looked more like plastic than metal, and a tab ran down the center. Perhaps for a retractable visor?

Isaac gave the odd ensemble an inward shrug; he'd seen stranger getups on ACs plenty of times before.

"You two know each other?" he asked Cephalie.

"You could say that." She winked at Viking. "Isn't that right, Philo?"

"Uhh, yeah." Philo rubbed the back of his neck bashfully. "We know each other."

"Friend of yours?" Kaminski asked.

"Not . . . precisely," Philo said.

"Philo and I go way back," Cephalie explained. "About eighty years back, actually. I arrested him once for pattern theft."

Philo slumped his shoulders, bowed his head, then gave everyone a brief nod.

"Really, a pointless crime, if you ask me," Cephalie continued. "More about the thrill of the act and the bragging rights for pulling it off." She flashed another sly smile. "*Almost* pulling it off."

Great, Isaac thought. *More personal baggage cluttering the room.*

"You staying clean, Philo?" Cephalie asked.

"Trying to."

"Staying out of trouble?"

"That's . . . been a little harder. But at least it hasn't been my fault this time."

"Look, you two can reminisce later," Kaminski cut in. He looked over at Isaac. "The main reason the *Kleio*'s here is to support the impeller tests, but our commissioner is *very* interested in tracking down who killed our agents. Is there anything we can do to help out?"

"Yes," Isaac said. "As a matter of fact, there is."

"Name it."

"First, what's Andover-Chen's condition? Has he returned to duty?"

"Yeah, though I hear he's somewhat disoriented. You likely have more experience dealing with the temporary dead than I do, but his condition sounds typical for what he's been through."

"Is he well enough to travel?"

Kaminski furrowed his brow. "Why do you ask?"

"I need him to come out to Saturn to be interviewed."

"What the hell for?"

"Because right now the motive for these murders is unknown," Isaac said firmly. "We have a few indicators that Delacroix was the target, but they're hardly conclusive. Nothing more than dubious business deals."

"I'm sorry." Kaminski blinked. "What dubious deals?"

"Your chief engineer was in bed with one of the impeller companies."

"The hell he was!"

"Would you like to review the evidence?"

"Well—I—" Kaminski stammered, unbalanced by the news. "Are you sure?"

"Yes," Isaac continued in an unwavering voice. "Your chief engineer was in a sexual relationship with Melody Quang, a manager in the Trinh Syndicate. It would have been best if Gordian had never signed a contract with the syndicate, but you did, so here we are. On top of their unethical relationship, I have reason to believe Delacroix conspired with Quang to flunk one of the Negation Industries impellers, resulting in losses for Negation Industries and the Trinh Syndicate purchasing the raw material at a significant discount.

"So yes. Something is very wrong here, and it includes the Gordian Division. Since Delacroix is dead, Andover-Chen is the next best source of information I have within your division."

"Hold on here," Kaminski warned. "You want the doctor—a guy who was just *murdered by transceiver*—to transmit out to Saturn?"

"That's right."

"Don't you think that's a little cold?"

"We're trying to track down his killer," Isaac countered.

"Okay, yeah, granted," Kaminski agreed, relenting somewhat.

"Is access to a witness too much to ask?"

"But he's missing the last six months of his life. What do you think you'll get out of him?"

"I don't know," Isaac admitted. "But that's the nature of our work. I *can't* know until I've had a chance to speak with him. He recommended Delacroix for the position of chief engineer; that, by itself, is a lead worth following, especially given Delacroix's questionable actions here on Janus."

"You don't think *Andover-Chen* was up to no good, do you?"

"I haven't seen any evidence both of them were involved in dubious behavior, but I can't discount the possibility. Not until I know why two Gordian agents were murdered. Which, again, brings us back to why I need to talk to him."

Kaminski let out a long sigh and nodded. He turned to Philo. "What do you think?"

"Seems reasonable to me," the Viking replied. "Plus, the doctor has to come out here eventually. We'll need him for impeller trials."

"All right." Kaminski faced Isaac again. "Is the doctor the only person you want?"

"Not quite. If you could help us track down Delacroix's former IC, I'd also like to interview him."

"That shouldn't be too hard," Philo said. "Komuso and I spoke before he left Gordian. Their breakup hit Komuso pretty hard, and he made sure Delacroix had a way to reach him if he ever wanted to talk again. We only need to check in with Argus Station and forward an interview request his way. I'd wager he'll transmit over as soon as he receives word from us."

"Good," Isaac said. "That'll help."

"Anything else?" Kaminski asked.

"Not at the moment."

"We're due to head over to Negation Industries, anyway," Philo said. "Ortiz wants to get the first round of tests rolling."

"Then we'll leave you gentlemen to it," Isaac said, and started for the door.

"Oh, actually, there is one more thing," Kaminski said.

"Yes?" Isaac turned back from the door.

"You from these parts?"

"I'm Saturn-born, if that's what you mean."

"Know any good places to stay around here?" Kaminski asked. "You see, Gordian set us up in the same apartment complex Andover-Chen and Delacroix used, but it's...well..." The big man shrugged.

"A dump?"

"I was going to say 'shithole,' actually." Kaminski held up a hand. "No offense."

"None taken." Isaac sent him the address and contact string for the Top Shelf Hotel. "I think this one will be more to your liking."

"Thanks. I'd rather sleep on the ship than that other place."

"We'll send your requests back to Gordian right away," Philo said.

"And we'll make sure they're taken seriously," Kaminski added.

"Right," Philo said. "With luck, we should hear back from them in about three or four hours."

CHAPTER FIFTEEN

WITH THREE-PLUS HOURS TO PASS, ISAAC DECIDED TO HOLD A second interview with Melody Quang. Cephalie analyzed the previous interview and cross-checked it with the new evidence in their possession, but she didn't find any places where Quang outright lied. Despite her unethical behavior, Isaac couldn't charge her with any crimes that would stick in court.

At least, not yet.

Cephalie scheduled the meeting, and they met once more at the Trinh Syndicate factory an hour later.

"Nice to see you again, Detective, Agent," Quang said after everyone had settled into their seats in the same conference room as before. Isaac would have preferred to question her at the precinct, depriving her of the home turf advantage and any comfort that might bring her, but if Quang was involved, then an aggressive move like that would tip her off, and she'd clam up, invoking her legal rights to impede his investigation.

If Quang had used the Ōdachi alias to order the Fanged Wyverns around, then she knew her relationship with Delacroix *might* get out. The police raid on the gang hangout would be public knowledge. But she didn't *know* he knew, and that ambiguity might present an opening he could tease new information out of.

He would need to tread carefully.

"What brings you here today?" Quang asked. "Is everything going well?"

"I have a few follow-up questions I'd like you to answer."

"Of course. I'm at your service, though your IC was lucky to call when she did. I fly out to Titan in a few hours. Anyway, how can I help?"

"I'd like to start with the impeller remains the Trinh Syndicate purchased." Isaac checked his notes. "Did you ever speak with Delacroix about the impeller?"

"Yes."

He looked up, surprised by her direct answer. The temperature in the room seemed to drop a few degrees.

"Once or multiple times?" he continued.

"Multiple."

"Did you discuss the impeller's test results?"

"Yes."

"Did you discuss the sale of the impeller to Trinh?"

"Yes."

"Did you—"

"Detective, I appreciate you're trying to do your job," she began, her tone icier than before, "but why don't we get the obvious out of the way. Yes, Delacroix and I were in a sexual relationship." She spread her hands. "There you go."

Isaac watched his only advantage fly out the figurative window.

"You didn't mention that fact in our last meeting."

"You didn't ask."

"Not quite," Isaac countered. "I asked about the nature of your relationship with Delacroix, and you told me he was sad. I'd characterize that as a dodge."

"The important part is I never lied to you. It's not my fault you didn't follow up your original question." She smirked at him. "You're the detective here, not me."

"Then describe the nature of your relationship with Delacroix," Isaac said firmly. "In *very* clear words."

"We would occasionally meet up and have sex." She raised an eyebrow. "Clear enough for you, Detective? Or would you like me to describe his favorite positions?"

"Was he in love with you?"

"How should I know? I'm not a mind reader."

"Did he ever say he loved you?"

"Yes."

"Did you tell him you loved him?"

"Yes."

"Were you in love with him?"

"Not in the slightest."

Isaac frowned, but Quang simply smiled back at him.

"Did you tell Delacroix to fail the impeller?"

"No."

"Then it was his idea?"

"I would assume so. Again, not a mind reader."

"Do you know why he failed the impeller?"

"Not for certain."

"Why do you think he did it, then?"

"To impress me." Her eyes twinkled, and she flashed a half smile. "He was showing off. Demonstrating the power he held over one of our competitors. He knew we could use the exotic matter, so perhaps it was intended as a gift as well. *I* simply took advantage of the opportunity."

"And you saw no problems with that?"

"I saw no *legal* problems. The impeller did fail, and Delacroix's actions fell within the contractual arrangement between Negation and Gordian. Furthermore, he wasn't the senior member of Gordian on site, Andover-Chen was, and *he* could have overruled Delacroix." Quang leaned back and crossed her legs. "But he didn't."

"What about moral problems?" Susan asked, speaking up for the first time in the interview.

"What about them?"

"Delacroix had just lost his wife unexpectedly," Susan pressed. "One might assume he was in a vulnerable state."

"And did I take advantage of that vulnerability? Absolutely. But morality isn't your jurisdiction, is it? If I want to be lectured on morality and religion, I have colleagues who were once Numbers. *They'll* talk my ears off about it. *You two*, however, should only be concerned with the legality of what I did, and there is *nothing* illegal about any of this. I'm free to sleep with any consenting man I choose, and Delacroix was *very* consenting. Just as I'm free to take advantage of a competitor's misfortune, which is all the failed impeller amounts to."

Quang leaned back in her chair with a self-satisfied smirk.

"You should have come forth with this information in our first meeting," Isaac said. "The fact that you didn't casts a cloud of doubt over your actions."

"Oh, I'm sure it does." Her eyes laughed at him. "But do I look worried to you?"

"You will need to register any travel plans with SysPol for the foreseeable future."

"As I said, I'm flying out to Titan later today. I'll be staying in Promise City for a few days' worth of meetings, then I'm coming straight back here. Will that suffice, or do I need to fill out some tedious forms?"

"That's sufficient."

"And is there anything else you're curious about, Detective?" Quang tilted her head. "Or would you like to hear about those positions?"

"Do you know anything about the murders you're not telling me?"

"No, Detective. Still don't have a clue who might have done it. Best of luck to you, there. I think you're going to need it."

Isaac paused in thought, trying to come up with a new line of questioning. Despite how forthright she now appeared, he suspected he wasn't receiving the full story, but however hard he looked, he couldn't find a crack in her armor. He'd been outplayed by the Trinh Syndicate manager in a game whose rules he didn't fully understand, and there was nothing he could do about it but retreat and explore other avenues of investigation.

"That will be all for now," he said at last.

"Good. Then I believe we're done here."

✧   ✧   ✧

"Komuso, thank you for coming," Isaac said, rising from his seat in the NFPD conference room to greet the AC.

"Don't mention it, Detective. And please, there's no need to stand."

Komuso's avatar wore a long, pale gray robe and what resembled a straw basket over his head. The basket came with a thinner weave across a square at the front, and a pair of green eyes glowed within the shadowed recesses. Isaac wondered if the AC had even bothered to model a head underneath the basket.

Komuso waited for Isaac and Susan to sit back down, then he conjured a plain wooden chair and seated himself, hands folded in his lap.

"I appreciate you transmitting in on such short notice," Isaac said.

"To be honest, I'm still in shock over the news. Breaking up with Joachim was hard enough, but now *this*." He shook his basket head, eyes dimming. "If there's anything I can do to help. *Anything* at all, I'll aid you without hesitation. Please understand, Detective, I want his murderer brought to justice. I want this very much."

"Let's start with some basic questions," Isaac began. "How long were you and Delacroix integrated?"

"Twenty-eight years. We met at his grandmother's going meat-less party when he was in his early twenties and stayed in touch."

"Who initiated the integration?"

"He did, though I welcomed the invitation. We both saw how compatible we were, and it turned out we were right."

"And what was your level of integration?"

"Low. Only sharing surface thoughts." Komuso raised a hand. "Except for a brief period in his forties. From October 2967 to February 2968. We experimented with a deeper level of integration, but neither of us liked it, and we fell back to our previous arrangement."

"Tell me about the accident that forced Delacroix into a synthetic body."

"I don't think I'm qualified to discuss the accident itself, but the emotional toll on Joachim was high." Komuso lowered his head. "He wasn't prepared for the transition and, as is sometimes the case, he began to question the nature of his own existence."

"Physical Separation Syndrome?" Isaac asked.

"Yes. Doctors prescribed a regimen including a synthoid set to maximum fidelity, which he followed, but the real healing came from Selene. I like to think I did my part, but Selene was the rock he leaned against in moments of weakness."

"How did Delacroix react to the death of his wife?"

"Poorly. He was on Mycene Station, assisting Doctor Andover-Chen with the c-bomb construction, when the Dynasty attacked the factory cluster. He clung to an irrational hope that search parties would eventually find her, despite the nuclear attack on the factory. I tried to explain to him how infinitesimal her chances were, but he wouldn't listen.

"In time, he did finally accept her death, though it took weeks. Or, I should say, accepted that she was dead. Selene was . . . she and Joachim connected in a way he and I never did. I've never had much of an interest in science, but the two of them as fellow engineers, well . . . they were meant for each other. They shared the same interests, the same passions. I'm hesitant to throw out concepts like fate, but for them, I'll make an exception. They were fated for each other. In a small way, I was jealous of the love they shared. Even after two centuries, I still don't understand human love as well as I'd like."

"What led to your separation from Delacroix?"

"I don't know, to be honest. Selene's death played a part, obviously. Joachim became increasingly distant after her death. I tried to help, but he rebuffed my efforts. Pushed me further and further away. I even suggested we lower our integration level as a means to save our friendship. Drop it to the point where we only shared thoughts when both of us gave active permission, but even that didn't help."

"Why not?"

"Joachim wanted to be alone. *That* much was clear. I didn't think the solitude would be healthy for him. I wanted to help, but I also wasn't about to defy his wishes, not after so many good years together. We separated on agreeable—if sad—terms, and I always made sure he knew where to find me. I left Earth after that. I needed the space and spent the time with some old friends living over Venus. That's where I was when I received word of his death, and I transmitted to Saturn immediately afterward."

"Did Delacroix ever contact you after you separated?"

"No." Komuso sighed. "I wish he had, though."

"Did he ever mention Melody Quang to you?"

"No, sorry. The name's not familiar to me."

"Did he discuss the impeller construction at Negation Industries with you?"

"No, but that's not unusual."

"Why not?"

"We rarely talked shop. That was always him and Selene, and I would politely leave them to it. They *loved* to get technical with each other, often spending the night debating the merits of one approach or another, delving into all manner of esoteric details before . . ."

"Before what?"

"Before their dialogue became . . . flirty."

"Ah."

"They both found smart to be sexy, and I'd slip out whenever the double entendres started showing up." Komuso shrugged. "Organics and their glands. What can you do about them?"

"Do you know of anyone who wanted either Delacroix or Andover-Chen killed or any reasons why someone might benefit from their deaths?"

"No, sorry. Wish I did, though." Komuso adjusted the basket over his head. "Feels like I haven't been much help."

Isaac glanced to Susan, who shook her head to indicate she didn't have any questions.

"Thank you for your time, Komuso. That'll be all for now. We'll be in touch if we need anything in the future."

Andover-Chen arrived in the Saturn State almost an hour before Komuso, but his connectome transmitted only as far as Kronos Station. The scientist had been unwilling to transmit directly to Janus-Epimetheus, so a SysPol corvette flew him down to the New Frontier Airport, and the delay placed his interview last in Isaac's schedule.

The short synthoid stepped into the NFPD conference room, snug in a Gordian Division uniform while ghostly equations shifted under the black, glassy skin of his face. He struck Isaac as a man of competing emotions: on one hand, he strode in with the confidence of one used to commanding the respect of those around him, and on the other hand, Isaac saw hints of timidity in a man trying to piece his shattered life back together.

"Doctor Andover-Chen, thank you for coming," Isaac said. "I'm Detective Isaac Cho. This is Agent Susan Cantrell, my deputy, and Encephalon, my IC. Please, if you'll be seated, we can get started and hopefully not take up too much of your time."

"What a difference six months can make." Andover-Chen grinned at Susan as he pulled out his chair and sat down. "Glad to see we're not at each other's throats."

"We're making progress," Susan agreed.

"You know, I took an immediate liking to the Admin. From the moment I learned of its existence, I could see the advantages of its stricter laws. Your 'Restrictions.' Oh, certainly, Admin culture is rough around the edges here or there; that's to be expected of any society still pushing through the painful transition to post-scarcity. But the underlying principles—the *cautionary* approaches to new technology—*those* I find greatly appealing."

"Thank you, Doctor," Susan replied. "We think the Restrictions are a smart approach, too." She paused in thought, then added, "Or most of us do."

"Doctor, if you don't mind," Isaac said, "shall we begin?"

"Yes. Of course, of course." Andover-Chen sat straight, leaning back against the chairback as confidence eclipsed those subtle hints of a shattered life.

"First, a few baseline questions given your integration level and recent time loss. Would you please identify both connectomes for the record as well as your current integration level?"

"Certainly. I'm composed of the connectomes for both Matthew Andover and Chen Wang-shu, and I'm a total integration of the two."

"And do you prefer to be referenced in the singular or plural?"

"Singular, please. And that's true legally as well. My former selves jumped through all the necessary hurdles to be legally recognized as a new, singular entity. You're probably aware of this, but I was revived from a single, consolidated connectome with First MindBank, and my death, also, was categorized in the singular." He leaned back. "So, yes. Singular, it is, if you don't mind."

"Describe for us why you chose to integrate."

"That's easy. My two minds cover for each other."

"Could you elaborate?"

"Certainly. Both of us were hired by the Gordian Division shortly after it was formed, and we began working together for the first time in our careers. We knew of each other's work, of course, and we knew we held similar views on the dangers of time travel. But we'd never collaborated in a professional capacity until we joined Gordian. How to describe the feeling." Andover-Chen rubbed his chin. "Ah! Yes, of course! Both of us had ... gaps."

"Gaps?"

"Weaknesses in our mental tool kits, you might say. For example, Chen was the true powerhouse when it came to theoretical work, while being a little ... scatterbrained? Too easily distracted? Andover, meanwhile, could brute-force his way through just about any problem. But that special spark, that leap of ingenuity Chen could make on a whim, had always eluded him.

"Separate, both were very good at our jobs. *We* saw the problems with time travel before anyone else did, and we tried to warn everyone. Oh, we tried!" He shook his head sadly. "But those earlier efforts were divided. At Gordian, we saw the synergy, and experimented with a low-level integration. The results were astounding!

"Separate, we were good. Together, I was brilliant! We increased the level of our integration step by step until Andover proposed to Chen a full, unbridled integration." The doctor spread his hands. "The rest is history."

"And you feel your integration has been successful?"

"Absolutely! Just look at what we achieved during the Dynasty Crisis!" A crack formed in Andover-Chen's mask of confidence, and he frowned. "At least, so I've been told. It's strange. You wake up one morning, and suddenly there's half a year's worth of actions and repercussions you don't remember. It's uncomfortable hearing about exploits I never partook in, especially when they involve the creation of a universe-obliterating superweapon."

"Does your involvement with the c-bomb bother you?"

"I'd be lying if I said it didn't. Seems to go against everything I've stood for in the past." He straightened in his seat. "But, as I understand it, we wouldn't be having this conversation if the Gordian Division had failed. I'm sure my other self realized this as well, and I'll take solace in that. Though . . . I could have done without the jokes."

"The jokes?"

"Yes." The scientist grimaced. "Gordian Division and their time travel jokes. I received a few messages that said 'Welcome to the Future!' after I was revived. I didn't find them funny."

"Moving on to your colleague, Chief Engineer Joachim Delacroix," Isaac began. "You recommended him for the post, correct?"

"Yes, that's right."

"Why was that?"

"Because while I have *some* engineering acumen, I'm most definitely *not* an engineer. My specialty is more on the theoretical side. Taking those theories and realizing them into physical hardware requires a different approach, a different mindset. That's where Joachim came into the picture. Though"—he shrugged—"sounds like I branched out with my work on the c-bomb."

"Why did you select him?"

"Because of his experience at the Antiquities Rescue Trust, TTV impeller enhancements in particular." Andover-Chen held up both hands. "Now, don't get me wrong. I'm no fan of ART, and my public record shows that clearly. But I know a talented mind when I see one. When I made the recommendation, Gordian Division was on the cusp of taking ownership of just about *every* time machine in SysGov, and we had to modify *all* of their impellers for transdimensional flight. That's no easy task, but I felt Delacroix was the right man to lead that effort."

"And was he?"

"According to my notes, yes."

"Your notes?" Isaac perked up at the mention.

"Yes, I'm a stickler for writing notes during or after any meeting I'm in." Andover-Chen smiled sadly. "Turned out to be a good thing in multiple ways, since I've been reading through my own personal record for the past six months. Anyway, you'd be surprised how fallible our minds are and how a written record of what was said and agreed to can save so much time and wasted energy."

"Then, you have notes from your most recent meetings with Delacroix?"

"I don't see why I wouldn't."

"Do we have copies already?" Isaac turned to Cephalie.

"Don't think so," Cephalie said. "They must not have been stored at his desks or the apartment."

"Not surprising," Andover-Chen said. "I would have kept them locally."

"I'd like a copy of those records," Isaac said. "If you don't mind."

"*I* don't have a problem with that, but I think some of my notes on the c-bomb are still classified."

"I'm only interested in any notes that pertain to the impellers being constructed on Janus or conversations you had with Delacroix, at least at the moment. If it turns out I require additional access, access that might be restricted, I'll submit an official request to Gordian. Does that work for you?"

"It does." Andover-Chen opened an interface with a long file list and began entering filter parameters.

"There's no need to provide the files now."

"No, no. This'll only take a moment." His fingers flew over the interface, but then paused. "Hmm? What's this?"

"Something unusual?"

"Not really." The physicist frowned at the screen. "It's a conversation I had with Joachim during our last trip to Janus. We were having a few beers after work. Normally, I wouldn't take notes on that."

"Can you tell why you made an exception in this case?"

"Let me see." He expanded the record. "Ah, there it is. We were talking about temporal replication. That's why I took notes."

"Temporal replication?" Isaac asked, and thought for a moment. "That would be the replication process outlawed by the Valkyrie Protocol, correct?"

"That's right. 'Temporal replication' refers to any method where a time machine travels to the past, grabs something, and brings it back to the True Present, essentially replicating that object. ART did quite a lot of that in the form of the antiquities and historical figures it brought to the True Present, although all of ART's efforts together were *nothing* compared to the Dynasty's! *They* used the same method as the primary engine of their post-scarcity society, and at face value it might seem like a good idea. However!" Andover-Chen raised a stern finger. "The process is not without cost, and it's the outer wall of our universe that pays it."

"What do you mean?" Isaac asked.

"The atoms of both the replicated object and the original resonate, and this resonance can damage the outer wall of a universe."

"Outer wall?"

"The barrier between our universe's 3+1 dimensional parameters and the 6+1 dimensions of the transverse. The barrier between our reality and the connecting fabric of the wider multiverse."

Isaac felt his brain congealing.

"You see, the resonance impacts upon that transdimensional membrane between a universe and the transverse. And with enough damage"—Andover-Chen made an exploding gesture with both hands—"the wall breaches."

"Doctor."

"When that happens, the barrier between two different levels of chronometric energy is gone. It's like a balloon bursting. Pressure will equalize, either by inrushing from the transverse into the universe, resulting in the implosive destruction of said universe, or expelling outward at a catastrophic rate, resulting in the *explosive* end of that universe."

"Doctor?"

"That's why the Dynasty imploded. Chronometric energy rushed in through the breach caused by the c-bomb, and this inflicted a phase state upon normally inert matter. Inert in a *temporal* sense, that is. In essence, their present flew back into their past, and the universe's timeline itself imploded inward."

"Doctor Andover-Chen?"

"Hmm? Yes? Am I going too fast?" He smiled brightly. "I sometimes have a habit of doing that. I can slow down you if like."

"That won't be necessary," Isaac said. "I'm more interested in why Delacroix would raise this topic with you. Do your notes mention why?"

"Let's see." Andover-Chen skimmed down the record. "Not really. He had a lot of questions for me, though. Wanted my opinion on a few matters."

"Such as?"

"He asked me if I ever thought limited temporal replication would be safe in our universe again."

"But it's outlawed because it's so dangerous," Susan said.

"Well, yes and no," Andover-Chen explained. "Before the Dynasty Crisis, the SysGov outer wall was in prime health. As I said, ART had replicated a few famous people and artifacts but never approached anything on the scale of the Dynasty. Under those conditions, some *limited* and *regulated* replication might be beneficial for our society to explore. For the moment, the process had been completely prohibited. That was before we made the c-bomb, however, and with the fate of our whole universe hanging in the balance, we took some risks."

"What sort of risks?"

"I..." Andover-Chen hesitated.

"Classified?"

"Let's just say the Gordian Division was up against the clock and used temporal replication to cheat our way to the finish line. I think that's what inspired Joachim to think about how the prohibition might ultimately be modified. But we did more damage in a few hours to our outer wall than the Dynasty did to theirs in *decades*. And that's the state the outer wall of our universe is in. Bruised. Bleeding. Throbbing. Not fatally; it'll heal with time, but we *need* to give it that time, and that's why the Valkyrie Protocol is so important."

"Is that the answer you gave Delacroix?"

"More or less. According to my notes, our discussion dug into the details a bit more, but the fundamentals are the same. The SysGov outer wall has a long way to go before we should even *think* about replication again."

"Do you know why Delacroix would ask you about this?"

"My notes don't give a reason, sorry. But I don't think his question is unusual."

"Why not?"

"Because it was his role to ask those sorts of questions. As an engineer, you see. 'Where are the limits?' and 'Should we push up against them?' Just like it's my role in Gordian to throw up the big warning sign when I see danger ahead."

"Then you don't see anything unusual in your notes regarding Delacroix?"

"Not at the moment. Let me take a closer look."

✧   ✧   ✧

Isaac and Susan spent over two hours with Andover-Chen going through his notes on Delacroix, and every last one of them ended with the doctor declaring the engineer's behavior normal and appropriate. He even defended Delacroix's decision to take a strict stance on the failed impeller, stating it fell under his authority as chief engineer, even if Andover-Chen didn't fully agree with the decision.

"Have we accomplished anything today?" Susan asked as they walked out to their car.

"If we did, I missed it," Isaac grumbled. The car door opened, and he dropped into his seat.

Susan sat down opposite him, and the door closed.

"Top Shelf Hotel," Isaac ordered.

"Destination set. Departing."

The car drove out of the NFPD parking lot and merged onto the main Shelf One highway.

"We learned Delacroix was in a dumb relationship," Susan offered.

"Which he was allowed to be in."

"And he made a dumb decision about the impeller."

"Which he was allowed to make."

"And he asked the doctor some questions about the newest time travel law."

"Which were perfectly normal for him to ask."

"Yeah." Susan crossed her arms and stared at the floor. "It's been one of those days, huh?"

"Yup."

Isaac glanced out the window and watched the detritus of New Frontier's lowest layer pass by.

"Oh, I-*saac*?" Cephalie asked in a singsong voice.

"Yeah?"

"I have something that might cheer you up."

He turned back to the small woman standing atop the LENS. "I'm listening."

"Check your mail. You have a message from Kronos."

Isaac gave her a dubious look, but he opened his mail regardless. He checked the title on the newest message and perked up immediately.

"Something good?" Susan asked.

"Possibly." He forwarded a copy to her. "We have an update from the Ballast Heights forensic report."

"Better than the nothing we have right now."

"Too true." He opened the report and read the abstract. "And they have a vector for the virus!"

"*Much* better than nothing," Susan said with a smile.

"Vector is a traveling artist named Neon Caravaggio," Isaac continued.

"Neon?" Susan blinked. "What, as in the noble gas? Are his parents Argon and Xenon? Does he have a little sister named Helium?"

"I know you're joking," Isaac said, "but you could be more right than you know. Caravaggio's registered as a Lunarian, and some of them have *very* loose ideas for what qualifies as a name. Says here he transmitted out to Titan and then almost immediately transmitted back to Ballast Heights, both shortly before the murders. The forensics team found evidence of the virus in both of his passes through the LifeBeam tower."

"That could be deliberate," Susan said. "A quick back-and-forth trip would give him two chances to infect the transceiver."

"Right." Isaac highlighted a note in the report. "Though, there's a warning here from the forensics team. They don't know if Caravaggio was the *origin* of the virus or simply a *carrier*. But you do raise a good point. If he was trying to deploy it, his travel schedule made that easier."

"What's this part about forwarding the report to LifeBeam?" Susan asked.

"Standard SysPol procedure to help the company plug their security hole. They need to check with us first before forwarding it." Isaac clicked the authorization box. "There. No reason to hold out, since the 'Internal LifeBeam' angle is dead."

"But how could a virus on a passenger affect the LifeBeam hardware?" Susan asked. "You'd think they'd have safeguards in place against something like that."

"You're right. The report should tell us how it slipped through." He scrolled down to the analysis of the virus. "Normally, a firewall prevents clients from accessing LifeBeam's internal infostructure. However, some LifeBeam employees have access to administrative holes in the firewall. The virus jumped from Caravaggio to one employee after another until it found someone with the access it needed. Very sophisticated. And *very* illegal."

"How illegal?" Susan asked.

"Just *writing* a virus like this could result in the death penalty, never mind *using* it." He glanced to Cephalie. "Wouldn't you agree?"

"Maybe. Depends on the judge and jury."

"Do we know where Caravaggio is?" Susan asked.

"I'm looking for that part right now." He tabbed over. "Hmm. Whereabouts unknown after returning to Ballast Heights."

"Suspicious."

"Quite. Public transportation records show he traveled to the Crystal Falls apartment complex. According to his government file, that's where he lives, but there's nothing after that. The forensics team sent SSP to Caravaggio's apartment, but no one was home. He also didn't respond to any of their calls."

"Then he's gone dark?" Susan speculated.

"Seems that way. I get the impression our colleagues on Kronos didn't believe he was the origin and wanted to examine his synthoid for more clues. But his activities since paint a different picture. Twice through the tower, and then he vanishes from his apartment and doesn't respond to calls."

"Sounds like we've got ourselves a lead," Susan said with a smile.

"We do indeed." He returned the smile then glanced to his IC. "Cephalie, get us a search warrant of Caravaggio's home and a pair of train tickets. We're heading back to Ballast Heights."

"On it!"

CHAPTER SIXTEEN

ISAAC CLIMBED OUT OF THEIR CAR AND SURVEYED THE CRYSTAL Falls apartment complex, which inhabited the midsection of a teardrop-shaped tower near the leading edge of Ballast Heights. Clear triple-layered walls held the frigid Saturn atmosphere at bay, and seven white apartment buildings formed a ring within a lush parkland with a lake at its center. The buildings all rose up to meet and support the tower's upper reaches, which formed a metal sky fifteen stories above, and a waterfall poured down from the ceiling into the central lake.

"Swanky," Susan said.

"Mmhmm." Isaac rubbed the sleep from his eyes. He'd grabbed a few extra winks during the train ride up, but he didn't feel fully awake yet.

The LENS floated out of the car and hovered to his side.

"I've cleared us with the apartment staff," Cephalie reported. "They were kind enough to provide his keycode without complaint. Caravaggio lives in Building 3, Floor 2B."

"How many apartments per level?" Susan asked.

"Three."

"He has a whole third of a floor to himself?" Susan asked. "Damn. Guy must be a big deal somewhere."

Night had fallen outside, but Ballast Heights refused to yield to the rhythm of Saturn's ten-hour-and-forty-two-minute days, and the city glowed with activity outside the tower's thick, transparent walls.

"Let's see what we find."

Isaac led the way into Building 3 and took the counter-grav shaft up a level to a circular waiting area with three doors. He palmed open the one marked 2B and walked in. A short corridor with black walls and a white floor and ceiling ended in a junction with an abstract diorama.

Isaac stepped up to the diorama, hands clasped behind his back. A party of adventurers atop an open-deck airship fought against a dragon in an endless animated loop. Little flickers of arcane light flew across the diorama, and the dragon drew in a deep breath and bellowed fire.

"Caravaggio's art?" Susan asked.

"I would assume so." Isaac turned to the LENS. "Cephalie, search the infostructure. Susan, with me. We'll look around, room by room."

He took a left and followed the hall down to a large master bedroom. A small bed with black-and-white-striped sheets sat in the corner of an otherwise empty living space with a pair of storage caskets built into the far wall.

Isaac palmed the first casket open, found it empty, then palmed the second open.

A bald synthoid rested back in the casket at a slight angle. His skin was powder white, his open eyes were black from end to end, and he wore black lipstick. His black suit sported a line of white faux buttons down the front, and a white streamer ran down from a white sash across his waist.

Isaac snapped his fingers in front of the synthoid, but he didn't react.

"Caravaggio?" Susan asked.

"Maybe. Cephalie?"

"Synthoid's empty."

Isaac glanced to the bed, then back to the empty casket next to Caravaggio's inert synthoid.

"Something on your mind?" Susan asked.

"The bed's too small for two people, but he has two synthoid caskets."

"And one's empty."

"Yeah." Isaac looked into the synthoid's eyes. The empty husk stared blankly at the far wall. He grimaced and palmed the casket shut. "Let's keep looking."

The bedroom led to a wide studio with abstract art lining the walls. Real lights turned on and an abstract workspace activated around what appeared to be an incomplete sketch. Isaac recognized a few characters and locations from games like *Solar Descent* and *Sky Pirates of Venus*, though combined or repurposed in ways not found in the originals, such as a buxom sky pirate in star seer armor from *Solar Descent* or a cyber-lich and his necro-drones dressed as pirates.

They circled around to a spotless dining area with a black glass table.

And only one chair.

Isaac rested a hand on the chairback and pulled it out.

"Hmm." He walked over to the food printer, opened its menu, and found it chock full of expensive, luxury patterns.

"I take it those aren't public domain?" Susan asked.

"Nope." Isaac closed the menu and looked back at the table. "He spent a lot of Esteem stocking this printer, but what kind of guy only prints one chair out?"

"An aloof artist?" Susan suggested.

"Then why the two caskets?"

"Do people keep spares in SysGov? Or swap bodies? Sort of like me and my combat frame?"

Isaac gave her a cross look.

"Minus the weapons, I mean," she added quickly.

"Sometimes, though they're *supposed* to be registered, and I didn't see two bodies on Caravaggio's file. Cephalie?"

"You rang?" The LENS floated into the dining room.

"I'm getting the impression this guy has an unregistered second body."

"You could be right. I'm seeing hints of a second ID in use, though I'm not sure who it's for."

"Why not?"

"Because I'm up to my eyeballs in hostile encryption. I've only been able to touch the infostructure's periphery."

"Come across any illegal software?"

"Not yet. I'd guess the encryption comes from a Stalwart'n' Steadfast home defense package. Expensive, but perfectly legit. I can crack it, but it'll take some time."

"Focus on that second ID. See if you can pull a name."

"Give me a moment. That shouldn't be too hard to grab."

"And if Caravaggio does have an unregistered synthoid?" Susan asked.

"Then he may also have a fake ID for it," Isaac said.

"Done," Cephalie said. "Got a name for you."

"And?"

"Second ID belongs to Grunt-Zero."

"That sounds like a Numbers name," Susan said.

"It does," Isaac agreed. "Run it through the SSP database."

"Checking . . . and we have a match. Grunt-Zero, former member of the Numbers. Real name is Douglas Chowder. Saturnite."

"Not Lunarian?" Isaac asked.

"Not according to SSP. Says he was born in the Howling Bow. How about that? He could be an old friend of yours. Right, Isaac?"

"Doubt it," he replied gruffly. "What else?"

"Doug Chowder, aka Grunt-Zero, has had multiple run-ins with the law. Several counts of pattern theft, illegal replication and sale, and a few assault charges related to gang violence. All while underaged. He spent some time in a panopticosm for those."

"And afterwards?"

"Oh, you'll love this," Cephalie declared. "The Trinh Syndicate hired him."

"You're kidding!" Isaac exclaimed.

"Another connection," Susan said.

"Yeah." Isaac scratched his chin. "I wasn't expecting this. Anything else?"

"Nope. Chowder has led a law-abiding life since hiring on with Trinh."

"And, let me guess." Isaac crossed his arms. "Chowder transitioned shortly after leaving prison, and Caravaggio starts making public appearances around the same time."

"Hey, no fair," Cephalie pouted. "You beat me to it."

"Then Trinh may have set up his 'artist' identity," Isaac said.

"If they did, you know how this'll go down," Cephalie said. "They'll have an excuse on hand for why the alias isn't properly connected to the original. At worst, they'd get a slap on the wrist."

"Maybe so," Isaac said with a grin, "but this is the best lead we've found so far, and we're going to tug it hard! It looks like Caravaggio has switched to his original ID and gone dark. We need to mobilize SSP to hunt him down, but we also need to get a dedicated forensics team in here to tear his home's infostructure apart, bit by bit. And then—"

The front door chimed and split open.

Isaac and Susan glanced to each other.

"SSP?" she whispered.

"No," he whispered back. "We're the only ones who should be here."

Susan's eyes narrowed with intense focus.

"Stay put!" She drew her sidearm and headed for the front door.

"Wait!" Isaac hissed under his breath.

Susan zipped around the corner with synthoid-enhanced speed, and Isaac hurried after her. He rounded the same corner, but Susan pressed a hand to his chest and held him back. He tried to push through, but her arm wouldn't budge.

"Stay back!" she whispered. "I'll handle this!"

"But—"

She swung out into the open and aimed her anti-synthoid hand cannon over the diorama near the entrance. A shadowed figure dressed all in black emerged from the short hallway.

"Freeze! Police!" Susan shouted, pinging everyone nearby with her virtual badge.

"Ack!" The man backed up against the wall. He held a thick, dark bundle in his hands. "Who are—"

"Drop the weapon!"

"But I don't—"

"Drop it or I will *end* you!"

"Eep!" He let go of the bundle, and it fell to the floor in a heap.

"Back away!" Susan ordered, advancing on the suspect. "Back away, I said! Hands where I can see them!"

The man raised both hands and backed away.

"Please don't shoot!" he begged.

Susan made her way to the pile and poked it with her foot.

"What the hell is this crap?" she demanded.

"It's—"

"You be quiet!" she snapped. "Cephalie, can you tell what the hell he was packing?"

"Sure thing." The LENS floated out behind her, descended to the dark pile on the floor, and extended a lone pseudopod. It lifted a cloth flap and peered inside.

"Well?" Susan asked, never taking her eyes or pistol off the suspect. "What kind of weapon is it?"

"It's a pile of shirts."

✧   ✧   ✧

The tea saucer shook in Doug Chowder's trembling hands. He sank into the dining room table's lone chair, raised the shuddering teacup to his mouth, and took a loud, slurping sip. The bundle of shirts sat in an unruly pile on the table, and Susan stood near the wall, frowning at the floor.

"Mister Caravaggio," Isaac said.

"Please. Call me Doug," the man replied, looking up with dark eyes. His features resembled the Caravaggio synthoid with a bald head and a somewhat lumpy physique. "I only use my professional alias while in public."

"Mister Chowder," Isaac said.

Doug cringed with a sour expression. He raised the shaking teacup, took another sip, then set it down. Spilt tea pooled in the saucer.

"I'm sorry for what just happened," Isaac continued, "but both SysPol and SSP attempted to contact you earlier regarding an ongoing investigation, and when you failed to respond to calls and couldn't be located, we came to search your apartment."

"I see," Doug muttered sadly. "I'm sure someone somewhere thinks this is funny. I have anxiety problems on good days, you see. Even had my connectome modified to reduce my stress level. Didn't work out." He made a vague painting gesture. "My art became mediocre, so I had the edit removed. Wish I'd kept it, at least as a toggle. Would have made her shoving a gun in my face a little easier to bear."

"Mister Chowder, I'm sorry my deputy shoved a gun in your face"—behind Isaac, Susan drooped her head even lower—"but we're here on official business, and I have several questions I need to ask you."

"I'm sorry," Doug groaned.

"What for?"

"I don't know. There are cops in my home. Whatever's going on is serious enough for her to point a gun at me. I figure apologizing is a good place to start." He looked up at Isaac with mournful eyes. "Did it help?"

"I suppose it hasn't hurt any," Isaac said guardedly.

"Am I going back to jail?"

"That remains to be seen."

"Well, I told him it was a bad idea." Doug shook his head. "But, no. He wouldn't listen."

"He?" Isaac asked.

"My manager at the Trinh Syndicate. Gordon Russo. He kept telling me no one'll buy art from *Doug Chowder*. He pushed me to develop an artist persona, and I came up with Neon Caravaggio, eccentric Lunarian artiste." He flourished his hand haughtily. "Russo said he could work with that, and he set up my alias."

"And?" Isaac urged.

"Trinh handles all my marketing, and they take thirty percent of my profits as compensation. It didn't work out too badly, I suppose. Except for the legal gray area." Doug smiled sadly. "Sorry about that, but Russo insisted. Can you imagine how people would laugh if they found out Caravaggio was actually some loser named Doug Chowder? I mean seriously! What were my parents thinking?

"And that's not the only time I've had bad luck with names. The main reason I joined the Numbers was for the gang name. Well, that and me bowing to peer pressure. Anyway, I thought it'd be a cool replacement for 'Doug Chowder.' I was *so* excited at the time. And do you know what happened? My turn with the deacon comes, and he rolls a zero. A *zero!*" Doug rested his chin in both hands. "I didn't even know that was possible! Obviously, I used my reroll, knowing I would have to live with the second result. And you know what that toss came up as?"

"Another zero," Isaac said dryly.

"Another [BLEEP]ing zero! When I saw it, I let out this long grumble, so you know what the deacon did? He dubbed me 'Grunt-Zero' right then and there!" Doug took a deep, shuddering breath. "I hate my life."

Isaac paused and regarded the man curiously.

"Did you just censor yourself?"

"Yeah. Sorry about that." He took another sip of tea, his hands somewhat steady now. "My girlfriend hates it when I swear, so I edited my speech to make her happy. This way, 'mother[BLEEP]ing [BLEEP] humpers' comes out like that. It's automatic, and it makes her laugh. I can turn it off if it bothers you."

"That won't be necessary."

Isaac felt off-balance questioning Doug Chowder. He'd been truly excited at what they'd found in the apartment, like a bloodhound sniffing out the trail, but now that he saw the man and heard useless information spill from his mouth, he sensed this lead transforming into another dead end.

"Mister Chowder, why isn't your alias properly registered?" Isaac asked.

"You mean how it has no official connection to 'Doug Chowder'?"

"Yes. That."

"I already told you. Who'd want to buy art from a loser like me? And if someone found out Neon Caravaggio was actually Doug Chowder, then the alias would lose its purpose." He gazed into his tea. "Honestly, I just did what Russo told me to do."

"After we're done here, we'll notify the Ministry of Citizen Services. They'll contact you to clear up this discrepancy."

"Will I go to jail?"

"For this? No, but there will likely be a fine."

"Oh. Okay, then." Doug let out a relieved sigh. "I guess that's not too bad. Perhaps I've worried about being found out too much. I have a habit of worrying unduly."

"However, there are other matters I'm far more interested in."

"Of course. Ask away."

"You're being awfully forthcoming."

"And why shouldn't I be?" Doug asked. "You're a SysPol detective. You'll get what you want out of me one way or another, even if I keep my mouth shut. There's no point in resisting; I learned that lesson when I was with the Numbers. Might as well just spill it all, save both of us the time and trouble. So, ask me anything."

"Very well. We'll start with your most recent trip. Why did you transmit down to Titan?"

"For AbyssCon. It's a small *Solar Descent*-themed convention in Promise City. The con chair asked me to judge the cosplay pageant."

"Then why did you leave Titan almost immediately?"

"Because AbyssCon can go [BLEEP] my [BLEEP]ing [BLEEP]!" Doug rose halfway out of his seat, then frowned as if realizing what he'd done. He sat back down and stirred his tea. "Uhh, I mean I had a disagreement with the con chair concerning my duties, which were *a lot* more than we initially agreed, and my compensation, which was *nothing* like what we agreed. In short, he was trying to take advantage of me and my brand, so I left."

"Both SysPol and SSP tried and failed to contact you afterwards."

"Yeah, sorry about that."

"Where were you and why didn't you respond?"

"I don't check my Caravaggio mail too often, and I was with my girlfriend Tomoe. Ito Tomoe." He looked up. "I suppose you'll want to confirm this?"

"Yes, we will."

"I figured." Doug sent them a contact string. "There you go. I needed to unwind after my aborted trip, so I spent some time with Tomoe. She's nice. Helps me recharge when I get down." He picked up one of the shirts. "She's not a fan of my work, though. I printed her some of my new artshirts, but she only kept one, just to be nice. That's why I came back with these. Honestly, it's less stressful that way. She doesn't pressure me to produce like other people do."

"I'd like your AbyssCon contacts as well."

"Sure thing." Doug sent them over. "There you go."

"We'll need to verify your story."

"I wouldn't expect anything else." He smoothed out one of the shirts. "My latest series has been doing quite well. I'm most well-known for my 'critical fail' posters as well as mixing elements from *Solar Descent*, *Sky Pirates of Venus*, *RealmBuilder*, and a few others, but I've tried a more traditional approach recently." He offered the shirt to Isaac. "Here."

"Here, what?"

"For you."

Isaac took the shirt tentatively. It featured Singularity, one of the abyssal gods of *Solar Descent*, checking his virtual schedule with a come-hither smirk. The caption read: WANNA BE THE EVENT ON MY HORIZON? The artwork winked at him.

He suppressed a strong desire to groan.

"And you, too." Doug picked up another shirt and unfurled it for Susan.

"Me?" she asked, pointing to herself.

"Sure. Here you go."

Susan took hold of a shirt featuring a voluptuous blue-skinned woman in a bodysuit, the front unzipped to reveal a *lot* of impressive cleavage. She levitated in a fiery, animated aura, with the words HOT DATE placed above her.

"Who is she?" Susan asked. She held the shirt up with the slightest hint of a smile on her lips.

"Natli Klynn," Isaac explained. "She's a prominent star seer in *Solar Descent* lore."

"Oh, are you a fan, too?" Doug's eyes lit up. "Did you hear the developers hinted they might kill her off this season? They mentioned it at their DescentCon Saturn panel. Were you at DescentCon this year?"

"No." Isaac tossed his shirt to the LENS, which caught it, folded it, and stashed it away in one fluid motion. The more Doug talked, the more Isaac felt like he was wasting his time with the man.

But perhaps I can still figure out where he contracted the virus, he thought.

"I can load some more images into your shirts, if you like," Doug offered. "I normally charge for that, but I'll make an exception for you two. Can I interest you in some critical fails? Or perhaps—"

"Mister Chowder," Isaac interrupted, "we still have a job to do."

"Right. Yes. Of course."

"Where were you before your trip to Titan?"

"DescentCon Saturn, obviously."

Isaac grimaced, sensing where this line of questioning was headed.

"And did you have a table in one of the artist halls?"

"Naturally. I'm such a regular nowadays, they set one up for me for free, and they always give me a great location. Lots of foot traffic."

"A high-traffic area," Isaac noted. "With thousands of people passing close by your table?"

"Oh, *tens* of thousands! Maybe even *hundreds* of thousands! The hall I was in was packed the whole time. There were so many people stuffed together, I had to call for an escort to my panels. I hear the con broke another attendance record this year."

"And did anyone know of your travel plans to Titan?"

"I would assume so. AbyssCon was advertising my appearance." Doug grumbled something under his breath, then said, "*Without* my permission."

Then literally anyone at the convention could have passed the virus to you, Isaac thought. *They knew where to find you, and they knew where you were going next and when.*

"Have you ever interacted with Melody Quang?"

"Who?"

"A junior manager at the Trinh Syndicate."

"No, I don't think so. Like I said, I deal almost exclusively with Gordon Russo."

"Have you ever been to New Frontier?"

"Where's that?"

"Bottom of the Shark Fin."

"No. I've been down as far as the Epimethean Divide, but that was *years* ago."

"Did anyone interact with you in a suspicious manner at DescentCon?"

"Suspicious, how? I deal with a lot of weirdos at these conventions."

"Someone trying to stay close to you. Perhaps to pass a virus to your synthoid."

"A virus!" he squeaked. "What sort of virus?"

"One that infected the LifeBeam tower and killed two police officers."

"*What?*" Doug's eyes grew wide with horror. "I was carrying around a virus that killed two cops? Is that why you're here?"

"It is."

"But that's *horrible!*" he cried. "Who would do such a thing?"

"That's what we're trying to find out."

"To think I was *used* to murder someone!" His eyes misted up. He grabbed the last shirt on the table and balled it up in his arms. "I'm *so* sorry! If there's anything I can do to help, I will!"

"I appreciate your cooperation, but unless—"

"Would you like another shirt?" He offered the garment.

"*No*," Isaac snapped.

"Okay." Doug cradled the shirt against his chest. "I suppose it's a rather lame way to apologize. I'm sorry."

"Again, did you witness any suspicious activity at the con?"

"No, none that I recall." Doug shook his head. "Nothing but the usual quirky customers one finds at conventions. Wish I can help, but..." He shrugged.

"Mister Chowder, you will need to notify SysPol of any travel plans while the investigation is underway. Furthermore, I advise you to contact Kronos Station and arrange for both your synthoids to be examined, for your safety as well as those around you."

"Yes, of course. I understand." Doug nodded. "I'll take care of that right away."

"Also, if you recall anything unusual from DescentCon, you're to contact me immediately." Isaac provided his contact string to the artist.

"I will. You can count on me, Detective!"

✧   ✧   ✧

"Well, *that* didn't go the way I expected," Isaac grumbled once they were back in the car.

"I'm sorry," Susan said, wringing her hands.

"As you *should* be. What were you—"

Susan's face tensed up, and her eyes moistened to the cusp of tears.

"Look." Isaac shook his head and let out a sigh. "Cephalie and I have handled violent people before. That's why we have the LENS, okay?"

"Okay," Susan replied softly.

"Your gun is a last resort. Please try to remember that."

"I know."

"That said..."

She raised her gaze.

"I couldn't help but notice how your first reaction was to shield me from danger." He gave her a slim smile. "Thanks."

"That's what STANDs do," she said, her eyes brightening.

"Yeah, I see that. Nervous artists beware."

She chuckled, but then cut herself off.

"I'll try harder from now on."

"I know you will." He turned to Cephalie's avatar next to the LENS. "Ask SSP to keep an eye on Mister Chowder, just in case."

"Will do."

"And contact the DescentCon staff. See if you can get security video that includes his table and panels."

"Do you really plan to hunt through the tens of *thousands* of possible suspects who could have given him the virus?"

"Only if we have no other choice," Isaac groused. "Until then, let's head back to New Frontier. Maybe there's something we missed. Vehicle, take us to the Pillar Station."

CHAPTER SEVENTEEN

"YOU TELL THAT LAZY BUM TO GET HIS PASTY ASS BACK TO TITAN or I'll sue!" Mei Hsi-mou, the chairman of AbyssCon, fumed over the comm window. "You hear me? I'll sue!"

"For the last time," Isaac seethed, "I do *not* represent Neon Caravaggio! I'm with SysPol Themis Division!"

Isaac's response took four seconds to cross the 1.2 million kilometers from Saturn to Titan, and Hsi-mou's reply took another four seconds on the return trip.

"Yeah, I heard you! And I don't give a shit! I'm a taxpaying citizen, you hear, which means you work for me!"

"No, I *don't*! I am *not* a civil servant, and even if I was, that's not how it works!"

"Then I'll sue both of you! Him for breach of contract, and you for not doing your damn job!"

"Mister Mei, on behalf of Themis Division, this conversation has been most informative, and I thank you for your time." Isaac closed the window before the irate chairman could say another word. He rested his head against the train cabin wall. "Good grief!"

"Well, you did confirm the AbyssCon story," Cephalie said. "There's that."

"But why'd he have to be so difficult?" He put his face in his hands and massaged his temples. "What a day!"

"At least I don't look like an electrified bumble bee," Susan chimed in brightly. "In that sense, today's been all right."

"Well, it doesn't *feel* that way," Isaac grumbled. "How'd your chats go?"

"Ito Tomoe checks out," Susan said. "No surprises."

"DescentCon hasn't gotten back to me," Cephalie said, "but I got in touch with Citizen Services and let them know about the Caravaggio alias. Trinh set up the ID, so they're the ones getting fined. Drop in the bucket for them, but poor nervous Doug's in the clear. His record's still spotless since leaving prison. Won't even get fined for this, though he'll have to deal with his 'secret identity' going public."

"I'm sure he'll manage somehow." Isaac eyeballed the Singularity shirt crumpled next to his seat. He snatched it up and rolled it into a cloth log. "What a day." He walked over to the cabin's reclamation chute and shoved the log in. It disappeared with a faint whirring sound.

"But..." Susan reached toward the shirt being mulched, then lowered her arm with a forlorn expression.

"Here." Isaac held out his hand. "Toss me yours."

"Do I have to?" She tucked her star seer shirt behind her back.

"You want to keep it?" Isaac asked.

"What's wrong with that?"

"Nothing, I guess. But why?"

"I like it."

"But it's just a silly sh—"

Cephalie jabbed her cane into his cheek. He hadn't noticed her climb up.

"Hey!" he exclaimed, rubbing his cheek out of reflex even though the pain was fake. "What was that for?"

"You're acting grouchy."

"I think I have a right to be." Isaac shooed her off his shoulder, and she floated back down to the LENS. He sat back down and gazed out the cabin window as the train descended past the Pillar Palaces.

"What's our next move?" Susan asked.

"Not sure," Isaac admitted, then let out a tired breath. "We should take a second look at the evidence, especially Delacroix's files on that tower. Maybe there's something we've missed."

"I can get started on that," Cephalie said. "But you"—she jabbed his thigh—"need to take care of yourself. You're hungry, and you get ornery when you're hungry."

"Do not," he said, a moment before his stomach growled.

Cephalie raised an accusing eyebrow.

"Okay, yes, you're right, I'm hungry. Let's talk about where we go next over some food." His stomach rumbled again.

"In the mood for anything in particular?" Cephalie asked.

"I could go for the Meal Spigot, actually." He turned to Susan. "You all right with that?"

"The meal what?"

They found the nearest Meal Spigot franchise outside the New Frontier train station on Shelf Six. A few cars and copters dotted the parking lot outside the squat, homey building, and a large abstract marquee animated overhead, featuring a cheerful man in coveralls working the lever on a waterspout. Pizza, burgers, noodles, beverages, ice cream, and all manner of other food poured out of the oversized nozzle to fizzle out above the open, inviting doors.

"The Meal Spigot," Susan said dully.

"Uh-huh," Isaac replied.

"Food any good?"

Cephalie shook her head.

"Oh, how would you know?" Isaac said.

"I've read the reviews."

"You can't trust those."

"Wanna bet?"

"It may not be fancy, but it's fast and filling," Isaac told Susan. "Personally, I love the food. There was a Meal Spigot near my parents' old apartment, so I grew up on this stuff."

"Are those SysPol drones?" Susan asked.

"Where?"

"Over there." She pointed to the parking lot where a pair of conveyor drones sat, heavy crates held tight in their flexible arms.

"Could be." His stomach grumbled. "Come on." He urged her inside with a hand on her shoulder. A hostess in a T-shirt and denim coveralls guided them to their booth, and Isaac opened the abstract menu and filtered through the selection. "I'm thinking pizza today. How about you?"

"I wouldn't mind a taste of whatever you're having," Susan said, dismissing her menu with a wave.

"All right, then."

A waitress in denim coveralls approached their booth.

"Hello everyone!" she said with a touch too much energy. "How are you— Oh! You're with SysPol!"

"We are."

"Are you here about the..." She nudged her head to the side twice.

"And what would"—Isaac mimicked her double head nudge— "be, exactly?"

"Oh, umm...never mind! My mistake!" She put on a forced smile. "My name's Melissa. Can I take your order?"

"Yes." Isaac traced through the menu with his finger. "I'll have a personal pizza with sausage and banana peppers. Oh, and an order of fried pickles. And a bottle of the Spigot's Tongue Melter, please."

"Very good, sir. Anything else?"

"No, that'll be all."

"And for you, ma'am?"

"Just an empty plate. I'll try some of his food."

"Got it!" She jotted their order down on her interface and transmitted it to the kitchen. "Your order"—her eyes flicked to the side and back to them, and she smiled once more—"should be up momentarily!"

Susan waited for her to leave.

"Are they always like that?"

"Like what?"

"Overly cheerful."

"Service with a smile," Isaac said. "I'll have to remember to give her a good tip."

"You know, I've been meaning to ask about the service here in SysGov."

"What about it?"

"I haven't seen much automation. Why does a place like the Meal Spigot need hosts and servers? In most places in the Admin, the food would be delivered by automation."

"Well, it's because of the Two Pillars," Isaac said, confused by her question.

"The what?"

"Don't they have the Two Pillars in the Admin?"

"I don't know. Maybe we call them by a different name."

"They're the cornerstone of our post-scarcity society. *Surely* you have them, too."

"Maybe not. Post-scarcity is still new to us. So, how do these Two Pillars work?"

"Basically, the Two Pillars are a guiding philosophy for how to be happy in a post-scarcity environment, where the need to struggle for necessities like food and shelter no longer exists. But humans with nothing to do, nothing to struggle against, aren't happy.

"Hence, the first Pillar is work. The pursuit of goals and the joy of achievement. Without something to struggle against and to strive for, life degrades into simply existing for the sake of existing. We view work as not only necessary for happiness, but also as a basic part of human dignity. That's one of the reasons why you see so many people gravitate to the service industries and why you don't see automation used in those industries as freely as it could be."

"Huh," Susan said. "Never thought of it that way. And the second Pillar?"

"Love, which many in SysGov pursue not only through conventional relationships, but also through integrated companionship."

"I hate to break it to you, Isaac," Cephalie tittered, "but I barely *like* you sometimes."

"I mean in a broad sense," he snipped back. "Love. Companionship. Fellowship. The basic need of humans to be with other humans. Or, at least, other sentient intelligences."

"The Two Pillars came about as a response to a period called the Great Depression in the late twenty-sixth century," Cephalie added. "It's a pretty dark time in SysGov history. That's when the post-scarcity effects of our technology really began to take hold, and a large percentage of the populace no longer performed any work at all. At the same time, high-fidelity abstractions gave people the chance to live out their lives completely free of normal human interactions, and both of these issues led to massive societal problems. Mass suicides, epidemic levels of depression, and rampant criminal activity, just to name a few highlights."

"Ouch." Susan grimaced. "Yeah, we don't have the Two Pillars."

"This explains so much," Isaac mumbled.

"Excuse me?"

"Nothing, nothing. We should really get back to business." He leaned against the booth's prog-foam. "Where do we go from here?"

"Not sure. What are you thinking?"

"We could interview more people from Gordian," Isaac suggested. "Maybe speak to the Negation Industries engineers who worked on that impeller. Perhaps interrogate those other three gangsters."

"Sounds like you're grasping."

"Because I am. There's also DescentCon and any surveillance video they might have of Caravaggio."

"That's going to be a long shot."

"I know, but if our leads dry up here, then that's all we have left."

"There may be a third option." Cephalie walked down the table between them and twirled her cane. "I ran through Delacroix's tower again and came across an interesting coincidence."

"A new lead?" Isaac asked.

"Not sure. I'll let you be the judge of that." She waved her arm, and a pair of reports appeared for Isaac and Susan. "First, the lead-up. Based on SSP's analysis of the Fanged Wyverns' wearables, Ōdachi contacted the gang through FR3G8, more commonly known as Free Gate. It's an abstract domain built on a *RealmBuilder* gaming seed. Now the coincidence. Delacroix has a *RealmBuilder* account."

"That's . . . rather tenuous," Isaac warned.

"Ah, but wait for it," Cephalie continued. "I scoured through Delacroix's files, and he's not much of a gamer. In fact, the *only* gaming account he used while on Janus was for *RealmBuilder*, and he acquired it two months ago. Furthermore, the login record on his tower shows he played *exclusively* on the Free Gate domain, and he was logged in shortly before he and Andover-Chen left for Earth at the end of their previous trip."

"Perhaps he was in touch with Ōdachi?" Susan said.

"Or, more specifically, whoever's behind that alias." Isaac rubbed his chin. "As far as leads go, it's a stretch, but I think it's the best one we have right now. Good work."

Cephalie took a bow.

"Okay, let's assume Delacroix was in touch with Ōdachi through Free Gate." Isaac leaned in with an elbow on the table. "How do we put this to use? Is Delacroix's *RealmBuilder* account still active?"

"Maybe," Cephalie said. "It might have been deactivated when his death certificate was posted. I'll have to check."

"Start there. We need to know what we're working with first. If Delacroix was using Free Gate to communicate with criminals, we could be on the verge of busting this case wide open."

His stomach growled again.

"I thought you said they were fast." Susan twisted in her booth and looked for their waitress.

"They normally are," Isaac said. "Maybe they're having problems."

"It's a *Meal Spigot*," Cephalie stressed. "It's having problems by merely existing."

"Oh, hush."

A spherical drone about the size of a LENS left the kitchen and floated out to the parking lot.

"Never a good sign," Isaac muttered.

"That drone looked familiar," Susan said. "Was it..."

Nina Cho ran out of the kitchen, two more drones behind her, and rushed over to her conveyor drones in the parking lot.

"Yep," Isaac finished. "It's one of Nina's."

"Sir?"

Isaac twisted around to face their waitress, only to find a gray-skinned, blue-eyed synthoid in coveralls beside her who he assumed was the manager.

"Sir, I'm very sorry!" the waitress said. "I tried printing your order four times, but this is the best I could manage."

Isaac peered at the tray held up by a floating remote the size of a fist. Steam rose from a cheese pizza covered in apple cubes and thin strips of apple, complete with tiny dark glyphs, and his fried pickle order appeared to be apple-based as well. He picked up the bottle of Tongue Melter, twisted the cap off, and sniffed.

"Apple juice," he breathed.

"I'm so sorry!" the waitress said. "At least this one has some bread and cheese! We tried our best, I swear!"

"Sir. Ma'am." The gray synthoid placed a hand to his chest. "On behalf of the Meal Spigot, I hope you'll accept our sincerest apologies. There is, unfortunately, nothing more we can do with your meal at the moment. One of your SysPol specialists just shut down all our printers, and we're not sure when she'll bring them back online."

"Oh well." Isaac shrugged. "I wouldn't worry too much about it."

"Sir?"

"Trust me. This isn't the worst problem we're dealing with." He grabbed a fried apple slice, bit into it, and chewed. "It's edible, and I'm hungry. You can leave the food here."

"Are you sure, sir?"

"Yeah, don't worry about it."

"Then, can I interest you in some virtual flavors to make your meal more...palatable?"

"Nah, it's fine." He sent both the waitress and manager larger-than-usual Esteem tips. "We live in apple-blighted times. It's all right."

The waitress looked to the manager, who nodded to her. She then served Isaac the corrupted pizza and fried "pickle" order. Isaac picked up an apple cube off the pizza and tried to tug it free of the cheese strands.

The waitress and manager walked off, and he overheard their quiet conversation.

"It's nice, you know, every now and again," the manager told the waitress.

"What is?"

"To get someone who doesn't scream at us over every little misprint."

"I know what you mean. I feel like I met a unicorn."

"Aww," Susan cooed. "That was nice of you."

"Mmhmm." He put the cheese-coated apple slice in his mouth and chewed slowly. Then he shrugged. "Eh. I've had worse."

Nina raced in through the front door with a trio of drones tailing her.

"Nina!" Isaac snapped at her.

"Wha!" She turned toward them with a start.

"There's apple in my pizza!"

"I know!" she snapped back. "I'm working on it!"

"I give this meal two stars out of five," Isaac declared, then wiped his mouth daintily with his napkin. "There's clear room for improvement." He gestured to Susan with an open hand. "And your judgment?"

"One out of five. The apple juice was refreshing. That's about it."

"I see." Isaac nodded thoughtfully, then faced Cephalie. "And from our abstract judge?"

"Zero out of five. It's a Meal Spigot."

"That seems a bit harsh."

"It's a *Meal Spigot*, Isaac. It's fast food. Your meat suit works on the same principle as database analytics."

"What's that supposed to mean?"

"Garbage in, garbage out."

"And not very tasty garbage at that." Isaac tossed his napkin onto the empty plate. "Back to business. Find anything on Delacroix's account?"

"Not much," Cephalie said. "But what I have is golden. The login records from his tower include the Free Gate coordinates of his last visit."

"Then we can use Delacroix's login to go to the same location," Isaac said.

"Not quite," Cephalie cautioned. "His account won't work in Free Gate anymore."

"Could we ask the publisher to switch his account back on?" Susan asked.

"It's not the publisher who's the problem," Cephalie explained, "but the Free Gate administrator, a reclusive AC named Gate Master. *He's* the one blocking Delacroix's account, probably in response to the death certificate, and the publisher won't meddle in how he runs his domain."

"Then we ask Gate Master to switch the account back on," Susan said.

"Sure, if you can find him. 'Reclusive,' remember."

"He'd have to respond to a search warrant, right?"

"Eventually, yes." Isaac leaned in. "But perhaps there's another approach."

"What's on your mind?" Susan asked.

"Free Gate is built on a *RealmBuilder* seed, which means there's a communal spawn point at the center of the domain. Sure, we could use Delacroix's login to go directly to his last position, but there's nothing stopping us from logging in with new accounts and traveling there ourselves. How far are those coordinates from the central spawn?"

"Not far," Cephalie said. "Might take you an hour or so to get there on foot with entry-level gear."

"Then this approach could work." He paused in thought, then began a slow nod. "Might even be better this way. Faster, too. Using Delacroix's account could let the wrong people know we're coming, and who knows how long it would take Gate Master to respond to our warrant."

"Sounds solid to me," Susan agreed.

"I'm not so sure," Cephalie warned. "How much do you know about Free Gate?"

"Never heard of it until today. Why?"

"I've been inside before, about twenty years ago. Gate Master runs it as an anarchy domain."

"Meaning?" Susan asked.

"No rules. All he does is prevent cheating and enforce the realm conditions, which are baseline physics for Free Gate. He'll also load the occasional balance patch or update, but the rest is left up to the players."

"So?" Isaac asked.

"It can get a little wild in there."

"It's a *RealmBuilder* domain," Isaac dismissed. "People play because they like gathering resources and building stuff. It's a creative outlet. How bad could it be?"

"Oh, you'd be surprised." Cephalie pushed up her glasses. "Also, I won't be joining you. I . . . may have cheated the last time I logged in. I'm on Gate Master's ban list."

"Cephalie!" Isaac said with faux shock. "You? Cheat in a game? Why, I never would have guessed!"

"Yeah, yeah."

"Where should we settle in to connect?" Susan asked. "Back at the precinct?"

"We could," Isaac said, "but I'd rather use a public gaming lounge. Less chance we'll draw attention that way." He opened an interface and performed a search. "Perfect. There's a lounge called the Gold Split not far from here. We could easily walk there if we wanted . . ."

He trailed off as Nina lurched over to their booth. She sank into the booth next to Isaac, plopped her forehead down on the table, and let out a long, agonized groan.

"Nina?"

"Isaac."

"Are you okay?"

"Sixteen."

"What?"

"I have sixteen sites left in my queue. I'm never leaving this damn city."

"Wait a second." Isaac thought for a moment. "Didn't you have thirteen sites last time we spoke?"

"Uh-huh. But more keep coming, and I can't work through them fast enough!"

"Well, I'm sure you'll manage." He patted her on the back.

"I wish someone would crack this stupid glyph code," she moaned into the table. "Even if the perp is crazy, we need to know what the code says so we can better track the bastard down."

"Doesn't Raviv have a team working on decryption?"

"Yeah, but no matter what cyphers they apply, the glyphs always come back as gibberish."

"You ever consider it might actually *be* gibberish?"

Nina looked up, a sudden gleam in her eyes.

"I hadn't thought of that." She pushed up off the table. "Oh. Hey, Susan."

"Specialist Cho."

"How's life in SysGov treating you?"

"It's going well." Susan shrugged. "More or less. I'd say it's been a nice change of pace so far."

"Change of pace how?"

"I get shot at less over here."

"You've been shot at before?" Nina asked with bright-eyed interest.

"Oh, yes. Tons of times. This has been ... pleasant by comparison." She smiled. "Nothing like my last assignment where I had my head blown off again."

"Your head?" Nina recoiled in horror. "Again?"

"It's a long story."

"Oh, come on!" Isaac snapped. "How many parts of you have been blown off?"

"Quite a few, actually." Susan turned to Nina as if it were nothing. "Thank you for asking, by the way. I think you might be the first person to ask how I've been since I got here."

"Oh, *really*." Nina turned to Isaac with ire flaming in her eyes.

"What?" he asked. "Why you giving me that look?"

"*Isaac?*"

"What?"

"You haven't asked her how she's handling all this?"

"Well..."

"Not once?"

"We've been busy, and I assumed if there was a problem, she'd let me know." He gestured toward Susan. "Isn't that right?"

"Of course. You can assume no news is good news when it comes to me."

"See?"

"Isaac!" Nina snapped. "She is literally living in another *universe*, and you haven't asked her how she's doing? What is wrong with you?"

Isaac opened his mouth to speak, but Nina placed a finger against his lips.

"No, no. You've done enough. I'll fix this." She faced Susan with an air of formality. "On behalf of the Cho family, I apologize for my idiot twin brother."

"Hey!"

"I'm okay." Susan's cheeks reddened. "Really."

"So, how's the murder case going?" Nina asked, ignoring her irate twin brother's glare.

"Most of our leads have dried up," Susan said, "but we have one left that looks promising."

"Hey, sometimes one is all you need." Nina nudged Isaac. "Am I right?"

"We think one of the victims might have been in contact with a criminal while in a *RealmBuilder* domain. We're heading to a nearby lounge to investigate further."

"Wait a second." Nina faced her brother. "You're telling me that while I'm slaving away with one defective printer after another, the two of you are going to be chilling out in a *gaming lounge*?"

"What's so strange about that?" Isaac protested.

"Isaac?"

"Yes?"

Nina narrowed her eyes at him. "I hate you."

CHAPTER EIGHTEEN

THE GOLD SPLIT NESTLED IN THE MIDDLE OF A LARGE STRIP MALL on Shelf Six with its virtual neon logo glowing over a black, windowless front. The door split open as they approached, and then flinched shut behind them.

Inside, the place bustled with crowded tables and overlapping conversations. Hostesses in skimpy outfits delivered food and beverages to young adults taking breaks next to their abstraction recliners as well as teenagers and preadults wearing interactive black bodysuits and headsets to compensate for their lack of wetware.

"For a gaming lounge, I'm not seeing much gaming," Susan observed.

"These places double as social hangouts," Isaac explained.

"Hello! Welcome!" A hostess who appeared barely above the age of consent headed their way. She wore a fluorescent pink halter top and miniskirt with striped thigh-high stockings and a small neck scarf. Glowing lines of code scrolled across the scarf. Despite her youthful appearance, she moved with ageless poise and grace. "My name is Molly. How can—"

She frowned and her eyes landed on Isaac's shoulder flash, then flicked to the LENS, and finally to Susan's gun.

"Is something wrong?" Isaac asked.

"Damn it," she breathed. "*SysPol* this time? And they were doing so well." She faced the wider room.

"I'm sorry?"

"Okay, listen up, you mushbrains!" Molly raged, and the racket died off at her command. "Which of you are the cops here for?"

No one answered. The lounge was quiet except for a slow, stealthy bite of a chip.

"Sebastian!" Molly shouted, fists on her hips.

"Ah!" cried a teenager in the far corner.

"Front and center!"

A lanky teenager weaved through the crowd and hurried to Molly's side.

"Yes, Miss Molly?"

"Have you been trolling people again?"

"No, Miss Molly."

"Been spreading prank mail?"

"No, Miss Molly."

"What about Dobromir? Has *he* been causing trouble?"

"I don't...think so?"

"Then why are the cops here?"

"I don't know, Miss Molly."

"Doby! Get your butt up here!"

"Perhaps there's been a misunderstanding," Isaac said smoothly. "Our business doesn't concern any of your patrons." He paused meaningfully. "Unless you feel it should."

"Oh, that's a relief." Molly smiled at Sebastian and tousled his hair, then turned back to the room. "Sorry everyone! False alarm! You know I love you!"

"We love you, too, Miss Molly!" the room chorused.

Sebastian scurried back to his corner.

"And sorry to you, sir." Molly extended a hand, which Isaac shook. "Margaret Downes, proprietor of the Gold Split. I thought one of the kids was causing trouble again."

Isaac ran a discreet search on Margaret Downes and found her listed as a one-hundred-and-three-year-old synthoid, no criminal record.

"Detective Isaac Cho, SysPol Themis. This is Agent Susan Cantrell, and my IC Encephalon."

"Purr."

Isaac's brow furrowed in confusion at the odd sound. Something rubbed against his pant leg, and he looked down to find a black cat slinking past. It padded over to Molly and curled around her legs.

"That's Siren, my IC. She sometimes hangs out in a cat synthoid."

"Meow," the cat said in a husky feminine voice.

"You always this busy?" Susan asked conversationally.

"Not until recently. There's been an uptick since all this Apple Cypher drama started." Molly pointed to the far wall. "I have a lot of new customers who only come here to eat because I keep at least one chef on staff at all times, you see. I bring in fresh groceries from Old Frontier twice a week. The kids appreciate the taste of non-printed food."

Isaac tilted to the side and caught a glimpse of the kitchen through the crowd. A pair of young women assembled sandwiches behind a counter, both wearing long black aprons over their halter top and miniskirt "uniforms."

"Your staff are..." Isaac began.

"Synthoids, all of us," Molly explained. "This is my business body. I have another docked at home that's based on my original meat suit. Do you need to see my registration and permits?"

"That won't be necessary."

"I run a respectable establishment, though you know how kids can be. You're not the first cop to come through that door."

"Do you ever have problems with your patrons getting a little"—Susan glanced over Molly's outfit—"handsy?"

"Sometimes, but we can take care of ourselves." She turned back to the crowd. "Hey, kids! What's the Gold Split's golden rule?"

"Look but don't touch!" the room chorused.

"See?" she told Isaac and Susan. "They're sweet. And even if a few do cause trouble now and again, better here than in a gang. Am I right?"

"I wholeheartedly agree," Isaac said.

"So, Detective." Molly clasped her hands together. "How can I assist you?"

"We'd like to use your facilities, if you don't mind," Isaac said. "Nothing more than that. We need to visit an abstract domain as part of our work, and your establishment was nearby. Do you have any private rooms we could use?"

"I do. I'll need to check if one's empty and cleaned up." She smiled apologetically. "The kids are sweet, but neatness is a scarce virtue among them."

"Not a problem," Isaac said. "We'll wait here."

"Be right back." Molly headed toward the back of the establishment.

"Meow. Pert," the black cat said before disappearing into the crowd.

Susan eyed another hostess as she passed in front of them, tray of drinks floating behind her.

"I must be the only woman in here not showing off her tits and ass," she grumbled.

"At least our work didn't lead us to a brothel," Isaac replied.

"Fair point," Susan conceded.

Molly waved at them from the far wall, and Isaac nodded and began weaving his way through the crowd. The few that realized a police officer was passing through gave him and Susan a wide berth, and he used the space to slip through more quickly.

"Business is good. What can I say?" Molly palmed the door, and it slid open to reveal a private room with four recliners arranged around a table. "Will this do?"

"It will." Isaac paid the Esteem cost and provided Molly with a generous tip. "Thank you for your assistance."

"Don't mention it." Molly refunded the base cost but kept the tip. "Always a pleasure to assist our friends in uniform. Just holler if you need anything."

"We will." Isaac closed the door and settled into one of the recliners. Abstract connection icons flared to life around him. "Need any help logging in?"

"I think I can manage," Susan said, dropping into the recliner opposite him.

"All right, then. See you inside." He entered the connection string for Free Gate, leaned back, closed his eyes, and toggled the commit icon with his mind.

Isaac materialized in a private, white-walled loading room. A doorway with FR3G8 written above it formed on one wall, and menus activated to either side of the portal, advertising virtual goods for purchase such as starter equipment sets and resource caches.

His avatar matched his physical body, though his attire had changed to a light gray undershirt and tough, dark gray pants held up with a leather belt. Susan appeared a moment later in the same clothing.

Cephalie popped into existence, her avatar full-sized for a change. She wore a long coat with a curious camo pattern of red and blue patches, and she'd replaced her hat and glasses with a helmet and thick goggles, as if to emphasize her concern for their venture into Free Gate.

"I thought you said you couldn't join us," Susan said.

"I can't. We're in a loading abstraction next to the domain. This is as far as I can go. Both of your accounts are set up, by the way. Be careful in there."

"It'll be fine." Isaac walked up to the advertisements and filtered for free gear. He harrumphed at the paltry selections and clicked the top icon. A tray opened in the wall to reveal a knife in a leather sheath. He toggled the "auto-equip" option, and it teleported to his waist.

"If you say so," Cephalie said.

"Don't worry," Isaac insisted. "I played *RealmBuilder* once or twice on a temporary account. Everyone in the domain I visited was working on buildings shaped like giant dishes of food. The players were nice enough, but it was so weird and boring."

"Free Gate's not like that."

"How bad can it be?"

"You'd be surprised."

"We'll be fine. It's just a game."

"All right." Cephalie held up her hands. "You'll see for yourself soon enough."

"Ready?" Isaac asked Susan.

"Ready." She patted her own knife.

"Then let's head out." He nodded to Cephalie. "Be back in an hour or so."

"*Zhù hǎo yùn.*" Cephalie waved at them. "You'll need it."

Isaac shook his head and passed through the threshold.

The loading room vanished, and a gray, craggy wasteland flashed into existence around them. Black clouds rolled overhead, and lightning streaked from cloud to cloud. Thunder boomed in the distance, and dry, dusty air blew across the rocks. The back of his undershirt and pants flapped in the wind, then settled back down.

"Oh dear," Isaac breathed as he turned around in a circle. Free Gate's central spawn formed a blasted plateau of rock and ash with deep, gaping trenches all around. The shattered remains of three bridges spanned the trench, but even if they'd been complete, impossibly tall walls farther out formed an incomplete ring around the central spawn, further locking in new players who would enter with few resources.

And then there was the tree.

It was the only tree on the plateau, and an arch with a wooden sign declared it the TREE OF WELCOME, but Isaac didn't feel welcomed. Not one bit. Thick branches spread across a leafless crown, and hundreds of pale corpses hung from them like rotting, diseased fruit.

"Now, that's just rude," Isaac grumped.

"Is this what central spawn is supposed to look like?" Susan asked.

"No. It's normally more...green. The players must have modified the landscape over the domain's lifespan."

"Which way to Delacroix's last login?"

"One moment." Isaac opened a virtual compass over his palm and turned to face the correct heading. "This way. Across what's left of that bridge."

"I could jump it in real life."

"Yeah, but not in here. You'll be limited to baseline human strength and speed."

"Then how do we get across?"

"Not sure." He looked around. The wind picked up, and pebbles chattered across the ground. "Maybe if we had a rope and grapnel? Normally, we could use the in-game crafting system to construct tools and equipment."

"I don't see *anything* we could—"

A gunshot rang out, and Susan's head exploded in a burst of gore.

"Ah!" Isaac yelped, flinching back. He turned to the left, then the right, searching frantically for the source of the gunfire.

A second shot barked, and the world turned black.

—LIFE LOST—

"Hey, kiddos," Cephalie sneered. "Back so soon?"

"Me and my big mouth." Susan picked herself up off the floor. She patted the sides and top of her head to make sure it was back in place. "Didn't expect to lose body parts so soon."

"Come on." Isaac rose from the floor and dusted himself off. "That doesn't count."

"What happened to you?" Susan asked.

"Same as you. Who would do something like that?"

"How'd they get you?" Cephalie asked.

"We were sniped," Susan said. "At least one player must be watching central spawn for new arrivals."

"Figured." Cephalie gave them an indifferent shrug. "Welcome to Free Gate."

She walked over to a blank wall. A chalkboard appeared, and she picked up a piece of chalk and drew a small, vertical line.

"What's that for?" Isaac asked.

"Just making a prediction. Please, don't mind me."

"What now?" Susan asked.

"We'll try again." Isaac stepped up to the menu, ordered a rope and grapnel, and paid the Esteem fee to start the game with it. One appeared coiled around his shoulder.

"Any guns in there?" Susan asked.

"Yes, but they're expensive."

"Fine by me." She filtered the menu, her face a stony mask of determination. "There. This one." She clicked her selection, and a long-barreled scoped rifle materialized in her hands. She raised it to her shoulder, released the safety, and viewed down the scope. "Now *this* is more my style. Antiquated, but lethal is lethal."

"We need to find cover as soon as we spawn in," Isaac said. "Fortunately, we can keep trying if we fail again."

"Unlimited lives?"

"Yes, but we lose our gear when we die."

"Oh." Susan glanced down to her hip and saw the starter knife was missing. "I see. Maybe I shouldn't have splurged so soon."

"First priority is locating and neutralizing that sniper. Ready?"

"Ready." Susan raised her rifle.

"Here we go!"

They charged though the threshold, vanished from the loading room, and popped into existence on a barren patch of the spawn plateau, close to where they first appeared but with a slightly randomized entry. Isaac swept his gaze across their surroundings, spotted a rocky outcrop, and sprinted for it.

"Come on!" he urged.

"Don't need to tell me!"

A shot rang out, zinged across the rocks at Isaac's feet, and he dove for cover. He landed prone behind the outcrop, and Susan struck the ground next to him with her shoulder and tucked in her feet.

A second shot blew shards off the outcrop.

"Did you see where those shots came from?" Isaac whispered.

"No. Did you?"

"No."

"Well, that's no good," Susan breathed. "He's going to blow my head off if I peek out of here."

"I know," Isaac whispered. "Maybe I can reason with him."

"You seriously think that'll work?"

"Worth a try." Isaac put his back against the outcrop and drew in a deep, virtual breath. "Excuse me, Mister or Missus Sniper!"

Another shot ricocheted off the rocks, and Isaac ducked deeper out of reflex.

"Look! I don't know what kind of grievances you have with new players, but I can assure you we don't plan to stick around!"

Two shots plinked off the stone.

"We're here on important business! I'm not exaggerating when I say this is a matter of life or death to some people!" Which, Isaac supposed, was technically true. "If you would kindly provide us safe passage beyond central spawn, we would greatly appreciate your aid!"

He paused and waited for another shot.

It didn't come.

"Are you going to shoot at us anymore?" Isaac shouted.

"No!" came the distant response. "I won't shoot you! Promise!"

"Thank you, sir!" He turned to Susan. "See? Even Free Gaters can be reasoned with."

"Guess so."

Isaac heard a soft *thoomp* from the sniper's general direction. Something clattered against the top of the protective rock, and he looked up in time to see a small cylinder fall past his head and land in his lap.

"Oh, for the love of—"

The rifle grenade exploded in a blinding white flash.

—LIFE LOST—

Isaac popped into the loading room on his back. He huffed out an angry breath and stared at the ceiling, arms and legs splayed around him.

"Why, hello!" Cephalie said brightly as she drew a second line next to the first. "Back so soon?"

"Well, that was a bundle of Esteem wasted." Susan sat up. "Didn't even get to fire once."

"Maybe we can force him to stop shooting us," Isaac said.

"How?"

"I don't know." He shrugged against the floor. "Just keep spawning until he runs out of bullets?"

"You really want to try that?" Susan asked.

"Nope," Isaac huffed. "'I won't shoot you. Promise.' And then he lobs a grenade at us."

"Not very civil of him."

"No, it wasn't." Isaac sat up and gazed at the menus by the portal and all their expensive, high-end gear. "That's it. No immature spawn camper is going to get the best of us!" He rose and opened the menu. "Forget cost, we're taking this guy down!"

He scrolled through the selection, picked out a set of full body armor, and hit the purchase icon.

"You could expense those, you know," Cephalie said.

"Are you kidding?" Isaac turned from the screen, voice muffled by his new helmet. "There's no way I'm expensing *RealmBuilder* equipment packs! Can you imagine what Raviv would say?"

"Nothing nice, I'd wager."

Isaac clicked an icon to purchase grenades. He kept clicking until his belt sagged with them.

"How about you, Susan?" Cephalie asked.

"I'm good. The Admin provides an Esteem stipend while I'm over here, and I've barely touched it."

"You really want to spend it this way?"

"Sure, if it'll help solve the case. Honestly, Esteem feels almost like play money to me."

"Fine." Cephalie rolled her eyes. "You two have fun. I'll be here when you're finished. Just let me know whenever you want me to get that search warrant."

"We won't need a warrant." Isaac's face hardened as he purchased a submachine gun. It materialized on a strap hanging from his shoulder. He tapped a secondary icon, and extra ammo phased into place along a bandolier.

"Good grief!" Cephalie exclaimed. "How much are you spending?"

"As much as it takes!" He gripped the submachine gun and released the safety. "You ready?"

"Ready." Susan stood away from her menu, clad in body armor and sporting a new, even larger rifle. "Just give the word."

"All right. Here we go!"

They charged through the portal.

CHAPTER NINETEEN

—LIFE LOST—

Isaac and Susan belly-flopped onto the loading room floor.

"Wow." Cephalie smiled as she chalked in the twelfth line on her board. "You two are *persistent.*"

"Did we get farther that time, at least?" Susan asked.

"Only if you count how far your head rolled," Isaac replied gruffly.

"Yay for head rolls," Susan groaned, rising from the floor.

"I don't think this is working." Isaac stood up and planted his back against the wall.

"What was your first clue?" Cephalie asked with unbearable glee.

"We almost had him four tries ago." Susan shook her head, upset with their lack of progress. "But then he called in some friends. There must be at least three of them out there now."

"And I bet they have even more players they could call on if we start making progress," Isaac said.

"You could be right."

"Cephalie, go ahead." Isaac waved for her to give him some-thing. "Let me have it."

"I told you so."

"Yep. You told me so," Isaac echoed wearily. "We've wasted enough time and money here. Let's log out."

"You're giving up?" Susan asked.

"We're not beating those players like this, that's for sure. I thought I was being clever with this approach, but it turned out to be a dumb idea, and I'm mature enough to admit when I'm wrong. We'll proceed through the regular channels by issuing Gate Master a search warrant and waiting for his response."

Susan lowered her head. An idea had been stirring in the back of her mind since the sniper received reinforcements, but she'd been hesitant to speak up, worried about how Isaac might react.

A small frown formed on her face, but she steeled herself.

"Before we go?" she began, turning to him.

"Hmm?" Isaac murmured.

"There's one last thing we could try." Susan swallowed and took a quick breath. "We could . . . play dirty."

"You mean cheat?"

She nodded to him.

"I don't know," Isaac said doubtfully. "As appealing as the notion is, haven't we burned enough time here as it is?"

"Bear with me," Susan said. "Cephalie, just for argument's sake, could you hack our accounts? Give us an unfair advantage?"

"Sure thing." Cephalie crossed her arms. "I've done it before, after all, but it won't take long for Gate Master to notice you and give you the boot. You'd never get to the coordinates in time on foot."

"What if we're not traveling on foot? Could you spawn us with a vehicle?"

"Yes, but that might not be enough," the AC warned. "You're still going to get shot at when you spawn in."

"And one of those new players brought a rocket launcher," Isaac grumbled and rubbed his shoulder.

"Actually, what if we used assets from a different game? Something to *really* give us an unfair advantage. Something with qualities above baseline physics. Perhaps with magical or science fiction advantages. Is that possible?"

"*RealmBuilder* shares the same Universal Abstraction Matrix common to most SysGov virtual environments, so yes, the assets can be imported. Did you have something particular in mind?"

"I do. What if we—"

"Aha!" Isaac snapped his fingers.

The two women looked over to find his eyes gleaming with malicious intent.

"I've got it!" he declared.

"You do?" Susan asked.

"Yes!" He pushed off the wall and joined them with a wide grin on his face. "Susan, this is a great idea, but I need to step in here. If we're going to play dirty, we should go all the way. No holding back. Cephalie, you know my favorite *Solar Descent* character? The one I leveled all the way to his capstone skill?"

"Oh!" Her face lit up and she gave him a cheerful clap. "That's perfect!"

"What is?" Susan asked, not following.

"You'll see." Isaac chuckled. "I call it 'Big Stompy.'"

✧   ✧   ✧

Geronimo-Sixty-Nine knew he was destined for greatness from the moment the deacon bestowed such a lucky, storied number upon him, and that greatness had continued long after he moved on from the Numbers. His old gang had been a useful, if problematic, stepping-stone in his preadult years, but they'd served their purpose in elevating his name within the *RealmBuilder* gaming community.

Sixty-nine. Lucky in love. Lucky in life.

He never once believed in the Divine Randomizer or any of the other intellectual refuse spewed by the sect deacons. Sixty-nine was just a number like any other, but the superstitious crowd he'd kept at the time didn't think so, and his popularity during the gang orgies only served to elevate him further.

If people *thought* he was destined for great things, and he *acted* the part, then greatness would follow. And people naturally wanted to be there when he achieved his destined success. His career as a livecast gamer and entertainer had followed so smoothly, so naturally, it had shocked even him.

It didn't hurt that Numbers and Divine Randos still thought of him as a true believer. He'd kept his gang alias, after all! Of course, he believed with all his heart! He even started each livecast with a prayer for favorable randomness and ended with a random number roll and a short theological discussion on what it could mean.

What a load of crap! But religious nuts made for a loyal audience, and they tipped *generously*. He might even move to Ballast Heights someday!

For now, he focused on his latest streak of luck in the form of two idiots who kept trying to break out of central spawn in the most boneheaded ways possible. He settled his fully upgraded Head Ventilator Mark X into position on its barrel-mounted bipod and scanned central spawn through the scope. The highlight reels alone would keep the Esteem rolling in for weeks!

"Think they gave up?" Stalwart-Eight radioed over from his own hiding spot on the opposite end of central spawn.

"No way," Geronimo said. "These two don't have the brain power for that. I give them five more attempts at least."

"Well, I'm using this lull to do some editing. You're going to love how a few juicy sound effects amp up that lady's head explosions."

"Nice!" Geronimo replied, chuckling. He pulled back from the scope and swept his gaze over central spawn, looking for the telltale light of an opening spawn portal.

Nothing yet.

These two knuckleheads must have known they were up against three experienced players, but what they didn't know was another *eighteen* were camped out around the plateau, under the bridges, huddled in cave mouths along the plateau's cliffs, or situated on the far side of the Great Spawn Trench, all waiting in case the situation at central spawn became too hot.

Geronimo and his fellow gamers were all experienced Free Gaters, players used to the harsh kill-or-be-killed environment of the anarchy domain, and they did *not* tolerate newcomers who tried to break out of central spawn like this was some *ordinary* abstraction. Free Gate was *their* turf, and they would defend it. Together with others of the same mindset, they'd transformed central spawn into the blasted, inhospitable hellscape it was today, depriving new players of the basic resources they needed to craft tools or even to survive. They'd dug the Great Spawn Trench and had begun construction on the Great Spawn Wall, further impeding new players.

All of them were veterans from Free Gate's most harrowing days, the bloody Flavor-Sparkle War. After surviving that harsh, punishing crucible, they could hold their own against any foe!

Markie Flavor-Sparkle—Lunarian actor, singer, and heir to the vast Flavor-Sparkle fortune—had learned about Free Gate during a concert tour of the Shark Fin and had become curious, since he enjoyed playing *RealmBuilder* in his free time. He'd wanted to experience the anarchy domain for himself.

And experience it he did.

Free Gaters killed him moments after he arrived, as was their way, but Markie didn't take the insult sitting down. He raged about his experience on a livecast, and his fans mobilized to punish his "killers."

The result was horror personified. Flavor-Sparkle fans logged into Free Gate in human waves, charging across central spawn in tides of bodies as outnumbered Free Gaters gunned them down frantically. The soil of central spawn ran red with blood and viscera that day, but his suicidal fans didn't stop, didn't relent. They kept coming at all hours, and desperate Free Gaters organized their defenses to ensure central spawn was never without its defenders. The war degenerated into a long bloody stalemate, and Geronimo-Sixty-Nine, representing his Free Gate brothers and sisters, challenged Markie Flavor-Sparkle to single combat in order to break the siege.

Ah, good times.

Fans bequeathed the singer with their finest virtual weapons and armor, but he proved no match for a player as experienced as Geronimo. The Lunarian superstar fell, and an armistice was signed between the Flavor-Sparkle hordes and the Free Gaters, declaring Free Gate off-limits to the singer's fans.

Geronimo pulled the magazine out of his sniper rifle.

"How about we mix it up a little?" he declared. "Everyone, load your incendiary rounds. Let's light their asses on fire!"

The room was cramped and dark with only a few green pin-points casting pale glows across the chair, console, and Isaac's face. Susan squeezed in and sat on a console to his left, her head pressed against the low ceiling.

"Here we go," she breathed, not sure what to expect.

A single button pulsed, and Isaac pressed it.

"Initiating startup," said a monotone feminine voice as read-outs flickered to life.

A large, circular gauge appeared, and a needle twitched upward into the green.

"Abyssal reactor online."

A rectangular display switched on with a red humanoid silhouette divided into blocky sections. The shade of each section turned yellow, then green.

"Reactive armor online."

Another display lit up, and a text list formed.

"Weapon systems online."

Pale light shone across Isaac's rictus grin.

"All systems online," the female computer said. "Pilot, have a nice day."

Isaac took hold of a pair of analog control sticks covered in buttons.

"Oh, I intend to."

"Portal light!" Stalwart-Eight radioed over.

Geronimo-Sixty-Nine raised his rifle and sighted down the scope. The portal began forming near the center of the plateau. He lined up his shot, but the two idiots didn't rush through this time. Instead, the portal grew larger and brighter.

"What the hell?" He lowered the scope and sat up for a wider view.

The top of the portal sped upward into the dark sky, and the sides ballooned outward. It grew and grew, like one disconnected side of a many-storied building, and Geronimo craned his neck to see the top.

"What's going on?" Stalwart asked.

"How the hell should I know?"

The portal stopped growing. Its edges firmed up, surface undulating like water.

A black, mechanical shape appeared a third of the way up the portal and pushed through. It was all flat surfaces and sharp angles that reached down close to the ground, with a wider section at the base. A column of angular purple runes pulsed along the side, each character taller than a human being. Hot, purple gas exhaled from the runic vents, and the base of the tall, mechanical shape crunched to the ground.

The earth trembled and Geronimo steadied himself with a hand against his stone cover.

"Is that...a leg?"

A second, identical form emerged, and then the upper body pushed through. The immense humanoid machine towered over them, covered in angular black armor with runic vents along its legs, forearms, and sides of the torso.

"A giant robot?" Geronimo protested. He rose and pointed

at the interloper. "You can't do that! There're no mecha in Free Gate! You're cheating!"

The portal closed off, leaving the giant robot standing atop central spawn.

"Screw this!" Geronimo raised his rifle. "Everyone, open fire!"

He launched a rifle grenade at the robot. The cylinder arched through the air, hit the side of the boot and exploded in a bright flash. A gust of wind blew the smoke away to reveal unscratched armor.

"Shoot it!" Geronimo shouted. Free Gaters opened fire from all sides. Two rockets flew in and boomed against the robot's back, and automatic fire pattered off its armor.

It didn't seem to notice or care.

More rockets screamed in, and a Gatling gun blared alive from the far side of the Great Trench.

Geronimo aimed at the head and fired. The shot plinked off the red glow of its singular eye.

The robot gazed down at him.

"Uh-oh."

The massive construct raised a giant boot. A shadow fell across Geronimo as he gazed up and, curiously, noted a strange pattern in the base of the sole. Grooves formed letters that spelled out: IF YOU CAN READ THIS, YOU'RE ALREADY DEAD.

He found little reason to disagree.

❖   ❖   ❖

"Aaaaand *splat!*" Isaac said as the giant robot's boot turned the sniper into paste. He yanked back on a control stick, and the robot smeared the sniper's guts over the ground until they formed a damp streak.

"You're in a better mood," Susan said.

"And why wouldn't I be?"

"You do realize giant robots are totally impractical."

"Not if they're rocking stats this awesome." Isaac checked the map screen, found his bearings, and pushed the throttle forward. The robot crossed the chasm around central spawn in a single stride. "Heh. And we were going to rope across."

"What game is this from, anyway?"

"*Solar Descent.* The same one Chowder was talking about. I've burned more hours in it than I care to admit."

"Is that so?"

"Big Stompy here is from my pilot character. You don't see many of those, since pilots are an unpopular class."

"Why's that?" She knuckled the side of the cockpit. "Who doesn't like a big, stompy robot?"

"Because pilots are a pain to level up. Sure, you get access to your giant mecha at level one, but the cooldown for the summoning skill is *atrocious*. Like, over a week real-time. Which means pilots get their one moment of brief glory, then spend the rest of their time underpowered.

"But I'm one of those contrarian gamers. I like finding ways to make suboptimal builds work. And besides, it's a giant robot. What's not to love? Plus, the capstone skill makes up for it."

"Capstone skill?"

"At max level, pilots finally come into their own. The cooldown for their summoning skill is removed, and since my pilot character is maxed out, I can call upon Big Stompy whenever I want. Honestly, *all* the class capstones are ridiculously overpowered, but that's compensated against *Solar Descent*'s endgame difficulty spike."

The giant robot jogged across a charred, barren landscape, and the ground thundered with each footfall.

"Personally, I feel the pilot class is highly underrated," Isaac continued. "In my gaming party, I would save the summon for after we completed a quest."

"Why?"

"Better rewards. Big Stompy can be an intimidating presence."

"You deliberately intimidate quest givers?" Susan blinked. "Wait a second. Do you play an evil character?"

"*Lawful*-evil, thank you very much!" Isaac corrected sharply. "He has a code of ethics. It's just a twisted one."

"Oh, like that makes it any better!" Susan rolled her eyes.

"What's wrong with a little bit of roleplay?"

"Nothing. I just assumed you'd play a champion of order and justice. A space-paladin or something."

"In my off time?" Isaac gave her a sour look. "Where's the fun in that?"

"I guess you have a point," she conceded. "You play this game often?"

"Sure do. We have a consistent gaming group on Kronos. Nina's in it, of course, and Grace Damphart, too. You haven't met her yet. She's a senior detective who works in the same department as us. Raviv used to be a part of our group, but he bowed out after being promoted. He didn't want it to look like he kept favorites, and I can understand that. There are a few other people who play less consistently, but Nina and Damphart are the regulars."

"Sounds fun." Susan scooched closer. "I have a gaming group like that back in the DTI."

"Really?" Isaac asked, sounding surprised.

"Oh, sure." Her face lit up. "*Worlds Beyond Ours* is the diversion of choice. It's a space exploration, resource gathering grindfest. This one time, I found a derelict ship on this barren, airless world. Some other player must have lost it there, and I know this won't mean much to you, but it was an Intrepid. An Intrepid Type-Q! Fully loaded, too. Only..."

"Only what?"

"Just about every onboard system was busted from the crash, but it was still the best thing I'd ever found in the game. I towed it back to port and broke the bank fixing it up. Named it the *Trash Heap*. I was going to suggest we import the ship into *RealmBuilder*, but you spoke up first."

"You wanted us to use a ship named the *Trash Heap*?"

"Why not? It's got a laser turret, and speed wouldn't be a problem with an FTL drive. We'd already be at the coordinates."

"I see your point."

"But this is better." She rubbed a hand over her console seat. "I doubt the import would have worked, since an Admin game isn't going to use that Universal Abstraction Matrix Cephalie mentioned."

"The *Trash Heap*." Isaac chuckled. "Sounds like it would be a lot of effort. Was it worth it?"

"It's still a work in progress." She glanced away guiltily. "This is going to sound silly, but I'll sometimes... spend real world money on upgrades for that ship."

"What's wrong with that?" Isaac asked.

She turned back to him and saw a complete lack of condemnation in his eyes.

"Nothing wrong with that in my mind," he added. "I do the same thing."

"You *do*?" Her eyes widened.

"Sure. You think Big Stompy came like this out of the box?

I've sunk at least three months' worth of pay into him. Yeah, I could grind it all out in-game, but who has the time for that?"

"*We* sure don't," she agreed.

"Too true. At a certain point, the time becomes worth more to me than the money. Besides, with all the travel this job entails, what else am I going to spend it on? A home in a gated community I hardly visit? Clothes patterns I never wear?" He shook his head. "What would be the point? This way, I'm spending my hard-earned Esteem on something I enjoy."

"I couldn't agree more. The Admin takes good care of us STANDs, and I don't have a family of my own. My parents are well off already, so what's there to spend it on? Put it into a retirement fund?" She laughed sadly. "That's nothing but a bad joke in STAND. We retire when we get blown up."

"Did your parents support you becoming a STAND?" Isaac asked.

"My mom was hesitant, but my dad..." She frowned and let out a slow exhale. "*He* opposed it. Strongly."

"That had to be rough," he said, watching the terrain.

"Yeah. Thing is, both of them thought I'd go pro someday."

"Go pro?"

"With *Legions of Patriots*. It's a competitive team-based strategy game popular in the Admin. I was so good at it, I had offers for sports scholarships and my pick of the best colleges. But my heart wasn't in it." She tilted her head. "Are there professional gamers in SysGov?"

"Oh, sure. Tons." Isaac looked over at her. "So, you almost ended up as a pro gamer?"

"Not really. I quit playing after high school. Dad held out hope I'd pick it up again, but that was before I quit college and joined the Peacekeepers."

"Sounds like there's a little friction between you and your father."

"Just a little." She held her thumb and forefinger close. "He's not the biggest fan of the Admin."

"Ouch."

"Yeah. He thinks we're a bunch of thugs."

Isaac blinked, then turned to her slowly and gave her a long, meaningful look, then turned away again.

"What was that about?" she asked pointedly.

"I didn't say a word."

"But you were thinking it."

"But I didn't *say* it." He adjusted their course around a snow-capped mountain.

Susan crossed her arms and decided not to press the topic.

"What about your parents?" she asked. "They approve of your career in SysPol?"

"I would certainly hope so. Both of my parents are *in* SysPol. My mom's in Hephaestus—our research and development division—and my Dad's in the patrol fleet. He didn't see any action during the Dynasty Crisis, though."

"Family reunions must be tough to arrange."

"Yeah, no kidding."

Susan leaned away from Isaac and pressed her back against the cockpit's arch. She looked around, taking in the carefully crafted abstraction with all its anachronistic dials, buttons, and levers. It put a smile on her face, but there was something else lurking on the edge of her mind.

And then, as sudden as a shock of electricity, everything clicked together.

"Oh, *shit!*"

"What?" Isaac stopped the robot. He swiveled the head left, then right. "Did I miss something? Are we in danger? Are those people from spawn chasing us?"

"No." She put a hand to the side of her head. "Sorry. It just hit me, is all. Holy hell. I never saw *that* one coming."

"What hit you? Are you okay?"

"I'm fine, Isaac," she said, then she started laughing.

"Are you sure?" He twisted in his seat with a worried expression.

"Isaac, don't you realize what just happened?"

"Umm." He checked his gauges and displays.

"Not out there. In here." She leaned toward him. "We've discovered something we have in common."

"We did?" He paused in thought, and his expression transformed, eyes widening. "Oh. *Oh.*"

"Yeah. Hard to believe, huh?"

"It's not the common ground between SysGov and the Admin I would have expected." His brow tightened in thought. "But now that look of yours makes sense."

"What look?"

"The enthusiasm on your face when you talked about the *Trash Heap.*" Isaac gave her a sly grin. "I've only seen you with that expression once before. It was back on the saucer while you showed off your combat frame."

"You notice things like that?"

"Well, I *am* a detective."

"Point taken." She glanced out the cockpit. "Hey, what's that?" She nodded toward a reddish light emanating from a distant hilltop.

"Trouble, I presume." Isaac took hold of the controls again and pushed the throttle forward.

A massive, scaly silhouette rose from the widening arcane circle. Great wings unfurled, and red light spilled from the creature's smiling maw. It was at least three times as large as Big Stompy.

"I thought Free Gate was baseline physics."

"Seems we're not the only ones cheating." Isaac clicked buttons on both his control sticks and maxed out the throttle. "Guess the Free Gaters *really* don't want us around. Well, bring it on!"

"Arming twin energy swords," the computer stated.

Big Stompy reached behind its back and grabbed the handles of two giant swords. Mechanisms clanked open, releasing the twin blades, and the giant robot brought them forward as its stride sped up from a jog to a full, thunderous sprint. Purple superheated gas vented from the runes on its forearms, and the swords ignited with purplish energy.

"Can you soften it up with guns or missiles?" Susan suggested.

"Don't have any."

"You serious?"

"Who needs guns when I have a pair of swords that can cleave mountains in half?"

"You built a giant robot that only fights hand-to-hand?"

"Don't judge. This isn't your character."

"Yes." She rolled her eyes. "*Obviously.*"

The creature unleashed a beam of red energy that slammed into Big Stompy's chest. The robot staggered to the side, corrected, and continued charging forward.

"Reactive armor compromised," the computer reported as a section of the armor display flashed red.

"That's not good." Isaac flipped open a button guard atop the throttle and held his thumb ready.

The winged monster gathered energy in its smiling maw once

more, and Isaac jammed the button down. Thrusters ignited on Big Stompy's back and the bottom of its boots. The robot launched high into the air, and the energy beam sliced past underneath.

The black, scaly creature raised its snout toward the airborne robot now holding its twin swords high. Thousands of virtual tons of armor and arcane machinery reached the peak of its leap, then began to fall back to earth. The monster gathered energy for another strike, but the robot plummeted faster.

Big Stompy's big boots smashed into the top of the monster's head, caving in its skull, and the twin energy swords sank deep into its shoulders. Molten ichor gushed from the wounds, and the force of the impact crushed the monster onto its back, wings draping the surrounding foothills.

"That'll teach you!" Isaac declared, moments before the landscape vanished outside.

"What?" Susan said.

The cockpit disappeared, and then darkness enveloped them.

✧   ✧   ✧

Isaac and Susan found themselves in the middle of an endless plain of black sand. Wind blew wisps of sand into the air that twirled around, tighter and tighter, until they formed into a swirling humanoid shape.

"What the hell do you two think you're doing?" the figure demanded in a coarse, grating basso.

"Gate Master, I presume," Isaac said.

"Correct, Detective Isaac Cho."

Isaac raised an eyebrow.

"Don't look so surprised," Gate Master said. "I know everyone who logs into my domain, just as I remember Encephalon's disastrous last visit. People call me a recluse. They imagine I sit back and let the players do whatever they want because that's what it *appears* I do. Do they think Free Gate became so popular, so notorious by accident? People flock to it for the challenge, and those less skilled spend exorbitant amounts to overcome its harshness. Do they think I don't watch this carefully crafted, Esteem-generating engine of mine like a hawk? Only a fool would assume so, and I don't take either of you for fools.

"Which then begs the question," Gate Master continued. "Why are the two of you acting like fools in my domain? I have precious few rules, and the ones I have are easy to remember. And yet you hacked your accounts and imported foreign assets into my abstraction. Why? What brings a SysPol detective and whatever *you* are"—the sand figure indicated Susan—"to my domain?"

"A crime has been committed," Isaac said simply.

He let the words hang in the air for long seconds, but the only sound was the rasping of airborne sand.

"And it's our job to bring the criminal to justice," Isaac added at last, not sure why that last part had been necessary.

"I should have suspected as much." Gate Master crossed the swirling sand of his arms. "Do you have a warrant?"

"Not at present."

"Yet its absence doesn't seem to worry you," Gate Master noted. "Then I must assume you could acquire one, if necessary. Why haven't you already?"

"We were concerned with how long you'd take to respond."

"You seemed to have found a way to bypass that."

"That was not our intention."

"Maybe not, but here I am anyway. If this search warrant proves disruptive to my business, I'll challenge it in court."

"As is your right," Isaac acknowledged. "But you'll lose."

"You sure about that?"

"I've been down this road before. All you'll cost me is time. It's a sum I'd rather not pay, but if I have no choice, I will." Isaac spread his hands. "But perhaps there's a way for us to both get what we want. Tell me, what concerns you about a potential warrant?"

"Don't be naive. I run an *anarchy* domain. As long as a player doesn't break my rules, they can do anything they want, meet with whomever they want, *say* whatever they want. As a cop, I'm sure you know what this space can be—and *has* been—used for."

Isaac nodded. "It's one of the reasons I'm here."

"My clients have an expectation of privacy, even if it is, to a degree, only an illusion. Shatter that illusion, and some of them will find other venues. In short, cops are bad for my business."

"Then let's see if we can come to an arrangement."

"What sort of arrangement?" Gate Master asked.

"You want to avoid an intrusive search of your domain, and what I'm after is very specific information. Information *you*, as the administrator of Free Gate, will be able to find much faster than we could on our own, I believe. If you'll hunt down and provide me that information, I'll have no need for a search warrant."

"Hmm," Gate Master murmured, sounding intrigued. "I can work with that. Depends on what you need, though."

"Here are the coordinates and timestamps I'm interested in." Isaac held out his hand, and a file appeared. "A murder victim was online here. I'm trying to find out who he met with."

Gate Master took the file. The sand within his body swirled with more energy, then settled again.

"Joachim Delacroix, recently deceased Gordian Division agent," Gate Master said. "I switched his account off the other day. Should have guessed this is what drew you. And yes, you're right. He was with someone. I can provide you with a local domain download that includes Delacroix and his 'plus one' for those timestamps."

"That would be perfect, though I'm surprised you keep domain downloads."

"The *illusion* of privacy," Gate Master reminded him. "Is that all you need?"

"There's always the possibility I may require more as the investigation unfolds." Isaac nodded to him. "However, if that happens, I'd prefer to contact you first. Directly and discreetly, of course. Do we have a deal?"

"We do."

Gate Master offered him both the domain download and his contact string, and Isaac copied them over.

"Thank you for your cooperation."

CHAPTER TWENTY

THE DOMAIN RECORDING PLAYED OUT IN MINIATURE ON THE table in the Gold Split's private room. Isaac and Susan sat on the edges of their abstraction recliners and watched the conversation unfold for the third time.

The recording started with Joachim Delacroix pacing back and forth in the gloom of a damp cave. A single lamp provided orange-tinged illumination, casting light across an array of stalactites reaching down toward the man like a thicket of daggers.

A second man arrived a few minutes later. If Isaac could pick a phrase to describe him, it would be "deliberate averageness." Average height, average build, and a face that was neither ugly nor attractive. This was the look of a man who could blend into any crowd. If his avatar was based on a real body, then he was most assuredly a synthoid. *No one* was that average by accident.

The two men began to talk, calm at first, but with escalating frustration. Isaac didn't know what they were talking about, because they were using SysPol security chat and he didn't have the key, but the tenor of their conversation was all too clear. Soon the two men were shouting at each at the top of their virtual lungs. Delacroix appeared ready to storm out, but then the other man spoke in a softer, perhaps conciliatory tone. Was he making a peace offering of some sort? If so, Delacroix begrudgingly accepted, and the two calmed down and finished their conversation on good terms.

The recording paused at the end.

"What do you think?" Susan asked.

"Whatever they were talking about, Delacroix *really* didn't want it getting out," he said. "He met this man deep in a cave within a hostile anarchy abstraction and used security chat to encrypt their speech on top of it all. These aren't the actions of an innocent man."

Cephalie popped into existence on the table.

"I heard back from the Ministries of Citizen Services, Finance, and Transportation."

"And?" Isaac asked.

"The second player is Thomas Stade, an eighty-two-year-old Oortan synthoid who immigrated to Janus seven years ago. His public profile lists him as a 'freelance consultant.' Formerly contracted by the Trinh Syndicate, but that was only for a year. No criminal record, though. His file's spotless as far as SysPol or SSP are concerned."

"And Delacroix's chat key?"

"Like you thought, Andover-Chen had it on him and was kind enough to provide me with a copy. I already tested it on the domain record, and it didn't work. Delacroix must have generated a new encryption key at some point."

"I'm not surprised." Isaac blew out a quick breath. "He *really* didn't want this getting out. Worth a try, though."

"What else do we have on Thomas Stade?" Susan asked.

"Very little, I'm afraid," Cephalie said, conjuring a virtual blackboard. "Public transportation and fiscal records, mostly. I'm not sure what kind of 'consulting' he does, but I haven't found much in the way of a digital presence. The banks show he has a modest sum of Esteem to his name. No permanent residence, either."

"Sounds like a man who operates mostly 'off the record,'" Isaac said. "Do we know where he is now?"

"We don't. Based on public transport logs, he last passed through the Howling Bow Airport on an inbound flight a day after the Free Gate cave visit, but there are some irregularities in what I received from the Ministry of Transportation. It may not be accurate."

"The Howling Bow," Isaac grumbled. "Of course."

"What's wrong?" Susan asked. "Why wouldn't the data be accurate?"

"Whoever Stade is, he knows how to be discreet," Isaac explained. "The Howling Bow is a city situated along the upper leading edge of the Janus crown. Structurally, it serves as a wind buffer for cities inland, like Ballast Heights. It's an old and not very popular place to live, though honestly, it's not as bad as people make it out to be."

Cephalie pulled a sign out of her purse, which read: NO, IT'S WORSE.

"To each their own," Isaac dismissed. "The important takeaway is certain areas of the Janus infostructure haven't been updated in decades, and a few spots are centuries old. Not all parts of the infostructure play nice together, which creates blind spots for SysPol and SSP. Or, at the very least, hazy spots where automatic data collection and collation are less reliable and searching for information is slower. If Thomas Stade flew into the Howling Bow, then there's a good chance he's purposefully trying to cloud his data trail."

"Then where does that leave us?" Susan asked. "Initiating a manhunt for Stade?"

"Perhaps not," Isaac said. "Cephalie, where was his flight inbound from?"

"The *Atomic Resort*. It's an Oortan dirigible currently stationed two hundred kilometers south of Janus." Cephalie's eyes twinkled. "Ah, and this might be interesting. Stade *left* Janus for the *Atomic Resort* less than an hour after his last conversation with Delacroix. He bought his ticket just before boarding."

"Sounds like he wanted to get out there in a hurry," Susan speculated.

"Indeed," Isaac said. "I wonder what sort of business he had on the dirigible. Regardless, we'll need to check it out for ourselves, though the fact that it's Oortan-owned is a potential problem."

"Why's that?" Susan asked.

"The Oort Cloud Citizenry isn't a SysGov member state, which places the *Atomic Resort* outside our jurisdiction, so our authority as SysPol detectives won't get us very far on its own. On the other hand, the OCC has applied for statehood in the past, unsuccessfully, and SysPol's services are one of the key benefits of statehood. That means its citizens, generally speaking, hold us in a positive light, but there's nothing on the books that compels their cooperation."

"Then we'll need to be discreet."

"And friendly." He gave her a meaningful look.

"I can do that."

"And you'll have to leave your gun behind."

She frowned at him. "If I must."

"Yes!" Cephalie thumped the air.

"Find something good?" Isaac asked.

"You could say that." She flourished a hand across the black-board. "Guess who else has been to the *Atomic Resort*? Why, none other than Delacroix himself! It was two months back, but Delacroix put in for vacation time and spent three days at the resort before he transmitted back to Earth. And it seems Stade was also at the resort during that very same week!"

"Another strong connection between those two," Isaac said, nodding. "And even more reason to head out there ourselves. Good work, Cephalie."

She took a bow from the table beside the recording.

"Then we're off to this resort next?" Susan asked.

"Yes, but let's not be hasty." Isaac glanced down at the two men in the cave. "Stade is a face we didn't have before, and I'm wondering if we might find connections elsewhere."

He opened a comm window.

"What's on your mind?" Susan asked.

"Just checking a hunch. This shouldn't take long."

The call went through, and a bald synthoid with powder white skin, black eyes, and black lipstick appeared in the window.

"Hello, Mister Chow—"

"Caravaggio!" the synthoid spat quickly. "The name's Neon Caravaggio!" He leaned toward the screen and spoke softer. "I'm working right now. Sorry for yelling."

"I understand, Mister Caravaggio. My sincerest apologies for the confusion. I was thinking of someone else. Would you mind if I trouble you with a few questions? Is now a good time?"

"Yes, of course. I could use the break." He stood up and began walking. "Did you two like the artshirts?"

"Umm..." Isaac recalled mulching the shirt on the train ride back. He glanced to Susan, who threw out a quick thumbs-up. "Agent Cantrell enjoyed hers."

"Oh, that's great to hear. Tell her there's more where that came from. Inspiration struck after you left, and I've started a new series." He spread his hands theatrically. "*Solar Descent* characters dressed as the men and women of SysPol! I think it'll be a hit. How about you?"

"Mister Caravaggio, I need to ask you about an individual who recently came to our attention. His name is Thomas Stade. I'm sending his picture over to you."

"Got it." Caravaggio studied the off-screen image. "Hmm. Talk about a plain face."

"Do you recognize him? Specifically, did you ever see him near your table or at any of your panels during DescentCon?"

"I don't think—" Caravaggio's mouth formed a sudden O. "Wait a second! That was the guy!"

"The guy?" Isaac asked.

"He must have been the strangest customer I had all convention."

"How so?"

"He came up to my table and said he wanted a gift for a friend. I began my normal intro where I go over the more popular items in my catalog, and he totally ignored me! He just pointed up at one of the shirts I had on display and said, 'That one.' So, I asked him if he'd like me to print a new one or if he'd prefer to purchase a single-use pattern license. You know, normal sales process.

"But the guy refused! Said he wanted the shirt hanging way up on my booth display! I again tried to offer him a freshly printed one, but he wouldn't hear it. He insisted I pull the display shirt down and sell him that one."

"How did you respond?" Isaac asked.

"Well, you know how it is. A sale's a sale, right? So, I got out of my booth, took the shirt down, and sold him that one." Caravaggio shook his head. "Weird guy. Didn't even wait for me to sign it."

"Did stepping out of the booth place the two of you in closer proximity?"

"Of course, it did. And he stayed close to me while I brought it down. Like, creepy close. In fact— Oh!" Caravaggio sucked in a quick breath. "Was he the guy? Did that [BLEEP]ing [BLEEP]sack give me the virus?"

"I can't answer that other than to say we are investigating the matter."

"I bet it was! That [BLEEP]ing creepstick! I knew he wasn't a real fan!"

"Thank you, Mister Caravaggio. You've been most helpful."

"Why that [BLEEP]ing piece of [BLEEP]ing [BLEEP] [BLEEP]! He'd better hope I never see his boring face ag—"

Isaac closed the comm window.

"Stade was at DescentCon," Susan summarized. "And he came into close contact with the virus vector."

"This lead is looking better by the minute." Isaac permitted himself a wolfish grin.

"We thought Caravaggio was a good lead, too."

"Let's keep a positive attitude, shall we?"

"You still want me to chase down the convention security video?" Cephalie asked. "They did finally get back to me, but it sounds like they intend to contest the warrant."

"Keep on it for now and widen it to include any video of Stade. It's possible Caravaggio wasn't his only errand at the convention." Isaac opened a new window. "Dispatch."

"Themis Dispatch here. How may we serve you, Detective?"

"I'd like to requisition a variable-wing aircraft. Our investigation is taking us off Janus-Epimetheus, and I'm not sure where it'll take us next."

"Understood, Detective. Would you like the v-wing to be armed?"

"Oh, no. I don't think that's nece—"

"Arm it," Susan interjected.

"We're only flying out to the resort," Isaac pointed out.

"We're also hot on the trail of a man suspected of killing two cops. We should prepare accordingly."

"That's . . ." Isaac hesitated with a grimace. He couldn't fault her logic.

"Better safe than sorry," she added.

"Will that be armed or unarmed, Detective?" Dispatch asked.

"Fine," he grumbled. "Arm it up. Just stay clear of anything too . . . flamboyant. We're heading for an OCC dirigible next."

"Not a problem, Detective. I'll see to it the v-wing is equipped with an appropriate defensive package. Where would you like your transport delivered?"

"New Frontier Airport, please."

"Understood. Your request is in the queue. The v-wing should be ready for pickup in about two hours. Is there anything else I can assist you with?"

"Not right now, Dispatch. Thanks."

"Our pleasure, Detective."

The comm window closed.

"Cephalie, how fancy is the resort?"

"Depends which parts we visit, but most areas are *very* high end."

"Then we should dress the part. Our uniforms will only serve to draw unwanted attention, anyway." He massaged his face, then glanced to Susan. "Did you bring any formal patterns with you?"

"No."

"You'll need to take care of that when we stop back at the hotel."

❖　　❖　　❖

In her hotel room, Susan activated the delivery port's attendant program.

"Hello, Miss Cantrell!" the program said. "How are you today?"

"I have a problem."

"I'm listening and ready to be of service."

"I have no idea how SysGov formal wear works."

"Could you please clarify the nature of your problem?"

"You don't understand." Her brow creased with worry. "I don't do formal. You see what I'm wearing now? *This* is formal for me." She sighed heavily. "I need help."

"I'm ready to be of assistance, Miss Cantrell."

"Can you help me pick something out? I need something classy to wear, and I need it fast. We're leaving for the airport soon."

"Of course, Miss Cantrell. We have a vast selection of Saturnite clothing patterns, ranging from Ballast Heights couture to the latest Epimethean trends, all ready for on-demand printing. Would you like to view a sample? It's recommended you select a base garment first, then choose a dynamic scarf or other accessory to complement the base."

"Sure. Let's see a few."

A bright green gown appeared.

"No."

The gown vanished, replaced with a black one-piece...bathing suit?

"No."

A gray business suit with a cleavage window popped up next.

"No."

A fluorescent pink...abomination with too many straps appeared.

"Hell no."

"Perhaps if you explain why a pattern isn't to your liking, I can better filter the catalog."

The previous selections arranged themselves in a row. Susan pointed to each in turn.

"Hate the color. Too much ass. Too much cleavage. Too much of both and a *terrible* color."

"I see. Filtering the catalog now."

A snug, light gray business suit came up next.

"Okay, now you're on the right track. Let's see some more like that one."

Isaac waited in the Top Shelf Hotel lobby and smoothed out the front of his black formal wear. He looked good in black; most people did, he reflected, but he'd added a splash of color with a dynamic purple scarf that feature electrified energy crackling along its length.

"She's taking longer than I thought she would," he commented.

"Want me to go check on her?" Cephalie offered, hopping to his shoulder.

Isaac checked his abstract clock. "Not yet. We'll wait." He glanced to the counter-grav shaft, then to Cephalie. "Did she seem worried to you?"

"Hadn't noticed." Cephalie yawned into a fist.

"She seemed worried. I wonder why."

Isaac checked his clock a few more times as he waited, and just before they were due to leave, Susan floated out of the shaft, dressed in a dark gray business suit with long sleeves and a high collar. She'd forgone a scarf in favor of a silver, shield-shaped pin at her throat. The gun at her hip stuck out, though.

She walked over and did a double take when she saw him.

"Something wrong?" he asked.

"Are those the same colors as Big Stompy?" she asked with a shrewd half smile.

"I exercise my right to remain silent." He gestured to her new clothes. "You look good, by the way."

"Thank you."

"You'll have to leave your gun in the v-wing." Isaac tapped the side of the LENS. "Same with this."

"Resort rules, I assume."

"As far as the guests are concerned. They'll have armed security."

"What about my body?"

"You have any projectile weapons or explosives in secret compartments? Anything like that?"

"No."

"Then we should be fine. Oortans don't judge when it comes to a person's synthoid. Let's go."

They both climbed into the car, and the door sealed shut.

"Vehicle, take us to New Frontier Airport, Bay Three."

"Destination set. Departing."

The car pulled out of the hotel parking lot and merged onto the main Shelf Six highway. It drove half a kilometer, then began taking down ramps, descending through the city.

"How do we approach this when we get there?" Susan asked. "Besides hunt and peck, I mean."

"I've given that question some thought, and here's what I've come up with." Isaac opened a profile and passed her a virtual copy. "Meet the owner of the *Atomic Resort*."

"'Fat Man,'" she read. "Lovely."

"Mmhmm."

The profile included images of a morbidly obese male, clothed in dark purple finery and seated in a plush recliner, the folds of his massive girth spilling over the armrests, legs and arms sagging with extra flesh.

"His physical shape is deceiving," Cephalie explained. "Fat Man inhabits a synthoid, and he's old. *Very* old. First entries in his SysPol file were from three centuries ago, and given all that time, he remains an enigma to this day. We don't even know if his connectome was originally organic or artificial, and we're pretty sure that body hides tech illegal in SysGov."

"Has he ever come into conflict with SysPol?" Susan asked.

"A few minor incidents," Cephalie said. "Most stem from customer complaints, but his Oortan status protected him without fail. Given the timespans we're dealing with, the volume is barely background noise for a business of his size."

"This is where I propose we start," Isaac said. "We have no jurisdiction over there, but that doesn't mean Fat Man won't give us what we want."

"We start by asking nicely?"

"Exactly. Let's see what that gets us and go from there."

"And if he turns us away?"

"Then we ask around until we find something," Isaac said.

"Sounds like we could be there for a while."

"There are worse places to be stuck. Remember Nina and her printers?"

"Yeah." Susan chuckled.

The car pulled away from a down ramp and drove toward the outer wall of Shelf Two. Abstract marquees lit up the outer wall around the three airport bays, listing pending arrivals and departures and providing directions to nearby waiting areas and restaurants. The car passed through an automatic security check-point, then drove up to Bay Three, the smallest of the airport bays and meant for private launches.

Isaac climbed out of the car and walked up to the hexagonal bay door. An airline AC with the avatar of an old-fashioned aviator materialized next to him.

"Detective Cho, is it?"

"That's right."

"Your v-wing came in from Kronos Station a few minutes ago. We'll have it shifted over momentarily. Please wait here."

The AC vanished, and a virtual caution sign pulsed over the hexagonal door. The airport stored private craft in hexagonal bins arranged below the launch bays, and when a craft was needed, a robotic storage and retrieval system (SRS) shifted the bin up to the correct bay. Some aircraft were too large for individual bins, and in those cases, multiple bins would be merged to make room in the storage system.

The SysPol v-wing only took up a single bin, and an abstract window in the bay door provided a view of the bin rising before it locked into place. The caution sign vanished, the hexagonal bay door split aside, and Isaac walked over to the aircraft.

"You know," he said, circling the v-wing, "when the dispatcher said 'appropriate defensive package,' this was *not* what I was expecting."

The variable-wing aircraft's body could dynamically shift through numerous configurations, and the current shape was optimized for Saturn's dense atmosphere at the bottom of the Shark Fin. Prog-steel formed a thick, gunmetal gray delta wing with a small crew cabin at the front, winglets at the edges of the delta, and a tall vertical stabilizer situated above the rear-mounted graviton thruster.

"What were you expecting?" Susan asked.

"Something less loud." Isaac used his boot to prod the bottom of the fat weapon blister beneath the v-wing's nose. A cluster of seven barrels protruded from the blister's front. "What's this supposed to be, anyway?"

"A thirty-millimeter Gatling gun?" Cephalie offered.

"And these?" Isaac gestured to racks underneath the wings. "What are these?"

"Those would be the precision micro-missiles," Cephalie said.

"Do we really need all this?" He turned to Susan.

"Don't look at me. I didn't pick the loadout. Though"—she caressed the Gatling barrels with the smallest hint of a smile—"I feel a lot safer now that I've seen it."

"But all we're doing is flying to an Oortan dirigible."

"You'd feel the same as me if you'd dealt with *Admin* Oortans before."

"This had better not cause problems at the resort," Isaac said. "Cephalie, do we have clearance to land there?"

"Yes."

"Do they know we're packing this much firepower?"

"Yes."

"All right, then," Isaac huffed, then shrugged his arms. "I guess I'm the only one who sees a problem. Who am I to complain?"

He climbed on board.

The v-wing rose through dark clouds lit within by the rare streak of lightning. The aircraft's sharp-edged delta morphed into a straight wing more suited for gliding through the thinner upper atmosphere. Night had fallen over Janus-Epimetheus, and the glittering lights of its crown turned nearby clouds into a glowing haze.

The v-wing sped away from the megastructure and toward a far smaller collection of lights that slowly resolved into a grand dirigible with an egg-shaped main body ahead of box-shaped rear fins, greatly resembling the "Fat Man" Mark III nuclear bomb from Earth's distant past. Lights glowed atop the dorsal landing bays and from the dirigible's sixty-level outer concourses, built along the outside of its primary exotic foam bladders.

A series of large hoops and pillars floated around the resort in a rough circle, and over thirty v-wings raced through the ever-changing obstacle course. More craft flew into the dorsal bays or departed through the ventral hangar.

"You think Fat Man will ever branch out with a second dirigible?" Isaac asked.

"Who knows?" Cephalie said.

"Think he'll theme it after the Little Boy if he does?"

"Hard to say."

"Why would he do that?" Susan asked.

"Well...I mean..." Isaac gestured to the dirigible, growing larger as they approached. "Just look at it."

"Yes, I see it," Susan said. "What does the resort have to do with little boys?"

"Not boys. Little *Boy*. As in the nuke dropped on Hiroshima."

"What are you talking about?" Susan asked with genuine confusion.

"You know. The two most famous bombs in Earth's history. Fat Man and Little Boy."

"I'm sorry. You've completely lost me."

"Isaac." Cephalie leaped to his shoulder and whispered into her ear. "World War II played out differently in her universe. The United States never nuked Japan."

"Oh, right." He smiled apologetically at Susan. "Whoops. Sorry."

"Did you just forget I'm not from around here?"

"Momentary lapse. Won't happen again," he assured her.

"Don't try too hard." She smiled back at him. "I'll take this as a compliment."

The v-wing slowed over the vast dirigible's dorsal hangar bays. A hexagonal port opened, the v-wing pulled its wings into its main body, and the graviton thruster eased them down. They touched down on the landing cradle with a small jostle, the bay door sealed above them, and the hangar SRS robotics maneuvered their bin to an empty egress point.

Their bin locked into place, the air finished cycling, and the v-wing's atmospheric indicators lit up green. The cabin hatch split open, and a stairway extruded to the floor.

"Fat Man approved our meeting request," Cephalie said, materializing on Isaac's shoulder. "He's at his personal balcony overlooking the arena. We can head up whenever."

"Then let's not keep him waiting." Isaac climbed out of the v-wing cabin and hustled down the steps.

One wall of their bin parted to reveal a long hallway connecting to other bins on one side and lined with open counter-grav shafts on the other. Guests in Lunarian, Martian, Saturnite, and Jovian finery headed to or from their own rides as Isaac and Susan approached the nearest shaft.

Cephalie entered their destination, and they stepped in. Gravitons whisked them upward at a diagonal toward the front of the dirigible, then deposited them in a wide circular balcony with rich, red carpeting, plush recliners, and windows angled outward for a better view of the arena.

Fat Man leaned against a railing by the window, watching the match play out, and an Oortan squidform synthoid stood guard near him, its eight tentacles tipped with projectile weapons. The squidform's mechanical, many-eyed head swiveled in quick, jerky bursts of motion as it scrutinized them with a variety of sensors.

"Well, if it isn't a SysPol detective and his entourage!" Fat Man beckoned for them to approach. "Please! Come here! Come here!"

"Thank you for agreeing to see us," Isaac said, walking over.

"Oh, it's no trouble, Detective." Fat Man let out a deep, boisterous chuckle. "I welcome all to my humble establishment, SysPol included. But before business, perhaps a dash of pleasure, if you'll indulge me." He spread an open hand toward the arena, and the fatty jowl under his arm wobbled. "Who do you think will win?"

Isaac gazed into the fighting pit below. Two synthoids battled each other amidst a ruined, urban landscape. One was a hulking brass-skinned brute sporting a pair of war hammers, the other a lithe, silvery acrobat brandishing a flexible whip-sword. If the brute landed a single hit, he'd crush the speedster.

"I'm not sure I'm the right person to ask," Isaac said. "Perhaps the—"

"The silver one," Susan cut in.

Isaac glanced her way but didn't say anything, and she gave him a quick wink. If that's who she thought would win, who was he to argue?

"You sure about that, my dear?" Fat Man asked. "Raging Hammersmith is a seasoned veteran of the arena. All the smart Esteem's on him, whereas Silver Slash is a relative unknown, just working her way up the ranks."

"I know a winner when I see one," Susan replied confidently.

"Oh ho! Is that so?"

"She has a good eye," the squidform said in a husky male voice.

"I'm inclined to agree. This is Thorn, by the way." Fat Man

laid a bejeweled hand upon the synthoid's shoulder. "Champion of the Atomic Arena and my personal bodyguard."

Thorn bowed with a sweep of two tentacles.

"Tell you what," Fat Man said. "How about I put in a small bet in your name? If Silver Slash wins, you can keep it. If not..." He shrugged, and several parts of him jiggled. "We'll call it a harmless bit of fun and move on."

"Sounds like I have nothing to lose," she said.

"Indeed not!" Fat Man opened an interface and entered a wager in Susan's name. "There. And now, I'm sure you're all eager to get to business." He clasped his hands. "How can this old devil be of service?"

"We're looking for information on two men." Isaac opened profiles on Delacroix and Stade. "Both have been to your resort in the past few months."

"Oh dear." Fat Man's jowls wobbled under his mouth. "I'm all for friendly cooperation with SysPol, but when you start talking about breaches of customer confidentiality..." He spread his hands in the way of an apology.

"One of them is a deceased Gordian Division agent."

"And the other?"

"Possibly involved in his murder."

"How dreadful. Well, that does change the arithmetic of the matter." Fat Man placed a thoughtful finger against his puffy lips. "If we're talking about a *SysPol* agent, and a *dead* one at that, then I suppose I can bend the rules in the spirit of respecting your organization's loss. But the other man..." He shook his head.

"I'll take any information you can give me."

"Which one is the agent?"

Isaac presented Delacroix's profile, and Fat Man copied it.

"Let's see what we find." He perused his records behind a privacy filter. "Yes, there he is. Joachim Delacroix. A rather focused individual, it would seem. He knew exactly what he wanted and where to get it."

"Why do you say that?"

"Because, according to my records, he spent almost three whole days at the Made-For-You brothel in the Nose Concourse. Very upscale, but *very* expensive."

CHAPTER TWENTY-ONE

"A BROTHEL?" SUSAN ASKED DOUBTFULLY.

"I know," Isaac said. "Doesn't make sense, but there it is."

"I looked over Made-For-You's pricing," Cephalie said, her avatar seated on Isaac's shoulder. "Fat Man wasn't kidding about them being expensive."

The counter-grav shaft deposited them near the bottom level of the Nose Concourse. Level after level extended out from a bulbous structural dome to press against a clear view of the Saturn night sky. An obstacle loop hovered near them, and v-wings streaked through in a blur of lights. Abstract displays updated the race's leading positions, and crowds along the giant window cheered for their favorites.

Isaac opened a resort map over his palm, then guided them to the right along the level's curve. They passed storefronts displaying Oortan goods, marquees listing the racing and arena odds, and advertisements for restaurants, hotels, and brothels.

"What a . . . colorful place," Susan remarked.

"Locations like these exist outside SysGov law," Isaac explained. "And the Oortans are a highly distributed society. Very little central control, which translates into limited regulation, and even what they have is difficult to enforce over such vast distances. The lack of a central authority was one of the key problems with their application for statehood."

"How so?"

"Who exactly does SysGov coordinate with in a society that decentralized? And there were other issues. During the application process, the Oortans tried to take a census three times in order to determine how many representatives they'd receive in the House, but they came up with three vastly different numbers. That doesn't exactly bode well for them in a representative democracy."

"I see."

Susan eyeballed an advertisement for the Tender Arms brothel featuring a naked woman wrapped in the strategically placed tentacles of an Oortan squidform. She shuddered as they walked on.

"Is most of this illegal on Janus?" she asked.

"Some of it. Depends on the local ordinance," Isaac said. "What are the Oortans like in your universe?"

"They don't run gambling resorts, that's for sure. Some of them are upstanding members of society, but their settlements are notorious hangouts for anti-Admin terrorists and criminal cabals."

"There seem to be a lot of 'anti-Admin' groups over there."

"That's why we must remain ever vigilant." An alert chimed in Susan's periphery, and she slowed down and opened it. "Oh, neat."

"What is it?"

"Silver Slash won the match, and the resort credited me with a generous chunk of Esteem. It's nice to have some spending money after everything I dumped into Free Gate."

"We can celebrate later," Isaac said dryly.

The entrance to Made-For-You stood in a discreet corner at the far end of the level's curve. Sheer white curtains covered the outer walls, and suggestive shadows writhed behind them. A tall woman stood at the podium by the door and looked up attentively as they approached. Her long, golden hair and the subtle points of her ears gave her an elven air, and her flowing white dress hinted at the sumptuous curves underneath.

"Yuck," Cephalie said. "Call me if you need me."

She vanished from Isaac's shoulder.

The woman at the podium waited patiently for them to approach. Then, and only then, did she acknowledge their arrival with a curt dip of her head.

"Greetings," she began in a light, ethereal voice, "and welcome to Made-For-You, the last word in personalized sensual experiences." She placed a hand against her bosom. "I'm Mistress Succulent, and may I say, you've arrived at the *perfect* time! We're having a special on all our couples-themed services. Pay once, come twice."

She winked at Isaac, and he suppressed the desire to groan at her joke.

"Oh, we're not a couple." Susan sidestepped away from Isaac for emphasis. "We only work together."

"That's quite all right, miss. Whether you're romantically involved or simply curious, we provide *ample* services for all our customers. From soft, loving scenarios for those with sensitive tastes to wild adventures the most daring minds can scarcely imagine. With us, you can experience everything from baseline roleplays to limitless fantasies impossible in the physical. Whether you wish to dive into a custom abstraction or experience your pleasure in the flesh, we'll cater to your every desire."

"Could you be more specific about the services you provide?" Isaac asked.

"Of course, sir." Succulent leaned forward on the podium, providing Isaac with a deep view of her cleavage. "Every experience is handcrafted by our award-winning team of experts, be they abstractionists for your virtual pleasures or cyberneticists behind the designs of your synthoid partners. It says it all in our name. Every experience, down to the last glistening drop of sweat, is made *especially* for you.

"And if that sort of handcrafting isn't to your liking, we offer more"—she flashed a sultry smile—"immediate relief in the form of our most popular scenarios, all expertly crafted with the same loving care and attention to detail."

Isaac frowned. What could Delacroix have possibly wanted here, other than the obvious?

"Are you the owner of this establishment?" Isaac asked.

"Yes, sir. That I am."

"And if we were to place an order, would you be the one to handle the specifics?"

"Initially, yes," Succulent said, "though I'd place you in the care of one of our specialists once we've narrowed down the services you desire."

"And do you handle all customer orders that way?"

"Most of them, yes, sir. I'm not here all the time, of course, but I make it a point to check in with every customer at least once to ensure they're being serviced to our high, exacting standards."

Isaac paused before his next question.

There's no good way to ask this, he thought. *Might as well go for it and see what happens.*

"What if I wanted to purchase the same scenario you provided someone else? Would that be possible?"

"Sir, please." She smiled sweetly at him. "We operate at our customers' pleasure. *And* their discretion. I couldn't possibly reveal that kind of sensitive, confidential information, unless this other customer you mentioned gave me explicit permission to do so."

"Unfortunately, the other customer has passed away. Permanently. Would confidentially still be an issue?"

"Oh, I *see* now! I was wondering about all your questions." Succulent grinned at him and folded her arms under her breasts. "You two are cops, aren't you?"

Isaac grimaced.

"Called it!" Succulent said brightly.

"Well," Susan sighed. "It was worth a shot."

"Mistress Succulent," Isaac began, "my name is Detective Isaac Cho, SysPol Themis, and this is Agent Susan Cantrell. We're in pursuit of a cop killer; the victim made extensive use of your services in the past, and we would greatly appreciate any assistance you can provide."

"Hmm." Succulent tapped her lips. "Cop killer you say. Show me who the victim is, and I'll think about it. No promises, though."

Isaac offered her Delacroix's profile over an open palm.

"'Delacroix. Joachim,'" Succulent read, entering the name into an interface fuzzed behind a privacy filter. "Yes, here he is." Her eyes scrolled through the entry, but then stopped suddenly. She paused, fixated by some unseen fact, then she composed herself and shook her head. "I'm sorry, I won't be able to help you. You're right that Delacroix and his boyfriend spent some quality time with us, but I simply can't in good conscience share the details with you. I'm very sorry, Detective, but that's the way it has to be."

His boyfriend? Isaac thought. He wasn't sure if Succulent had made a genuine slip or if she'd provided him with a tidbit on the sly, but either way, he wasn't sure what to make of it.

"I understand," he said stiffly. "Thank you for your time, then."

He and Susan left the brothel and headed back toward the counter-grav shafts.

"His *boyfriend*?" Susan asked under her breath and in security chat.

"I caught that, too. What's going on here?" Isaac looked around. "Cephalie?"

She appeared on his shoulder. "You done talking about yucky stuff?"

"We are. I need you to check Delacroix's files again. Look for any indicators he might have been bisexual."

"Will do, though I doubt I'll turn up anything," Cephalie said.

◆   ◆   ◆

"As far as I can tell, Delacroix's as hetero as they come," Cephalie reported from the small coffee table.

"Figured." Isaac took another sip from his coffee. He and Susan sat next to the concourse window outside Supercharged, which advertised itself as "The Best Brain Fuel Around."

"This coffee is a little on the strong side," Susan complained, setting her cup down.

"Really?" Isaac swirled his own cup and gazed into it. "Seems just right to me."

"You think Stade is the 'boyfriend'?"

"That seems the most likely explanation. Stade was here at the same time Delacroix was two months ago."

"And then Stade came back three weeks ago, right after their argument in Free Gate."

"Mmhmm."

"But why?" Susan wondered.

"Don't know." Isaac drummed his fingers on the coffee table. "What could they possibly want in a brothel?"

In SysGov, the answers would have been a search warrant away. He'd have access to all the resort's records, and he'd sit down and interview all the key players. The mechanisms of SysPol would grind forward, churning out the truth piece by piece.

But not here.

Which is why they did whatever they did at the resort and not on Janus, he thought. *But what did they do here? Why did they argue about it in Free Gate? Why was Delacroix killed on the way back to Saturn?*

"Something on your mind?" Susan asked.

"Just trying to figure out where we go next."

"The way I see it," she began, "there are two people who know what we need to know: Fat Man and Succulent."

"And neither of them will give us what we want."

"Perhaps..." Susan said slyly, and Isaac looked up at her. "You're right they won't *give* us the information." She gazed out as the v-wings raced past in another circuit. "But that's not how this place works."

"Are you suggesting we *purchase* what we need?"

"In a sense."

"I don't know," Isaac said. "It'll take a *lot* of Esteem to make Fat Man budge, assuming it's even *possible*, and I doubt Succulent's business is doing poorly either. Sex sells, as they say." He blew out a breath. "But I also don't know where to go next. Tell you what. I'll give Raviv a call after we finish our coffee. Let's see if he'll free up some funds for us to try buttering them up with."

"Actually"—Susan's eyes twinkled with mischief—"I had something else in mind."

✧　　✧　　✧

"Detective Cho!" Fat Man bellowed boisterously. "And Agent Cantrell! What a pleasant surprise! What brings you back so soon?"

"Hello, Fat Man." Susan leaned against the railing and glanced down at the arena, now modeled after a sweltering bog with twisted, diseased trees rising from the muck. Two teams of three synthoids each battled it out across the swamp, engaging in quick bursts of melee combat before breaking off and circling each other again.

"Care to make another wager, my dear?" Fat Man gestured to the arena. "The combatants are just getting warmed up. I'd love to hear what your young, insightful eye sees this time."

"That can wait." Susan crossed her arms. "Tell me, do you hold exhibition matches here?"

"I have on occasion." He regarded her with a guarded expression. "Why do you ask?"

Susan held up an abstract image of a Peacekeeper-blue synthoid with white racing stripes, festooned with weapons.

"What's this?" Fat Man took the image into his palms, and Thorn elongated four "foot" tentacles to peer over his master's shoulder. Fat Man spun the model around and opened the weapon and performance specifications. "Oh my! What a beauty!"

"What you're looking at is a Peacekeeper Type-99 STAND combat frame," Susan announced with glee. "*My* combat frame. Top-of-the-line Admin technology. It's fast, tough, and deadly." She pointed a thumb at the arena. "Got anyone you think could hold their own against me?"

"A military synthoid!" His eyes sparkled with the possibilities. "A military synthoid from another universe! In my arena? No one else can claim that! We'll be the talk of Janus for years!"

"This is worth something to you?"

"Oh, I knew you were something special from the moment I met you!" Fat Man turned to Thorn. "Didn't I just tell you that?"

"I don't seem to recall—"

Fat Man clunked the top of the squidform's head.

"Oh wait," Thorn added dryly. "Now I remember."

"Agent Cantrell—or, Susan. Can I call you Susan?" He took her delicate hands into his fat-fingered hams. "We're going to make a mint off this idea of yours! But there are a few issues, I fear. First, some of those weapons won't work in my arena—they'd blow holes clean through the walls."

"Not a problem. All the weapon systems are modular."

"Fantastic. The incinerator can stay, but the rail-rifle and grenade launcher need to go. We can provide you with a selection of weaponry to replace them. And with that, there's only one other teeny, tiny problem left to consider."

"Which is?"

"Who are you going to fight? I can't throw any old riffraff at you! No, this needs to be something grand. Something *special!*" He turned to Thorn.

"Do I get a say in this?" the squidform asked.

"No."

"I thought not." Thorn said, and his tentacles drooped sadly.

"Oh, I can see it now!" Fat Man gazed up and spread a hand over an imagined future. "Thorn the Destroyer, Champion of the Arena, versus..." He paused as he tried to come up with something suitable, then: "The Thug from the Admin!"

"*Excuse* me?" Susan asked crossly.

"Or something else," Fat Man assured her. "We can figure out your arena name later. What matters is we're both going to be swimming in Esteem over this deal!"

"That's all fine," Susan said, leaning toward him, "but Esteem doesn't interest me. I'm not from around here, so it might as well be play money you're offering. I want something else. Something of far more value to me and the detective."

"Name it, my dear!"

"I want your full record of both Joachim Delacroix's and Thomas Stade's activities on the *Atomic Resort*."

"Oh ho!" Fat Man chuckled. "I should have known. I see what you did there." He put a hand on Thorn's shoulder. "You see what she did there?"

"I saw."

"I'm expecting complete access," Susan stressed. "No holding back."

"Of course, you are." Fat Man ran a finger down his many chins. "In that case, I'll want some extra assurance. Let's say, an exclusivity clause in the contract. A guarantee you won't fight in any arenas but mine for one year."

"Done."

"Then it seems we have a tentative deal?"

"We do."

"Well then, I'll get started on the contract." He rubbed his hands together, fat jiggling under his forearms. "And after that, all that's left is to set the date and start advertising."

"The sooner the better," Susan stressed. "We have a killer to chase down."

"Of course, I understand you have other commitments. With an event like this, an advertising blitz across all concourses should only take a day to saturate."

"That should work for us as well," Isaac chimed in. "We need time to collect her combat frame out of Kronos storage."

"Wonderful. Let's all meet later today and finalize the details over dinner. In the meantime"—he offered Susan a keycode—"please accept this complimentary room for use while you stay. It's for the Ring Suites penthouse atop the Starboard Concourse. I'm sure you'll find it to your liking, but if anything is wrong, please don't hesitate to let me know."

"Ring Suites?" Susan noted with a frown. "Will it be furnished?"

"Why wouldn't it be?" Fat Man replied, brow furrowed with confusion.

✧   ✧   ✧

"Furniture," Susan said with a smile, surveying the lavish furnishings in the penthouse's central space.

"Speak for yourself." Cephalie conjured a miniature recliner atop the kitchenette counter and leaped into it.

Isaac peeked in one of the bedrooms.

"And they already have my favorite bed printed out," he said. "Nice."

Susan walked up to the window and watched the Saturnite dawn.

"Am I breaking any rules by doing this?" she asked suddenly.

"A little late for that, don't you think?"

"But am I?"

"Eh." Isaac shrugged. "You might be bending them uncomfortably. I don't think SysPol detectives as Oortan gladiators is the preferred look."

"Want me to stop?"

"No, no," he clarified. "By all means, please continue. Raviv might complain, but we can sell him your idea easily enough. All we have to say is we're trying to crack this case as fast as possible, like he told us. 'Innovative out-of-the-box thinking.' That's how I'll word it. At worst, he might scold us." He joined her at the window. "What about your government? Are they going to be fine with this?"

"They're the ones who sent me over with the combat frame. I assume they intended for me to use it."

"Fair enough. I'll call it over, then." Isaac opened a comm window. "Dispatch."

"Themis Dispatch here. We read you, Detective Cho. How can we help?"

"I had a storage crate consigned to the station's logistics centers a few days ago, and I need it retrieved and brought to my location at the *Atomic Resort*. Sending my case number now."

"Case number received. Give me a moment, sir," the dispatcher replied. "Ah, here we are. Seems there were additional instructions attached to the storage order. Pulling it out may take longer than usual."

"Oh? What seems to be the problem?"

"You tell me, Detective. I have a message here to, and I quote, 'Shove this thing into the deepest, darkest pit of the station's logistics centers, never to see the light of day again,' unquote."

Susan raised an eyebrow at him, and his face reddened.

"I ... don't remember saying that." He cleared his throat and glanced over at Cephalie. "Did I say that?"

She held up a sign that read: YOU DID.

"That doesn't sound like something I'd say."

"Detective, I see there's an audio file attached to the note. I could replay it for you, if you like."

"Uh, no." He made a point of avoiding Susan's gaze. "That, umm, won't be necessary."

"Fortunately, it seems the crate has yet to be shifted to long-term storage. There. I've halted the deep storage order and will queue a new one for delivery to your location. You should have it in about three hours. Will that be sufficient, or do you need expedited delivery?"

"No, that'll work. Thank you, Dispatch. That's all for now."

"You're welcome, Detective."

The comm window closed.

"'Deepest, darkest pit'?" Susan asked, a quirky smile on her lips. "'Never to see the light of day again'?"

"I'm sure I didn't mean it like that."

Cephalie held up a new sign that read: HE MEANT EVERY WORD.

"*You*"—he pointed at the avatar—"are not helping!"

✧   ✧   ✧

Thorn sat down at the square, steel table in the center of the bland abstraction. Six of his eight tentacles folded like baseline human legs, and he placed two of his tentacles on the table, contracted and bent like human arms. His head revolved in quick jerks, regarding the figure seated on the opposite side through various inputs. None of them elucidated the mysterious individual's identity, since the person's avatar was a black silhouette with a thick white border.

"Who are you, and what do you want?" he demanded.

The response took eight seconds to arrive, which made Thorn suspect the signal came from one of Saturn's moons.

"Like my message said, just think of me as a fan," the figure replied in a synthesized voice as fake as its avatar. "Though if you insist on a name, you can call me Ōdachi."

Thorn wondered at the wisdom of meeting this anonymous individual, but the message he'd received had piqued his interest. The exhibition match was unusual in and of itself, his opponent was unlike anyone he'd ever faced, and then a mysterious "fan" sends him a carefully worded message an hour after the first advertisement aired.

I KNOW HER WEAKNESS, the title had read.

And so, curious to learn more, he found himself here, seated in an encrypted abstract domain across from a shadowy "fan."

"Whatever," Thorn said at last. "Keep your real name to yourself. Just get to the point. What is it you want?"

"To help you."

"I don't need your help."

"You think you can take that Admin killing machine on your own?"

"She's never fought in the arena before. That gives me the advantage."

"She's an Admin Peacekeeper. A STAND. A synthetic soldier on the front lines of her universe's hottest conflicts."

"That's not the same thing."

"No," Ōdachi said confidently. "It's worse."

Thorn leaned back. He was Fat Man's champion, and he enjoyed the benefits of the old synthoid's patronage. Would their relationship change if he lost? Would he start to lose some of his luster? Would Fat Man seek out another champion to stand at the top of his roster? This was an exhibition match, sure, but that meant little to Thorn. He fought to win, always. The audience deserved no less than his best.

"Do you think she understands the etiquette of the arena?" Ōdachi asked. "The unspoken rules of engagement you and the other gladiators live by? Of course not. She's going to come at you with everything she's got, because that's all she understands."

The same thought had occurred to Thorn as well, and it worried him. Dueling this agent of the Admin would be unlike any match he'd ever fought. Would a little extra help—a little insurance—really injure his pride that much?

"What are you offering?"

"This." A glowing file appeared between them.

"What is it?"

"The Gordian Division's tactical analysis for the Peacekeeper Type-92 combat frame," Ōdachi said.

"Where did you get this?" Thorn asked.

"I have my sources."

"Few people have access to the Gordian Division's databanks."

"Yes," Ōdachi said in an oily tone. "Few people do."

"Why give it to me?"

"Let's just say I'm not a fan of hers and leave it at that."

"Fine. Keep your secrets." He leaned closer and scrutinized the schematic. "Type-92?"

"It's not an exact match for the Type-99 Agent Cantrell is using, but you should find the information valuable, nonetheless."

Ōdachi opened the file, and the outline of a skeletal machine appeared. Its malmetal armor turned to glass, revealing the locations of actuators, power cells, booster fuel, infosystems, structural joins. It was all there.

But it was all for the wrong frame.

"Worthless," Thorn concluded.

"Don't be so hasty," Ōdachi urged. "You're missing the one critical difference between this combat frame and gladiator synthoids."

"And what's that?"

Ōdachi highlighted a single component in the heavily shielded center of the STAND combat frame.

"This. The connectome case."

"Case?"

"The Admin doesn't allow wireless transmission of connectomes, so the minds of their STAND agents inhabit a singular case, and this case must be transferred manually from one synthoid to the next."

"So what?"

"Susan Cantrell has no backup save of her connectome. She *only* exists within that case."

A chill of realization ran through Thorn's mind. Susan Cantrell could *die* in the arena? No gladiator would take such a risk! Every last one of them knew the infosystems in their synthoids could be wrecked beyond repair, and he personally created a connectome backup before each match because of the danger.

"This location is in the most heavily shielded part of the chassis," Thorn said.

"How you deal with that problem is up to you."

"How I *deal* with it?" he spat back.

"You want to win, don't you?" Ōdachi replied with smarmy confidence.

"Don't pretend like you know me."

"Oh, I don't need to pretend. You're an easy man to read, if 'man' even applies to you anymore," Ōdachi said. "Born Tyrone Hoag in orbit around the dwarf planet of Makemake twenty-three years ago. Received his wetware implants at the age of four and left his organic body behind at the age of fifteen. Look at all you've given up in the pursuit of your gladiatorial dream. Not only your flesh, but your humanity as well. You crave victory, and because of that hunger, you'll take this, whether you like it or not."

Thorn's temper flared and he almost closed out of the abstraction right then and there, but he hesitated. The file hung over the table, tempting him, seducing him with the promise of victory.

He was afraid; he admitted that to himself. Afraid of losing. Afraid of no longer being "The Champion." Afraid of Cantrell and her military synthoid humiliating him. And this mysterious person was right; Cantrell was going to hit him with everything she had. Shouldn't he do the same? Shouldn't he press every advantage, exploit every weakness.

Yes, but...

He hesitated.

Hesitated.

Hesitated.

And then he snatched the file up and left the abstraction without saying another word.

CHAPTER TWENTY-TWO

"I'VE DUG THROUGH THORN'S PAST MATCHES LIKE YOU ASKED," Cephalie said from Isaac's shoulder as he and Susan entered their v-wing bin. The crate containing the combat frame had been delivered by SysPol corvette and was now stowed in the v-wing's elongated main body.

"What did you find?" Isaac asked.

"About the only thing you can expect is the unexpected. He's famous for switching between different synthoids for each match, with little in the way of consistency in combat style or weaponry."

"Improv it is, then," Susan said with a shrug. "Should be fun."

Isaac palmed the release on the side of the v-wing, and prog-steel split open to reveal the storage crate. Susan entered her access code, and the crate's malmetal plating shifted to either side.

The combat frame stood tall inside the cramped space, a lithe war machine ready for battle.

"How does this work, exactly?" Isaac asked.

"I'll need you to remove my connectome case from my spine and install it in the combat frame." She tapped an open slot halfway down the combat frame's back. "It fits in right here. The frame will activate automatically after that, and I'll have complete control."

"And if it doesn't switch on?"

"It will."

"But if it doesn't?"

"Then pull the case out and put me back in my general purpose synthoid. Easy as that."

"Okay. Got it."

She removed a knife from the crate's back wall and handed it to him, grip first.

"What's this for?" Isaac asked, taking hold the knife.

"You'll need to cut through the epidermis to reach my case."

"The Admin makes people knife you in the back to transfer your connectome?" Isaac asked. "Who designed this system and what were they thinking?"

"It is what it is," Susan said with indifference.

"I can handle the transfer with the LENS, if you like," Cephalie offered.

"Thanks, but no thanks," Susan said. "No offense, but I'd prefer it if Isaac do this."

"Suit yourself." Cephalie vanished from Isaac's shoulder.

"I'm ready. Let's do this." Susan turned around and pulled up the top of her business suit, revealing her naked back and a small U-shaped indentation halfway up it. Abstract art materialized over her whole back in the form of a woman in flowing white robes with a skull wearing a silver circlet for a head. Isaac wondered if the image was supposed to represent death. The figure held a scroll of parchment in her hands, and it took a moment for his senses to translate the Admin version of English.

"Uh, Susan?"

"What?"

"There's a message on your back."

"So?"

"It says 'If you can see this, you're in big trouble.'"

"Oh. Whoops. Must have left it on default."

The scroll text changed to graphic instructions for removing her case.

"You can start cutting whenever."

"Right." Isaac lined up the tip of the knife with the top of the U-shape indentation and pushed in.

Slowly.

"What's taking so long?" Susan asked.

"I'm being careful."

"Why? You think you're going to hurt me with that little toothpick?"

"Hey. Do you want to do this yourself?"

"I *can't* do this myself. Otherwise I would."

"Then let me work in peace. This is my first time carving into someone's back."

"All right," she sighed. "Sorry."

"Almost got it." He curved the knife around, then drew it up through the U's remainder. He lifted the flap of flesh. "Okay, I see a slot in your spine."

"That's it. Ready?"

"Ready."

"Sending the release code."

The slot opened, and Susan's synthoid twitched, then locked in place.

Isaac reached into the slot, gripped a slender cartridge, and pulled it out. The cartridge was a square about the size and thickness of his palm with arrows on either side indicating the correct direction. He held it with both hands and walked—slowly and with great care—over to the back of the combat frame. He lined up the case with the slot and pushed in until he felt the first hint of resistance.

The combat frame shuddered, and he backed out of the v-wing.

Malmetal plates closed across the combat frame's back in three layers, and the head swiveled toward him.

"Susan?" he asked. "Everything okay?"

"Good work." The combat frame gave him a thumbs-up. "All systems green. I'm ready for action." The audio came over his virtual senses.

Susan-the-combat-frame pulled the shirt down over her general purpose synthoid's naked back. She picked up the empty husk, cradling its back and the crook of its knees with both arms, and placed it gently on the floor in the storage crate. Then she detached her rail-rifle and shoulder-mounted grenade launcher, stashed them next to her body, and sealed the container.

"Showtime!" she said with glee.

✧   ✧   ✧

Susan waited at her assigned position by an archway just outside the gladiatorial arena. A virtual window provided her with a view of the new landscape, now featuring a rolling, windswept desert with red craggy rocks dotting it like oblong stone pillars. It was a good combination of solid cover and open sight lines well-suited to her combat frame's maneuverability.

She switched on the vibro-axe in her right hand. Its leading edge blurred with deadly, rapid oscillations, and she swung it experimentally through the air. The arena weapon was solidly built with good heft and balance. She raised the incinerator in her left arm and fired a small test belch. A hot blue puff exhaled from the nozzle.

She had no idea what to expect from Thorn's combat synthoid, but flame and blade would see her through this.

"Ladies and gentlemen and abstracts!" the announcer began. "Welcome to our main event! Tonight, the *Atomic Resort* is proud to present a surprise exhibition match, held exclusively for your entertainment! In the bow corner, with an unprecedented fifty-seven match winning streak, your reigning champion! Please give an atomic welcome to Thorn the Destroyer!"

The archway on the far side opened, and Thorn stepped out in a black chassis wrapped with the silhouettes of green, thorny vines. He stood atop two flexible limbs, and another two limbs of equal length held dual vibro-swords. Heavy pauldrons sat atop his shoulders with graviton thruster assemblies arranged behind and above them like skeletal wings. He crossed his swords in an X before him, then swished them out to either side.

Susan couldn't hear the crowd, but Fat Man had told her the stadium seating was packed and half the resort had prepaid to watch remotely.

"And in the aft corner, his challenger. The soldier from another universe! The Thug from the Admin!"

If Susan had possessed a mouth and lungs, she would have sighed.

"Put your hands together for the Unbreakable Shield!"

The archway split apart, and Susan strode into the open. She changed the variskin over her left forearm to silver, expanded the malmetal to a door shield, and slammed its lower edge into the sands. Her shoulder and leg boosters heated up, and sand blasted out to either side.

She glanced up at Fat Man's balcony and saw Isaac wave at her from the railing. Both archways closed, and a giant number three rotated in the center of the area. It changed to a two, then a one, then finally spelled out FIGHT!

Thorn swiveled his thrusters and energized them, darting to Susan's left, and she engaged her own propulsion and flew to the right. They circled the arena, each wary of the other, the distance between them contracting as they both closed with the center.

Thorn cut in toward her, and she fired a burst from her incinerator, more as area denial than a full-on attack, and Thorn pulled back. They continued circling each other, now dangerously close. A single burst of speed inward from either combatant could bring them into direct conflict.

Her onboard infosystem analyzed Thorn's synthoid, and estimated performance data scrolled in her virtual vision.

"A little slower than me, it would seem," she murmured to herself. "Well then!"

She fired her boosters at full power and streaked toward the champion. He steadied himself with retro-thrust and held his ground with a rocky pillar at his back. He raised his swords as if ready to strike, but then both his pauldrons detached from the main body and flew at her.

"*What?!*"

She swung at the first pauldron, but the drone or whatever it was darted around her swipe and flew past. She caught a glimpse of chittering insect-like legs hidden within the pauldron's armored shell.

The second pauldron charged at her, and she bashed it away with her shield. The drone spun out of control, flared its thruster wings, and regrouped with the other pauldron behind her.

Thorn energized his back thrusters and shot in, faster than her projections without the pauldron weight. He brandished both swords and swung at her. She deflected one attack with her shield, but the other scraped against her thigh armor and hewed through the outer layer of microplates before she pulled away.

She landed on the side of a tall reddish rock and tracked Thorn's movements. All three segments of his synthoid docked, and he hovered in the air on a column of excited gravitons.

"Well, that was a neat trick." Susan spun her axe in a taunting flourish. "Seems I should be taking you a little more *seriously!*"

She kicked off the rock and lit her boosters, flying toward her opponent. Thorn detached one of his pauldrons and sent it arching around her. She ignored it and closed the distance. Thorn tried to dash to the side, but she tracked him and crashed into him shield-first. His vibro-sword sparked against her shield, and she raised her axe for a heavy cleave.

The pauldron zipped in from behind, and the twittering insect legs inside its shell latched onto her forearm.

"Not good!"

The pauldron's thrusters fired, and she found herself whipped to the side. She tried to correct her course, but the pauldron drove her into the ground. Sand blasted high as she cut a juddering groove through the dunes. She turned her back to the ground and fired her shoulder thrusters in an attempt to gain some altitude, but the pauldron twisted her arm and shoved her back down.

"Oh no you don't!"

Susan jammed her incinerator into the pauldron's shell and let loose. Blue flame enveloped the drone, and its mechanical insect legs began to glow. She smashed her free fist into it and yanked her forearm out of its grip, but she wasn't done yet.

The pauldron tried to flit away, but she grabbed hold of it. It struggled to flee, thrusters firing in frantic, random bursts, and she accelerated toward the arena's outer wall, her own propulsion overpowering it.

She flew up to the outer wall, following it in a long curving course, and she smashed the drone against it and kept flying. Sparks showered from the contact point as friction ate through the pauldron, one layer at a time. She sped on, grinding it down until its thrusters died out, and its twitching mechanisms fell still.

Then and only then did she pull back toward the arena center, where Thorn waited, holding the distance open. She tossed the pauldron toward him, and it landed at his "feet" in a glowing, smoking ruin.

"You'll have to do better than that," she taunted.

Thorn regarded the ruined drone with concern.

Her combat frame was faster and tougher than he'd expected. He'd chosen and equipped his gladiatorial frame based on the Type-92's specifications, but her Type-99 far exceeded the older model's thrust-to-mass ratio.

She may have never battled as a gladiator, but this was not the first time she'd fought in a synthetic body, *that* much was certain! She couldn't have predicted the nature of his attack, and yet she'd adapted to it with remarkable ease.

He had to admit, he found that level of talent...admirable. In another life, she would have made an excellent gladiator.

But admiration would not win him this match. He was down one drone and he'd barely scratched her armor. He'd employed a tricky, overly complicated opener, and perhaps that had not been the best choice. It would have been a crowd pleaser, to be sure, but she'd overpowered the attack with brute force, and he feared she would do the same to his follow-ups.

His frame was too light to go toe to toe with her for long.

He needed an edge.

The Type-92's schematic glowed in his virtual vision, and he raised his twin swords.

He knew what he had to do.

Thorn sped in, and Susan flew out to meet him. She fired her incinerator, but Thorn climbed over the flames, then dove at her. They collided in a flash of weapons and armor, broke, then slammed into each other again. Shield and axe clashed with twin swords, and Susan sprayed bursts of flame that charred Thorn's armored skin.

She struck his remaining pauldron with her axe and split the armor, but Thorn swung with a rising sword, and deflected her second attack. He swatted her shield with a "leg" once, twice, and she found her guard forced upward, moments before he thrust straight at her chest with one of his blades.

The tip pierced into her chest plating, and the oscillating weapon ate through malmetal layers. Warning lights flashed in her virtual vision as her onboard infosystem projected the attack would cut through her case.

"Shit!"

She punched the flat of his blade and shattered it, then reversed her boosters and pulled back. Thorn dove after her and thrust with his remaining sword, again toward her chest. She brought her shield around, and the attack glanced off. He dashed to the left, thrust again, and his blade cut into her side, again angled toward the same internal systems. She bashed his attack aside with her shield and pulled away.

Susan yanked the broken sword tip out of her chest and tossed it away. Malmetal microplates sealed the wound and reinforced the path to her connectome case.

That was three attacks in a row aligned with a specific point within her torso. Was he deliberately going after her case? Or was he simply targeting the combat frame's primary systems in the torso?

Either way, she needed to be careful! One false move, and that was it!

Thorn pointed the tip of his sword at her and hovered on his graviton thrust, and she switched to a more guarded posture, shield forward, axe at the ready as she levitated on her exhaust plume. They circled each other, neither willing to make the first move. Thorn darted in, and Susan pulled back, but he reversed course just as quickly as they felt each other out, both searching for an opening.

Thorn charged first, and Susan raised her guard. His sword bit into the top of her shield, and then one of his tentacles wrapped around the barrier and jerked it to the side. Thorn aimed his sword with deadly intent and thrust.

In desperation, Susan swung her axe to deflect the attack, but Thorn pulled back at the last moment.

"A feint!" she hissed.

His blade struck her axe arm's shoulder, then sawed through armor layers to reach her internal systems. He pushed the blade in, cutting through the fuel line, and one of her shoulder boosters burped and sputtered.

She compensated with added thrust elsewhere and pulled back, trying to break free, but the blade in her shoulder and the tentacle around her shield delayed her long enough for Thorn to cut upward through her shoulder. He pulled his blade free, and her right arm spasmed and fell limp.

She kicked him in the center mass, and his grip on her shield loosened. She kicked once more, and they finally broke apart. She put some distance between them and regarded the slack arm hanging by a few malmetal microplates and cables.

"Well, this isn't good."

Thorn pressed the attack, and Susan lit him up with her incinerator. Hot, blue flame engulfed him, scalding his armor, but he pushed through and swatted her shield aside. He thrust, and his blade tore a deep gash through her incinerator. The output faltered, and he grappled with her, tentacles wrapping around her limbs.

His sword glinted in the light as he raised it, then brought it down in a slivery sweep that cleaved through her left shoulder. Her shield arm and ruined incinerator dropped to the sands.

She pulled back and landed, weaponless, unsure what to do next.

"We have a winner!" the announcer said. "Victory by disarmament! The winner is Thorn! Let's hear it for our champion!"

Thorn landed across from her, swept the sword-wielding tentacle in front of him, and bowed.

"Well, shit," Susan pouted.

Isaac regarded the combat frame, now back in its crate. The right arm hung from a few tentative cables, and the left arm sat on the floor.

"You did great," he said, turning back to Susan, once again in her regular synthoid.

"But I wanted to win," she said, sounding frustrated with her performance. "I almost had him, too."

"Don't be too hard on yourself. As long as Fat Man provides the information we need, I consider this a win."

"I suppose you're right." She pushed the hanging arm and it rocked back and forth. "What are we going to do about repairs?"

"Kronos Station can take care of it, assuming you have the necessary patterns."

"I do."

"Then let's plan to drop it off whenever we turn in the v-wing. If the case drags out, we can call dispatch and arrange transport, but I'd rather not bug them over this. Repairing your combat frame isn't a priority."

"It's a priority for me," Susan insisted.

"It'll be fine." Isaac smiled at her. "Don't worry. I'm sure the station will take good care of it."

The entrance to their v-wing bin split open, and Thorn walked over on four tentacles, back in his original squidform synthoid.

"Detective. Agent." He dipped his mechanical head to them. "My benefactor sent me here to personally provide you with the data you seek." He held up a tentacle, and a file transfer request appeared.

"Cephalie?" Isaac said.

The LENS floated over, and the transfer request vanished.

"Got them. Looks like everything we're after."

"Start digging through the data."

"On it!"

"Thorn," Isaac said. "Please express our thanks to Fat Man."

"I will, though there's another matter I wish to bring to your attention." Thorn's head swiveled, and a camera lens focused on Susan. "Agent Cantrell, I feel I owe you an apology."

"What for?"

"I assure you I would never have struck your connectome case intentionally. Accidents do happen in the arena, but such an attack is considered dishonorable amongst us gladiators."

"Then why use it?" she pressed.

"You were, quite frankly, more of a challenge than I had expected. And so, I used the threat of harm to your case to force you into a defensive posture and gain the upper hand. That's all."

"Damn." Susan crossed her arms and shook her head. "You certainly had me fooled."

"And I'm sorry for that." He bowed his head. "I hope you'll forgive me."

"It's all right," she said. "We have what we came here for. I'm more concerned about how you knew where to strike."

"Yes, about that." His eyes focused on the damaged combat frame. "A third party contacted me before the match"—he offered her a file—"and gave me this."

She took the file and opened it.

"Uh-oh. *Isaac.*"

"What?"

"We've got another problem." She transferred the file to him. "Someone gave Thorn classified intel from the Gordian Division. That's their analysis of the Type-92 combat frame, which is the model their agents faced while unraveling the Gordian Knot. The contents of this report are old news to me, but I'd assume Gordian doesn't want it circulating outside their division."

"You're right." Isaac perused the file before closing it. "Kaminski's not going to like this one bit."

"Who gave you the report and why?" Susan asked.

"I wish I knew. The individual avoided answering those same questions when I posed them, though he or she used the name Ōdachi."

"Ōdachi?" Susan turned to Isaac and they exchanged a knowing look.

"It's possible Ōdachi saw an opportunity to slow us down," Isaac suggested. "Susan, if you'd been killed..."

"Yeah. Someone's playing for keeps here."

"I think it best if you two exercise caution," Thorn said. "Someone is watching your progress."

"You could be right." Susan glanced over the classified file once more, then closed it. "Thanks for the help, Thorn."

"You're welcome." He stepped closer to her combat frame and made a throat-clearing sound, despite his lack of a throat or mouth. "You know, Agent Cantrell."

"Yes?"

"Your combat frame is quite impressive."

"Thanks. I think so, too."

"It's a shame to see it in such a state." He poked the broken arm and let it wobble. "I would be happy to offer you the services of my pit crew. They'll have it fixed up in no time, I'm sure."

"I doubt we'll be sticking around much longer," Isaac interjected as he climbed into the v-wing. "Cephalie?"

"Most likely, but I'm still waiting on a response from the Ministry of Transportation."

"I see." Thorn sighed, which was odd given his lack of lungs. "I understand, of course. Though, Agent Cantrell, I hope you'll contact me when your combat frame is repaired. It would be nice to duel you again under less...strenuous circumstances." He dipped his head to Susan. "Farewell for now."

Thorn departed the v-wing bin, and the doors sealed shut behind him.

"I think he likes you," Isaac said.

She shuddered and boarded the v-wing.

CHAPTER TWENTY-THREE

"WHAT DO WE HAVE?" ISAAC ASKED.

"A name." Cephalie walked across the v-wing console in front of their tandem seats. "Thomas Stade's business contact on his most recent trip to the *Atomic Resort* was an Oortan programmer named Adrian Kvint. Age twenty-seven, born on the dwarf planet of Haumea, and *technically* no criminal record."

"Another Oortan," Isaac breathed. "Great."

"And a programmer," Susan said.

"Yeah," Isaac said. "Sounds like we have the source of our virus."

"You could be right." Cephalie provided both of them with Adrian Kvint's SysPol file. "We don't have much on Kvint, I'm afraid. His name is referenced in a handful of other cases as a provider of illicit software, but all of the transfers took place in Oortan territories, like the *Atomic Resort.*"

"Which means he hasn't committed any crimes we can prosecute him for." Isaac sighed. "Even if he's violated the spirit of the law."

"We're going to run into jurisdiction problems again, aren't we?" Susan asked.

"Yup. Software is almost completely unregulated in the OCC, and he's free to sell it to SysGov citizens. He just can't do it *in* SysGov, and *they* can't bring it back legally, either." Isaac pushed the file aside. "Do we know where he is now?"

"He's on a flight from the Atlas Shoal to Ballast Heights,"

Cephalie said. "That's the Ministry of Transportation response I was waiting for. He's due to arrive within the hour."

"Then we can pick him up at the airport," Isaac said. "Send word to SSP. Have him brought in for illegal software trafficking."

"Is that charge going to stick?" Susan asked.

"No, but we can inconvenience him, and right now that's the only leverage we have. Best use it before he goes somewhere we can't touch. From the looks of it, Kvint conducts his business in a smart way. He'll know the laws and he'll know we can't prosecute him, but he'll *also* know he's within a hairsbreadth of breaking the law. I'm hoping that means he'll want to convince us he's clean, and there's the opening we need to pump him for information."

"Sounds like a long shot," Susan said. "He could just keep quiet until we're forced to release him."

"Maybe," Isaac said. "We won't know until we try. Cephalie, take us back to Janus."

❖   ❖   ❖

Isaac watched Adrian Kvint through the interrogation room's virtual window on the thirty-third floor of the BHPD 51st Precinct. The young man was barely an adult by SysGov reckoning, but that meant little in the OCC, and his body showed signs of extensive modification. He wore his brown hair in a long braid, which did nothing to hide the metallic back half of his skull, and Isaac wondered how much of Kvint's original brain remained or how heavily his mind was integrated with illegal programming.

The customizations didn't end there. His legs looked normal enough, but the joints in his hips afforded a greater range of motion, and his feet ended in elongated, prehensile toes, granting Kvint the equivalent of four hands and arms if he kicked off his sandals. He sat in his chair with arms crossed and a defiant glower affixed to his face.

"Is there such a thing as a normal Oortan?" Susan asked. Both had changed back into their uniforms at the airport, and her sidearm hung heavy from her waist.

"They're out there," Isaac said, and palmed the door open.

"I want you to know I'm *very* unhappy about this situation," Kvint started as soon as they entered. "Whoever you're looking for, I'm not him."

"Then perhaps you can help us clear things up." Isaac sat down and waited for Susan to seat herself. "We have a few questions for you. If you're innocent, as you say, and your story checks out, I'm sure we can have you on your way shortly."

"No, no, no." Kvint wagged a finger. "Forget it. I fly into Janus for a well-earned vacation, and this is the welcome I get? Grabbed by state troopers the moment I step off the saucer? And for what? Software trafficking? Give me a break! I conduct all my business in the OCC. It's all perfectly legit. This game didn't work out for the last SysPol stooge who tried to charge me, and it's not going to work out for you either."

"Be that as it may, we still have questions we need to ask you."

"Forget it. I'm not answering any questions."

"Then I'm afraid we'll have to hold you until—"

"—the charges are dropped," Kvint cut in. "Yes, I know. I've been down this road before, and this dance will play out the same way as the last time, mark my words."

"If you simply cooperate with us, I'm sure we can have this misunderstanding resolved in short order."

"Then consider this a 'screw you' from me for ruining my vacation. Software trafficking! I mean really! How dumb do you people think I am? I was going to tour the Founding Sector and everything today, and now I'm stuck here!"

Isaac leaned back with a grimace, unsure how to proceed.

Kvint looked over at Susan and regarded her uniform curiously.

"Which SysPol division are you from?" he asked, then gestured to Isaac. "He's from Themis, obviously, but I have no idea which you're from."

"I'm not from a division."

"What's that supposed to mean?" Kvint opened an interface and ran a search.

"Warning!" Cephalie yelled. "Firewall breached!"

"Oh, don't get so worked up," Kvint said. "It's not my fault this precinct's so-called data isolation is full of holes. Just running a search, is all. Perfectly legal."

"I think SSP might have a different take on the matter," Isaac warned.

"You can monitor my traffic if it'll make you feel better." He tapped in his parameters. "Strange uniform. Peaked cap. Blue with white stripes. Shield insignia. And..."

Kvint put his head on a fist and read the data scrolling down his interface with a somewhat bored expression. But then his face slackened. His jaw dropped, his eyes grew wide, and he pushed away from the table.

"You're with the *Admin*?!" he cried, chair back pressed against the wall.

"Is there a problem?" Isaac asked.

"You keep her away from me!" Kvint pointed a shaking finger at Susan.

Isaac and Susan looked at each other, and both kept their faces carefully neutral. He saw an opening; the question was, did Susan? He was about to spell it out for her when he noticed a brief glimmer of amusement in her eyes.

"Permission to act like a scary Admin thug?" Susan asked, her speech encrypted in security chat.

"Permission granted," Isaac replied with a guarded expression, also in security chat.

"That's correct, Mister Kvint," Susan said, returning to normal speech. "My name is Susan Cantrell. *Agent* Cantrell of the Admin's Department of Temporal Investigation, and *you* are a person I've been greatly looking forward to meeting."

"What does the Admin want with me?" Kvint asked, hands trembling on the table.

"That depends." She tilted her head. "Tell me, Mister Kvint. Do you know what we do with criminal scum in the Admin?"

"It says here you forcibly extract their connectomes, dump them in abstract prison domains, and recycle their bodies."

"That's correct." She smiled malevolently at him. "I'm glad to see our reputation precedes us."

"But I don't live in the Admin!"

"You're also not a citizen of SysGov." Susan knitted her fingers on the table. "Mister Kvint, let me be plain with you. I'm here concerning a matter of great importance to the Admin. A matter that involves the construction of time drives and injury to agents of the Gordian Division." She gestured to Isaac. "And since you've declined to cooperate with our colleagues in Sys-Pol, it is up to me to explore... other avenues of acquiring the information we need."

"You wouldn't dare!"

What does he think she'd do to him? Isaac wondered. *Oh well. Doesn't matter, I suppose.*

"Mister Kvint." Susan flashed a sharklike grin. "The Admin

has no formal relationship with the OCC. You have no legal recourse with us."

"But! But!" Kvint faced Isaac. "You wouldn't let her take me away, would you?"

"Well, I don't *want* her to do anything to you," Isaac said, putting on his best good-cop face, "but I'm afraid this is out of my hands." He rose from his chair. "Good day, Mister Kvint. I wish you well."

"WAIT!" Kvint screeched.

"Yes?" Isaac said.

"We can all be reasonable here, right?"

"That depends," Susan said. "Are *you* willing to cooperate with the detective?"

Kvint nodded emphatically.

"I'm glad to hear it." Isaac sat back down and placed the LifeBeam code fragments over the table. "First, you can start by taking a look at these."

"Hmm." Kvint arrayed the code fragments in front of him, eyes zipping through the porous code. "Where did you get these?"

"From a LifeBeam transceiver in Ballast Heights."

"Seems an odd place for these to end up." He toyed with his braid, then nodded. "I can't be certain what they were originally, but this is at least based on my code."

"How can you tell?"

"You know what every programmer says about every other programmer's work?"

"No."

"We say 'Sure, that'll work, but *I* wouldn't do it that way.' A programmer's habits come out in the way they write their code, and I can see some of my own markers in these fragments. See this looping structure here? There are eight spaces between each of the different syntax segments."

"Meaning?"

"I wrote the loop. I like the number eight and try to include it in my code wherever I can. It's my good luck charm." He glanced at Susan, who watched him with unblinking intensity. "Can I go now?"

"Not yet," Isaac said. "Tell me about Thomas Stade."

"Which one?"

"I'm sorry." Isaac blinked.

"'Thomas Stade' is a fake ID," Kvint said. "I've sold software to at least four of them over the past few years, all different people. Which one are we talking about?"

"This would likely be the most recent one. You met him three weeks ago on the *Atomic Resort.*"

"Oh, that guy!" Kvint's eyes lit up. "I've sold software to that one twice. Strange customer. Annoying, too."

"How so?"

"Normally, I conduct all my business in person. That way, there's zero chance of my work ending up somewhere it shouldn't. But the first time I dealt with this latest Stade, about two months ago I think, the guy *insisted* I provide the goods remotely. We were to meet on the *Atomic Resort,* but he still wouldn't come to me in person! What a bother! I had to craft these Trojan layers to wrap his package and route it discreetly over. Made him pay extra for it, too."

"What did he purchase?"

"A copy protection codeburner."

"Copy protection?" Isaac asked, brow creased. Codeburners were a class of software that combined decryption algorithms with delete functions. Why would Stade need to remove something's copy protection, and what might that "something" be?

"Don't look at me," Kvint said. "I didn't ask. Seemed like a waste of my time for something so simple, but whatever."

"Was that all he purchased the first time?"

"Yeah."

"And the second meeting?"

"We met three weeks ago, again on the *Atomic Resort.* Don't ask me why, but he met me in person that time. I wasn't about to complain, since it made my job easier."

"Is this him?" Isaac produced an image.

"Yeah, that's him. Or at least a synthoid that looks the same."

"What did Stade purchase during your second meeting?"

"An attack virus. Nastiest one I ever wrote, too. It's not sentient, but I did imbue it with a certain...animal cunning. You see, I used pieces of my own connectome as the foundation. The *synthetic* half of my connectome, of course." He plinked the metal back of his skull. "Haven't got a clue why the Trinh Syndicate would touch software this hot, though."

"*Trinh?*" Isaac raised an eyebrow.

"Yeah. Didn't I say so earlier?"

"Say what?"

"You know all those Stades I've dealt with the last, I don't know, five or six years? The Trinh Syndicate established the fake ID they use."

"Is that so? You wouldn't by any chance know which manager set up their fake account?"

"Sure, I do. After the third Stade, I hacked into their infostructure." He indicated their surrounds. "It's even more porous than this, if you can believe it. Anyway, I did it as a lark. More out of curiosity than anything else."

"And the manager in question?" Isaac pressed.

"Turned out to be a big letdown. Some junior nobody named Melody Quang created it."

"Nicely played," Isaac told Susan once they were alone and Adrian Kvint had been sent on his way.

"Thanks. I gave him my best Dahvid Kloss impression."

"Who's that?"

"Scariest guy in the whole DTI. Pray you never have to meet him."

"I'll take your word for it." He crossed his arms. "So. Melody Quang created Stade's fake ID." He made a *tut-tut-tut* sound. "Very naughty of her."

"Enough to charge her?"

"You better believe it. Identity fraud for one. From there, we're one step away from tying her to Stade, which means conspiracy to commit murder could be on the table. Cephalie?"

"You rang?" She appeared atop the LENS.

"Contact Citizen Services. Have them audit all of Thomas Stade's records and especially his ID application and immigration forms. Ask them to check for any irregularities in the process and any inconsistencies that lead them to believe multiple people are using it."

"On it!" She vanished.

"And if we find some dirt?" Susan asked.

"Then we grab Quang and turn up the heat."

Melody Quang hated everything about Titan.

She hated the light, bouncy gravity and the way it made walking a chore. She hated the cramped, claustrophobic corridors of its domed cities. She hated the brown haze of its atmosphere. She hated the dumb enthusiasm of her Titanite coworkers and how they always argued for more investment in this frigid, Esteem sinkhole.

But most of all, she hated the people, and how *cheerful* they were, how oblivious they could be about living on this frozen fart of a moon.

"But the promise of a better tomorrow is within our grasp! Just look at the park we built!" they would argue, and to that Quang wished she could cackle in reply. In her imagination, she did. In her *imagination*, she told them what she really thought instead of affixing her best politically correct smile and humoring their stupidity.

What a waste of resources. Sure, Titan already had an atmosphere, and that counted for something in the grand scheme of SysGov's terraforming projects, but why would anyone want to *live* here when they could run all their industries remotely? Just build another Saturnite megastructure, for goodness' sake! It'll be easier!

She rubbed her face as the car pulled up to her spaceport bay. Her jaw muscle hurt from all that smiling, but at least it was over, and she could go home now. She wished she could participate in these stupid meetings remotely, but the four light-seconds between Saturn and Titan made that approach untenable. She needed to be in the room, reacting to her colleagues' brain-dead ideas in real time if she were to protect them from themselves.

She rose out of the car with a weary sigh and walked toward the waiting v-wing bin at the Promise City spaceport. A rectangle opened in the hexagonal bin side, and she passed through it. Her red-and-gold company v-wing sat on the landing cradle, wings and stabilizer retracted for storage. She palmed the side hatch open, climbed in, and dropped heavily into the seat.

The hatch sealed shut, and she sent Promise City Spaceport Control a request for departure. The spaceport's SRS robotics latched onto her bin, pulled it out of the loading bay, and maneuvered it toward an empty departure pad.

She wasn't looking forward to the seven-hour flight back to Janus, but at least it provided her with time to catch up. She was four seasons behind on her *Solar Descent* viewing; her idiot boss had already spoiled most of it, but she loaded the show with a resigned sigh.

She wasn't a fan, but *he* was, and *he* enjoyed talking about all the dumb character intrigue and obvious plot twists, so it might benefit her career to be up to speed. Men were gullible that way, especially those still in their original meat suits, and he wouldn't say no to a little natural-on-natural action, if she presented the opportunity.

Quang settled into her seat and was about to queue up the next episode when the bin jostled. She decided to wait until after takeoff, and she activated a virtual window to better watch this sad moon recede behind her.

Only, she wasn't at any of the departure pads. For some reason, her bin had been returned to the storage stacker.

"Of all the—" she began, but then she shook her head and opened a comm window. "Spaceport Control."

She waited for a response, but none came, and several seconds later a red message flashed over the comm window.

CONNECTION UNAVAILABLE, it said.

"Oh, come on!" she griped.

She tried again, but the same message appeared.

"Don't tell me I'm stuck here!"

She opened the v-wing hatch, stepped out, and looked around. Virtual windows turned the bin walls transparent, revealing the tight press of hexagonal bins above, below, and to either side of her. The front led to an open chasm the robotics used to maneuver bins between the stacker and the various bays and pads, and the back was a solid prog-steel wall sealing off Titan's deadly atmosphere.

There was no way for her to get out of the bin on foot because bins with occupants were never supposed to be brought to the stacker.

"Well, this sucks!" She planted her hands on her hips. She tried reaching Spaceport Control again, but her connection failed once more. "They're going to hear about this when I get out! It's going to take more than a refund to make this problem go away!"

A massive robotic arm sped past her, halted, and drew a nearby bin out of the stacker. It began ascending toward the departure pads atop the spaceport, but then it stuttered, brakes whining against powerful servos.

"What the hell?" Quang muttered. "Guess I'm not the only problem they're having."

The stuttering stopped, and the bin dropped at a diagonal until it came to rest, perfectly aligned outside her own bin. New brakes locked into place, others disengaged, and the robotic arm began loading the second bin into her occupied slot. The front of her bin crumpled inward, and she flinched from the advancing wall of metal.

"Oh, no!" she cried.

The rolling front of twisted prog-steel touched the nose of her v-wing and shoved it back off the cradle. The main body screeched across the floor until its thruster pressed against the rear wall, and the delicate propulsive system crumpled under the implacable force pressing in. The wall advanced toward her, slowly but relentlessly, driven by a robotic arm that could lift up to twelve max-capacity bins at once and designed by engineers who believed in built-in spare capacity for future expansions.

Even with Titan's anemic gravity, the arm pushed forward as if her already-loaded bin wasn't even there.

Quang cowered against the back wall, heart racing as death came at her in a slow advance of metal. Immense pressure crushed her v-wing, causing its mangled body to balloon outward to either side, and she looked around, frantically searching for something—*anything*—that could save her.

"Stade, you bastard!" she screamed.

Who else could be behind this?

The plan had seemed so simple at first, so deliciously *deniable*, and with such a rich payoff on the horizon. The plot would have seen her star rise within the Trinh Syndicate. No longer would she be a disposable *junior* manager with the guillotine ready to fall on her neck at a moment's notice if her superiors were ever threatened. Oh, no! She'd *become* one of those superiors after this job!

It would have worked, too, if Stade hadn't fucked everything up by overreacting!

"Stop this, Stade!" she shouted. "Stop this right now!"

Contorted panels and crumpled machinery advanced on her, forcing her back against the bin's rear.

"Let me go!" she pleaded, tears weeping from her eyes. "I won't talk, I swear!"

She braced her arms, elbows against the wall, hands against the advancing scrap, but the forces opposing her were too many magnitudes beyond what a mere human could defy. The cold, unthinking machinery didn't care about the life in the way, and her forearms snapped like twigs. Pressure mounted against her chest and skull, and air wheezed out of her lungs.

"STAAAAAADE!" she cried as the wall of metal squeezed the life out of her.

CHAPTER TWENTY-FOUR

THE SYSPOL V-WING DESCENDED THROUGH THE OCHRE HAZE OF Titan's atmosphere, long wings extending out from the fuselage as it slowed. Winds buffeted the craft, and restraints bit into Isaac's shoulders for a moment before the v-wing pushed through. He stretched out his legs and massaged his thighs, but the act had little effect on the fatigue he felt from the seven-hour trip.

The v-wing may have been designed primarily for flight through Saturn's varied atmospheric layers, but its airtight cabin and thruster capacitors allowed for short-range space travel within the Saturn State.

Their craft dipped underneath the main haze layer, revealing a chocolate-hued landscape of dark mountains shot with paler, rocky veins that led down to smooth plains stripped by eons of erosion. Not from the flow of water, but from the rain of liquid methane across the moon's desolate surface, which pooled in vast, dark lakes and rivers.

Their v-wing veered around a puffy cloud with liquid methane drizzling from its flattened bottom in sporadic hazy columns. The lights of the Promise City dome and its surrounding cluster of terraforming towers glowed through the methane-nitrogen fog directly ahead.

The black dome had been built in the center of a wide, pale plain, and covered transit arteries formed spokes leading to lesser domes nearby. A ring of six immense, spindly towers with open tops encircled the city, drawing in air to form hazy, ochre funnels at their peaks.

"Where's the spaceport?" Susan asked from the seat next to him.

"At the top of the main dome." Isaac pointed to a shallow, black cylinder rising from the dome's apex. A pair of private v-wings took off from departure pads, and a luxury saucer slowed for its final descent. Floodlights bathed the upper surface with light, and green strobes pulsed along the borders of the structure.

"We have landing clearance," Cephalie said. "Taking us in."

Their craft pulled in its glider wings, and the graviton thruster eased back, giving way to the moon's 0.14 gravities. They came to rest on a landing cradle, which latched onto their v-wing, and the bin sealed and descended into the spaceport complex. The atmosphere cycled outside their craft while the bin moved to their designated bay.

"I hope someone's monitoring this system," Susan said.

"They are," Isaac said. "Most of the spaceport is operated by Polaris Traveler, including the machinery that killed Quang. Both they and SSP are monitoring the stacker like hawks."

"And if the stacker tries to crush us, too?"

"Then this'll be your big chance to blast our way out."

Isaac may have flippantly dismissed the risks, but he couldn't help but feel anxious until their bin locked into the correct position, and the side opened to reveal the arrival concourse. Several SSP and Polaris Traveler personnel stood waiting outside the bin entrance, though given their positions, Isaac wondered if they'd been in the middle of an argument.

"Here we go," Isaac breathed.

The v-wing's side split open, and stairs extruded down. Isaac stood up, grimaced at the stiffness in his back, then climbed down the stairs and walked over to the crowd.

"Detective Cho." An SSP officer with a ghost-white buzz cut stepped forward and extended a hand. "Good to see you again."

"Likewise, Lieutenant." Isaac shook his hand.

"You two know each other?" Susan said.

"We do, indeed." He extended his hand to Susan. "Lieutenant Alfons Garnier, Twenty-ninth Precinct, PCPD."

"Agent Susan Cantrell, acting deputy detective."

"A pleasure, ma'am."

"A year ago," Isaac began, "Raviv and I helped the lieutenant with a rash of disappearances in the Fridge, which is the nickname for an unfinished subterranean expansion to Promise City. Officially, it's known as the Ice Grotto."

"Which has turned into nothing but a headache for our precinct," Garnier grumped. "What did the city council *think* would happen when they left an area that large unfinished and unsupervised? Didn't take long for job dodgers, addicts, gangsters, and far worse to move in, but our spineless councilors refuse to let us clear them out and lock down the Grotto."

"Raviv and I caught a serial killer preying on the gangs. Gruesome piece of business. The killer was into collecting trophies, and teeth were his favorite, especially if extracted while the victim still lived."

"The Bloody Dentist, people called him." Garnier cringed at the memory. "How is Raviv doing these days?"

"Promoted."

"Oh, I'm so sorry." Garnier was of the mind that promotions could inadvertently distance good officers from the people they served, and he'd refused all attempts by his superiors to make him a captain during his long years on the Promise City police force.

"Yeah, I think he's sorry, too," Isaac conceded.

"Anyway, I'm glad you're finally here. I understand this mess may be related to a case you're working on."

"I'm almost certain it is," Isaac said. "We have evidence Melody Quang was at least tangentially involved in the deaths of two Gordian Division agents. I had hoped to pull her in for questioning. In fact, we were about to contact your precinct when word of her death reached us."

"Not the best way to collect a witness," Garnier said, in the manner of a massive understatement.

"No. It's hard to have a conversation when they're sloshing around in a beaker." Isaac sighed and rubbed the small of his back. "What have you found so far?"

"Not much," Garnier confessed. "Physical examination of the crime scene is obvious enough. One bin crushed another, but we're struggling with the question of how. The captain put our best data forensics team on the job; they've been scouring the infostructure but have found jack all in the hours since her death. Honestly, it's looking more and more like a glitch of some—"

"Excuse me!" A man in a pastel green business suit pushed through a pair of SSP troopers and took a long, floating step over. Polaris Traveler logos scrolled across his neck scarf. "I think I've waited long enough."

"Not now," Garnier breathed irritably.

"And you are?" Isaac asked.

"Emanuel Voit, Polaris shift manager on duty when this so-called 'glitch' occurred."

"I didn't say it was a glitch," Garnier protested wearily. "I was merely pointing out for the detective that we haven't found evidence of a deliberate criminal act. Not *yet*."

"Which means you're trying to pin this death on our company!"

"Mister Voit, please. Our investigation is ongoing. No conclusions have been drawn yet, and I'm sure the detective will have his own input to provide. Now, if you'll excuse us, I need to bring his team up to speed on—"

"Oh, no!" Voit glowered at the Garnier. "Not without me! I'm not going anywhere until I know this case is being handled properly."

"Please, stop right there, Mister Voit," Isaac said sharply. "I believe I can help sort this out."

"That would be most appreciated, Detective," Garnier said.

"First, have we identified the infosystem where the failure occurred?"

"Yes, that part's clear enough," Garnier said. "Stacker Control Seven was the infosystem responsible for shoving one bin into another."

"The lieutenant's right," Voit agreed. "SC7 interfaces with numerous other systems, such as the MTC. The Master Traffic Controller. But SC7 is the only system responsible for positioning bins within Stacker Seven. No other systems track what's in which bin, and no other systems provide orders to the SRS robotics, so it's the only one that could have caused this."

"And do we have a save state from the time of the failure?"

"We do," Garnier said. "Polaris provided us with the file, but we haven't had much luck analyzing it. Everything checks out so far."

"And has Polaris performed their own analysis?"

"We're . . . working on it," Voit said.

"Have you found anything?" Isaac pressed.

"Well, no. But I'm sure it's only a matter of time."

"I'll need a copy of the file."

"Of course." Voit offered him a file exchange, and he copied it to the LENS.

"Cephalie, contact Kronos Station, and have them analyze the fault state. See if you can get it assigned to the same team who looked over the LifeBeam tower file. Regardless, have them check for any similarities between the two failures. Oh, and tell them I need the results expedited."

"On it."

"What's LifeBeam have to do with this?" Voit asked.

"Nothing, until we've determined there's a link between the two incidents," Isaac deflected. "Mister Voit, I assure you both SysPol and SSP are approaching this incident with all due seriousness, but I need to inspect the crime scene next. *Without* any interruptions."

"All right," Voit said. "But you two better not keep me in the dark over this."

"We won't," Isaac said. "Thank you for your time, Mister Voit. I'll be in touch if I need anything else from Polaris."

"This way, Detective." Garnier led them to a counter-grav lift that whisked them down into the lower levels of the spaceport. They came out in a utility area at the base of the stacker trench.

Isaac craned his neck and watched the stacker robots pull a pair of bins out of storage, shift speedily at a diagonal, then slot the bins into position higher up and on the opposite side of the trench. A clear roof separated the robot from the basement level except for a wide-open maintenance bay where the robot could temporarily store bins removed from service.

"That's the calmest I've seen their shift manager all day," Garnier commented.

"Glad I could help, Lieutenant."

Isaac walked around the circumference of the maintenance bay and the compressed forms of two bins. It made him think of a reclamation plant compactor. A small pool of blood collected underneath one corner, where a coffin-shaped segment had been cut away and removed.

"Melody Quang, I presume," Isaac said.

"That's right," Garnier said. "Her body's back at the precinct. We made a positive ID from her DNA and confirmed it with her data signature in the spaceport as well as with surveillance video of her entering the bin."

"I'll need the full autopsy report," Isaac said. "Cause of death seems obvious enough, but the autopsy may reveal other valuable information, such as the data contents of her wetware."

"You'll have it, though I wouldn't get your hopes up. Her wetware's pulped. I doubt we'll get anything useful out of it."

"Still worth a look," Isaac said, staring at the crushed bins. "What about the v-wing's infosystem?"

"It's in there, somewhere."

"Can you bring a team in to retrieve it?"

"Sure thing, though again, I wouldn't get your hopes up."

"The v-wing's outer hull should have provided some protection to the nodes," Isaac countered.

"Yeah, but maybe not enough." Garnier shrugged. "Doesn't matter. We'll pull out whatever we can find."

"That's all I ask, Lieutenant."

✧   ✧   ✧

"What now?" Susan asked as they sat down at their booth. The bottom level of Promise City Spaceport included a large cluster of restaurants, and several featured tinted floors and wide windows where visitors could observe the sprawl of Promise Park far below.

Promise Park, as the name implied, represented a preview of the moon's final terraforming stage. Their booth provided a bird's-eye view of a vast lake, filled not with liquid methane, but crystal-clear water. A single artificial landmass of green, rolling pastures floated atop the lake with pontoon bridges connecting outward to the park's boundaries. Virtual images along the walls displayed clear, blue skies dotted with cottony clouds.

Titan's gravity was so low and its atmosphere so thick that human-powered flight could be achieved with relative ease, and Promise Park was the best place on the moon for the activity, since adventurous citizens could take flight without environmental gear. A young woman flapped past their window, arms wide with the added length of her glimmering wing membranes, while a young man pursued her, a small harness-mounted propeller buzzing on his back.

"Thoughts?" Susan asked.

"Analysis of the fault state may link this to the LifeBeam tower virus." Isaac turned away from the window.

"And what if it does?" Susan pressed. "Where do we go from there?"

"I don't know. Quang was our connection to Stade, and now she's dead. Maybe there's something on her v-wing, but..." He shook his head.

"That seems doubtful."

"Yeah. I wouldn't expect Quang to be so careless. We'll have to wait and see what turns up."

"And if nothing turns up?"

"Well then." Isaac leaned back in his booth. "That's the question, isn't it? We don't have the slightest clue where Stade is, and he's demonstrated a knack for hiding in the shadows. Other than a statewide manhunt, I'm not sure where we go with this."

"I'm kind of doubtful even *that* would find him."

"Yeah." He placed his cheek on a fist. "*Zhù hăo yùn.*"

"Sorry. That didn't translate through."

"We could use some good luck right about now."

"You'll get no arguments from me."

"Let's review what we know," Isaac said. "Maybe something will come to us."

"Fine by me," Susan said. "I'll start. We're almost certain Stade killed both Delacroix and Quang."

"Andover-Chen, too, but he was just collateral, unless we've missed something big."

"Right. Also, either Quang or Stade used the Ōdachi alias to contact the Fanged Wyverns and had them clean out Delacroix's apartment."

"The information we recovered from his apartment led two places," Isaac recounted. "Quang and Delacroix were in a relationship, and Delacroix had met with Stade on Free Gate."

"And before that, they met on the *Atomic Resort.*"

"Where Delacroix and Stade spent time together in a brothel... for whatever reason."

"That's also where Stade purchased a copy-protection code-burner from Kvint." Susan frowned. "That's another strange part. Why that piece of illicit software?"

"Yeah," Isaac agreed. "The attack viruses Stade purchased later make sense; he's clearing out his accomplices and covering his tracks. *Atomic Resort* is also where Ōdachi—again either Quang or Stade—tried to convince Thorn to kill you."

"After which, Kvint revealed Stade is *also* a false name, set up by Quang."

"Which begs the question," Isaac continued. "Who, exactly, is Thomas Stade?"

"Yeah." Susan glanced down at the park. "Do we even have a motive yet?"

"Nope."

"If we had that, I bet all of this would slot into place."

"We can dream," Isaac said wearily. "But let's keep working through this. Both Quang and Delacroix have been offed. What did they have in common?"

"The Gordian Division contract with Trinh."

"And the failed impeller." Isaac leaned back and stared off for a moment.

"You think that could be involved?"

"Maybe. Not sure how, though. It seemed like a dead end last we talked with Quang, but that was before we could link her to Stade."

"A time drive is a valuable commodity," Susan noted. "The wrong people could do a lot of bad things with one."

"True, but Negation Industries chopped up the impeller before handing it over."

"Could they reassemble it?"

"I would assume so, though I'm not sure what would be involved. We could ask Andover-Chen, but I imagine the repairs would be difficult. You'd need to supervise them with an experienced..."

He trailed off, and they both exchanged looks of simultaneous realization.

"Chronometric engineer!" they said in unison.

"Which Delacroix was," Susan finished. "Trinh could be after an off-the-books time drive."

"This might be it." Isaac rubbed his chin. "They *tell* us they'll use the exotic matter for other work, but instead, they switch it out behind the scenes and reassemble the impeller in secret."

"And Delacroix helps them do it."

"But there's a problem with this theory," Isaac said. "When would Delacroix have had the opportunity? He's been either joined at the hip with Andover-Chen or back at Earth this whole time."

"Or 'on vacation,'" Susan pointed out.

"Hmm." Isaac nodded slowly. "Maybe he assisted remotely during the time he and Stade 'spent' at the brothel?" He pulled up dates for their resort visits and compared them to the sales records for the failed impeller. "No, it doesn't line up. Their time together on the *Atomic Resort* came two weeks too early. Trinh hadn't taken possession of the impeller cubes yet."

"Damn," Susan breathed. "Thought I was on to something."

"It's all right." Isaac flashed a smile at her. "That was a good guess. If the dates lined up differently, we'd be all over this lead."

"Then you don't believe it's the impeller?"

"I wouldn't go that far. The failed impeller *is* shady business, and it links Delacroix and Quang. The stink coming off that deal is related to this whole mess. *Somehow.* I'm just not sure how."

"Where are the impeller pieces now?"

"Quang said they were moved to their new Kraken Mare plant on Titan."

"And here we find her crushed while leaving Titan. Coincidence?"

"Hmm." Isaac leaned back in thought.

"Hey, kids," Cephalie said, appearing over the LENS resting at his side.

"News?" Isaac asked.

"Some. You already have a preliminary report on the Polaris infosystem fault state."

"And?"

"They found strange code fragments in one of the buffers which bear some striking similarities to the fragments recovered from LifeBeam. Not a conclusive match, but..."

"Good enough for our purposes," Isaac said. "We can assume Stade killed Quang. Anything else?"

"Looks like the flight recorder in Quang's v-wing is recoverable. Imaging shows at least one of the redundant nodes wasn't crushed. SSP's cutting their way to it now. We should have the contents within the hour."

"Good. That might be interesting."

"How so?" Susan asked.

"Remember what Quang said about Trinh's Kraken Mare plant?" Isaac said. "She made it clear she's not involved. But what if her flight recorder shows she visited the facility during this trip? That would be unusual for someone in her position."

"You're thinking she stopped by to check on the progress?"

"Maybe. If so, Stade might even be at the facility."

"Perhaps that's how he infected her with the attack virus?"

"Speculation aside, it's clear we need to check out that facility," Isaac said. "Cephalie, put in for a search warrant."

"Understood. I'll take care of it." She vanished.

"What are we going to do when we get there?" Susan asked. "Neither of us knows much about exotic matter."

"No worries. I'm one step ahead of you." Isaac opened a comm window and waited for the call to go through.

"Raibert Kaminski here."

"Agent, this is Detective Cho."

He waited eight seconds for the light-speed delay to play out.

"Hey, Detective," Kaminski replied. "Been wondering when I'd hear from you next. You find the murderer yet?"

"No, but that's actually what I'm calling about. You remember the impeller Negation Industries sold Trinh?"

"Sure do. What about it?"

"I have reason to believe the remains of the impeller may no longer be in a disabled state."

"What? You think they might be putting the impeller back together without authorization?"

"That's one possibility, yes. However, Agent Cantrell and I aren't qualified to inspect exotic matter devices. We were hoping your division could assist us."

"Sure, we can help out. Andover-Chen would be perfect for the job. I bet the man could *lick* an impeller and tell you if it's configured right just from that. Besides, it'll do him good to stay busy. We just finished a round of tests and won't have any more until tomorrow while Negation performs some recalibrations. Where do you need us?"

"One moment." Isaac pulled up the coordinates for the Kraken Mare plant and transmitted them. "I'm sending the location over. It's a Trinh Syndicate facility south of Titan's Kraken Mare."

"Got it. Bit of a trek to get from here to Titan, but with just me, Andover-Chen, and Philo, we can max out the *Kleio*'s thrusters and be there in about three hours. I'll leave the rest of my crew behind and spare them the high gees. That work for you?"

"It certainly does," Isaac said. "Just let us know when you leave. We'll coordinate our departure from Promise City so we arrive at the same time. Much appreciated, Agent."

"Don't mention it. See you at the Kraken Mare."

CHAPTER TWENTY-FIVE

"SSP SENT US THE FLIGHT RECORDER CONTENTS," CEPHALIE SAID.

"And?" Isaac asked, staring out the virtual canopy. The v-wing sped across a jagged labyrinth eroded by methane and ethane precipitation between the teeth of two mountain ranges. A dark brown stormfront loomed in their flight path as they fought through headwinds gusting at eighty kilometers per hour.

"Quang's v-wing landed at the Kraken Mare facility before heading to Promise City."

"Not of note by itself," Isaac said. "She did declare her business trip to Titan."

"But given what we know now," Susan added from the seat next to him, "it's another piece that fits our theory."

"It does indeed," Isaac said. "Pass on my thanks to Garnier for the quick turnaround."

"Will do," Cephalie said. "Also, the TTV *Kleio* is about to begin orbiting the moon. They're on schedule to reach the facility a little after us."

"Good. Then maybe we'll finally have some answers," Isaac said. "Any pushback from Trinh concerning the warrant?"

"No. They seem to be playing it cool, letting things play out. They *say* no one's at the facility right now. They're still in an automated construction phase with on-site inspections every three days." Cephalie leaned onto her cane. "If you believe them."

"It's possible their management doesn't know what's going on at the facility," Susan suggested. "You did mention the syndicates like to compartmentalize."

"Either way, I'm sure they're lining up the heads they intend to let roll." Isaac watched the rough terrain speed past underneath the v-wing. "It's the syndicate way of life, after all."

"What state is the facility in?" Susan asked. "Officially, according to Trinh?"

"The building's structural work is complete," Cephalie said, "but the exotic printer isn't finished yet."

"And the supporting industrial printers?" Susan asked.

"They should be operational. Says here they were flown in seven weeks ago."

"Then we're dealing with a lot of unoccupied building space," Susan noted. "They could be hiding anything in there."

"We'll sweep the whole complex," Isaac said. "And we should have Andover-Chen inspect the exotic printer, too. I have a feeling it's not as unfinished as they claim."

The v-wing shuddered as it shot through a fierce downpour. Liquid methane pounded the craft in sheets and ran across the skin in tiny rivulets. The ship rocked as it fought through the storm, and lightning flashed in the distance.

"Let's wait for Kaminski to arrive before we head in," Isaac said. "We'll move in as a unified—"

A two-tone alarm he'd never heard before warbled in his virtual hearing, and virtual displays flashed alive in front of him.

"Cephalie, what's—"

"Collision alert!" she shouted. "Hold on!"

The v-wing spun onto its side and banked away as restraints dug into Isaac's shoulder. He gasped at the sudden gee forces and clenched his fingers over the armrests. The two tones of the alarm began switching faster and faster.

"Damn! It's tracking us!"

"What's tracking us?!" Isaac wheezed.

"Not sure! Here we go!"

The v-wing corkscrewed through the storm, and the two-tone alarm rattled off so quickly it almost became a single grating noise. A brief flash of orange lit up outside the cockpit, a shock wave smashed into the v-wing, and Isaac's head thumped against the headrest so hard he saw stars.

A schematic of the v-wing appeared, and damage indicators lit up red across the back half.

"We're hit!" Cephalie cried. "Thruster's out! Going down!"

Rough, icy terrain rushed to meet them, and Isaac barely had time to gulp before the v-wing crashed through a jutting spine of ice. The impact tore the left wing off, and the broken plank somersaulted through the air as the fuselage bobsledded forward over the Titanite surface.

The right wing caught against a dark, ragged outcrop, spinning the craft like a sluggish top, and the side of the v-wing crunched against a tall slope of ice. One entire side of the cockpit bulged inward, and escaping air hissed.

The impact threw Isaac to the side. His head struck the bulging wall, hot blood splattered from his temple, and his world turned to black.

✧   ✧   ✧

Susan released her seat restraints and executed a quick internal diagnostic. Her synthoid was undamaged, and she twisted around in her seat.

"Isaac!"

His head lolled against the deformed cockpit wall, and blood dribbled down his cheek. His chest heaved as he drew in unconscious breaths, but sensory clusters in her nasal cavity showed the temperature dropping and the air composition turning lethal for baseline humans.

"Cephalie, you still with me?" she shouted.

"Here!" The LENS floated up to her side.

"Quick! The air's going to kill him! Where are the pressure suits?"

"Stand back. I've got something better."

Susan shifted away until her back pressed against the far wall. The LENS flew up to Isaac and shed its outer layer in a rain of quicksilver. Flexible prog-steel poured over his face and ran down his body until it hardened into a full gunmetal gray cocoon. A tube extended from the mass and connected to the cockpit's ventilation duct.

"He's safe for now," Cephalie said. "The v-wing's still producing breathable air, but some of the prog-steel power circuits are fried. I can't close the hole in the cockpit. I've configured the suit to form a vacuum insulation layer, which'll keep him warm once the temperature starts cratering."

"What do we have left?"

"About two thirds of a v-wing. Our SOS beacon activated, so there's that. We're calling for help, but something must be wrong with our data transceiver. I can't get it to boot up. Infosystem might have been damaged in the blast or the crash. Or both."

"What the hell hit us?"

"A missile of some kind. Must have been launched from close by. I hardly saw it coming."

"Stade," Susan breathed.

"Or an accomplice."

"He's going to pay for this." She drew her sidearm.

"What are you doing?"

"Making sure help has time to arrive." She swept a finger in a wide circle. "Can you guide me to where you think that missile came from?"

"Sure can."

"Then give me a nav beacon. I'm heading out."

She stiffened the fingers of her free hand, jammed them into the cockpit breach, and curled the digits upward. She disabled all performance limiters and clenched the artificial muscles in her arm.

"Hold up," Cephalie urged. "I'll try to reroute . . . and you've already ripped it open."

Susan tore the prog-steel hull upward, and frigid air blasted her in the face. She pounded the jagged edges aside with the flat of her forearm, then climbed out. A torrential downpour of liquid methane beat on her in heavy sheets. Temperatures below negative one hundred eighty degrees Celsius snap-froze her cosmetic layer. Her skin solidified and her sense of touch faulted out, but the artificial muscles underneath pushed through, cracking her skin open with each step, each flex of her limbs.

Warnings lit up in her virtual vision, cautioning her against staying in the cold too long, lest viscosity build up in her joint lubrication. Ice froze over her eyes, and she wiped them clear with her sleeve; they only *looked* like human eyes, and the complex sensory suite built into each orb continued to function in the piercing cold.

The v-wing was partially imbedded in an icy slope, minus a wing, the vertical stabilizer, and the thruster assembly. The thick seven-barreled tip of the 30mm Gatling gun stuck out from the nose and appeared intact, for all the good that would do, but one of the micro-missile racks had survived mostly intact underneath the right wing. Her busted combat frame and—more importantly—its weapons might have survived the crash, but she'd burn a lot of time trying to dig them out.

Time she likely didn't have.

<Cephalie?> Susan transmitted over her virtual hearing, her lips frozen shut. <You hear me?>

<Loud and clear.>

<Can you open the way to my combat frame?>

<No can do. Power's out to that part of the hull.>

<What about the micro-missiles? Do they still work?>

<Don't know. What are you thinking?>

<Not sure yet. Just see if they're good to go.>

<On it.>

<Where's that nav beacon?>

<Coming right up.>

A blue triangle blinked in her periphery.

<Got it. Heading out.>

She took long, bouncy strides in Titan's gravity and cut across the groove torn by the v-wing's impact, then hurried through a series of icy dips and rises eroded long ago by the moon's weather, staying low whenever possible. The storm grew fiercer, pounding her back with fat droplets of liquid methane as she came to a steep, rocky rise.

She scaled the hill, crouching low as she approached the top, and peeked over the rise.

A teeming swarm of industrial drones floated over the drenched terrain with a solid core of disk-shaped conveyors flanked by smaller spherical remotes. The conveyors lumbered toward the crash site, some carrying what looked like heavy rifles or grenade launchers in their malleable arms, and a few of the remotes zipped around with pistols grafted to their bodies. Other drones carried only construction welders, vibro-saws, or other tools that could double as lethal weapons.

<Damn, there are a lot of you.>

<Micro-missiles online,> Cephalie reported. <I can launch them, but that's about it. Can't see a damn thing from here.>

<But I can.> Susan permitted herself a vicious grin, even though it tore open the skin around her cheeks. <I have eyes on a mass of converted construction drones. They're not built for combat, but there are a *lot* of them. I'd guess someone's been

printing weapons and installing them on the facility's construction force. About two thirds of them have guns, and they're heading straight for you.>

<Sounds like you're right about them being from the factory. Weapons could have been printed out in haste when they realized we were closing in, which is why not all of them are armed.>

<Let's make it clear SysPol expects better hospitality than this,> Susan sent. <Transmitting coordinates. Hit these bastards with *everything* you've got.>

<Locked. And firing.>

Susan hunkered down behind the rise and glanced back in the direction of the crash. A flurry of tiny lights arced upward, formed a glittering cloud, and then zipped toward her. Dozens of tiny missiles, little larger than guided grenades, flew past her position and onboard systems "saw" the oncoming horde.

SysPol micro-missiles were precision weapons, designed to take down high-threat armored targets with minimal damage to their surroundings. Their infosystems networked in the brief moments after the criminal drones came into direct view, and quick whiskers of data spread target acquisitions and prioritization across the munition cluster.

The micro-missile hive mind selected its targets and assigned them to individual micro-missiles. The collective intelligence locked its final attack plan, tiny thrusters redlined, and the micro-missiles rushed in for the kill.

Shaped charges wracked the construction drones with tongues of flame. Gutted conveyors dropped to the ground or sputtered forward until they buried themselves in ice.

But the drones were not an army made of skin, meat, and bones. They were a collection of nonsentient machines that didn't care about losses, that didn't understand hope or shock or resolve. They had a job to do, and they would execute their assigned tasks with the unfeeling calculation of computers following a designated path to completion.

Half of the conveyors fell to the barrage, but the other half pressed on.

Susan steadied her hand cannon over the rise and opened fire. Her first shot punched through the side of a conveyor and blew its arm clean off. Her second shot pierced its graviton thruster, and it teetered to the side before ramming its nose into the earth.

Susan blasted a second conveyor before gunfire chattered against her cover. Icy splinters flew into the air, and she ducked behind the rise and reloaded.

<You okay over there?> Cephalie asked.

<Never better!>

Susan shifted her position and popped up between a narrow V of slick black rock. She sighted down the top of her pistol and blasted another conveyor with a quick, three-shot burst. Smoke poured out of its body, and it settled to the ground.

A conveyor toward the back of the swarm spun to face her and launched a pair of guided grenades. Estimated trajectories played out in her virtual vision, and she pushed off her cover. The grenades cracked against the rocky V, obliterating it in a flash, and smoking pebbles rained down around her.

She sprinted to the side, firing until her pistol was empty, then dove for cover. A lucky bullet grazed her face, tearing frozen flesh from metallic bone at her cheek. Her ear flopped freely, and she reloaded her pistol, numb to the concept of pain.

A trio of remotes crested the rise, and one shot a quick burst at her. Bullets cracked against her face and shoulder, and she swung her aim up and returned fire, obliterating the remote in a single shot. Static danced over the feed from her right eye, but she compensated and blew the second remote to pieces.

The last remote darted in and a pincer latched onto the barrel of her pistol. A blue flame burning bright from the drone's underslung welder cut into the barrel of her pistol. She grabbed the remote like a baseball, ripped it free of her pistol, and smashed it against the rocks.

More remotes swarmed over the rise, and she slid down the slope, then raced into the eroded labyrinth. Bullets zinged past her, blasting ice into the air, and she kept her head down and quickly inspected the pistol.

The welding flame had melted and warped the barrel. It wouldn't shoot straight, if it shot at all.

<Damn it!> Susan holstered the pistol and hurried back to the crash site. <Cephalie, we've got a problem!>

<Tell me something I don't know.>

<A drone damaged my pistol! They'll tear me to pieces without a weapon!>

<Okay. That's a problem.>

<Is there anything left in the v-wing?>

<Nothing but the Gatling and your weapons in the hold. I used all the micro-missiles.>

<Then I'll take the Gatling.>

<What? You mean the gun that's the size of a small car?>

<I can lift it no problem, even in standard gravity. Can you get it free of the nose?>

<I'll try. The prog-steel in the nose still has an active power circuit.>

<Do it!>

Susan caught sight of the downed v-wing and cleared the space to it in four long, gliding strides. She halted herself with a stiff boot to the side of the nose, which began to flower open around the Gatling gun assembly.

She grabbed the gun by the bracket around the barrel tips and slid it out of the expanding prog-steel. The barrels were over two and half meters long, and the discharge capacitors took up another meter with a feed belt connecting back to the drum-shaped ammo sorter, which gave the whole assembly most of its bulk.

Susan braced the weapon against her hip and shook out the feed belt, which snaked back into the v-wing. She interfaced with the weapon's manual controls; ballistic trajectory, weapon status, and ammo count lit up in her virtual vision.

She raised the weapon, spun up the barrels, and aimed it toward the hillside blocking her view of the approaching drones. Despite the physical strength that allowed her synthoid body to heft a weapon half again its own height, it had far too little body mass to absorb its mammoth recoil—a problem the low gravity only made worse. But the enemy's angle of approach would let her keep the muzzles high, directing the recoil energy into the ground. *That* had plenty of mass.

She lowered her stance and braced one foot against the v-wing wreckage; she'd fought in low gravity before, and her training and field experience were about to pay dividends.

<The gun suits you,> Cephalie said.

<This is what a thug like me is good for,> she quipped, despite the danger. <Blowing shit up.>

<Here they come.>

<I'm ready.>

A pair of conveyors crested the hill, and she lit them up with a stream of sixty-seven bullets per second. The conveyors evaporated under the sleet of metal, but more crested the hill, and Susan hosed them down, too. The drones charged in, unthinking, unfeeling, unable to be broken. They rushed her all at once, and she chewed through them with the constant thunder of metal and fire and death.

<Hell yeah!> Susan cheered.

Her ammo count plummeted. She wouldn't last long burning through at this rate, but she didn't let her mind dwell on it. She existed purely in the moment, feet braced, giant weapon in her hands spewing metal as she eliminated threats and moved on in a vicious cycle of roaring death. She would either have enough shots, or she wouldn't. She would either survive this ambush, or she wouldn't. She couldn't put more rounds in the drum, not stuck out here in the freezing rain.

But the one thing she could control—the one thing she'd be *damned* if she left this mortal coil without doing—was to fight on till the very end. *That* was the very essence of what it meant to be a STAND, to be a warrior who gave up her flesh to serve the greater good. It didn't matter where evil lurked. Bad guys were bad guys, whether they melted the flesh off children or crushed women in stackers, and they *all* deserved her wrath.

Shattered drones toppled over the hill, forming a twisted, sparking, smoking pile at its base, but they kept coming without end. Five guided grenades soared through the air, and she pulled her aim up. One blew apart. Two. Three.

A pair crashed down around her, exploding in spasms of scything shrapnel. A red-hot chunk imbedded itself in her forehead, and more shrapnel slashed across her body. Static fluttered over her right eye's feed. Her synthoid's diagnostics pulsed with damage, while the Gatling gun whined from heat and friction where shrapnel caught in its rotary mechanism.

Susan fought on, undeterred, unflinching, holding her ground against the enemy. She selected a target, blew it to hell, then selected another, killed it, then another and another.

A conveyor rose above the hillside and its heavy rifle boomed.

The massive round punched through her knee.

Her joint gave out, and she dropped to one knee and raked the top of the hill with cannon fire. Tiny explosions tore through the conveyor, but more rose to take its place. Drone gunfire blasted her left shoulder to pieces, and the limb dropped away.

She let go of the Gatling gun with her right arm, twisted her wrist for a better angle, and grabbed the weapon again, compensating for the loss of her left arm with one quick, fluid motion. The Gatling never stopped firing, and she adjusted her aim and savaged the drones assaulting her.

More drones crested the hill, and she took aim and triggered her weapon, but all that came out was a quick burp of rounds.

<Shit!> she hissed. A bullet struck her face, and the feed from her right eye flickered out.

She drew her sidearm and squeezed the trigger, but the BARREL OBSTRUCTED fault lit up next to the weapon.

More shots rang out, and damage pulsed across her shoulder, torso, and legs. She collapsed back, and the drones swarmed in around the crashed v-wing. She tried to rise, but the artificial muscles in her legs and remaining arm strained with the effort, and critical faults lit up in her mind.

She dropped back onto the icy ground, liquid methane raining over her ruined face.

The world seemed to slow around her, and a strange sense of contentment draped her mind, almost as if covering her thoughts with a warm blanket. She had fought as hard as she could, had stood between the innocent and the guilty, had defended those who could not fight from the monsters who dared threaten their lives.

Wasn't this what she'd always wanted? Wasn't this the end she'd hoped for when she joined STAND and willingly surrendered her blood and bones? If she died here, fighting desperately to save an innocent life—fighting to save *Isaac's* life—was it really such a bad way to go?

No.

No, it wasn't.

Susan rolled onto her stomach and forced herself up just enough to turn her good eye toward the approaching drones. If death truly came for her, she would face it head-on, not cowering in the dirt.

A pair of conveyors floated toward her, vibro-saws buzzing in their arms. She pushed herself up higher, rising in defiance of their advance, spitting in the face of her impending death in what little way she still could.

The lead conveyor raised the vibro-saw high overhead—

—and then fire and brimstone and the wrath of Hell itself consumed the world.

Explosions split the conveyor open, threw its ruined carcass back. More explosions blasted ice, rock, and metal high into the air in a rolling pattern that radiated outward from the crash site in expanding arcs. The inferno consumed the closest drones first, then spread, shattering those farther away. The cacophony shuddered through her body, but she braced herself against the ground, refusing to topple over until the worst had passed.

She craned her neck to see a massive gunmetal ellipsoid slide into view overhead, gun pods open, Gatling guns raking the ground with fire. The long spike of a time drive impeller protruded from its back.

The TTV *Kleio* had finally caught up with them.

CHAPTER TWENTY-SIX

ISAAC BLINKED HIS WATERY EYES OPEN.

"Wha..." he croaked. "Where?"

"Hey, Isaac," Cephalie said, sitting on the side of his pillow. "You with us again?"

"What?" He licked his dry lips. "What happened?"

"Quite a bit, actually. How do you feel?"

"Like something crawled down my throat and died."

He sat up to find himself atop a medical casket in a sterile white room, covered with nothing more than a blanket. The hum of distant, powerful machinery filled his ears. Was he on a ship? He looked around for someone besides Cephalie, but the room was vacant except for his LENS, a row of glass-topped medical caskets, and, for some strange reason, Susan's combat frame.

"Not surprised." Cephalie floated up to his shoulder. "You breathed in a few whiffs of Titan's atmosphere, so we slathered your lungs with medibots. You should feel fine in an hour or so."

"Thanks," he said hoarsely. He looked around again. "Where are we?"

"Onboard the *Kleio*. Kaminski picked us up after the crash."

"The crash." Isaac rubbed his eyes. "Yeah. I remember that. Something hit us, right? Where's Susan?"

"Over here." The combat frame waved at him with its only arm, a milky white shell around the shoulder.

"Susan?" Isaac blinked the blurs away.

"Yes?"

"What's that on your shoulder?"

"A microbot cast from the *Kleio*. It's repairing the joint. This way I have at least one good arm."

"And why are you in your combat frame in the first place?"

"Because my other body's all shot up."

"It's *what*?" Isaac's exclaimed. "What did I miss?"

"Oh, you should have seen it!" Cephalie pointed to Susan-the-Combat-Frame with her cane. "Your deputy here held back a swarm of weaponized construction drones all by herself! Bought enough time for the *Kleio* to reach us, and after that it was all over! Those drones were a danger to us, but against a TTV, they were flinging spitballs."

"Wait a second," Isaac said. "Hold up. A swarm of construction drones?"

"Like fifty plus. Not itty-bitty ones, either, and with plenty of guns and explosives mixed in."

"All by herself?"

"Yep."

"With just her pistol?" Isaac asked, confused.

"Well, initially." Cephalie pushed her glasses up her nose, and the lenses gleamed. "But then she grabbed the v-wing's nose cannon and started using *that* monster!"

Isaac's mouth flopped open.

"It's lighter than it looks," Susan said.

"You should have seen her mow them down!" Cephalie grinned. "Actually, you *can* see her. I took video."

"Please!" Susan shooed the suggestion away. "You're embarrassing me!"

Isaac had never expected to see a bashful Admin death machine, but there she was.

"Come on," Cephalie pressed. "Don't be shy. I put together a highlight reel while Isaac was out."

"You might think a firefight is something special, but to us Peacekeepers, that's just another day ending in *y*."

"You're exaggerating." Isaac massaged his temples in an effort to clear his head.

"Maybe, but I feel like I earned that one."

"Now, what do you say, Isaac?"

"Huh?"

Cephalie poked his cheek with her cane.

"Ouch!"

"What do you say, Isaac?"

"Thank you for saving my life, Susan!" He rubbed his cheek. "I was about to!"

"Glad to be of help," Susan said.

"You did a lot more than that." Isaac glanced down at his blanket. "Is my uniform still in one piece?"

"Got it right here." Susan grabbed the folded uniform off the next casket and set it in his lap.

"Thanks. We should talk to Kaminski. Get our bearings. Does anyone know where we're headed? Feels like we're in flight."

"Still on track for the Kraken Mare," Cephalie said. "And it's not just us, anymore. Argo Division sent a pair of corvettes down from orbit, and SSP is getting in on the fun, too. They've dispatched six heavy v-wings from Promise City, all loaded down with state troopers. If Stade's at the facility, we're about to *seriously* ruin his day."

"Serves him right." Isaac pinched the blanket between two fingers and lifted it a hair. "Would you two mind?"

"Oh. Right." Susan stepped outside the medical bay.

❖   ❖   ❖

The time machine's bridge was a circular room built around a command table with abstract charts glowing over its surface. Kaminski's big blond synthoid and Andover-Chen's smaller model both turned when Isaac and Susan entered.

"Detective!" Kaminski grinned at him. "Good to see you up and about. You gave us quite the scare when we picked up your SOS."

"Good to *be* up." Isaac joined them at the table. "I understand I owe you thanks as well for our survival."

"Not as much as you owe your partner, I think." Raibert grimaced. "Which brings me to an important piece of business, now that you're here to witness it."

"Witness what?" Isaac asked.

"Oh, wow. Here it comes." Andover-Chen grinned. "You two have no idea how difficult this is for him."

Raibert made an annoyed shooing gesture, then cleared his throat and faced Susan.

"Agent Cantrell?"

"Yes?"

"Look, I'm going to level with you. I'm not the biggest fan of the Admin."

"Understatement of the century," Andover-Chen quipped.

"Would you *please* let me do this? It's hard enough as it is." Raibert fumed over his shoulder. He sighed and turned back to Susan. "Truth is, the Admin and I got off on a bad foot. A *really* bad foot, so I approach anyone from your government with a healthy dose of paranoia salted with pessimism and a bad attitude."

"That's ... understandable, given what I know of your history."

"But!" He held up a finger. "That doesn't mean I'm blind to reality, and what I saw when we came over the horizon was a genuine fight-to-the-last-round, fight-to-the-last-breath moment, with you holding the line to protect Detective Cho here."

"He's my partner. Of course, I'd do that for him."

"Exactly!" Raibert smiled at her. "And that's part of what I'm beginning to understand about you people from the Admin, and from the DTI in particular."

"What's that?"

"One thing I've seen over the course of my ...."—he swirled a hand vaguely—"various interactions with the DTI is when you guys get pointed at a problem, it tends not to last very long. Being the problem you're trying to solve is *not* pleasant, believe me! I speak from experience there!

"But being on the same side as you guys?" He smiled again, and with genuine warmth. "That's ... a pretty all right place to be."

"Which is high praise coming from him," Andover-Chen said.

"Hey! I'm not finished yet!"

"Whoops. Sorry." Andover-Chen didn't sound sorry at all.

"Geez!" Raibert sighed. "Anyway, Agent Can ... *Susan*. The big thing I want to tell you is you did good out there—*real* good. You're all right in my book, and that means you're welcome on board the *Kleio* any time you like."

"Thank you. That means a lot to me, though I couldn't have done it without your help."

"Don't mention it. I'm just glad we were able to reach you in time. *Both* of you. Now, to our other business." Kaminski pointed to a tactical map of the terrain with icons for the factory and various SysPol and SSP craft. "Here, take a look. Argo

Division's been keeping an eye on the factory from orbit. Nothing's departed since they started watching, but that's a small comfort. The reassembled impeller, or whatever they're working on, could be long gone by now."

"Perhaps, but the attack on our v-wing suggests otherwise," Isaac said. "The evidence trail Agent Cantrell and I have followed tells us this crime was carefully planned, but those drones she fought..." He shook his head. "*That* feels like the hasty, desperate act of a cornered criminal. They weren't even all armed, which tells me they're protecting this facility because the impeller is still there."

"Well, we'll know soon enough," Kaminski said.

"Doctor," Isaac said. "We're proceeding on the theory the criminal—an individual using the alias of Thomas Stade—means to reassemble the impeller fragments, and he's doing so at this facility. Your thoughts?"

"Putting those pieces back together is a tall order," Andover-Chen said. "The dismantling process Negation used is designed to prevent such an act. You'd *really* need to know what you're doing."

"Delacroix's involvement seems to satisfy that requirement."

"Yes, it would." Andover-Chen let out a heavy sigh. "Hard to believe he was wrapped up in this."

"Believe it. We have evidence Delacroix and Stade were in contact."

"But that know-how isn't enough on its own. You need support equipment to rejoin the segments. High-precision atomic printers, for one."

"Which the Kraken Mare plant has."

"Or a different facility with the same equipment," Kaminski countered.

"The Trinh Syndicate only has two exotic matter facilities," Isaac said. "Kraken Mare and New Frontier. I think it's safe to assume those are the only two facilities Stade has access to, and of them, only Kraken Mare is free from regular audits."

"It fits." Andover-Chen crossed his arms. "If Stade is trying to put the impeller back together, his new ride is stuck at Kraken Mare until it's done."

"And he's just about out of time." Kaminski expanded the view from an external camera and zoomed in on a red rectangular block built along the coast of a deep, blackish lake. Rain lashed at its broad flanks, and huge pipes lined one side of the structure, ready to drink deeply of the lake's liquid methane.

The ellipsoid of a SysPol corvette dropped beneath the haze layer and angled toward the facility, while a second one sped across the lake from the opposite direction.

"Looks like we barely got here first," Kaminski said.

"We should surveil the interior remotely," Isaac said. "Does this ship have reconnaissance remotes?"

"Sure does. Once we're alongside, I'll—"

Three separate charts over the command table began flashing red.

"Uh-oh," Kaminski breathed.

"Raibert!" Philo's Viking avatar materialized on the other side of the table. "There's an active impeller in the facility! It's about to phase into the past!"

"Not good!" Kaminski seethed through clenched teeth. "Are we in weapons range?"

"I can't *see* it! It's in the middle of a factory! Which part do you want me to shoot up?"

"Fine, then! Lock onto that signature! Wherever it goes, we go!"

"Got it." Philo vanished. "Bringing the impeller online. All systems ready for phase-out."

"Agent?" Isaac stepped up next to Kaminski. "What's going on?"

"Looks like Stade finished his work. He's getting ready to leave the True Present, but don't worry. When he does, we'll be hot on his tail. He won't get far. No DIY time machine is going to outrun *this* ship!"

Isaac blinked. "We're about to enter the past?"

"Sure are." Kaminski grinned broadly at him. "Bet you didn't think this was in the cards when you woke up today."

"No," Isaac replied dryly. "No, I didn't."

"Phase-out detected," Philo said. "Engaging impeller... now!"

Exotic matter in the TTV's impeller morphed to block chronotons flowing up the timestream while allowing those traveling in the opposite direction to pass through freely. Temporal pressure built along the mechanism, the craft's phase state began to shift, and the TTV slipped into the past.

Isaac blinked again. Everything in the room was as it had been moments before. The past felt exactly like the present.

That seemed strange to him for some reason.

He glanced over the command table and took note of a pair of clocks, one displaying absolute time in the True Present, which still ticked forward at one second per second, while the other counted backwards rapidly, denoting their relative position in the timeline.

"Stade's time machine has a slight head start, but we're closing," Philo reported. "Distance is negative three days to target and dropping. Phase-lock in less than a minute, absolute."

"Phase-lock?" Isaac asked.

"Our term for matching temporal course and speed," Kaminski explained. "Think of it like two ships in space coming alongside each other. After that, Stade better play nice, or I'll send him straight to hell."

"Try to take him alive, if you can," Isaac stressed.

"I will, but only if he lets me."

The ship noise changed, lessened slightly, and Kaminski leaned forward and his brow furrowed.

"Philo, why did we stop all of a sudden?"

"I lost him."

"*What?*" Kaminski snapped. "What do you mean you lost him?"

"Just that. One second, our scope had a clear read on his impeller, and the next it was gone. I thought I saw a phase-out at negative two months behind the True Present, but..."

"There's no time machine at negative two months!"

"Yeah. I noticed that."

"We lost him?" Isaac asked.

"*Temporarily*," Kaminski clarified.

"Of course." Isaac glanced over the command table. "Is there anything we can do to help?"

"Look, Detective." Kaminski took him by the shoulder and guided him away from the command table. "I appreciate the offer. I really do, but honestly, the hard part's over. You already took care of that for us by discovering the crime and bringing us here. We'll handle the rest."

"I'm sorry, Agent. I meant no offense. You're the experts when it comes to time travel, obviously. I only asked in the off chance you needed assistance."

"You know which TTV you're on, right?"

"The *Kleio*?"

"The frickin' *Kleio*!" Kaminski slapped him on the shoulder with surprising force. "The ship that cut the Gordian Knot and saved fifteen universes. Fifteen! The ship that made first contact with the Admin, survived *two* imploding universes, and helped end the Dynasty Crisis."

"That's quite the résumé," Isaac said.

"It is! Philo and I were there for every part of it, and the doctor's a regular addition to our team."

"Technically, you and I were on the command ship during the Crisis," Andover-Chen clarified.

"Details, details," Kaminski dismissed. "What I'm driving at, Detective, is you have nothing to worry about. So, sit down. Relax. Take a load off. Between the three of us—"

The ship's feminine voice cleared her nonexistent throat.

"—*four* of us," Kaminski corrected, "the situation is in good hands. So, pardon me if I scoff at the idea some asscave's do-it-yourself time machine is going to give *us* the slip!"

✧   ✧   ✧

An hour later, Isaac couldn't help but notice how unhappy Kaminski looked as he leaned over the command table, glowering at the array of charts. The big man let out a long, frustrated exhale then glanced up.

"You have any idea where it went?" Kaminski asked Andover-Chen from across the table.

"Nope," he replied with frayed patience. "I didn't the last time you asked, and I still don't."

"He gave us the slip, didn't he?"

"So it would seem."

"But he can't have gone far! We would have seen him!"

"I agree."

"Then where is he?"

"I don't know."

"Arrhhh!" Kaminski ran harsh fingers through his hair.

A prog-steel chair formed out of the wall, and Isaac dropped into it with a tired sigh. He rested his forearms on his thighs and stared at the floor.

"You and me both." Susan's combat frame leaned against the wall beside him.

"It's a strange concept to grasp."

"What is?"

"That I'm in the past."

"Yeah?" She shrugged. "So?"

"But I'm in the *past*."

"You've been here before."

"No, I haven't," Isaac said, but then he paused and considered his words more carefully. "Okay, granted, yes I have. But not like this. Not out of sequence."

"We're only two months back. Where I work, this barely counts."

"Well, this is a new experience for me. Is what we're doing dangerous? Could we branch the timeline by being here?"

"No way," Susan assured him. "Sure, the *Kleio*'s in the past, but it's flying in a non-congruent state."

"Meaning?"

"We're out of phase with the rest of reality. Yes, we're two months in the past, but we're not *interacting* with it. Not yet, at least."

"And if we have to?"

"The *Kleio*'s equipped with a metamaterial shroud for sneaking around, which reconfigures into laser-refracting meta-armor in a combat situation. This close to the True Present, we'll need to be cautious around a population center, but we shouldn't have any issues in open space."

"You seem to know a lot about this ship."

"I—" The combat frame looked away. "Yeah, I guess I do."

"I seem to recall you mentioning DTI smash-and-grab missions into the past."

"Yeah. We're more careful nowadays."

"But did any of them branch the timeline?"

"Not as far as we've seen."

"Then we should be safe to swoop in and nab Stade," Isaac said. "Assuming we can find him."

"Yeah. A little, piddly interaction like that is a nonissue. We'd only be grabbing another foreign element. Risk is as close to zero as it gets with time travel."

"Good to know. I suppose I'll wrap my head around this eventually. How about you?" He knocked on the combat frame's hip joint. "You doing okay in there?"

"I've been stuck in combat frames for days at a time, so this is nothing." Susan flexed her arm. "Would be nice to have all my limbs, though."

"I'd ask Kaminski, but..."

"Yeah. He seems busy."

"Very."

"We should leave him be."

"Let's."

"You realize I can hear you two!" Kaminski grumbled with his back turned.

"Sorry," Isaac said, then spoke softly to Susan. "Glad to hear you're doing well. It's hard to tell how you feel in there, since your face doesn't emote."

"What do you mean? It can emote."

Isaac glanced up at the combat frame's blank, featureless face armor and raised a doubtful eyebrow.

"Sure, I can. Here. Watch."

The variskin on the combat frame's head formed two bright white dots, and then an arc lit up underneath.

"See?" Susan said. "This is happy."

"You drew a smiley face on your frame's dynamic camouflage?"

"Why not? And here's sad."

The arch under the two dots inverted.

"Very convincing." He grinned wryly. "I can feel the emotion radiating off you."

"I do what I can."

"Aha!" Kaminski exclaimed with glee. "There he is!"

"Find him?" Isaac stood up and joined them at the command table.

"More or less." Andover-Chen brought up a map of the Saturn State and highlighted a point between Saturn and Titan. "I'm still not sure how he eluded us at the outset, but his ship really did phase out at negative two months. He's been moving away from us in a non-congruent state ever since."

"He almost got away with it, too." Kaminski wagged a finger. "If not for his second-rate impeller."

"It must be compromised in some manner," Andover-Chen continued. "Every so often, it's creating an unusual chronometric ripple. Subtle, but detectable to our scope. Now that we know what to look for, we can plot the earlier occurrences..." The doctor spread his hands, and a series of dots formed a rough arc leaving Titan.

"He's well on his way back to Saturn," Isaac observed.

"We'll catch him," Kaminski said. "Based on his progress,

he's pushing three gees. We can hit five when we mean business, which'll see us to Saturn's atmosphere a little after him. Your meat sack will need to sit out the flight in a compensation bunk, though."

"I'm fine with that," Isaac said. Long flights at high gees were a standard part of training for organic SysPol officers. "Where are the bunks?"

"Along the bridge wall." Kaminski pointed, and a panel slid aside to reveal five upright glass caskets.

"Right." Isaac sidestepped into one, and it closed and began to fill with a milky microbot soup that would fortify his body against the high acceleration.

"Philo, take us into orbit once the detective is situated. Maximum thrust."

"You got it."

Kaminski turned to Susan and scowled at her.

"What?" she asked.

"Why are you frowning at me?"

"Oh, sorry." Her face armor reverted to Peacekeeper blue.

✧　　✧　　✧

The *Kleio* descended through thick, billowing clouds in a storm band two hundred kilometers north of Janus-Epimetheus. Winds gusted at three hundred kilometers per hour, and the deck rocked under their feet. Isaac steadied himself with a hand on a railing built into the rim of the command table.

Visual feeds showed a brief glint of metal in the raging storm of reddish ammonium hydrosulfide, and tactical displays rendered the rogue time machine in a vivid schematic. The ship bore a striking resemblance to the *Kleio*, with an elliptical main body attached to the long spike of an impeller.

"Try again, if you don't mind," Isaac said.

"This is TTV *Kleio* of the Gordian Division to the unauthorized time machine," Kaminski said stiffly over the direct laser link. "There's no point running, and even less point ignoring us. We're faster than you, both temporally and in realspace, and our main gun is locked on your hull. You are hereby ordered to surrender and prepare to be boarded. Respond."

He muted the comm window.

Isaac gave the other ship a full minute to reply, then shook his head.

"I hate being ignored," Kaminski grunted.

"He must really want to do this the hard way," Susan said. The *Kleio*'s microbots had finished repairing her combat frame on the flight over, though her general purpose synthoid remained a work in progress within the *Kleio*'s printers.

"Fine by me." Kaminski cracked his knuckles.

"Any indication his craft is armed?" Isaac asked.

"No, but I've noticed something else." Andover-Chen tapped the other ship's schematic where the spike met the hull. "The impeller is equipped with devices similar to Admin-style stealth baffles."

"Figured it had to be something like that," Kaminski growled. "How else could he have given us the slip?"

"Wait a second," Susan put her hands on her hips. "How does Admin tech end up on a SysGov time machine?"

Andover-Chen and Kaminski exchanged guarded looks.

"Gentlemen?" she pressed.

"I suppose there's no harm in telling her," Andover-Chen said.

"Tell me what?"

"Fine." Kaminski waved for Andover-Chen to continue. "Be my guest."

"It's nothing unexpected," the doctor began. "Admin impellers are superior to ours in many respects, and we've been research-ing ways to close the performance gap. Delacroix was heading an initiative to replicate Admin stealth technology." He passed a hand underneath the schematic. "This looks like a crude first attempt to apply some of our new theories."

"It may be crude," Kaminski said, "but it still fooled us."

"Only once the time machine stopped at negative two months. We could clearly see it in normal flight."

"Yet another sign of how deeply Delacroix was involved," Isaac said.

"We're going to have to rescreen all of his associates when this is over." Kaminski leaned over the table and eyeballed the other time machine. "Want me to try calling Stade again, or shall we move in and grab him the hard way?"

"We've given him ample time to turn himself in peacefully," Isaac said. "Move in."

"Philo?"

"Yes?" The Viking avatar appeared across the table.

"Get us close enough to send over a few remotes and the

detective's LENS, but keep that ship in your sights." Kaminski opened a comm window. "TTV *Kleio* to the unauthorized time machine, since you have declined to respond, we're coming to you. Any hostile action on your part will be met with lethal force. Hold position and prepare to be boarded."

He closed the window, then nodded to Philo.

"Taking us down," the Viking said.

The *Kleio* descended through the lashing winds at a diagonal and came to rest directly behind the criminal vessel. They eased forward until their bow almost touched the tip of Stade's impeller.

"This should be close enough. Sending the remotes over now."

Prog-steel along the *Kleio*'s bow blossomed open, and a cluster of six spherical remotes and a heavy conveyor left the bow hangar. They flew across the other ship's impeller, struggling to fly straight in the fierce crosswinds.

"I'll need to make an opening," Philo said. "If it's laid out like our ship, the bow hangar's the easiest place."

"Do it," Kaminski said.

The conveyor reached the bow. It latched onto the hull with one arm and stabbed a slender spike deep into the prog-steel.

"Virus is taking hold," Philo said. "There. We have partial local control."

The bow prog-steel opened at the conveyor's command, and the remotes zipped into the dark interior. They switched on their tiny lights, and video feeds opened on the command table.

"The hangar was already equalized with Saturn's atmosphere at this depth," Isaac observed.

"Wonder why," Susan said.

"Layout looks familiar," Kaminski said.

"It's a design Delacroix would have easy access to," Andover-Chen noted.

"Yeah." Kaminski exhaled the word more than spoke it.

The remotes left the barren, three-story hangar through a ground-level airlock at the rear. They cycled past it and spread throughout the rogue time machine, mapping it in quick order. The craft was mostly empty rooms and corridors, with only a few critical systems installed.

"Reactor output is normal for a TTV," Andover-Chen observed. "Stade could park here for a century or two and still have power to spare."

"Bridge doesn't look finished," Kaminski noted. "There's a command table, but not much in the way of a supporting info-structure. No attendant program on board that we've seen so far. Stade must have flown it manually."

"Not many people could do that." Andover-Chen turned to Isaac. "Who did you say Stade was again?"

"I didn't. We still don't know his true identity."

"Lot of empty space in the floor plan," Kaminski said. "This bird was pushed out of the nest early, if you ask me."

"Mmhmm," Isaac murmured, watching the feeds.

"Where's Stade hiding?" Susan asked.

One of the remotes entered the rear hold, where six towering printers formed a row underneath a high, rounded ceiling.

"Stop remote number four," Isaac said. "Back it up and pan left."

The remote retreated and spun to face one of the printer's output ports with a chair positioned next to it. Folds of slick, pale material lay in a haphazard pile in front of the chair, along with a few small metallic cylinders.

"What is that?" Susan asked.

"Not sure." Isaac took direct control of the remote and brought it close to the pile. The material was coated in clear gel on one side and colored like pinkish flesh on the other. One patch of the surface was coated in brown fur.

No, not fur. Hair.

Synthoid hair.

"Oh dear," Isaac breathed. "Stade replaced his synthoid's epidermis."

"Why would he do that?" Kaminski asked. "Doesn't matter what he looks like. There's hardly anywhere left on the ship for him to hide."

"Because he's not on the ship," Isaac said coldly. "That's why the pressure was equalized in the hangar. Stade isn't here!"

"He must have brought a v-wing with him," Susan said. "Do you think he's heading for Janus?"

"Probably. It's the closest settlement."

"But why abandon the time machine and head there?" Kaminski asked.

"To continue what he's been doing this whole time," Isaac said, "which is blending in. He's changed his identity, and now he's heading to Janus to disappear. For good, this time."

"We need to stop him!" Susan said urgently.

"I agree, but how?" Isaac asked. "You see those metallic disks next to the skin? I'm guessing he changed the dimensions of his limbs, too. He's a totally different person now. Which of the billion people on Janus is he pretending to be? We need to figure that out or we don't have a prayer of finding him. Cephalie, send the LENS over. I need you to tear that printer's infostructure apart. Find anything we can use."

"I'll take care of it."

"Philosophus, keep sweeping the ship with the remotes. Look for anything unusual. Any clues Stade might have left behind in haste. We're up against the clock here."

"Will do."

"Umm. Isaac?" Susan leaned toward the video feed of the skin pile.

"Agent Kaminski," Isaac continued, his mind laser focused on mobilizing everyone as quickly as possible. "We'll need to move fast if we're to catch up with Stade. Once we've grabbed everything we can, can you get us onto Janus without being noticed?"

"That shouldn't be too hard. This isn't the first time we've been sneaky with the *Kleio*, and no one over there is looking for a shrouded TTV."

"Good to hear."

"Isaac?" Susan repeated more forcefully.

"Yes, Susan?"

"The chair."

"What chair?"

"*That* chair." She pointed at the image of the chair next to the skin pile. "Look at the armrest."

Isaac did so, then frowned. "You mean how the foam on the armrest is torn up?"

"Yeah. We saw Delacroix do that a few times."

"It's true," Andover-Chen said. "Quite the annoying habit. Those foam crumbs go everywhere."

"Okay, granted," Isaac said patiently, "but I'm not following where you're taking this. We know Delacroix helped with the time machine, and all this tells us is he claimed another armrest casualty before Stade killed him."

"But he was never on Titan." Susan tilted her blank face. "Was he?"

"He, umm..." Isaac scratched his chin. "Yeah, you're right. We never came across a record of Delacroix traveling to Titan. And furthermore, he's been dead for days."

"Those crumbs look fresh," Susan pointed out.

"That they do. Even a simple housekeeping remote should have cleared them out by now. That implies they were ripped free recently. Perhaps as recently as the flight over from Saturn."

"Then who tore the foam off the armrest?" Susan asked.

"Can't be Delacroix, so I suppose it must be—"

Realization struck him like lightning, and his eyes widened. He finally understood what was going on.

"Isaac?"

"I know where Stade is headed."

CHAPTER TWENTY-SEVEN

THOMAS STADE STROLLED DOWN THE SIDEWALK OF NEW FRONTIER'S Shelf One, his new face shadowed under a black hoodie. A car drove past, as oblivious to the temporal intruder as all the others, and he kept walking toward the Oasis apartment complex at the end of the darkly lit street. His attack virus swept ahead of him through the infostructure, purging his image from any recording devices.

He put his hands in his pockets and wrapped his fingers around the textured grip of the PA20N "Whisper." Unlike most Popular Arsenal weapons, the Whisper fired silent, subsonic darts that injected the target with neutralizing microbots. Once his victim was paralyzed, it wouldn't take Stade long to chop him up for disposal.

Disposing of the body would present a challenge, but Stade had plenty of time. No one would ever suspect the victim was dead, because Stade intended to take his place, and he'd transport the body to his shrouded v-wing one piece at a time before consigning the remains to Saturn's depths.

No one would ever know.

It would be the perfect crime.

Yet, he felt no elation. *None of this should have been necessary!*

You fool, he raged in his mind. *You damn fool. We almost had it. Almost had* her *again! We were so close!*

How had it all come apart? How had he been reduced to this? To nothing more than a common criminal with access to uncommon tools? The job had seemed so simple at the start. Build the time machine for Trinh and use the maiden flight to collect his "payment" before the syndicate took ownership. That was all he had to do, and he'd done it, by God! He'd fulfilled his end of this Faustian deal.

But that fool ruined everything.

Anger simmered in his mind, but he wrapped it up tight and kept walking. There would be time to vent later. Now, he had yet another distasteful task to do. The plan was in shambles, his coconspirators were both dead, and this was his last chance to shake SysPol off his trail. If he failed now, it would all be for nothing. All his sacrifices, all the stains on his consciousness.

All to see her again.

All for nothing.

He reached the Oasis cul-de-sac and took the path on the right to the second building. The doors split open, and he rode the elevator up to the fifth-floor balcony. His attack virus reported in; the apartment's surveillance systems were as brain-dead as ever, and he walked around the fifth balcony until he came to room 516.

He sent the keycode, and the door slid open. He stepped in, locked the door shut behind him, and drew the silenced pistol.

A part of him considered what he was about to do. The black thought weighed down his feet, and he hesitated in the living room, pistol aimed at the floor. Yes, he'd killed before, but this was different in so many ways, and so very, *very* personal. The victim slept just around the corner, and circumstances demanded he bloody his own two hands this time.

It mattered not. Death was death, and his hands were already caked in blood. This time would be no different.

Any price for her, he thought again, letting his mantra from the last two months gird him with strength, fortify his will.

He strode into the bedroom and raised the pistol until the barrel came level with Delacroix's slumbering form. His aim shook, and he braced the pistol with a second hand. His vision blurred as tears welled up in his eyes, draping the dark room in a watery haze.

"This is all your fault," he choked, and pulled the trigger.

The subsonic dart shot out of the barrel, but it never reached the bed. Instead, it flattened against an unseen shape and dropped to the carpet.

Stade caught the briefest impression of sudden, powerful motion, and the pistol flew out of his hands. Light refracted around a humanoid shape between him and the bed, and the ghostly image coalesced into a lithe humanoid machine with light blue armor and a broad door shield attached to one arm.

Something struck him from behind, and he pitched forward, unable to escape the grasping prog-steel arms looping around his limbs. He collapsed to his knees, metal binding his arms and legs. The naked core of a LENS floated in front of him and shined a bright light on his face.

Delacroix cast the sheet aside and stood, but it wasn't Delacroix at all! It was that SysPol detective! The STAND combat frame stepped aside and allowed the detective to approach.

"We finally meet in person, Stade," Isaac Cho said, hands clasped in the small of his back. "But that isn't your real name, is it ... Joachim Delacroix."

"You know!" Stade gasped.

"Indeed, we do. I'm afraid the past version of yourself received an urgent message from Negation Industries, calling him back to the factory. A fake message from us, of course, but his presence here might have been ... problematic with you trying to kill him." The detective nodded to the LENS. "Cephalie, take him away."

The drone core rejoined Stade's bindings and injected his body's circulatory maintenance loop with powerful microbots that consumed his own onboard colony and disabled his data connections. He still had the attack virus, but it was useless to him now. The LENS's graviton thrusters powered up, lifted him off the floor, and hauled him toward the exit.

He hung his head in acceptance of utter defeat. And in an odd sort of ... relief. This wasn't the end he'd wanted, but at least it was all over now.

✧   ✧   ✧

Isaac checked on Stade through the virtual window. The prisoner sat at a table in a makeshift holding cell on board the *Kleio*, head hunched and limbs bound by the ever-vigilant LENS floating behind him. He gave the impression of a broken man who no longer cared what happened to him, but Isaac wasn't about to take any chances. The *Kleio* had imposed strict data isolation on the room, and Cephalie continued to monitor the microbots she'd injected into his maintenance loop. He wasn't simply a prisoner on the ship, but a prisoner in his own body.

The *Kleio* had returned to the True Present, and they would arrive at Kronos Station soon to off-load the criminal, but Isaac had unfinished business to see to first.

"Shall we?" Susan asked, back in her regular synthoid now that the *Kleio* had completed its repairs for her.

"Let's." Isaac palmed the door open and took one of the two seats opposite Stade.

The criminal never looked up.

"Hello, Stade," Isaac began. "Or should I call you Delacroix now?"

"Stade will do. I'm...not that man anymore."

"Suit yourself." Isaac opened his case file and scrolled down to his prepared questions.

"What do you want?"

"To wrap up the loose ends. We know the basics of what you did, but I have a few lingering questions I'd like you to answer. Given the weight of evidence against you, your only hope is to throw yourself at the mercy of the court, which means it's in your best interest to start cooperating with us."

"Who cares? It doesn't matter anymore. I lost and you won. Isn't that enough?" Stade shook his head. But then he paused and looked up. "Except for one thing."

"What would that be?"

"How did you catch me?"

"Answer my questions, and I'll tell you."

"Fine." Stade sighed and lowered his head again. "Ask your questions, Detective."

"Let's start with the most basic one. Why?"

"For Selene."

"Your dead wife?"

"Yes. I did it all for her. Have you ever been in love, Detective? Ever known someone who fits you so perfectly you believe you were destined to be together? Ever loved someone who filled your days with so much joy, you realized you were living a stagnant half-life before you met her? That's what it was like with me and Selene. Before her, I existed. After I fell in love with her, I *lived*."

"And then she was killed in the Dynasty attack on the L5 Hub."

"I couldn't accept that. Not when I knew a way to bring her back to life. It's so simple. 'Temporal replication.' Go back in time, pick up the past version, and bring it to the True Present. That's all you need to do to rewind a tragedy like Selene's."

"Possible," Isaac said, "but illegal."

"The Valkyrie Protocol be damned!" Stade spat. "Mark my words: Schröder, Andover-Chen, and all the others will use temporal replication if they have to. They may sit in judgment over me now, staring down at me from their ivory towers, but they'll break their own vaunted law when the time comes. You just wait and see.

"You know how I know this? Because they've done it before. We didn't have time to finish the c-bomb, and so what did that hypocrite Schröder order us to do? He had us replicate the weapon over and over again until we fatigued the outer wall of our own universe!"

"Ah," Isaac remarked. "The doctor mentioned having to 'cheat' during the Dynasty Crisis. This must be what he referred to."

"The lunacy of it all! That's when it became clear to me. The Gordian and Valkyrie Protocols will only be enforced when it's *convenient*. Why shouldn't I be able to save my wife—an action with almost no risk—when Schröder can march all of us up to the very edge of doom?"

"And based on that belief, you decided to bring back your dead wife. What then?"

"I knew I couldn't use any of the Gordian Division time machines. Everything is too closely monitored back at Argus Station. I'd never get away with it. That's when I decided to look elsewhere for assistance. Fortunately, I was heavily involved in the development and construction of Gordian's next-generation TTVs, and the bidding process brought me into contact with individuals who possessed... flexible outlooks on the law."

"Such as Melody Quang."

"Our deal was a simple one. I would provide the technical expertise needed for Trinh to build a time machine in secret, and I would use the maiden flight to travel back in time to just before the Dynasty attack on L5, rescue Selene, and bring her to the True Present. In the end, both Quang and I would have what we wanted."

"Then your sexual relationship with Quang was...?"

"A fabrication. We knew we would need to stay in regular contact, which involves a certain degree of risk if people became suspicious and started snooping around. We decided to use the guise of her preying on the 'poor, vulnerable widower' to mask our communications and meetings in the event someone nosed around."

"Did you receive support from other Trinh employees?"

"I'm not sure. I don't think so. That's not to say others weren't involved, but I worked exclusively with Quang."

"I see." Isaac made a note. "How did your deal with Quang proceed at first?"

"Well enough, though I had my work cut out for me. I needed to be in two places at once in order to avoid suspicion from my colleagues in the Gordian Division, and the easiest way for me to do that was to illegally copy my connectome.

"About two months ago, I took a 'vacation' to the *Atomic Resort*, though my real purpose was to establish my illegal copy. Quang provided me with the Thomas Stade alias and put me in contact with Adrian Kvint. The Oortan sold me a copy-protection codeburner, which I used to break the protective locks around my own mind and copy it. One of the resort brothels constructed my new synthoid, and with that, 'Thomas Stade' was brought to life."

"So, that's why you couldn't meet Adrian Kvint in person the first time," Isaac noted. "You didn't exist yet, and you wanted to avoid Kvint meeting Delacroix in person. And afterwards, as you said, you could literally be in two places at once."

"A useful talent when breaking the law," Stade said. "The original Delacroix kept up appearances at Gordian and waited for an opportunity for us to grab some exotic matter, which Negation Industries provided with that marginally failed impeller. Quang bought up the exotic matter and had it shipped to me at Kraken Mare, where I handled the time machine's fabrication using Trinh's construction drones. I kept in touch with both using another alias—Ōdachi—as an added layer of protection, much in the same way we used the fake relationship with Quang."

"It sounds like you almost pulled this off," Isaac said. "What went wrong?"

"*Delacroix* went wrong," Stade growled. "The original. The idiot got cold feet. Started talking to Andover-Chen about the dangers inherent to temporal replication. Ridiculous! We weren't talking about large-scale replication industry like the Dynasty had. This was just one person! Barely fifty kilograms of matter!"

"Did you explain this to him?"

"You better believe I did! We met in Free Gate right before he was due to transmit back to Earth. I tried to talk some sense into him, but the idiot wouldn't see reason! Kept going on about how frail the SysGov outer wall is and how the Valkyrie Protocol needs to be followed as strictly as possible.

"I explained to him we were in too deep. We *needed* to stick to the plan. Trinh expected a time machine from us, and if we didn't deliver, they'd throw us to the wolves! And then where would we be? In jail or worse, with Selene still dead! I couldn't let that happen!"

"So, what did you do about it?"

"I lied to him," Stade said. "I put on a kind act and told Delacroix we should both try to calm down and think it over. We'd see each other again when he returned for the inspection rounds. We could talk it over then, but it was *absolutely critical* neither of us did anything stupid before then. He agreed, and we went our separate ways on seemingly amicable terms."

"But you had other plans."

"Of course I did. I knew I couldn't risk Delacroix blabbing to Gordian. He was always the weak link in our scheme. It was his job to keep up the normal act while I got to spend the rest of my life with Selene. He would carry the burden to the end of his days while I reaped the reward of our crime. I should have known he—I—would find that hard to swallow. His focus on the replication dangers was simply how his doubts manifested."

"When did you decide to kill him?"

"Right before I told him to calm down. After I logged off Free Gate, I arranged another meeting with Kvint, traveled to the *Atomic Resort*, and purchased the deadliest attack virus he offered. A transceiver accident seemed the cleanest, most deniable way to proceed, and the virus would handle most of the heavy lifting, keeping me clear of the crime. Fortunately, the timing of DescentCon this year provided me with numerous suitable candidates to serve as the vector. I narrowed the list based on public records of future guest appearances and eventually settled on an artist named Neon Caravaggio. I met the man at his booth and infected him. The virus did the rest."

"Did Quang support your decision to kill Delacroix?"

"She didn't know until the deed was done. After that, she had no choice but to support me."

"What about the infosystems in Delacroix's apartment?"

"I couldn't risk him leaving evidence behind, intentional or otherwise, but I also couldn't move on his property too quickly. I had to wait until Delacroix was dead because if gangsters cleaned out his apartment while he was away, he would have been notified. That might have made him suspicious, which could have led to him changing his transit schedule or even canceling it entirely. I needed him back on Janus, so I had no choice but to wait."

"It seems your caution was justified," Isaac said. "Delacroix changed his apartment keycode before he left. He may have already suspected you were lying to him."

"But he wasn't suspicious enough," Stade pointed out. "Quang tidied up Delacroix's files on his syndicate desk, but there was nothing I could do about the local files at Negation Industries. Delacroix was *supposed* to keep our business off those towers, but we had no way to verify this. We simply had to risk it and hope for the best. After the virus took out Delacroix, I used the Ōdachi alias to mobilize the Fanged Wyverns, and they emptied the apartment while making it look like a petty, unrelated crime."

"And then we came into the picture," Isaac said.

"Yeah," Stade breathed. "You did. I had a program searching for news on the case, and Quang kept me abreast of developments on her end. For a while, I thought we'd stumped you, so imagine my surprise when I learned your partner would star in an exhibition match at the *Atomic Resort*." He chuckled sadly. "I mean, *really*! You weren't there to compete! You were wheeling and dealing with the Oortans, and I needed to put a stop to that."

"Did you provide the combat frame schematics to Thorn?"

"Yeah, that was me. I figured the death of an Admin officer would trump my case and bury you neck deep in unpleasant politics, providing the delay I so desperately needed. But Thorn didn't have the balls to go through with it, so I knew it was only a matter of time before the noose tightened. Quang visited Kraken Mare during her Titan trip, and I infected her with the virus there and set it to deploy when she tried to leave the spaceport."

"Then it was you who killed Quang."

"That's right."

Isaac made a quick note. "We suspected as much but hadn't confirmed it yet. What happened after you eliminated your partner?"

"The rest of my time was spent finishing the time machine as fast as I could. Any drones I didn't need, I set up as a makeshift speed bump for when SysPol and SSP inevitably came knocking."

"And that might have been enough," Isaac noted, "if we hadn't called in the *Kleio* for support."

"That was another shock," Stade confessed. "I figured they'd be over a million kilometers away when I phased out, which would have made it difficult, if not impossible, for them to track me. And even if they knew I'd left, the baffles would mean they'd never find me. *Should* never have found me. But instead, they were right next to the plant when I phased out!"

"And the rest was you trying to give us the slip one last time." Isaac made one final note, then closed his interface. "Thank you, Stade. That was most informative."

He rose from his seat.

"Wait," Stade said. "I need to know. How did you figure out I was Delacroix? How did you know where to find me on Janus?"

"Agent Cantrell?" Isaac asked. "Would you like to do the honors?"

"Crumbs," she said simply.

"What?" Stade asked.

"Prog-foam crumbs. You have a bad habit of picking chunks off your chairs."

"*Crumbs?*"

"Once we knew you were a copy of Delacroix," Isaac elaborated, "your plan to hide on Janus seemed obvious. You were going to replace Delacroix, the one person in all of Janus you could emulate the best. Because, ultimately, all you'd be doing is retracing your steps."

"You've got to be kidding me!" Stade stared blankly at the table. "*That's* how you found me?"

"Why don't you ponder this—and all your *other* bad habits— while you await your trial?"

Isaac and Susan left the room.

"You found me because of fucking crumbs!" Stade blurted as the door slid shut.

CHAPTER TWENTY-EIGHT

"ISAAC?" CEPHALIE ASKED, SITTING ON THE EDGE OF HIS HALF-empty pizza dish.

"Yeah?"

"Why are we here?"

Isaac blinked and paused with a pizza slice halfway to his mouth. He frowned and set it back in the dish. The table was laden with three personal pizzas: one with spinach, feta cheese, mushrooms, and sausage; another with chicken, bacon, and onion drenched in barbeque sauce; and a third slathered with mozzarella, cheddar, gorgonzola, and provolone cheeses with a drizzling of the Spigot's Tongue Melter sauce. Side dishes of buttered sweet rolls, hearty meatballs, thick-cut potato fries, and fried pickles added to the clutter, though they'd already emptied a big glass bowl of the house salad.

Isaac looked over to Susan, who shrugged at him and dipped another fried pickle into her ranch dressing.

"You mean in a philosophical sense?" Isaac gave his IC a doubtful frown. "I don't think I'm the right person for that."

"No. I mean why are we *here*"—Cephalie tapped her cane against the table—"at the Meal Spigot?"

"We're celebrating. We cracked the case and turned in a mountain of irrefutable evidence. Stade-slash-Delacroix is almost guaranteed to receive the death penalty, and the only people he permanently killed were his coconspirators! Why wouldn't we celebrate?"

"But it's a *Meal Spigot*."

"So?"

"Don't you think this is too lowbrow for such a tough case?" Cephalie stood up and rounded the pizza dish.

"Nah, it's fine. Besides, remember what happened the last time we were here?" He gestured over the hot food. "Now look at it. Not an apple in sight!"

"I hardly call this an improvement," Cephalie griped.

"Speaking of apples," Susan said, "is Nina going to join us?"

"Yeah, she's on her way," Isaac said. "Said she was finishing up her very last printer in New Frontier, so this'll be a celebration for her, too."

"Did you ask her where she'd like to eat?" Cephalie asked.

"No, but I'm sure she's fine with this."

"Uh!" Cephalie shook her head. "You're hopeless sometimes, you know that?"

"Honestly, I don't see the issue with this place," Susan said. "These fried pickles are great. I might have seconds."

"We can come back tomorrow if you want," Isaac said.

"Really?" Susan's eyes brightened.

"Sure. We'll be in town at least another day to wrap things up. I'd like to stop by the NFPD once more and offer our thanks to Lasky and MacFayden; we really lucked out with those two. Plus, there's the Trinh audit to consider. Sounds like every ministry and division in SysGov is taking a crack at them, so we should check in to see if they need anything from us." He smiled brightly. "Couldn't have happened to a nicer syndicate."

"What'll happen to their New Frontier factory?" Susan asked, dipping another fried pickle.

"Long term, it's anyone's guess. Short term, the whole place is shut down and swarming with cops. Same with Kraken Mare. Gordian took ownership of both the legit impeller and the DIY TTV, and they're hitting Trinh for multiple contract violations. Trinh's management will find themselves on the receiving end of some very pointed questions, but they're a slippery lot. Hard to say how much long-term damage will be done, but regardless, other companies are going to look at their legal mess and see the benefits of establishing partnerships elsewhere."

"And once we're done here? Where to next?"

"We'll head up to Kronos Station." Isaac grabbed a fry and bit it in half. "Which reminds me," he continued as he chewed, "I need to show you your desk."

"I have a desk?"

"You sure do. Right next to mine."

"You think I'll get much use out of it?"

"Probably not." He smiled apologetically. "Such is the life of a SysPol detective."

"Fine by me," Susan said. "I'm not cut out for desk work. By the way..."

"What's wrong?"

"I've been getting...mail."

"Oh?"

"From Thorn."

"Asking for a rematch?"

"No. He wants to go on a date. He even said I could pick the synthoid he'd wear. He...sent pictures."

"Explicit pics?"

"Yeah."

"You going to do it?"

Susan shuddered.

"Hey there!" Nina called out from the entrance.

"Hey, Nina!" Isaac waved for her to join them and scooched over to make room. "You done with food printers finally?"

"Even better than that." She sat down next to him with a mischievous grin. "Have you seen today's *New Frontier Times*?"

"No, we've been so busy I haven't read any news in days," Isaac said. "Why? Did they post an article on the Apple Cypher? Did you get a mention?"

"Check it out and see."

"All right." He opened an interface and logged into the *New Frontier Times*. A flattering full-body image of Specialist Nina Cho filled the front page, and he read the headline out loud. "'Rising Star in SysPol Cracks the Code'?"

"Oh? You hadn't heard?" Nina leaned back in the booth, grinning ear to ear.

"*You* cracked the Apple Cypher?" Isaac asked.

"Yup."

"Congratulations," Susan said.

"Thanks." Nina eyed the table. "Ooh! Fried pickles! Don't mind if I do!"

"But how?" Isaac asked. "I thought no one could make sense of the code. How'd you find time to decrypt it while fixing printers?"

"Eashy." She swallowed. "Easy. Turned out the cypher *was* gibberish."

"Then how did you catch the criminal?"

"Well, more specifically, the cypher was randomly generated. And we all know who worships randomness."

"The perp didn't turn out to be some Numbers punk, did he?" Susan asked.

Isaac skimmed the article for the answer.

"No, but close," Nina said. "Try *former* Numbers gangster. A few of the senior detectives, Damphart included, thought someone at Flavor-Sparkle might be involved, and when I clued her in on this angle, the search narrowed in a hurry! Turns out there's only one guy in Flavor-Sparkle's entire Saturn branch with that background. He was packing his changes into the official updates being sent from F.S. That's why we took so long to find the source of the corruption. We thought it must have been an external factor, but it turned out all along to be riding a built-in update feature."

"I see we have a quote from the criminal." Isaac cleared his throat and read. "'I'm on a mission from the Divine Randomizer to make people eat healthier.' Charming."

"The guy was clearly nuts," Nina continued. "Smart, but nuts. Damphart personally made the arrest, and Raviv held a press conference shortly thereafter. He credited me with busting the case wide open. I even made the front page of the *Saturn Journal*."

"Wait a second." Isaac blinked. "You're mentioned in the *Saturn Journal*, too?"

"The *Saturn Journal*, *Horizon Post*, *Ballast Life*, *Ring Spectator*—"

"How many articles are you in?"

"—*Epimethean Crier*, *Engine Block Weekly*, the *Janus Vindicator*, the—"

"There's no way." Isaac navigated to the *Saturn Journal*'s front page. "No way."

The page loaded, and a shot of Nina appeared, the viewpoint low and angled up with her gazing valiantly to the side. The headline read A HERO IS BORN in big, bold letters.

"Oh, come on!" Isaac griped.

"You should see my Esteem account. I'm getting *so* many tips right now!"

"All you did was say the cypher might actually be gibberish." His eyebrows shot up, and he pointed at her. "Wait a second. That was my suggestion! I told you that!"

"Yeah." She grinned and patted him on the shoulder. "Thanks!"

"Is our case in the news?" Susan asked.

"I doubt it with the Apple Cypher coverage sucking all the oxygen out of the room." Isaac crossed his arms.

"I'm going to run a search." Susan opened an interface with a smile. "This is rather exciting. I've never seen my name in the news before."

"I wouldn't get your hopes—"

"Found one!" Susan spun the article around for them to see.

"'Cop Killer Was a Cop. The Dark Side of Gordian Division Revealed.'" Isaac frowned. "Well, that's not a promising start. Do we even get a mention in there?"

"Umm." Susan turned the article back around and began to read.

"No," Cephalie said. "I read that one this morning. Kaminski and Andover-Chen get all the credit."

"Typical," Isaac groused. "Gordian gets all the attention these days. It's like the other divisions hardly exist anymore."

"Maybe someone wrote a better article." Susan started another search.

"We can only hope." Isaac slouched back in the booth.

"By the way, Susan," Nina said. "You still liking Themis? Even after all the chaos on Titan?"

"Absolutely. Like I said before, it's a refreshing change of pace. I get shot at less over here."

"But didn't your v-wing get hit by a missile?"

"Yes."

"Right before your synthoid received a bullet massage?"

"And your point is?"

"Wow. Guess I don't have one." Nina shook her head and turned to Isaac. "Remind me never to volunteer for the exchange program."

"Hate to break it to you, but I didn't volunteer either."

"Found another one!" Susan presented another article to the group.

"'Gordian's Chief Engineer Commits Elaborate Suicide,'" Isaac read. "Oh, good grief."

"It's not...totally inaccurate," Nina said.

"Does the article at least mention us?" Isaac asked.

"Nope," Cephalie said. "I read that one, too. Kaminski gets all the credit yet again."

"Of course, he does," Isaac sighed.

"He *is* better known than us," Cephalie added in a comforting voice. "It's not a big deal."

"It'd be an even smaller deal if my sister wasn't on the front page of the *Saturn Journal*!" He opened his own search window. "We've got to be mentioned somewhere. Maybe a footnote or reference?"

"Actually," Cephalie began, "I did come across a *Ballast Life* article with Susan's name in it."

"You did?" Her eyes gleamed. "Can you show me?"

"Yeah, but you may not like it."

Cephalie opened the article and shifted it over.

Susan's eyes flitted over the article, and the joy drained from her face.

"'Admin Thug Terrorizes Oortan Vacationer. Are You Next?'" she read in a dull monotone.

"Oortan vacationer?" Isaac asked. "Is that really how they characterized Kvint?"

"Yes, but I'm more concerned about the 'Admin Thug' part."

"*Journalists.*" Isaac ran his fingers back through his hair. "I suppose there's an upside to being overlooked in the news. Right, Cephalie?"

The small woman glanced away and whistled.

"Cephalie?"

She sent a link to his interface, and the page updated.

"What's this?" he asked. "The *Free Gate Newsletter*? 'Banned Player Returns with a Vengeance. Famous Livecaster Traumatized'?"

"My name appears in the article."

"What about me and Big Stompy?"

"Big Stompy, yes. You, no."

"Seriously?" Isaac asked. "You mean to tell me I'm the only one here not in the news?"

"Be glad you weren't," Susan said as she skimmed through her unflattering article. "You want to hear a quote from Adrian Kvint?"

"Sure."

"'You people better do something about that woman. She's a menace! Why, she'd sooner recycle your body than look at you!'"

"Oh, please." Isaac rolled his eyes.

"Quit whining, you two." Nina swept the table clear of interfaces. "We've got more important matters to discuss. The new season started. Time to choose."

"Can't I just stick with my usual?" Isaac asked.

"No way. This season requires new characters, so your pilot is way outside the level range."

"I'm sorry," Susan said. "What are you talking about?"

"The latest *Solar Descent* season started," Nina explained. "Have you heard of it? Isaac and I have a gaming group, but sometimes we have trouble keeping a regular schedule. Anyway, for this season, we've got to create new characters if we want to play the season scenarios."

"What's Damphart rolling?" Isaac asked.

"Combat medic."

"Again?"

"She likes playing support classes."

"In that case, can I create another pilot?"

"Nope. They're not allowed this season."

"Fine. Do you have the list of allowed classes?"

"Here you go." Nina opened an interface.

"Hmm." Isaac perused the list. "Abyssal harbinger might be fun to try."

"Is that an evil class?" Susan asked.

"Not...inherently so."

"Sounds like an evil name to me."

Nina elbowed Isaac in the ribs. He gave her a tired look, and she nudged her head toward the Peacekeeper.

"Susan?" He glanced her way. "Would you like to join us?"

"Oh!" Nina clapped her hands together. "What a wonderful idea!"

"Are you sure?" Susan asked. "I wouldn't want to impose."

"Perish the thought," Nina said. "These scenarios scale to the number of players, but four is considered the sweet spot. Almost all the professional teams use four players, though speedrunners might devise more optimized strategies after the scenario goes public. Anyway, we'd love to have you join us."

"Absolutely." Isaac sat up. "Besides, the only game you've seen so far is *RealmBuilder*."

"Oh, we have to fix that!" Nina exclaimed with a grin. "We can't have that lame diversion be her only impression of our games."

"All right, then." Susan leaned closer. "Then, yes, I'd like to join."

"Wonderful!" Nina eased the interface toward her. "First step is to select a class. What sort of play styles do you enjoy most?"

"Something that fights on the front lines and shields the rest of the party."

"That's good, because we could use someone like that," Nina said. "I was toying with the idea of playing a laser mage, and if Isaac's going to be a harbinger, we'll have two glass cannons on our team. We could use someone tough to protect us."

"I could do that," Susan said.

"Here." Isaac highlighted one of the classes. "Why don't you check out the stellar vanguard?"

Susan enlarged the image of a humanoid in iridescent blue armor, heavy shield in one hand and glowing sword held aloft in the other.

"They're tough to kill, even at level one," Isaac explained. "They start off with tiers in Health Regen Aura and Impact Reduction Aura. Plus, their class weapons are a shield that doubles as an upgradable drone, and a sword that shoots spell beams. What's not to love? Basically, they're space-paladins."

"It's perfect." She smiled at him. "When's our first session?"

EPILOGUE

ONE AND A HALF BILLION KILOMETERS AWAY AND A DAY LATER, Under-Director Jonas Shigeki had a problem.

It wasn't a bad problem, all things considered, but he still needed to deal with it somehow.

He sat at the conference table deep within Argus Station and listened as Chief Lamont and Commissioner Tyrel reviewed the exchange program's first resounding success, and he struggled— truly *struggled*—to keep all his smugness bottled up.

He'd been mostly successful up until now, but then Tyrel and Lamont began discussing how surprised and relieved and happy they were that Detective Cho and Special Agent Cantrell had not only failed to embarrass themselves—and, by extension, the superpowers they represented—but had actually solved an important case thanks in part to *both* of their strengths.

"I must confess, Oliver," Tyrel continued, "I expected the results to be...worse."

"You and me both," Lamont said, scrolling casually through Detective Cho's report. "What a surprise."

"A *pleasant* surprise," Tyrel stressed.

"Very pleasant," Lamont echoed.

"Agent Kaminski's report, and his *glowing* review of Agent Cantrell's actions, stands out as particularly significant. Especially given his...history with the Admin."

"Indeed."

"I thought this pair was doomed from the start, but it seems I've been proven wrong. Granted, I'm *glad* to be wrong this time. Cho and Cantrell have quickly formed a team that showcases both SysGov *and* Admin strengths. Wouldn't you agree, Director?" She twisted in her seat.

The smugness began to leak across his face, forming the precursor of a rude, condescending smirk, and he forcibly aborted it with a pained, almost constipated expression. Too pained, it turned out, because Tyrel regarded him with a puzzled face.

"Director?"

"Yes?"

"Are you all right?"

"I think it might be something I ate," Jonas strained.

"Ah." Tyrel shrugged her hands. "Well, the canteen's Sichuan cuisine did have a lot of heat today."

"That was probably it," Jonas managed. "Too much spicy tofu."

"Do you need to take a break?" Lamont asked.

"No, no. Please continue." He put on a courageous smile. "I'll be fine."

"Very well." Lamont regarded the report with satisfaction. "Any recommendations, Vesna?"

"I'd like to keep them on Saturn for the immediate future. Certainly, for the initial three months we've agreed to, but I'm perfectly happy talking about an extension, even at this early stage." She gave Jonas a sideways glance. "Assuming our partners in the Admin consent to one."

"The Admin will happily loan you Agent Cantrell for as long as you like."

"What did you have in mind?" Lamont asked.

"Perhaps a rotation through other jurisdictions in the solar system," Tyrel said. "There are a lot of benefits to be had for a detective working in unfamiliar states, such as exposure to differences in local laws and police operations. I make it a point to rotate a small percentage of my detectives each year; it helps cross-pollinate best practices across the different stations as well as promote the development of new talent. Their success with the Gordian murders shows they have promise, and such a rotation would be good for Cho's growth as a detective."

"It would also further our goals in the exchange program,"

Lamont observed, "granting Cantrell greater exposure to our culture."

"That, too," Tyrel agreed. "But I think that's a discussion for another day. For now, I'd like to keep them on Saturn."

"And I see no reason to object," Lamont said.

"Speaking of cultural exchanges..." Tyrel tapped her copy of the report and turned toward the director. "There's something I've been meaning to ask you."

"Oh?" Jonas said. "What's that?"

"You knew these two were going to work out from the start."

"Well, I wouldn't say I *knew*. But I did *suspect* they were a good match."

"Yes, I remember. You seemed quite confident when we selected Cho 'at random,' and nothing since has shaken your faith in the program. That strikes me as... curious."

Jonas smiled at her but said nothing.

"It also strikes me as curious that the 'random number' used to pick Cho came from you, the only person comfortable in his selection, *and* the only person who defended that selection despite how poorly Cho did during his brief interview."

"Your point?" Jonas asked, grinning ear to ear.

"My point, Director, is I'd like to know why you *deliberately* chose him while also trying to hide that fact."

"Impressive." Jonas gave her a short, congratulatory clap. "You're not in charge of the SysPol detectives for nothing."

She dipped her head toward him.

"And you're right, of course. The number I provided may have been... less random than I let on, shall we say? There was still some element of chance in the process, since I don't have full access to your division's roster, but I worked with what I had."

"Yet the question remains. Why these two?"

"Because my goal this whole time was exactly what I said from the start. To demonstrate cooperation between our two governments needn't involve the highest echelons of those governments. That lower levels of our societies could not only work together, but *like* each other, too."

"I must admit I'm still confused on that point," Lamont said. "How did you know Cho and Cantrell could even tolerate each other? They seemed poorly matched to me, at least at first."

"That's easy. I simply identified the most prominent point where our two cultures intersect and ensured both candidates were well versed in the subject. With that in place, I was confident their shared interests would come to light during their time together and help them ease through the friction our cultural *differences* undoubtedly cause."

"And this intersection of cultures is..."—Tyrel raised an eyebrow—"what, exactly?"

"Isn't it obvious?" Jonas grinned at them. "Both Cho and Cantrell are avid gamers!"